Also by
SARAH BETH DURST

Ice
Enchanted Ivy

DRINK SLAY LOVE

SARAH BETH DURST

Margaret K. McElderry Books

New York   London   Toronto   Sydney

MARGARET K. McELDERRY BOOKS
An imprint of Simon & Schuster Children's Publishing Division
1230 Avenue of the Americas, New York, New York 10020
This book is a work of fiction. Any references to historical
events, real people, or real locales are used fictitiously. Other
names, characters, places, and incidents are products of the
author's imagination, and any resemblance to actual events
or locales or persons, living or dead, is entirely coincidental.
MARGARET K. McELDERRY BOOKS is a trademark of Simon &
Schuster, Inc.
For information about special discounts for bulk purchases,
please contact Simon & Schuster Special Sales at 1-866-506-
1949 or business@simonandschuster.com.
The Simon & Schuster Speakers Bureau can bring authors to
your live event. For more information or to book an event,
contact the Simon & Schuster Speakers Bureau at 1-866-248-
3049 or visit our website at www.simonspeakers.com.
Book design by Mike Rosamilia
The text for this book is set in Apollo MT Std.
Manufactured in the United States of America
10 9 8 7 6 5 4 3
Library of Congress Cataloging-in-Publication Data
Durst, Sarah Beth.
Drink, slay, love / Sarah Beth Durst.
p. cm.
Summary: After sixteen-year-old vampire Pearl Sange is
stabbed through the heart by a were-unicorn, she develops
non-vampire-like traits that lead her to save her high school
classmates from the Vampire King of New England.
ISBN 978-1-4424-2373-2 (hardcover)
ISBN 978-1-4424-2375-6 (eBook)
[1. Vampires—Fiction. 2. Conscience—Fiction. 3. High
schools—Fiction. 4. Schools—Fiction.] I. Title.
PZ7.D93436Dr 2011
[Fic]—dc22
2011001449

For my brother John

Acknowledgments

I'd like to thank the Edwards, Spikes, Eric Northmans, and Draculas of the world for not turning me into a vampire. I hate the taste of blood. I'd also like to thank my amazing agent, Andrea Somberg, and my brilliant editor, Karen Wojtyla, as well as Jusin Chanda, Paul Crichton, Emily Fabre, Siena Koncsol, Lucille Rettino, Anne Zafian, and all the other fantastic people at Simon & Schuster for making this book a reality. And finally, many thanks and much love to my wonderful family for being wonderful. You fill my life with sunlight.

Chapter
ONE

"One hour until dawn," Pearl said. She leaped off the roof and landed catlike on the pavement. "Oodles of time, if we steal a car."

Her boyfriend, Jadrien, stretched out on the roof of Outback Steakhouse. He was a shadow, a lovely shadow, against the green tin. "Come back up, Pearl," he said. "I'll compare your eyes to stars, your lips to rubies, and your breath to industrial-strength air freshener."

"Your charm and sincerity overwhelm me."

Rolling onto his knees, Jadrien clasped his hands to his heart. "Oh, Pearl, jewel of my heart, light in my darkness, grace me with your nearness so I might feast upon your loveliness."

Pearl laughed, even as she admired his silhouette. His silk shirt rippled in the night breeze. "I want to feast on mint chocolate chip. Or maybe Chunky Monkey."

"You can taste the difference?"

"Mint chocolate chip, sharp and clean like an ocean breeze. Black raspberry, rich and smooth as a summer night. Bubblegum ice cream . . ." She faked a shudder. "Oh, the horror, the horror."

Pearl scanned the parking lot. This close to dawn, the pickings were slim. Brand didn't matter, but she'd like a car that could handle curves without threatening to somersault.

She selected a sporty little Kia. Curling her hand into a fist, she slammed her knuckles into the back window. The car alarm wailed as cracks spread through the glass. She hit it a second time, and the shards crumbled. Pearl reached in and unlocked the door.

On the roof, Jadrien jingled a set of car keys. "Want these?"

She examined the flecks of blood on her knuckles. "Your timing needs work." The cuts were already healing, but still. . . . "Where did you get those?"

"My waitress was obliging," he said. "Or, at least, disinclined to protest." He winked, and then he tossed the keys as he jumped off the roof. Pearl caught the keys, beeped the alarm off, and slid into the driver's seat.

"I can drive," Jadrien offered.

"I'm sixteen," Pearl said. "By human laws, I'm allowed." She flashed him a grin as he climbed into the passenger seat. It occurred to her that she'd never driven with Jadrien in the car. He was in for a treat. She stuck the key into the ignition and turned the car on.

The radio blared to life, country music.

Pearl winced and flipped the station. She stopped on "Bohemian Rhapsody." Smiling, she cranked up the volume. Shifting into drive, she said, "Seat belts."

"I'm immortal," he said. "Why do I need a seat belt?"

Pearl floored the gas, and they whipped through the parking lot. Jadrien grabbed the door and the dashboard to brace himself.

"Cute," Jadrien said.

"Always," she said.

"Do you know how to drive?" he asked.

"Sure," she said. "This one is the gas."

The wheels squealed as Pearl spun the steering wheel to the left and zoomed out onto the street. She rolled down her window and let the wind whip into the car. At near dawn, Greenbridge, Connecticut, was nearly dead. Streetlamps (every other one out) lit the sidewalks in circles of yellow. Trash rolled down the streets like tumbleweeds. Storefronts—a deli, a dry cleaner, an antique store—were dark. The local homeless man slept under a pile of filthy blankets with his shopping cart close beside him. Pearl loved this time of night: just before the cusp of day, when the humans were still caught in their last dream of the night and her kind had one final moment of delicious darkness to drink down.

She inhaled deeply and tasted a hint of onion in the air.

"Your waitress had onion soup, didn't she?" she said to Jadrien.

He licked his fangs and then retracted them. "Mmm, yes. Why?"

"You're fragrant," Pearl said.

He scowled, an expression that suited him well. His high cheekbones looked extra high, and his cleft chin looked extra clefty when he pouted. As she admired him, Pearl swung into the Dairy Hut parking lot and slammed on the brakes. The Kia fishtailed, and she parked diagonally across two spots.

"You clearly don't know how to park," Jadrien observed.

"Nonsense," Pearl said. "I simply know how to make an entrance." She opened the car door and stepped out. Her leather skirt rode up her thighs. She flashed a smile at the flock of humans that clustered by one of the picnic tables. Earlier in the night, the flock would have been bigger, but now, so close to dawn, only a few remained. *Seniors,* she guessed, *pulling the traditional spring-semester all-nighters.* Otherwise known as *dessert.*

"Care to join me?" Pearl asked.

"Nah. Full." He patted his stomach. "But you have fun."

"Always do," Pearl said.

"See you next dusk, my loveliest night rose."

She felt the humans' eyes on her as she walked toward the door. She added a little strut to her walk for their benefit and was gratified to notice that she'd stopped all conversation. A smile played on her lips as she entered the Dairy Hut. The bell rang as the door closed behind her.

Open twenty-four hours, the Dairy Hut had the look of a

store that didn't close for long enough to be cleaned. The door of the soda fridge was streaked with so much dirt that it looked clouded. The newspaper bin was tilted sideways and missing a shelf. The sign listing flavors and specialty drinks was missing key letters (like the *i* in "drinks," which someone had replaced with a scrawled *u* and someone else had then erased).

The kid at the counter—skinny, freckled, and not quite grown into his nose—ogled her as if she were a movie star.

"Hi, Brad," she said as she leaned against the counter.

His eyes darted down to her black lace blouse. "Y-you know me?" he asked her breasts.

She did, but he didn't remember that. "Name tag," she said, nodding at his my-name-is-Brad, how-may-I-serve-you name tag.

His face flushed pink, which made his freckles stand out like polka dots on a dress. "C-can I get you something?"

"You," she purred.

Slack-jawed, he stared at her. She laughed. She loved playing with Brad. He never failed to follow the script perfectly. "And a cup of mint chocolate chip," she added.

"R-right, you want ice cream! Of course!" Stumbling over his feet, he managed to yank open the cover to the ice-cream container. She watched, amused, as he tried to scoop ice cream into a cup. His hands shook so badly that it took him three tries. As if delivering myrrh to Baby Jesus, he held out the cup of ice cream to her.

She shook her head. "It's not for me; it's for you."

"Huh?"

"You have a break, don't you? Come share some ice cream with me." Pearl winked at him and then tossed her sleek black hair. With Brad, the hair always did the trick. Tonight was no exception. She strutted to the back door of the Dairy Hut. Listening to his shuffling sneakers, she didn't have to glance back to know he was following her. "Bring the ice cream," she said. She grabbed a napkin from a dispenser.

Behind her, she heard him scramble to fetch the ice cream. She pushed the door open and walked out to the employee parking lot behind the Dairy Hut. It wasn't the loveliest of environments. The air-conditioning unit jutted out, blocking the sidewalk, and half the parking lot was dominated by twin dumpsters. Hulking, rusted vats, they overflowed with black garbage bags and crushed cardboard boxes. She wrinkled her nose at the stench. At least the dessert was worth the odor. Pearl turned to face her ice-cream boy.

"H-have we met?" Brad asked.

Pearl didn't answer him. Instead, she walked up close to him, closer than friendly, and lifted the cup of mint chocolate chip ice cream out of his hands. "Try a bite," she said. She scooped a spoonful and raised it to his lips.

Automatically, he opened his mouth.

"Good boy," she murmured. She slid the ice cream in between his lips.

"Why are—," he began.

"Shh," she said. "Nearly dawn. No time for talking."

Snuggling against him, she continued to feed him ice cream. He swallowed mechanically, as if her proximity erased all brain function. When he finished the cup, she tossed it and the spoon aside. Pearl pressed closer and pushed his straggly hair back away from his neck.

And then she extended her fangs and sank them into his jugular.

At first his body jerked, but the vampire venom worked fast. His shoulders slumped as his muscles relaxed. He stared at the dumpsters with wide, empty eyes, as if watching a fascinating television show.

Sweet blood spilled into her mouth. *Lovely,* she thought. She sucked, and her tongue darted out, licking up the drops that seeped out. He tasted sweet and minty fresh, exactly as she'd told Jadrien.

She quit after a few swallows. Withdrawing her fangs, she licked the two tiny wounds clean. The marks healed seconds after her saliva touched them, smoothing out to pink skin, only slightly rosier than the rest of his neck.

"There now," she said. "Run along inside. We'll play again another day."

With glazed eyes, he stumbled to the back door of the Dairy Hut. By the time he reached the ice-cream counter, he'd have forgotten all about this incident. Again. She wiped her mouth with the napkin and checked the sky.

Twenty minutes until dawn.

In the bare branches, birds twittered as loudly as frat boys at the end of an all-nighter. Not that she needed the birds to tell her about the approach of dawn. Stretching, she yawned. She could *feel* the coming sunrise. It was time to head home. She turned away from the Dairy Hut—

—and saw the unicorn.

The unicorn stood between the dumpsters. At first she thought she was mistaken. Unicorns didn't exist, which made his presence here unlikely at best. But there was no chance that he was simply an ordinary white horse (which, she quickly realized, would have been an odd addition to the parking lot too). Despite the thick shadows by the dumpsters, he sparkled like a horse-shaped disco ball. His traditional spiral horn beamed like a toy light saber.

Pearl burst out laughing. "Seriously? A unicorn? Please."

He pranced out of the shadows and across the parking lot. His silver hooves jingled like bells as they struck the pavement.

"You sound like Santa's reindeer," Pearl said. "Must be embarrassing for you."

The birds chirped even louder. She had to leave. But this . . . Her cousins were going to pee themselves laughing when they heard she'd seen a unicorn behind the Dairy Hut.

"Why are you here? Are you dumpster diving?" Pearl asked. "I can see how the horn would be useful in sorting through trash. But is that really appropriate behavior for a mythical creature? Shouldn't you be eating honey and sunshine?"

The unicorn didn't speak. She supposed she shouldn't

be surprised—horses didn't speak, and he was horselike. He paced toward her. She eyed his shimmery neck and wondered what a unicorn would taste like. "Thanks, but I'm stuffed," she said.

He bumped his nose against her shirt.

"Hey, no equine drool on the blouse," Pearl said. Did he expect her to pat him? She wasn't an animal lover. She'd never been the type to plaster her bedroom walls with posters of horses or of fluffy kittens dangling from limbs above the caption HANG IN THERE. "Well, this is all very nice, but I have to run. Go on, shoo. Go . . . poop rainbows . . . or whatever it is you do." She wiggled her fingers at him to wave good-bye, and then she turned her back on the unicorn and started to walk away.

Ow! She felt a sharp sting between her shoulder blades. Her breath hissed out. *That hurt!* And then the pain intensified until it buzzed through her head. She heard a wet slithering sound, and a burning sensation spread through her lungs.

Pearl looked down at her chest. Two inches of unicorn horn protruded from between her ribs. Red blood dripped from its point. She stared at it. The buzz in her head increased to a steady pounding as loud as a bass drum. Slowly, her brain caught up with her eyes.

He staked me.

The pretty sparkly horse had staked her.

"Crap," she said.

She clutched at the bloody horn, and the world went dark.

Chapter
TWO

Pearl's eyes snapped open.

Huh, she thought. *I'm awake. That's a lovely surprise.*

She was lying on Uncle Felix's couch. She felt the cracked leather against her cheek, and she smelled the mix of old leather and almost-as-old blood. Family legend said that Uncle Felix had stolen this couch from a high-profile socialite—back in the days when a dead body didn't summon a fleet of forensic scientists—and carried it on his back down thirty-six flights of stairs from the penthouse. Usually, he spent every night stretched out on it with the latest *New York Times*, open to the obituaries, spread across his stomach. It wasn't a couch that Pearl had ever woken up on. Why was she here?

Mother leaned over Pearl, and Pearl flinched at her expression. "Idiot," Mother said. She poked a manicured nail at Pearl's shoulder. "I should stake you myself."

Pearl pushed herself to a sitting position and hissed as pain shot through her ribs and radiated out her arms. Fighting to steady her breathing, she fixed her eyes on the print above the marble fireplace. It was *Nighthawks*, also "borrowed" by Uncle Felix. (He considered it demeaning to pay humans for their goods.) He'd lifted it from the dorm room of an overly emo freshman who (he'd said) had seen it as a reflection of the loneliness of human existence. Uncle Felix considered it an ironic addition to their living room since vampires, unlike humans, were never truly alone. There was always the Family.

Several members of the Family watched as Pearl inhaled and exhaled. None of them bothered to breathe anymore. At Pearl's age, her body behaved (mostly) like a human's, though she could control her breath if she tried, but the vast majority of the Family had abandoned the habit in their first century. The silence made the stares worse. She needed to bury the pain fast.

The Family didn't like weakness.

Only Uncle Pascha ignored her. He was contemplating his chessboard. She doubted that he'd move his piece today. It had been his turn for only six months. Once, he had gone three years between moves. He preferred a leisurely game.

"What happened?" Pearl asked.

Cousin Jocelyn snorted. "Oh, not the old amnesia-for-sympathy ploy. You nearly died. How horrible. How traumatic. Blah-blah-blah." Curled up in the window seat (light-block black shades drawn, even though it was night), Jocelyn returned to typing on her laptop. The monitor's soft glow lit the tattoos on her knuckles.

"Terribly sorry to bore you," Pearl said, "but the question stands."

No one answered her.

Mother paced back and forth over the Oriental rug. Cousin Jeremiah crouched by the hearth, rocking slightly and grinning at her. Near him, occupying their usual positions on twin wingback chairs, Aunt Rose and Aunt Lianne continued their embroidery work. Uncle Pascha contemplated his chessboard near the china cabinet, while Uncle Felix perched pseudocasually on the armrest of the couch. Pearl guessed she had only a few minutes before he demanded that she remove herself from his couch. She intended to stand before that happened, just as soon as the sharp pain in her ribs quit feeling as if hot pokers were being rammed into her torso. Until then, she had to concentrate on appearing as if she were sitting by choice, not necessity. She put her feet up on the coffee table.

"Down," Uncle Felix said.

She ignored him.

"Feet off," Mother said. "A brush with extinction does not excuse unladylike behavior. You weren't raised in a barn." She paused. "No offense meant, Cousin Jeremiah."

As if on cue, Cousin Jeremiah issued a high-pitched wail.

Pearl lowered her feet.

"You could have been destroyed," Mother said. "Permanent death."

Gingerly, Pearl touched her chest. The horn must have missed her heart by millimeters. It had felt as if it had hit dead on, no pun intended. She fingered the tear in the fabric of her shirt. You'd think someone would have changed her clothes. Blood, her own, was caked on her front. It smelled like rusted iron. There wasn't as much blood as she would have expected. Someone must have helped themselves. They probably expected a thank-you for cleaning her up, but a shower would have been nicer.

"I am fine," Pearl said.

Mother fixed her with a stare.

"I am perhaps in dire need of a snack," she amended. She'd lost everything she'd absorbed from her ice-cream boy and from her meal before him.

Pearl saw Jadrien glide into the living room. His shoes were silent on the wood floor, but his entrance was, for a vampire, loud. Like Pearl, he was young enough to breathe, and the sound of his breath drew the attention of everyone in the room. Each vampire noted his entrance, mentally cataloged him as safe, and then lost interest in him. Pearl, though, continued to admire him. His shirt was unbuttoned, and she could see the rise and fall of his chest.

"You found me before dawn?" she asked him. He must have. She hadn't burned to a cinder, and she would have if she'd lain in that parking lot for another ten minutes. She was rather surprised that he'd stuck around the Dairy Hut to wait for her. She'd thought he'd already hightailed it home. He never liked to cut it as close as she did.

"Nope," he said. "You know I'm not the hero type. I prefer to personify the brooding, mysterious, and inherently unreliable archetype."

Pearl rolled her eyes at him. "You need to quit those night lit classes."

"But coeds are so tasty."

"We found you at sundown," Mother said, interrupting, "tucked up against our front door." She pursed her scarlet lips in a thin line, as if Pearl had been caught naked out in public.

"Very close call," Uncle Felix said. He sounded enthused, but then he always perked up whenever anything new happened. Daddy said Uncle Felix was easily bored, a hallmark of his vast intellect. Uncle Pascha said it was a hallmark of a small mind. "Given the angle of the porch, your fingers must have been three inches from direct sunlight at the sun's zenith. You could have lost your hand."

"You could have lost everything," Mother said, pacing. "*We* could still lose everything. You may have been left as a message."

"Told you we need voice mail," Pearl said. She touched the dried blood on her blouse. It flaked under her fingernails. She didn't think her voice betrayed how disturbing all of this was.

"Search your memory, Pearl: Does the hunter think you are rogue, or does he know about the Family? We must know how great the danger is." Mother punched her fist into her hand for emphasis, and all the younger vampires flinched.

"I am *not* moving," Aunt Rose said. "Stake me where I sit. I like it here." She added another stitch to her embroidery, another tiny rose to a silken counterpane that was already covered in so many minuscule flowers that it looked as if it were infested with ants. "If the child wants to bring destruction on us, so be it."

As the youngest vampire in the Family by a full century and the only one who had yet to attend the Fealty Ceremony that marked vampire adulthood, Pearl was often "the child." Normally, she protested the title, but these weren't normal circumstances.

"It wasn't a hunter," Pearl said. "It was a unicorn. I know, I know, mythical. But I remember everything right up until the moment after the stupid horse skewered me." If Jadrien hadn't brought her home (and now that she thought about it, it was obvious that he hadn't—he would have taken her inside and downstairs to the "safe" rooms, not left her on the porch), then who had? It couldn't have been the unicorn. Logistically, it wasn't possible. No hands. So who was her knight in shining armor? (She dismissed the idea of Brad the ice cream kid. The bite should have erased his memory—and even if it hadn't, her dessert didn't know where she lived.) Perhaps she'd dragged herself home and then forgotten.

Cousin Jeremiah giggled. But then, Cousin Jeremiah always giggled. He wasn't "right in the head," as some of the older vamps put it. Unlike Pearl, he'd been made, not born, a vampire, and there had been a problem with the turning. Pearl had never known what. She knew better than to ask, especially since Uncle Stefan had performed the transformation. Nobody criticized Uncle Stefan.

"Sorry, dearest," Aunt Lianne said, "but did you say 'unicorn'?"

"Horse. Pointy horn. Kind of sparkly," Pearl said. "Frankly, it was ridiculous. Mythical creature hanging out behind the Dairy Hut like it was on a smoke break."

Silence filled the room.

Even Jadrien paused his breath.

"Pearl," Mother said, "exactly how much blood did you lose?"

"I saw him," Pearl said. Like all vampires, she had excellent eyesight, and it wasn't as if the creature had been far away. "Unmistakably unicornish."

Mother nodded at Uncle Felix, who, with a sigh, handed over a half-full pint of thick red blood. "It's AB-negative, so sip," he said. "Don't waste it with a chug."

"No, thanks," Pearl said. She wasn't *that* thirsty.

"Drink," Mother ordered, "and then tell me again what you saw."

"I told—"

"Drink."

Pearl drank. She wrinkled her nose at the taste—stored blood was stale at best, moldy and sour at worst. Uncle Felix had developed a taste for it in the seventies when he'd worked the night shift at the hospital. He'd snacked from the blood bank. Aside from Uncle Felix, "dead" blood was reserved for the very ill and babies. She was neither. She couldn't let herself be either.

The Family watched her.

After three gulps of the AB-negative, she said, "I saw a My Little Pony refugee. Horselike. Kind of glowy. Big sharp horn. It looked as if it had jumped off a poster from the bedroom of an eight-year-old girl. It walked toward me. I mocked it. It stabbed me. Chalk this one up as my most embarrassing moment ever."

Mother knelt beside her. "Pearl, sweetie."

Pearl tensed. Mother never said "sweetie."

Uncle Felix reclaimed his pint. "What Mother is trying to say, prettiest Pearl, jewel of our hearts, is that you're off your rocker. One bulb short of a lit chandelier. One kitten less than a litter. One—"

"Enough," Mother said.

Uncle Felix stilled.

Across the room, Uncle Pascha lifted a pawn and then placed it down again without moving it. He leaned back in his chair and rubbed his chin. "Or rook could take knight," he murmured. "'And thou were the sternest knight to thy mortal foe that ever put spear in the rest.'" Aunt Rose added another stitch to her quilt. Cousin Jeremiah tapped on the hearth with his feet. It made Pearl want to tie his feet together so he'd hold them still.

"Unicorns do not exist," Mother said. "Either your memory is false, or else you are deliberately lying." She caught Pearl's chin in one hand. "Frankly, I do not care which it is, but it will cease. Here is the truth: You were beset by a vampire hunter. You let yourself be identified and nearly slain. Your carelessness may have exposed us all." Mother released her, and Pearl felt crescent-moon indents on her cheeks from Mother's nails. "We will summon Uncle Stefan. He will determine the degree of danger—and, if necessary, reply to this 'message.' None of us will speak of this to anyone." Mother leveled a look at each of the aunts, uncles, and cousins, as well as Jadrien. "Rumors cannot be allowed to spread, not at this time." She fixed her eyes on Pearl again. "As for you . . . for the next month, you will not participate in history lessons but instead will devote an extra hour each day to additional training. Jadrien will join you for failing to notice the hunter tracking you."

Pearl swallowed, and her throat felt dry. The blood she'd drunk tasted flat on her tongue. As punishments went, this was tame. In fact, she *liked* sparring with Jadrien, or at least she did when her internal organs weren't feeling like shish kebab. She waited for more.

"Good," Mother said, rising to her feet. "Dinner is ready."

Pearl couldn't hide her surprise. She was gratified to see that others registered the same emotion. Jocelyn halted typing. Uncle Pascha raised his head, interrupting his contemplation of the chessboard. Aunt Rose and Aunt Lianne did not react, but that meant nothing. Their clothes could be lit on fire and at most that would elicit a "Hmmm" . . . before they slaugh-tered the arsonist, of course, and then burned to a crisp. (All vampires, no matter how unflappable, were inflammable.) No one ever brought in dinner, at least not in Pearl's memory. These days most of the Family drank their meals in alleys and backyards and dark corners of movie theaters—a sip here and a sip there, leaving their prey like Brad, alive and memoryless. It was safer for the Family that way.

Pearl racked her brain to figure out what had caused this special occasion. She couldn't imagine Mother had brought in dinner to celebrate Pearl's escaping extinction, but she couldn't think of another reason. Pearl pushed herself off the couch. Her ankles wobbled, and she felt Aunt Lianne eyeing her posture. (Aunt Lianne believed civilizations rose and fell due to posture.) Pearl straightened her shoulders and forced herself to ignore the fresh jolt of pain.

"Jadrien, you may join us," Mother said.

He bowed. "Thank you, ma'am." Crooking his arm, he extended his elbow toward Pearl. "May I escort you, O Mythic Beauty of the Night?"

Pearl flipped her hair. Even that movement made her want to double over and howl, but she felt Aunt Lianne's eyes still on her. She fixed a smile on her face. "But of course, O Legend-ary Escort of Delight."

He waggled his eyebrows. "Indeed. I am at your disposal."

Of course he is, she thought, *except when I need saving from annihilation.* She wished she knew who had saved her. If her savior was human, why not bring Pearl to a hospital? If he or she was vampire, why leave Pearl on the porch instead of taking her to the basement? The mystery of her savior was almost more alarming than the oddness of her would-be killer.

Silently, all the vampires glided out of the living room and into the dining room. Their dinner had been presented on a bed of lettuce. Carrots had been stuck in candelabras on either side of the boy's torso, and his hands had been positioned to hold a decorative cabbage as if it were a bride's bouquet. He wore a bellhop uniform. Pearl smirked. Clearly, this was Daddy's work. She loved his sense of humor. Craning her neck, she looked for him.

The Family circled the table. Pearl and Jadrien, as the youngest, positioned themselves by the feet, while Mother and Uncle Felix chose the head. Stepping away from the shadows in the corner of the room, Daddy joined them.

"Daddy!" Pearl said.

Across the table, Daddy winked at her.

He was dressed for his standard hunt: a pin-striped black suit and a silver hoop in one ear. His shirt was starched and pressed as stiff as paper. He never allowed an errant wrinkle. Mother forgave his frequent absences, and in return he ironed all her clothes. Judging from his outfit (and from the boy's), he had recently returned from one of his favorite hotels. Typically, he frequented the Hartford airport hotels. No airport hotel bar ever raised an eyebrow at a slickly dressed man who picked up traveling businesswomen on a regular basis. Only once had a bartender warned off a woman, but Mother had taken care of the problem—or at least that was Cousin Jocelyn's claim. She did like to embellish Family stories. She was fictionalizing her favorites, she claimed, for eventual publication. So far, Mother had prohibited her from submitting her stories anywhere, but Jocelyn still carted her laptop to Starbucks to write each night. She had developed a taste for coffee-laden blood. Pearl preferred to avoid the extra caffeine, but to each her own.

Since Daddy had presumably selected their meal, Pearl could count on his not being overly caffeinated or having a high blood-alcohol level. Daddy had taste. The boy was young, twentyish, with dirty blond hair that had been combed neatly across his forehead. In the dim light, the pale freckles reminded Pearl of Brad, the ice-cream boy. Staring vaguely up at the ceiling, the boy crooned, "Ninety-nine bottles of beer on the wall . . ."

"I have an announcement," Daddy said. His voice was quiet and smooth, yet it filled the room like smoke. All eyes fixed on him, even Aunt Maria's, which was unusual because of her propensity to stare at walls as if she were reading tarot cards. Cousin Jeremiah softly whistled.

Jadrien cleared his throat. "Should I leave, sir?"

As Pearl's boyfriend, not mate, Jadrien wasn't Family. He wanted to be, of course. Really, who wouldn't? Their clan was rising in prominence. Daddy owned real estate throughout western Connecticut, including multiple businesses in Hartford, and Mother had a head for business that rivaled any

CEO's. Until Jadrien and Pearl were formally joined, though, he had to be careful not to overstep his bounds. Fortunately, he was always careful. Witness the fact that he'd been snug at home by the time Mr. Sparkly-and-Pointy had made his debut.

"Not necessary," Daddy said with a wave of his hand. Pearl noticed he wore his gold ring. She thought the diamonds encrusted in gold were a bit much, but it was part of his "look." He preferred to hunt women who didn't mind the wedding band—he claimed the venom worked best if the victim *wanted* to forget the encounter. His women didn't want more than one night, and the ring served as a signal to them that he was a man who wouldn't ask for more. Pearl wondered if their dinner had interfered with Daddy's hunt or if he'd simply been in the wrong place at the wrong time.

Their dinner was still singing. "Eighty-eight bottles of beer . . . no, ninety-eight, no, fifty-six bottles of beer on the wall . . ." Pearl wished she had earplugs. Some victims reacted to bites this way, but thankfully not many. She wondered if part of him knew what was happening or not. But why on earth should she care? He was *dinner,* for goodness' sake. Lions didn't pity the antelope. Bunnies didn't feel sorry for their carrots. All of the other vampires were ignoring him with ease. *Focus,* she told herself. *There's an announcement coming!*

"Thank you, sir," Jadrien said.

"This news will spread quickly enough," Daddy said.

Now everyone was paying attention. Except for the dinner, of course. And Jeremiah, who was rubbing his cheek against the velvet curtains. Uncle Pascha murmured, "'An honest tale speeds best, being plainly told.' 'Speak the speech, I pray you.'"

Daddy smiled, intentionally displaying a hint of fang. "His Majesty has announced the next Connecticut Fealty Ceremony."

The Fealty Ceremony!

Even Pearl quit breathing for at least a full minute. The Fealty Ceremony was held once a century. She'd been hearing descriptions of it in hushed, awed tones for years. She'd seen the magnificent gowns in Mother's closet, glorious concoctions of lace and jewels and sweeping trains, and she'd read Jocelyn's descriptions of feasts that surpassed imagining! But the heart of it (no pun intended) centered around a ceremony in which the king and his vassals sipped one another's blood and swore oaths of allegiance.

Daddy looked as if he could wait an eon for someone to ask the obvious question. A smile played on his lips, and his fangs remained fully extended.

Pearl scanned the faces of her relatives, each affecting his or her own version of calm or boredom. Oh, good grief. *Someone* had to ask for details. "When?" Pearl demanded. "Where? Who will host it?"

Mother exhaled loudly, as if Pearl had committed some horrific faux pas.

Daddy beamed at her. "Us," he answered. "At a location of our choosing. Six weeks from tonight."

Aunt Rose clutched her chest. Uncle Felix let out a whistle. Various cousins whispered to each other. Several looked to Mother for confirmation.

Mother fixed her eyes on Pearl. "And *that* is why we cannot draw the attention of hunters, or allow the rumor of hunters. The king of New England will be coming to us. Mistakes will not be tolerated."

"Yes, Mother," Pearl said.

On the table, the human sang, "Ninety-nine bottles of beer on the wall . . ."

Upstairs was the perfect suburban home: couches and TV in the living room, marble counters and stainless steel appliances in the kitchen, and color-coordinated lacy bedrooms. Downstairs, hidden from human view, was a catacomb of tunnels and rooms that included sleeping chambers, training rooms, torture rooms, a few storage areas, and the treasury. Unbeknownst to humans, the tunnel system extended under most of the town.

Pearl and Jadrien had claimed one of the nearby training rooms. She'd chosen her favorite, a room styled after a Japanese dojo with rice-paper walls and dark beams that crisscrossed the ceiling. Across the room Jadrien stripped off his shirt, flexed his muscles, and began a series of rapid punches into the air, as if the air had offended him.

Pearl threw a test punch, and pain blossomed across her chest. Black spots danced through her vision. Oh, this was going to hurt. A lot. She glanced over at Jadrien. Thankfully, he hadn't seen her wince. She needed to guard her expressions better. She crossed to a wall that was covered in weapons: swords, knives, maces, staffs. She selected a staff. She lunged across the room, striking the air with each step. Each strike felt like a mini-explosion inside her torso.

"Ready?" he asked.

She wasn't.

"Yes," she said. Pearl whirled the staff as fast as fan blades. It hissed as it sliced the air. He fetched a second staff and joined her in the center of the dojo.

"Your Family has a lot to live up to," Jadrien said. "I heard that the last Connecticut ceremony depopulated an entire town. How do you intend to stock the feast?"

Before Jadrien could strike, Pearl pivoted and slashed. He sprang back and landed in a crouch. "If I know Mother, she already has a plan."

"If there's a new hunter in town, he could cause problems."

Yes, she knew. The reason that the hosts were chosen less than two months in advance was to limit the risk of exposure. Every hunter in the world would love access to vampire royalty, and the king of New England in particular was very serious about security. He defined paranoid. Rumor had it he didn't even leave his stronghold to feed. His minions delivered his meals to him, like pizza-delivery boys minus the pizza. "We can handle it," she said. "Don't you worry your pretty little head."

"You should try to remember what happened last night," Jadrien advised.

What happened was a unicorn. Her memory was crystal clear about that. She changed the subject. "I suppose you think you're good enough to be my escort to the ceremony?" Pearl asked.

"Of course." He charged toward her, swift as a blur. She swung up as he sliced toward her head. The wood hit as she blocked the blow, and the staff shuddered from the strength of the impact. She swayed as pain rippled through her, but she shoved.

He stumbled backward.

"I have heard there's waltzing," Pearl said.

"All the more reason you need a handsome prince to complement your stunning beauty."

"Your brothers are handsome as well," she said. She swept her leg out, caught his knee, and yanked. He twisted away before her foot could pull him down. "And perhaps more coordinated."

He smacked her side with the staff, and her breath hissed through her teeth. Clearly, she'd misjudged Mother. Mother had indeed intended this as punishment. She knew that Pearl would never admit weakness to Jadrien, and she knew he wouldn't hold back. Of course, there was a way to escape the intended beating: Kick his ass first.

He struck again with the staff. Right, left, down, left. "You are destined to be with *me*," he said. She blocked. One, two, three, four. She spun and landed a second strike on his side. He swore as he danced away. "You are the most beautiful creature in all the state," he said as he swung his staff toward her neck. She bent backward as the tip pushed against her jugular.

"Just the state?" Pearl asked. Continuing to bend backward, she reached out with one hand to touch the floor and then kicked up hard as she flipped over. Her feet caught Jadrien on the chin, and he reeled back.

"Let's see how well you clean up before we invest in too many superlatives," he said.

"I think I'll 'clean up' right now," she said. She swept her staff low, aiming to sweep his feet out from under him.

He was too fast. He leaped over the staff and struck out with his fist. It caught her in the solar plexus, and pain from her wound lanced through her. Another blow came at her, and she was a second too slow to react. It knocked into her stomach, and she flew backward across the room. She slammed into one of the wood pillars.

"You're slow today," he commented.

"Just lulling you into a false sense of complacency." Pearl sprang away from the pillar and attacked. The spinning staff whirled into a blur. She struck at his neck, his legs, his shoulders, his arms. He ducked as she rained blows down on him.

Jadrien struck back, and she raised her staff over her head with two hands, catching his staff dead center. *Crack!* Her staff split in two. Splinters flew like shrapnel. She withdrew, holding half a staff in each hand.

"Surrender," Jadrien said.

"Oh, I don't think so." With one stick swirling in each hand, Pearl leaped through the air and attacked. With each hit, she felt stronger. She felt a smile tug at her lips. Her torso ached and burned, but she could think through it. She could do this. She'd survived a near staking. She'd been chosen with her Family to host the Connecticut Fealty Ceremony. She could do anything! Her breath raked her throat as she swung the sticks faster and faster. He blocked. Each strike became as loud and rhythmic as drumbeats. "Our ceremony will be spectacular," she said. "I'll make sure of it." No human, no hunter, no mythical beastie with a Day-Glo horn was going to ruin this for her. "Better than spectacular. It will be perfect."

Catching her waist with one hand, he drew her tight against him. "I believe you," he said. And then he kissed her. The sticks dropped from her hands and clattered to the ground.

Midkiss, she yanked his staff out of his hand, hooked her foot around his ankle, flipped him to the ground, and pinned him down with his staff pressed against his throat. "Surrender?" she said.

"To you," he said, "I surrender my heart and soul."

She rolled her eyes. "Very romantic, considering you have neither."

Chapter
THREE

Five nights later, Pearl surveyed the "perfect" location that Mother had found for the ceremony: wine cellars beneath one of Greenbridge's historical sites. Leading the tour, Mother swept through the cellars. Her trench coat brushed against the barrels. Pearl eyed the cobwebs that draped across the wine racks. They were so thick they looked like cotton strung up as a Halloween decoration.

"Bit dank and dark," Pearl said. "Even for us."

Daddy smiled. He'd been jovial ever since his announcement. "You haven't met His Majesty," he said. "He has a flare for the dramatic."

Cousin Antoinette snapped her gum. "Massive understatement."

"Indeed," Mother said. As she strode ahead, her entourage of Pearl's aunts, uncles, and cousins fanned out behind her. "We can install sconces on the walls. . . ."

"Only if you want to burn the place down," Uncle Felix said, "which wouldn't be a bad idea." He slapped one of the timbers. It shuddered, and dust sprinkled down on them. "Except, of course, that we'd burn too. Immolating oneself is not particularly festive."

Raising an eyebrow at him, Mother dusted flecks of dirt from her shoulder.

"Sorry," he said, unrepentant. "But this place is in shambles."

"Then we shall build it up," Mother said. "Once we clear the racks, wash the floor, and remove the rats, it will be perfect."

Antoinette flicked a spider off her arm. "Perfect," she said drily.

Pearl wrinkled her nose. Here? This was supposed to be where she attended her first ball, where she would become an adult in the vampire world, where they'd feast? She tried and failed to imagine the cellar transformed into splendor worthy of a vampire cotillion. Granted, if you shifted the wine racks to the walls, the vast chamber rivaled the size of a high school gymnasium, but the floor was sticky with grime. It felt like a solid layer of chewing tobacco, and it stank like a Porta-Potty in August.

She had to admit that the mansion above the wine cellar was nice. The Family had purchased it two centuries ago— just one of the hundreds of properties that the Family owned. Daddy had had plans to have it bulldozed and replaced by condos, but the town had declared it a historic landmark.

Daddy had failed to defeat the motion, mostly because the town meetings had been held in daylight. So they employed a squadron of landscapers and a cleaning service. An elderly woman gave tours on a regular basis, and they rented out the place for an obscene amount of money to wealthy humans who wanted an elegant location for their fashionable soirees. The tours and the events paid for the upkeep. But that upkeep obviously didn't extend to the cellars.

"We would need to pay the cleaners a bonus to have this place scoured within a year, much less before the ceremony," Aunt Rose said. She eyed the grime as if daring it to touch her starched white blouse.

Antoinette snorted. "Even humans wouldn't wade willingly into this filth."

Who said they had to be willing? Pearl tiptoed around a gummy patch on the floor. "Threaten to feed a few of their children to the rats," she suggested.

Mother planted her hands on her hips. "It will be done by us," she said. "We cannot afford to risk any security leaks."

Hosting the ceremony was sounding less glamorous by the moment.

Mother pointed to three of Pearl's uncles and two aunts. "You, move the wine racks and clear the tunnel entrance. We need to open the underground access for our more paranoid guests. You and you, collect trash. Sponges for the floor are"— another cousin tromped down the stairs with an armload of sponges—"here."

"Looks like a job for our youngest and most energetic," Uncle Felix said. He clamped one hand on Pearl's shoulder and one hand on Antoinette's. "I'll fetch the buckets."

Also not glamorous: living in a hierarchal society. Antoinette was more than a century older than Pearl, but in the Family tree, she and the other cousins all counted as the same generation and were stuck with the same chores.

Pearl spent the next four hours side by side with Antoinette and three other cousins. Jocelyn had escaped tonight (Aunt Lianne had conscripted her aid in designing the invitations), but Pearl, Antoinette, Jeremiah, Shirley, and Charlaine were all given sponges. Charlaine was instructed to watch Jeremiah, which she did by commenting every time he popped a centipede in his mouth. Antoinette kept up a steady string of commentary as well, informing them all of every speck of dirt that touched her precious skin and every strand of cobweb that caught her luscious hair. By the end of the four hours, Pearl was so heartily sick of listening that she was entertaining thoughts of drinking from Antoinette until she shut up. It wasn't as if the rest of them were spared from the filth. Pearl felt coated in grime. Cobwebs clung to her hair and tickled her neck. Her fingernails were full of black gunk. "Mung" was the appropriate word. She was coated in mung. Her skin felt gummy, and her clothes . . . *I'll burn them,* she decided. And the worst part of it all was that the cellar didn't look much better. It was going to take every night until the ceremony to scour away all the mung. Fun, fun, fun.

Dumping her black and sticky sponge into an equally filthy bucket, Pearl wiped her face and arms with about a thousand paper towels. Antoinette continued to complain as if her flawless skin was some sort of national treasure that had been defiled. All vampires had flawless skin (with the exception of Uncle Stefan, who had been burned with holy water about two centuries ago, but it wasn't like his skin was the first thing you noticed—his propensity to chew off birds' heads was much more unsettling than the puckering on his cheeks).

She wondered if Uncle Stefan had had any luck in his search for her hunter (or savior). She figured she would have heard if he'd discovered her unicorn. He could have, though, discovered Brad, her favorite snack. She pictured him dining on Brad's neck. . . . "I need ice cream," Pearl said, interrupting Antoinette's tirade. A nice sweet drink would make at least her insides feel clean again.

Antoinette gaped at her. "You know you were nearly skewered there, right?"

Pearl shrugged. She was sure she'd notice if the unicorn reappeared, and if he dared to show his horsey face, then . . . well, she would see if unicorn blood tasted sparkly. And she wouldn't share with Antoinette. "I like your spider earring," Pearl said.

"I'm not wearing—" Antoinette's eyes grew wide, and she swatted at her ear, shrieking. The spider that clung there flew across the cellar. Antoinette glared at Pearl. "You put it there."

"He was drawn to your magnetic personality and charm,"

Pearl said. She swept past Cousin Antoinette to approach Mother.

Mother had established her command center in the middle of the cellar. She'd instructed the aunts and uncles to set up a banquet-size table, and she'd covered it with paper. On it she'd scribbled lists and sketched diagrams—a massive to-do list. She was deep in discussion with Uncle Felix and Daddy, who flanked her.

Uncle Felix was speaking. ". . . It would destroy us. Massacres aren't practical anymore."

Mother clucked her tongue. "Such a pity."

"We still need to provide sustenance for the king and his guards," Daddy said. "His Majesty will expect it. He will cancel the ceremony if we can't provide some semblance of a feast."

"True," Uncle Felix said.

"Then we need tables, napkins, handcuffs for the meals. . . ." Mother added items to her list. "Bottled blood for the other guests?"

"But the source of the 'sustenance' remains problematic . . . ," Uncle Felix began. He stopped when he noticed that Pearl was listening to them. All three adults looked at her.

"Mother, has the Dairy Hut been cleared?" Pearl asked. She'd been dining elsewhere lately, per Mother's orders.

"Yes, Uncle Stefan has approved the area." Mother scanned the cellar, as if evaluating their progress. "You may go." Raising her voice, she said to Pearl and Pearl's cousins, "You are all dismissed for the night."

"Thank you, Mother," Pearl said. Others echoed her.

Pearl headed toward the stairwell, following her cousins up into the ballroom. She told herself that it didn't matter if Uncle Stefan had found Brad. So long as he could survive the loss of a few sips more, she'd have her snack. Still . . . he'd been hers.

Upstairs, the darkened mansion was silent. Moonlight spilled across the marble floor of the ballroom and was reflected in slivers by the chandelier and by the gilded mirrors. One by one, the vampires drifted out through the ballroom. Antoinette and Pearl crossed last. As Pearl passed the row of mirrors, she thought she saw a shadow flicker across the surface. But she dismissed the image as a figment of her imagination— vampires don't have reflections—and she joined her cousins as they walked out into the night.

Behind them, through the open door, the mirrors reflected the moon.

As Pearl entered the Dairy Hut, the bell rang cheerfully.

Brad was on duty.

She flashed him a brilliant smile, but he hadn't noticed her yet. With his slumped shoulders and listless eyes, he looked as if he were part zombie. Not that she'd ever met a zombie. Jocelyn often tossed them into her stories, but the last real zombie sighting was in Florida a few decades ago. An alligator-farm owner had been using them as cheap labor and then, when they'd decayed beyond usefulness, as alligator food. . . . All rather disgusting, in Pearl's opinion. Thinking of zombies made Brad slightly less appetizing. She fixed her attention on his customers.

Two teenage boys leaned against the counter. Based on their bleary eyes, both were up late, not up early. One was skinny and tall with a hook nose and pierced ear. He wore baggy gray pants that pooled around his ankles and a shirt with a peace symbol in bloodred streaks, the irony of which Pearl appreciated. The second was tubby with chipmunk cheeks and uneven facial hair on his chin. He sported a backward baseball cap and a sweatshirt that read, inexplicably, GO, X! Neither had looked at her yet, which further confirmed her up-late theory.

"Two scoops vanilla," the tall boy said. "Whipped cream on top. And a scoop of jimmies on the side." Brad shuffled to the vanilla vat to fulfill the boy's request.

"Dude, they're called sprinkles," the chubby boy said.

"Jimmies," Tall said. "I bow to the regional flavor of American dialect."

Chubby shook his head. "Oh, dude, no, only the chocolate ones are jimmies. Those are rainbow colored. You're getting sprinkles. Know thy ice-cream condiment."

Tall interrupted Brad. "Hey, if all you have are sprinkles, then I desire the crushed Oreos, *por favor, s'il vous plaît.*"

Chubby said, "You can't possibly taste the difference between sprinkles and jimmies."

"I have a discerning palate," Tall said.

While Brad served them, Pearl drifted closer to the ice-cream counter. She felt the need for a special flavor today to combat the gunky feeling that still clung to her hair and skin despite a shower and change of clothes. Pistachio almond. Or cherries jubilee. Or maybe rainbow sherbet, in honor of her vicious mythical attacker. As she checked the case for other flavors, she leaned over the glass—and then she froze, staring at a face that flashed ghostlike across the glass. It was a thin and pale girl, face framed with black-so-dark-it-was-almost-blue hair, beautiful as . . . as Mother. As Pearl stared, her reflection vanished. She blinked at the glass, trying to convince herself that she'd imagined it. All she saw reflected was the faded floral wallpaper.

She could *not* have a reflection. It was as impossible as . . . well, as impossible as a unicorn. For the first time she admitted the possibility that her Family was right and there hadn't been a unicorn. Certainly, she couldn't have just seen her reflection—no vampire had one. It was one of those inexplicable quirks, like their aversion to silver, garlic, and holy water.

Pearl studied the glass, but the ghostlike image didn't reappear.

Perhaps she was suffering hallucinations and these—the unicorn and her reflection—were the early signs of a mental illness that would leave her gibbering and biting heads off sparrows.

That would be unpleasant.

She noticed that Tall and Chubby were also staring at the

glass. Their eyes darted first to the glass in front of her and then to their own reflections (mouths open so wide they were perilously close to drooling). Pearl shifted backward, away from the glass, and flashed the boys her most reassuring I-am-harmless smile.

Brad presented the Dynamic Duo with their ice cream, and Pearl waited for them to leave. Instead, they continued to stare at her. Perhaps her miniskirt counteracted her harmless smile.

"Can I help you?" Brad asked her.

"Rocky road," Pearl said. "Small. Cup."

He scooped it and handed her a cup of ice cream that looked suspiciously like some of the muck she'd scrubbed off the wine cellar floor. She should have picked pistachio.

Rosencrantz and Guildenstern still didn't leave.

Brad rang up the ice cream. "Two ninety-five."

She fished three dollars out of her pocket. If they didn't leave, she'd need to pretend to eat the ice cream. Yuck. Pearl shot them a glare.

That did the trick.

The two boys fled the store.

Pearl turned the full force of her smile on Brad. "Want a break?"

His jaw dropped open. "Whaa . . ."

Oh, good grief, she didn't have time for this today. The Bobbsey Twins had delayed her, and dawn was creeping closer. She abandoned subtlety. "You. Me. Out back. Now."

"Uh, okay," he said. He shuffled behind her as she strode out the back door. Out by the dumpsters, she fixed her eyes on her snack and said, "Wait."

"I don't know what—"

Pearl flashed a smile at him. "I just want to be sure we're alone. Start eating."

She peered around the dumpsters. "Oh, pearly unicorn! Where are you?" She didn't know what she expected to find. Silver hoofprint. Extra-glowy horsehair. Given that Uncle Stefan had found nothing, her assailant was most likely long gone. Hitched a rainbow to Never-Never Land or whatever. She wasted several more precious minutes searching for proof that she hadn't flipped her lid, but she uncovered nothing more interesting than empty soda bottles and a moldy copy of *Catcher in the Rye*. She'd read that once, back when Mother was on an "understand your prey" kick. She'd thought the Holden guy was whiny. She wondered if this copy was Brad's. If so, she approved of the mold.

Pearl returned to him. She noticed puckered skin on his neck and knew Uncle Stefan had found him. Uncle Stefan was . . . an enthusiastic eater. She wondered if Brad had screamed.

"Relax," she told him as she ran her fingers through his greasy hair.

His glassy eyes stared at her. He'd had enough vampire venom in his system over the past year to be completely compliant. He reminded her of a dog tied up in a yard. *I should release him,* she thought. *Let the puppy run free.*

Pearl shook her head. Where on earth had that thought come from? He wasn't a puppy; he was a walking Happy Meal. Had she really just worried about how her snack *felt*? Seriously? She must just be overtired. Pressing herself against Brad, she bent his head to expose his neck.

In the distance, she heard a car. Dairy Hut must have a new customer. Brad would be missed if she didn't quit dawdling. Distracted, she hesitated—and the kid flinched as if his body remembered the pain.

Maybe I shouldn't. . . .

Pearl stepped back. *What's wrong with me?* First she'd seen a creature who didn't exist. Now she was seeing weird reflections and hesitating over her favorite snack.

She heard a yell. She was rattled by her bizarre reaction to Brad, and her reflexes were a second too slow. Turning, she saw the tall boy from inside the Dairy Hut leap out of a dumpster and toss a black sheet over her head. As the sheet fluttered around her, instinct (finally) kicked in, and she whirled, punching and clawing at the sheet.

Car wheels squealed.

Pearl yanked the sheet off her face as a pickup truck, driven by the chubby boy, slammed into her. For the second time in the same week, she blacked out.

When she woke again, she was in a cage in the middle of a backyard. On one side was an empty swimming pool half hidden behind hip-high weeds. On the other was a pile of old bicycles, rusted grills, and other junk. Squatting on top of a picnic table were the two boys.

"Time to burn, vampire," Chubby said.

He pointed toward the east.

Pearl screamed and threw her hands in front of her face as a sliver of sun appeared on the horizon. She felt her skin . . . Okay, wait, she didn't feel anything. She felt totally fine. Pearl lowered her hands. She should have burst into flame like any self-respecting vampire. But to the shock of everyone (Pearl, the boys, and quite probably the sun itself), she didn't.

Chapter
FOUR

Sunrise.

It pooled on the horizon like liquid gold. Seconds later it spilled over the hills and houses and coalesced into a puddle of light. As it rose higher, molten light dripped from the curve of the sun as if it were wet. Sunlight painted the clouds, tinting them cute, cheerful colors like pink lemonade. Above, the sky paled into a blue that washed out the stars.

Fumbling with the keys, the two boys unlocked the cage.

"Oh, crap, crap, crap," Chubby said. "You're going to tell the police, aren't you? So screwed. She's so telling the police. And then they'll tell my dad. Crap, I'm dead."

"You gotta understand," Tall said as he yanked off the padlock, "we're totally impressionable youth. Blame the video games. Corrupting our innocent, corruptible minds. Late-night TV, bad for the soul. Nearly bought a Bowflex last week, that's how impressionable. I own a Snuggie! We aren't the sorts to normally kidnap innocent girls."

"Just tell the police not to tell my dad, okay?" Chubby said.

"'Kidnap' is a harsh word," Tall said. "I prefer 'protective custody.' Really, when you think about it, we were protecting you. Or protecting someone from you, which is almost the same. Except for how it's totally not."

"He's had a rough time at work," Chubby said. Bracing himself, he dragged the cage door open. It shrieked and whined. "Recession. He can't take this right now. Last Tuesday he flipped about late garbage pickup. Tears, screaming, snot flying out of his nose all over the wall until it looked like a Jackson Pollock painting. Not a pretty sight."

Pearl felt the sun on her face. It felt like a warm breath.

"Kind of funny when you think about it, us believing we had to protect a dude from you," Tall said. "In a few weeks we can all grab a cheeseburger together and laugh about this. I mean, a hot chick like you couldn't possibly be a vampire. Seriously, though, you might want to cut down on the black garb."

She walked out of the cage.

"Not that you were in any way 'asking for it,'" Tall said. "A woman can wear whatever she chooses without fear of being mistaken for a fiendish bloodsucking nightwalker. But have you thought green? Green would look great with your eyes."

"She's got killer eyes," Chubby agreed. "I mean, awesome eyes. And legs. Dude, did you say you own a Snuggie? Seriously?"

Pearl waved her hand at the wannabe vampire slayers. "Shut up."

Both of them shut up.

She tilted her head back to look at the sky. She'd seen daylight in photos and on Antoinette's TV. But it couldn't compare to this feeling of the sky widening above her as it brightened, as if the world were opening up like a flower blossom. Around her, color flowed into the buildings, into the rust on the metal scraps, into the green-brown grass of the lawn, into the feathers of the birds that clustered on the telephone lines.

"You need a ride home?" Chubby asked, all solicitous.

"'Sorry' doesn't begin to cover this situation," Tall said. "Anything we can do to make this up to you, you just say the word. Consider us your knights in shining armor, milady."

Pearl brushed past them, eyes fixed on the horizon. As it rose higher, the sun, now a semicircle, bleached whiter and brighter. "You're still not shutting up."

"Do you need us to call anyone?" Chubby asked.

As she picked her way across the yard between rusted spare parts and unloved lawn equipment, the two "hunters" trailed her like puppies. She considered biting them to keep them quiet, but she didn't want the distraction from the sunrise. Plus there were two of them, which would make it awkward. She couldn't bite them both simultaneously, and there were too many rusty tools around here that the other could use as weapons if she bared her teeth at one of them. She didn't want to survive dawn only to be sliced up by Tweedledum and Tweedledee. It would be simpler to just walk out of here, eastward into the sun.

"Think she needs an ambulance?" Chubby asked his friend. "We did, you know, hit her with a car. And she seems a little . . ." Elbows flapping, he imitated a drunken bird.

"My sister would have been having hysterics," Tall said. "Granted, she has hysterics when a squirrel threatens her personal space." He caught Pearl's elbow. "We should take you to a hospital. You could have internal bleeding. Or, I don't know, a bruise or two."

Pearl fixed her gaze on his fingers.

He peeled his fingers away from her elbow and held up his hands in surrender. "No touchy. Got it. Sorry."

She spoke slowly as if to a pet, "No touchy. No talky. I'm leaving now. You stay here. Don't follow me. Stay. *Comprende?*"

Both of them nodded as vigorously as bobble heads.

Chubby cleared his throat. "Are you going to . . . tell?"

Pearl smiled. "Just my Family."

Both of them exhaled in unison, as if this news was a relief.

She wiggled her fingers in a wave and then strode away from them. She left the yard by squeezing between a fence and garbage cans piled high with empty pizza boxes. She inhaled the smell of stale pizza and was suddenly hungry—she'd been interrupted before her snack last night. She was tempted to turn around and revisit her two friends, but sunlight flooded the world in front of her and she kept walking toward it down the center of the street.

The sun filled the horizon with pale yellow. Around her . . . look at the trees! The sun painted each bare branch in highlights. She'd always seen trees as a morass of shadows, but in the dawn light, the warm brown branches wove into a lacy pattern as delicate as anything Aunt Rose had ever embroidered. Pearl could see the nascent leaf buds, waiting for enough warmth to let them grow. Spinning in a circle in the street, she gawked at the trees, transformed into artwork.

It was more than just the look of everything; the world even sounded different. From every direction, she heard the cacophony of birds. From the trees, the roofs, and the phone lines, they trilled and twittered and chirped and cooed until she felt like jumping out of her skin with the very loud wrongness of all of this.

Vampires did *not* walk into the dawn.

Or if they did, they didn't come back. It was a euphemism for suicide. Walk into the dawn equaled cease to exist. Painfully. Her skin should have bubbled and blackened. Her insides should have boiled. Her eyes should have been seared out of her head. And all of this charmingly crusty splendor should have been followed by crumbling into charred dust. Yet, somehow, she'd missed this delightful fate.

She lifted her face and tasted the sun as it poured over her. Dawn had a taste akin to the smell of a summer lawn mowed late enough to still smell fresh after dusk. It was crisp and sweet. She liked it. A lot.

Behind her, a car horn blared.

She decided not to step aside. If it were night, she might have skittered to the sidewalk. Vampires were supposed to be all sneaky in the shadows. But the rules had changed. Today she strode down the middle of the street into the arms of the dawn.

A red Buick veered around her. The driver, a middle-aged man in a blue suit, shot her a glare, and Pearl smiled and waved and then laughed out loud. Her laugh startled a flock of birds above her. "Fly, my pretties, fly!" she called, and laughed again.

Another car approached. She heard this one park on the street behind her, but she didn't bother to turn around. These were only the first of many humans to wake. Soon the morning commute would begin. Inside all these houses, humans were stirring, little mice scurrying through their nests. Alarms beeping. Showers running. Coffee percolating. She pictured the humans brushing their teeth, bleary-eyed, dreams still clinging to their sticky skin. She wondered what a human tasted like first thing in the morning.

Quit thinking about food in the middle of a miracle, she told herself.

A car door opened and shut behind her. She heard footsteps. Trying to ignore the human and focus on the miracle, she deliberately did not turn around.

A few seconds later a boy—peripheral vision said he was tall, male, weaponless, and about the same age as she was— matched her stride. "Hey, are you okay?" he asked.

"Perfect," she said. "You can leave me alone now." Maybe walking down the middle of the street wasn't the best idea. Skulking had its perks. You were never asked to chat and skulk at the same time.

"Are you sure? You look like you need help," he said. His voice was smooth and deep, older than he was. "Sorry to push, but, you see, I have this Good Samaritan hero-complex issue. And, in the interest of full disclosure, a bit of OCD. But don't worry—I only alphabetize my own books."

About to reply, Pearl glanced at him. Words died in her throat, and she was left with *sweet*. She felt her fangs poke at her gums, and she sealed her lips shut, running her tongue over the fang tips, forcing them back in. Hands down, he was the yummiest-looking human she'd ever seen outside a magazine. He wore a brown suede coat over a white T-shirt and jeans, and he made even his clothes look delicious. She noticed he had car keys in one hand. Pearl glanced down the street and saw a blue Honda Civic parked under a maple tree. Its windshield flashed in the sunlight. Even an ordinary car that she'd never consider hijacking at night looked luminous in daylight. She looked again at the boy. Sunlight danced in his hair so it looked as if the black strands were laced with tiny gems. It was the sun that made him look so sumptuous, she decided. It erased all the shadows that she was used to, and it deepened all the colors into richer hues.

She kind of wished she wrote poetry. This sun-bathed world and beautiful boy deserved to be captured in brilliant words. Hey, maybe she'd try a sip of a poet instead. "Do you write poetry?" Pearl asked him.

He blinked at her for an instant, but then he struck an actor's pose. "'Shall I compare thee to a summer's day? Thou art more lovely and more temperate. But thy eternal summer shall not fade nor lose possession of that fair thou ow'st.'"

"Uh-huh," she said. "You didn't write that."

"I can do haiku," he said.

"Never mind," she said. She continued walking down the street, and he continued to walk with her. "Is there something you want?"

"Just to help," he said. He sounded so earnest that she half expected him to glow with sunlit sincerity. *Humans are ridiculous,* she thought.

"Thanks, but I really don't need any help to watch the sunrise. Managing fine on my own." Pearl squinted as she looked into the sun. Streaks of white laced her eyelids when she blinked. A full, fat orb now, the sun squatted above the horizon like the mass of incandescent gas that it was. It blazed just like every book claimed it did.

He withdrew a pair of sunglasses from his coat pocket and slid them onto his face. "Yellow sun, daybreak; covers the earth with new hope; new promises made."

Pearl cocked her head at him. "Seriously?"

"You asked for a haiku," he said. "Cheesy?"

"I'd say so," she said.

"Parmesan-cheesy or Swiss-cheesy?"

The ridiculously bright morning sun was filling every crevice and chasing away all the familiar shadows, transforming the world into a colorful Disney-esque tableau. She wondered what the rest of town looked like. Ooh, she wondered what the sunlight would look like through stained glass! "How far are we from the library?" she asked.

"Library?"

"You know, place with books. Smells like dusty prunes. Overemphasis on alphabetization. You'd like it." It had stained-glass windows in the reading room. She wanted to see that place with sunlight streaming in. She'd only seen it on winter evenings, when the sun set before closing time.

"Five miles," he said. "Are you lost?"

She considered it. She could walk, but then she'd miss the early sun through the windows. She could take this boy's car . . . but she wasn't one hundred percent sure where she was. She could lose time finding her bearings. All these cookie-cutter neighborhoods were a rabbit's warren of cul-de-sacs, nestled between patches of trees. "You will drive me," she said—and then, after they reached the library, she'd say hello to her chauffeur's neck. Loving her new plan, Pearl spun on her heel without waiting for a response and strode toward the blue Honda Civic.

"Can I take you home?" he asked, following her. "Or do you need . . . I don't mean to pry, but what kind of trouble are you in?"

It was actually a valid question. So far, she had no idea

why she hadn't burned to cinder. She quickly dismissed the thought that there was anything special about her. It was also equally unlikely that the sun had transformed its rays.

Maybe the vampire aversion to sunlight was merely an urban legend. Maybe all vampires could walk in the sun. After all, when was the last time anyone had tested it? The whole vampires-and-sun thing could be as mythical as leprechauns and gold.

The Family was going to be so stunned when they learned that all the hiding from day they'd done for centuries was unnecessary. It was going to rock their world. Some of them might burst into flames from the mere shock of the discovery.

Pearl let a smile play on her lips. "Why do you think I'm in trouble?" she asked. "Do I look like trouble?" Brad would have melted into a puddle of ice cream if she'd trained that look on him, but this boy merely opened the car's passenger door.

"Yes," he said.

"Fair enough," she said with a light laugh. She scooted into the car. He closed the door and trotted to the driver's seat. "And you? Are you dangerous?" she asked him as he settled into the seat and attached his seat belt.

"Oh, extremely," he said. For a second she thought he meant it, but then he continued, "I'm a menace to road-crossing rodents everywhere. Also, I don't like bullies, no matter how rotten their childhood." Losing interest, she located the sun again. It had slipped behind a cloud, and the light had dimmed into a muted glow across the street.

She nearly missed him adding, in a softer voice, "But I'm not dangerous to you."

"Hmm?" She glanced at him, all earnest and yummy.

"My name's Evan," he said. "Evan Karkadann."

"Nice to meet you, Evan," she said. "To the library, please."

He shifted the car into gear and peeled out. To her delight, he sped down the street at her favorite velocity: alarmingly fast. She upgraded her impression of him from "delicious breakfast" to "attractive lackey." Too bad the Family didn't keep lackeys. In the old days, before she was born, vampires used to keep humans as butlers, servants, and favorite snacks. Half a century ago the king outlawed it. He claimed lackeys drew hunters, but rumor had it that the king simply didn't like humans, except to drink, of course. He didn't trust them.

Her discovery was brilliantly timed with the king's arrival. She imagined Mother presenting the news at the ball, bringing Pearl forward. . . . Certainly Mother would be happy with Pearl for freeing their kind from darkness, even if she had let herself be caught by Tweedledum and Tweedledee first.

If the king were pleased enough, maybe he'd let her have a pet human.

"Do you want to tell me what happened?" Evan asked.

On the other hand, a pet human would probably require far too much maintenance. Nosy critters, weren't they? "No," she said.

"Okay," he said. "I am an excellent listener, if you change your mind."

"You're just the whole package, aren't you? Kind to kittens and puppies. Don't park in the handicap spot. Never leave the toilet seat up. I'll bet all the girls melt every time you walk by."

"That's why I always carry a towel. Clean up the meltwater."

She laughed out loud and then instantly stopped as she realized she was laughing at a human's wit. Surely this was a sign of a coming apocalypse. Turning away from him, Pearl looked out the window.

As they drove across town, Pearl watched the sun glint off car windows and houses. It danced over fences and sidewalks. At a traffic light she leaned forward to study the pedestrians. The sunlight reached everywhere all at once. Everything from the shape of their faces to the depth of their shadows looked different.

Pearl fantasized about throwing the curtains open in her Family's living room and lounging on the couch in the sunlight. . . . Of course, if daylight was theirs, it would change more than just house lighting. For one thing, they could hunt in the day. But, to be honest, she also liked the idea of just sitting on a sunlit couch with a magazine.

As the last pedestrian hobbled across the street, Pearl said, "I didn't realize so many people were up and about this time of day."

"Not a morning person?" he asked.

"You could say that."

"I always wake at dawn," he said. "Doesn't matter what time I fall into bed. The birds and me, we're pals. I know, it's weird."

"Coffee drinker?"

"Nope."

"Oh?" She perked up. No coffee in the blood was a plus.

"Mountain Dew, every morning."

Uh-oh, there went her perfect meal. Also, it explained his puppylike cheer. She wrinkled her nose. "Ever think of switching to apple juice or milk?"

"Didn't figure you for a health nut," he said.

"I watch what I eat." She smiled sweetly at him.

Evan turned into the library parking lot, and Pearl was disappointed to see it swarming with early risers—librarians arriving to work, a father with a set of toddlers, a pair of senior citizens. Oh, well, she didn't really want secondhand Mountain Dew anyway. She could wait longer for her breakfast, but the day wouldn't wait. She unclipped her seat belt as Evan parked.

"You sure you're okay here?" he asked.

He sounded genuinely concerned, and for the barest of seconds, Pearl was flustered. Why on earth should this random boy care? *Because he thinks you're human,* she answered herself. "I can take care of myself," she said as she opened the car door.

"Of course you can," he said. "That's why you were walking down the center of the street at dawn in hooker wear."

Pearl felt her eyes bug. "I am *not* wearing hooker clothes." She surveyed herself: black leather corset top, lace skirt, knee-high boots. "It's Goth."

"Sure it is."

"And it's ironic."

"The *Titanic* labeled 'unsinkable' is ironic. Your skirt is just short."

"I happen to know I have nice legs."

"All the world happens to know you have nice legs."

Her mouth opened and shut like a fish. She *knew* there was a reason she avoided talking to humans. She stepped out of the car and slammed the door.

He opened his door and stepped out too. Leaning his arms on the roof of the car, he said, "I stuck my foot in my mouth. I'm sorry. It's just . . . All I'm trying to say is that you give off a cry-for-help vibe, and I want to help." Again he radiated sincerity nearly as bright as the sun. She wondered if all humans were this intrusively nice. It was obnoxious.

"So you criticize my clothes. Very helpful." Pearl glanced down and saw streaks of black reflected in the car window. She saw a hint of a pale face, ghostlike, that drifted over the glass and then vanished. Shaken, she retreated from the car and the impossible reflection. "Thanks for the lift. See you around." Spinning on her heel, she strode away.

"Hey, will I see you at school?"

"Nope, sorry," she said. "Homeschooled."

As she walked up the ramp toward the library, she swayed her hips. Let him watch *that*. He had zero right to judge her.

She didn't slow as she strode through the library doors, breezing past the librarians at the front desk and past the set of toddlers clustered around their daddy by the return bin. Her indignation lengthened her strides. Snacks didn't have the right to criticize her. He was so far beneath her. In fact, he was so below her on the food chain (literally) that she wasn't going to waste a second more of daylight in thinking about him or his ill-conceived and ill-considered and just all-around ill opinions.

In the reading room, she halted in the center of the carpet. Colored sunlight streamed through the stained glass. Slices of ruby and emerald split the room and overlapped on the wood bookshelves. All of her irritation drained out of her. She turned slowly in a circle, drinking in the blues and reds and purples. Colored light tinted her pale skin, and Pearl raised her arm and turned it over to watch the stained-glass light dance over her blue veins and bring hints of color into the whiteness, as if her skin were Formica.

Well, look at that, she thought. *I'm a sparkly vampire.*

But it was only a trick of the light through the glass. Entering the reading room, a girl with strawberry-blonde hair also glistened as if sparkles were imbedded in her skin. For the first time, Pearl looked at a human as if she were a work of art rather than a meal.

The girl never looked at Pearl, never knew how lucky she was to be here safe in the sun, rather than meeting Pearl in the shadows. Oblivious, the girl curled up in a sunlit chair with a book. Pearl resumed studying the light.

Slowly, the sunlight drifted from window to window, tossing colors and lighting up different panes of glass. She tracked it around the room like a cat after a mouse. She ignored the looks of the humans, and she dismissed the several librarians who asked if she needed help—what was it with these humans and their offers to help? She resolved to find a different wardrobe for her next foray into day. Maybe she could ask Antoinette. Assuming, of course, there *was* a next foray into day. . . .

This could be a one-day miracle. If so, she'd better drink down every second.

Abruptly, she strode out of the reading room. The girl with the strawberry-blonde hair put down her book as Pearl passed by.

Pearl's heels clicked on the library lobby's parquet floor. She shouldered past an elderly couple. She smelled their blood, pressing against their thin skin, but she didn't even slow. The sliding doors opened before her and she walked out into the light. Across from the library was a school yard. She crossed the parking lot and squeezed through a break in a chain-link fence.

A field stretched before her. She began to run. Feeling the wind in her face, she ran faster and faster. Her legs blurred as she raced, sun on her shoulders, across the field.

In the center of the field, she flopped down on the grass. She lay on her back and looked up at the blue sky. Around her, all traces of darkness had disappeared. The overhead sun had rid the world of shadows. Yet here she was, a child of shadows.

Soaking in the sun, she lost track of time.

After a while, in the distance, she heard laughter and lifted her head above the grass to see real, live human children pouring out of one of the school buildings. They swarmed like gnats over the playground. They swung themselves up onto the jungle gym. Screeching, they flew on the swings. In pairs and solo, they zipped down the slides.

Pearl had never seen so many children at once. Sometimes she'd see them in the evenings, especially in summer, but never en masse. She felt pressure against her gums as her fangs began to poke into her mouth. Drooling at the children, she sat up. Even across the field, she saw their plump faces, flushed pink as their sweet blood rushed through them.

She also saw, across the field, a blue Honda Civic.

Rising to her feet, Pearl shielded her eyes from the sun. The sun on the windshield obscured her view of the inside, but she was certain that it was Evan's car, even though he'd dropped her off ages ago in a different parking spot. The guy really did have some serious Good Samaritan issues. If he wanted that badly to help her, he could oblige her by donating a pint. She crossed the field toward the car.

Before Pearl reached the parking lot, the strawberry-blonde girl from the reading room climbed into the Honda Civic. Pearl watched the car sparkle and flash in the light as it zipped backward and peeled away.

Chapter
FIVE

On the roof of her house, Pearl drank in the sunset. She watched the light paint the sky colors she'd never known existed. As the sun dipped lower, it darkened to a burnt orange, and the clouds around it were streaked with rose and purple. Above her a few stars poked through as if someone had pricked the blue with a needle and caused it to bleed light.

She'd spent the day outside. She'd lain on park benches, wandered into stores that were closed at night, and watched the humans scurry about like (tasty) squirrels. In the backyard of a random house, she had kicked off her boots and walked through the empty flower beds. The sun had warmed the dirt in a way that the moon never did, and she could feel the tips of bulbs, waiting to burst out of the earth, as full of promise as a freshly risen vampire. It had been a marvelous day.

As the sun melted behind the hills and trees, Pearl felt a

lump in her throat like a clot of cotton. Her eyes itched. She wiped her eyes with the back of her hand, and she noticed a streak of blood decorated her skin. She stared at her blood tear for a moment, the tear of a vampire.

"Seriously?" she said out loud. She was all choked up over the sunset? She was a vampire, a nightwalker. She shouldn't mourn the end of day. It had been nice. It had been fun. It had been kind of pretty. But her kind ruled the night.

Right now, though, she didn't feel like ruling anything. She felt exhausted down to the marrow of her bones. As the last drop of sun disappeared, she slipped down the roof tiles, hopped off the porch roof, and let herself inside.

The house was silent.

Slipping into the hall closet, she unlocked the seven locks on the hidden door. She tiptoed down the stairs into the catacombs beneath. In the underground chambers, she heard the Family stirring as they woke for the night—a door squeaked, voices murmured, Cousin Jeremiah crooned in half Latin and half gibberish. Pearl let herself into her bedroom and collapsed on her bed. She'd rest a little, she told herself, and then she would tell everyone about her discovery.

She was asleep in an instant.

She snapped awake when her door clicked open. Lit by the hall light, Cousin Antoinette drifted into Pearl's bedroom and peered down at Pearl. Antoinette had styled her hair like Cyndi Lauper, circa 1984, and she wore neon-red lipstick and yellow eye shadow.

"Congratulations," Pearl told her. "You have now instilled in me a fear of being woken by a deranged clown."

"You skipped lessons," Antoinette said. "It's nearly dawn. You are so dead, pun totally intended. Your mother wants you upstairs."

Pearl shot up to sitting. She tossed off the sheets and was out the door before Antoinette could issue any comments on Pearl's rumpled clothes or the fact that she'd slept in her boots. As she mounted the stairs toward the main house, she dragged her fingers through her hair until she'd smoothed it straight.

Catching up behind her, Antoinette chattered cheerfully about the plans for the Fealty Ceremony. Daddy had lined up a source for night-blooming flowers. Aunt Rose intended to embroider every tablecloth with gold thread. No one had a lead yet on a feast for the king and his guards, which was a worry.

Reaching the upstairs living room, Pearl halted in the doorway.

Ever the master of the obvious, Antoinette proclaimed, "Found her!"

Mother rose from her chair. "Go to bed, Antoinette. It is nearly dawn."

Antoinette fled back downstairs.

For a moment, caught in Mother's gaze, Pearl was frozen. Her voice locked in her throat, and her muscles tightened into knots of rope that wouldn't unwind.

"Jadrien informs me that you missed your training with

him tonight," Mother said. Her voice was soft and even. There was no hint of anger or judgment, but still Pearl jerked backward as if she'd been hit. "You also missed lessons with Aunt Lianne and Aunt Fiona. Fiona in particular was most upset."

Pearl clasped her hands behind her back and schooled her expression to one of bland interest. She didn't know if it was Family legend or truth, but Aunt Fiona was reputedly descended from banshees. When she was upset, her screech could shake the plaster off the walls.

"Uncle Felix informs me that this is normal teenage rebellion," Mother continued. "Is it, Pearl? Do you feel an unusual surge in hormones that is unbalancing your common sense?"

Pearl wondered if that was rhetorical or if Mother wanted an answer. As she waited for Mother to speak again, she felt a familiar itch across her skin: morning was coming. Outside, she heard the chittering of birds on the bushes by the windows. Pearl looked at the thick curtains drawn across the living room window. "Mother, would you please wait by the bookcases?" She pointed to a corner of the room and then crossed to the window.

Pearl opened the shades. It was predawn. The sky was a dirty blue, speckled with a few stubborn stars. Dim early light lengthened the room's shadows.

"Pearl." Mother's voice was sharp. "If you plan to immolate yourself, you should know that it is an exceedingly painful way to die."

"Just . . . wait for a few minutes," Pearl said. "You have to see to understand." She positioned herself directly in front of the window and looked out at the east.

Behind her, Mother was silent.

A few moments later Pearl heard Daddy speak. "Kitten, why don't you step away from the window." She felt his hand on her shoulder. "You don't need to do this. A few skipped lessons . . . Your punishment will not be so harsh as this." He stroked her hair lightly as if she were a child. "You have a long and glorious existence ahead of you, my dear."

"I know," Pearl said. "Please, just . . . step back with Mother." She turned to point and saw that all of the Family stood there. They clustered together in the far corner of the living room: Cousin Antoinette, Cousin Jocelyn, Uncle Pascha, Uncle Felix, Cousin Jeremiah, Uncle Stefan, Aunt Rose, Aunt Fiona, Cousin Shirley. . . . Each of them watched her silently. A few, like Aunt Lianne, had their hands pressed across their hearts.

Cousin Jeremiah began to croon softly in a minor key.

Cousin Antoinette smacked him on the shoulder.

He quieted.

"Can I have her room if she dies?" Cousin Charlaine asked.

"Pearl, be sensible," Jadrien said—they'd invited him, too, even though he wasn't Family. Perhaps they thought he'd have influence over her. "If you won't think of yourself, then think of me. I can't have a fried girlfriend."

Uncle Pascha intoned, "'All our yesterdays have lighted fools the way to dusty death. Out, out, brief candle!'"

Daddy cupped his hand under Pearl's chin and lifted her face to look at him. "Think of all the glorious times that await you. You are only sixteen years into an existence that could stretch for centuries. You have not even tasted the blood of our king!"

"I don't want to die, Daddy," Pearl said. "You'll see in a minute. The sun won't hurt me. Yesterday I spent the day in the light. Our vulnerability to sun is a myth!"

The Family murmured.

"Daddy, step back, please," she said. "It's possible this was a one-day miracle."

He shook his head. "You are my legacy. Your fate and mine—"

Sharply, Mother said, "Step back. *Now.*"

He obeyed.

Outside, the sun poked a drop of brilliant golden orange above the hills. Pearl watched it as it lifted higher into the air, and the light spilled across the town, the trees, the yard, the shrubs, and through the window in the living room. It poured over her skin, and she stretched her arms toward it.

Again, she didn't burn.

"Oh, my, wow!" Cousin Charlaine said. "We can face the sun!" She strode forward into the beam of light that fell across the living room. In a millisecond, her skin smoked and flame burst onto her face and arms. She screamed.

The Family stood motionless in the shadows.

Smoke billowed into the room, and the Family and Jadrien watched as Charlaine's hair was wreathed in flame. Pearl took two long steps across the living room and shoved Charlaine out of the sunlight. She fell backward over Uncle Felix's couch into the shadows.

"My couch!" cried Uncle Felix.

Aunt Rose tossed her embroidered quilt on top of Charlaine. Cousins, aunts, and uncles piled pillows on top of the quilt, smothering the flame beneath. All of them kept their distance—vampires are as flammable as gasoline-drenched kindling. Mother fetched a fire extinguisher, and the room was suddenly full of white foam that sprayed through the air, lingering in the smoke.

Pearl shut the shades over the window.

"Take her downstairs," Mother ordered. "All of you, downstairs, *now*. Speak of this to no one. Understood? Consider yourselves sworn to secrecy. Pearl, stay."

All the aunts, uncles, and cousins filed downstairs. Only Mother, Daddy, and Pearl remained. Mother frowned at the char marks on the couch. She tossed Aunt Rose's quilt on the floor and stamped on it, extinguishing the remaining embers. Pearl waited without breathing, watching her.

Finally, Mother looked at Pearl.

"Well," Mother said. "Isn't this interesting?" Her inflection told Pearl nothing. She remembered once Cousin Jocelyn had dipped Jeremiah's hand in holy water out of curiosity. Holy-water scars never faded. Mother's retaliation had involved tattoos of matching scars on Jocelyn's palms and knuckles. She wondered if Mother would recognize that this was different.

Pearl glanced over at Daddy. He was beaming with a smile so wide that he resembled a very happy shark. "My dear child," he said, "this is indeed interesting."

She didn't feel comforted.

A few minutes later Mother, Daddy, and Pearl were seated at the kitchen table. Sun poured across the linoleum floor, and Pearl sat in a shaft of light. She felt the warmth caress her shoulders like a cat curled around her neck. She wanted to turn her face toward it and feel the dawn rays on her cheeks, but Mother and Daddy were staring at her.

Mother and Daddy had claimed two chairs in the shadows and had pushed them as far against the pantry door as possible. Still, the light spread across the table only inches from where Daddy rested his hands, clasped together in front of him.

"Serve us tea," Mother said.

"Sorry?" Pearl asked.

Mother pointed at the stove. "Heat water in the kettle. You'll find packets of dried type B-positive in the left cabinet." Her voice was calm, even casual, which made it all the more unnerving.

The chair scraped on the floor as Pearl pushed away from the table. She crossed to the stove and lifted the kettle. She felt Mother's and Daddy's eyes boring into her back, and she wished she knew what to expect. You didn't sit down to tea with someone you were about to punish, but then she'd once seen Mother wait an entire week before slicing off the toe of a distant relative who had crossed into their territory without permission. This could be a prelude to much unhappiness.

Behind her, Mother and Daddy were silent.

Pearl filled the kettle at the sink. Through the window, she saw the sun perched on the horizon. Pink and lemon clouds dotted the roofs of the neighboring houses. She saw cars pulling out of driveways and wondered if the neighbors ever thought it odd that her family's cars never moved in daytime.

"We could talk downstairs," Pearl offered.

"This is a private conversation," Mother said.

The water from the faucet sparkled and glistened like crystal. Drops landed on her hand and vibrated there, catching the sunlight on their surfaces. She studied her hand in the light and tried not to think too much about what Mother meant. It never paid to try to predict what Mother would do.

Pearl placed the kettle on the stove and studied the knobs. She'd never touched a stove before—only Daddy and Mother ever drank tea. It was an acquired taste, like Uncle Felix's penchant for stored blood. From the diagrams, she identified which knob controlled which burner, then she turned the closest knob to high.

"Please add sugar to mine," Daddy said.

She located the sugar and the tea bags in the cabinet and placed them on the counter. She wondered when they were going to begin the conversation—or if they'd already had it. Mother and Daddy knew each other so well that sometimes Pearl swore they had telepathy.

Pearl searched the various cabinets until she found three teacups and saucers. She set them out next to the tea bags and then checked on the kettle.

"Wait for the whistle," Daddy instructed her. "The kettle will whistle when the water is ready to pour. Place a tea bag in each cup."

Pearl obeyed.

"You weren't anything special when you were born," Mother said.

Pearl froze in the middle of fetching the third tea bag. Mother's tone was clinical, also unreadable. She wasn't certain what response Mother wanted. "Next time I'll try better?"

Daddy said, "All vampire babies are special, of course. It takes a powerful magic to grow life inside dead flesh. It's far simpler to turn a human. But the results of turning are so . . . unpredictable. Look at Jeremiah. Even Charlaine . . ."

"You were supposed to be pure and predictable," Mother said. "You are descended from a line that stretches back two thousand years. Your flesh bears the ancestry of the earliest nightwalkers. You were conceived to be nothing special." Her voice hadn't risen or changed, yet Pearl felt as if each word were a bullet. She flinched at that last phrase.

Both of them fell silent again.

Pearl studied their faces and tried to gauge how much trouble she was in. Mother's face was as flawless as a porcelain doll's. She didn't breathe, and she didn't smile. Daddy, too, wore a mask. His lips were curled in an expression of bland interest.

The kettle wailed, and Pearl jerked.

Mother and Daddy didn't move.

She turned and poured the water into the teacups. If she had disappointed them, it didn't matter that she wasn't facing them. It didn't matter that she was across a stretch of sunlight. She'd seen Mother in the training room. Her aim was incredible. Daddy could have a half dozen weapons within his suit coat. If they wanted to punish her . . . or worse . . . she couldn't stop them. Pearl poured the water with both hands, not permitting the stream to shake. She picked up one cup in each hand and carried them to Mother and Daddy. She placed the cups in front of them and fetched her own.

She knew she should sit at the table, but she stayed with her back against the sink. Sunlight wrapped over her shoulders and warmed her neck. She studied the tea. Rust red leeched from the tea bag into the water. It smelled pleasantly spicy.

Without looking up from the tea, Pearl said, "It must have been the unicorn."

Neither of them responded, so she risked a peek up. Daddy's eyebrows were raised in delicate arches. Mother's lips were pressed together in a thin red line.

"It's the only 'special' thing that has ever happened to me," Pearl said.

In a kind voice, Daddy said, "Unicorns do not exist."

Mother looked at him, and then she sipped her tea. Daddy added sugar to his tea. He stirred it and then laid the spoon on the table. Sunlight kissed the tip of his finger, and Pearl heard a soft sizzle. He withdrew his hand and patted a tendril of smoke that swirled from his fingernail.

"I was stabbed, that's undeniable," Pearl said. "Maybe the near-death experience? . . ."

"Do not worry, dearest Pearl," Daddy said. "We'll discover the cause. But you must look to the future!" He flashed her his most brilliant smile, the one meant to charm his meals. She felt herself start to smile in return. She couldn't help it. His smile was so wide and free that she suddenly felt as if everything would be okay. This was, of course, the same smile his victims saw before their blood loss began. She didn't move from the beam of sunlight.

"You will solve a problem for us," Mother said. She began to smile too. This was more alarming than Daddy's smile. Pearl wasn't sure she had ever seen Mother's face curve into a smile. It looked unnatural, as if the porcelain-doll face had cracked. Her eyes didn't change. Only her lips curved.

"Oh?" Pearl said. "Wonderful."

"For the Fealty Ceremony, we need to supply enough humans for the king and his guards to quench their thirst. However, obtaining the dozen humans needed with our current hunting grounds is problematic at best and extremely risky at worst," Daddy said. "One or two at a time can always be managed, but that many at once . . ."

Mother chimed in, "Our hope is that with this new development, new opportunities will present themselves."

"You want me to find the king's dinner in daylight?" Pearl guessed.

"Precisely," Mother said.

Daddy smiled. "We want you to attend high school."

Pearl dropped the teacup. It shattered on the linoleum, and blood tea spattered over the white floor. Scooping up a towel, Pearl bent to clean the mess. Mother and Daddy watched without moving as Pearl scrubbed away the blood that glistened in the stream of sunlight.

Chapter
SIX

Antoinette bounced on her bed and clapped her hands. "Girls' night!"

Underneath the house, in her cousin's room, Pearl contemplated an ignoble retreat. "Yeah, thanks, but I'd rather chug holy water. All I need is one outfit." She shot a look at Antoinette's closet door and wondered if Antoinette had rigged it with any booby traps. If not, Pearl could sneak in there while Antoinette was out hunting. . . . She'd most likely laced it with holy-water traps. Antoinette loved her clothes. "Maybe two outfits. Just until I have a chance to shop."

"Oh, glorious shopping! Helpful sales staff waiting on your every wish! 'Miss, can I bring you another size? Another color?'" Antoinette hopped to her feet on top of her bed and pointed at imaginary clothes. "Yes, please, I'd like a size four. Or do you think I'm a two? And could you send me that boy at the cash register, please? I'm feeling peckish. No, not the one with the tattoo. *That* one. Mmm." She flopped down on the bed and sighed in delight.

"Okay, then," Pearl said. "You enjoy yourself. I'll come back later."

"Pearly, no!" Antoinette flipped off the bed and darted to the door. She blurred into a streak of pink and blonde. Pearl shifted backward, prepared to strike if she had to. Antoinette's speed was alarming. "You've never, ever asked me for anything before. You can't blame me for being excited. We have the potential for a real bonding moment here, you and I. We could become BFFs." Antoinette wrapped her arm around Pearl's shoulders.

Pearl considered breaking her arm. Just a spin and a chop, and the deed would be done. Regretfully, she decided that she needed the clothes more than the satisfaction. Plus Antoinette was fast, and a failed arm break would be a bad idea. "I'm not playing truth or dare with you. We aren't going to start texting. All I want is one standard high school outfit."

Antoinette laughed, a high-pitched squeal like a squeezed pig. "Silly, Pearly! That's why you need the girls' night." She bounded across her room and inserted a DVD into her TV. Antoinette was the only vampire in the Family who was addicted to TV.

Wielding the remote, Antoinette sped through the nondescript opening credits. "You're joking," Pearl said as the image of a high school appeared.

"I never joke about Molly Ringwald." Antoinette plopped back on her bed and patted a spot next to her. "Listen well, young padawan, there's no such thing as one 'standard' outfit." She hit play on the remote. "The first thing you need to decide before you can choose an outfit is which clique you plan to join. And you announce that by your clothes." She upped the volume for the movie's opening voice-over. "You can be a brain, an athlete, a basket case, a princess, or a criminal. Or if you prefer: nerd, jock, dirtbag, mean girl, et cetera." She pointed to each human.

Pearl drifted farther into the room, compelled by the TV. "Humans don't . . . Did he just set his shoe on fire?" As Antoinette skipped through scenes, Pearl watched the boy in a blue tank top bounce his fluffed hair as he played air guitar. A girl in a baggy sweater and a redhead danced on a railing. A scene or two later, they were crawling through ceiling ducts. "This can't be an accurate portrayal of the human education system."

"Wait, wait! I skipped the best part." Antoinette rewound and then stopped and said in sync with the actor, "You're a neo-maxi-zoom-dweebie." She shook her head in admiration. "Best insult ever."

"You *like* this movie?"

"After *Breakfast Club,* you must watch *Sixteen Candles.* 'What's happenin, hot stuff?'" Antoinette jumped up again, and Pearl wondered if she'd drunk from an overly caffeinated donor tonight. "Oh, and we have to do your nails!"

Pearl put her hands behind her back. "Clothes, Antoinette. Focus."

Antoinette pouted. "You didn't select your type."

Pearl considered it for a moment. "Not hooker."

"Surprisingly, that does narrow it down," Antoinette said. She got off the bed and opened her closet. As Pearl watched, Antoinette flipped through clothes. "No, no, definitely no, don't trust you with that, no, hate that, ooh must wear that, no, no. . . ." Pearl's eyes slid back to the TV, where the "dirtbag" that Antoinette had identified was charging through empty hallways singing, "'I wanna be an airborne ranger. I wanna lead a life of danger.'" Antoinette selected three skirts and tossed them on the bed. A pair of jeans joined them, plus two blouses. She then dumped a pile of jewelry on top of them. "Okay, choice number one. This says, 'I am innocent yet possess many exotic secrets.'" She held up a flowy skirt with a midriff-revealing top. "Works best with a belly-button ring or a tramp stamp."

"Yeah, no," Pearl said.

Antoinette selected jeans plus a formless sweater. "This says, 'Too hot to care what I wear. Worship my wit instead.' Best if worn without a bra."

"I'd like a simple 'I'm human. Move along.'"

"Ah, you want a 'These aren't the droids you're looking for' look." Rifling through her dresser, Antoinette emerged with a soft pink sweater. She paired it with a black skirt. "Wear your boots with this. Plus this necklace." She tossed a tangled strand of charms at Pearl. Pearl caught it and examined it. One charm was Hello Kitty, another was the Eiffel Tower, a third was a silver pair of tiny flip-flops. It looked as if someone had deliberately assembled meaningful pendants.

"Yours?" Pearl asked.

"Memento from an extra delicious type O," Antoinette said. She gestured at the other necklaces strewn on the bed. "I like souvenirs."

Pearl supposed it was better than Uncle Pascha's collection of dried ears, his souvenirs from days when vampires didn't have to be so cautious.

"Now, let's discuss payment," Antoinette said.

"You aren't going to lend me this out of the goodness of your heart?" Pearl scooped up the skirt and the sweater. The sweater felt as soft as dandelion fluff. She checked it for bloodstains.

"I have no goodness in my heart," Antoinette said. "In fact, the existence of said heart is open for debate, given the whole no-pulse thing, which, by the way, I've never understood, because how does the lovely, delicious blood travel through our body if we don't have a pulse? Maybe I'll eat a scientist someday and ask him."

"You could borrow one of my outfits in exchange," Pearl said.

"Hmm, again, no," Antoinette said. "No offense, sweetie, but black is so cliché. You might as well wear a cape and befriend a bat." She clapped her hands together. "I know!

Your boy. You won't have much time for him once you're up all day. He'll be so lonely without you to brighten his nights. I could keep him company."

Pearl considered chucking the clothes back in her face. "Hands off Jadrien."

"Or . . . oh! You could let me give you a makeover!"

"You'll let me borrow these if I let you decorate my face?" Pearl said. That seemed a small price to pay, especially in comparison to Jadrien. She wondered if she was missing something. She'd say no to anything that involved tattoos or branding.

"Not decorate, highlight!" She fluttered around Pearl. "You would look astounding in natural-tone eye shadow. You have tremendous eyes, you know." She laughed. "Of course you don't know. How could you?"

As silent as a breath, Daddy drifted into the room. "Her eyes are fine as they are, Antoinette. We thank you for your contribution to the cause." He flashed Antoinette a smile intended to knock grown women off their feet.

Antoinette simpered. "Of course! My pleasure!" She wiggled her fingers in a wave at Pearl. "I'll tell Jadrien you said hello."

Before Pearl could reply, Daddy wrapped his arm around Pearl's shoulders and guided her out of the room. Her eyes readjusted to the dim light. All the corridors under the house had been created to appear as basementlike as possible, a final disguise in case defenses were ever breached. Pipes were exposed in the ceiling. Bare bulbs illuminated the space. The walls were cement painted a dark gray.

"Congratulations!" Daddy said. "You are enrolled as a junior in Greenbridge High. Your first day is tomorrow."

Pearl stared at him. She should have been sitting down for that sort of announcement, not standing in the middle of a corridor. "That's . . ."—a string of adjectives ran through her mind: exciting, great, wonderful, or more accurately, horrifically nightmarish—". . . soon."

He turned the full force of his magnificent smile on her. "You're nervous! You shouldn't be. This is your moment to shine!"

"Or sparkle," she said.

Daddy let out a hearty laugh. She felt her shoulders unknot. If Daddy was pleased with her, that was a good sign. She couldn't be too much of an abomination if she could make him laugh. But before she could truly relax, he switched to serious. "You won't have much time to ingratiate yourself. Get the lay of the land quickly and become a trusted member of the community as fast as you can."

"I'm not the only source for the king's dinner, am I? You have a backup plan, right?" She'd overheard Daddy say that without dinner, the king would cancel the ceremony. She didn't want so much responsibility. She was only supposed to swear allegiance, not worry about the success of the whole event.

"You'll do fine," he said. "Just remember: Sometimes the trick to blending in is to stand out." He cupped her face in his hands. His steel-gray eyes didn't waver or blink. "Also remember: You are my flesh and blood. You cannot fail."

"I won't, Daddy," Pearl said. "I promise."

He smiled. "That's my girl."

Putting his arm around her again, he escorted her upstairs. "Your aunts and uncles insist on speaking with you. Try to be civil to them."

Upstairs in the living room, the tableau matched the usual scene with only slight variations: Uncle Pascha occupied his chair at the chess set, Uncle Felix stretched on his (slightly charred) couch, Aunt Rose and Aunt Lianne sat like bookends on either side of an embroidered quilt. Another two aunts reclined on chairs by the bare fireplace. One, Aunt Fiona, read a book of poetry in a dead Celtic language. The other, Aunt Maria, simply stared at the wall. Her lips moved as if she were speaking, but she didn't make a sound. Cousin Jocelyn was ensconced in her window seat. Cousin Charlaine was curled up in a chair. Her head was wrapped in bandages, and her body was cocooned in a blanket. Cousin Jeremiah had tucked himself underneath an end table. He had what appeared to be a mouse's tail wrapped around his fingers. Pearl decided not to look too closely at it. Better not to know.

Uncle Felix clapped his hands together. "Aha! And there she is! Out to do battle with the dragons of day and taste the delights of this world in sunshine!"

Jocelyn said, "You don't mind if I record your experiences in verse, do you? Or if I fictionalize bits here and there?" She waved her fingers over her laptop. "I plan to make you more alluring in my version."

As Pearl considered what insult would be a worthy retort to that statement, Uncle Felix said, "Let me give you some words of advice before you sally forth, my dear. Americans invented adolescence. It is not a natural phenomenon. Adolescence is a social construct, created by an urban-industrial society that keeps its young at home far past puberty. Teenage angst is a luxury of a successful and complacent society, a purely modern human conceit that isn't condoned by our superior species."

Pearl waited for a point.

Uncle Felix stretched his legs out on his couch.

She sighed inwardly and wished it were possible to have a conversation without the little power plays. The older vamps liked to make the younger ones ask for clarification. It confirmed the hierarchy of power and satisfied them in some obscure way. It was annoying. "And?" she prompted.

"In another age or with another species, the parents would have told these teenagers to 'suck it up.' Because they don't . . . you should find it quite easy to suck *them* up."

A few aunts chuckled.

"Funny," Pearl said. "I never noticed you having much luck hunting teens."

The laughter cut off abruptly, like a TV switched off.

"Unnatural," Aunt Maria said. She continued to stare at the wall. "Vampires own the night, not the day. She shouldn't be hunting in daylight."

Daddy still had his hands on Pearl's shoulders. As she

opened her mouth to respond, he tightened his grip and said, "Now, Maria, bit of pot calling the kettle black, don't you think? We're all an affront to nature."

From her nest of blankets and bandages, Charlaine said in a muffled voice, "She'll condemn us all. She should be destroyed. The king will blame us for harboring a freak."

Daddy squeezed Pearl's shoulders again. "His Majesty appreciates results. If Pearl can demonstrate the effectiveness of her new skill, the king will reward us, not punish us."

"So say you," Aunt Maria said.

"So say I," Daddy said. "Continue, Felix." He directed Pearl to the hearth. "Sit and learn. Felix is an expert at gaining trust, and that is exactly what we need you to do. Befriend the students and gain admittance to their homes. From there . . . it should be easy to invent an excuse for them to invite us in after sundown." Vampires needed to be invited to enter a home. It was one of the fine-print details that came with vampirism, like the lack of a reflection and aversion to holy water.

"'Look like the innocent flower,'" Uncle Pascha said, quoting his beloved and not-exactly-contemporary Shakespeare again, "'but be the serpent under 't.'"

With a sigh, Pearl sank down on the hearth. She held Antoinette's clothes on her lap. Daddy leaned in the doorway, effectively blocking her path downstairs. Pressing her lips together to keep from insulting those relatives who hadn't advocated for her murder, Pearl listened as a centuries-old vampire counseled her about the modern teenager.

Chapter

SEVEN

High school.

Pearl placed her hands on her hips and surveyed the monstrosity. It hulked on a hillside, a fortresslike block with narrow slits for windows as if to allow the teachers to shoot arrows at the kids in the parking lot. *Not a bad idea,* she thought.

She'd refused to ride the school bus. She'd also turned down the neon-pink My Pretty Pony backpack that Uncle Felix offered her after a far-too-long anecdote about its acquisition. It sported bloodstains on one shoulder strap. Instead, she'd borrowed a military backpack from Uncle Pascha (actually used in WWI—it came with an anecdote too) and hiked across town.

Now that she was here, the temptation to keep walking was nearly suffocating. She'd rather walk across Connecticut (eastward into the sun) than walk into this shadowed prison and spend hours shoulder to shoulder with her supper. Humans didn't have to hang out in a chicken coop before having chicken nuggets. With this many humans, she bet it even smelled like a chicken coop. But she couldn't explain to Mother and Daddy that she'd balked because of the stench.

A familiar voice said behind her, "I thought you said you were homeschooled."

She nearly flinched. She hadn't heard the boy approach, which was inexcusable. Even in a parking lot with humans swarming in every direction, she should have been aware of her personal space. "Just enrolled," she said.

"Been inside yet?" Evan asked. He stood beside her, and she studied him from out of the corner of her eye. He wore a button-down shirt, slightly wrinkled, with jeans that had worn through in one knee. His neck looked soft and sweet against his collar.

"Nope," she said.

"Planning to?"

"Undecided."

"Fair enough." He fell silent, studying the school beside her. "Look, I feel like I owe you an apology. . . ."

Jumping up and down like a demented kangaroo, a girl screeched from across the parking lot and waved. "Evan! Over here!" Backpack bouncing on her back, she ran past the cars. She was puffing by the time she reached the sidewalk. "Hey, Evan," the girl panted. She then beamed at Pearl. "Hi, I'm Bethany."

Pearl raised her eyebrows at the newcomer. She never understood why any human would presume she wanted to talk. This human was of the perky sort. Her eyes sparkled, her teeth sparkled, and her strawberry-blonde hair sparkled. She carried a hot-pink backpack emblazoned with Hello Kitty. Pearl hoped she carried it ironically, but given the girl's chipper smile, Pearl had her doubts. She elected to ignore Bethany and returned to her assessment of the high school.

On all sides the school was framed by woods. To the left, the woods were broken by athletic fields, complete with bleachers and a track around a football field. Looking up at the school itself, Pearl noticed the mascot for the first time. Beside the words GREENBRIDGE HIGH SCHOOL was the white silhouette of a unicorn. In smaller letters, it read, HOME OF THE RAMPANT UNICORN. Automatically, she placed her hand over her heart, as if her hand could keep her vital organs safe and whole inside her. Her chest still ached, despite the pale skin that had sealed over the wound. Glaring at the unicorn silhouette, she decided that she hated coincidences. Or cosmic signs. Whichever it was. She felt as if the universe were laughing at her.

She heard Bethany stage-whisper to Evan, "Is she okay?"

"She has issues," Evan said.

"Oh," Bethany said. "Parents?"

"She didn't say," he said.

Bethany heaved a sigh. "I wish it were socially acceptable to walk up to strangers and say, 'Tell me your life story.' Every time I see someone interesting, I just about die from curiosity.

Luckily, there are so many boring people in this town that it's rarely a problem." She inserted herself between Pearl and her view of the school. "Hi! New here? Welcome!"

Pearl frowned and wondered what had given her the clue that Pearl was new. She hadn't spoken. She hadn't even moved. Surely, this girl didn't know all the students at Greenbridge High. For a second Pearl was tempted to ask. But then the temptation passed. She did not want to be sucked into a conversation with Miss Perky. "I have to check in at the school office," Pearl said. "Delightful to meet you." She strode forward.

Flanking her, Bethany and Evan walked with her. Each of them was close enough to lock arms with her and skip down the yellow brick road, or more accurately, the cracked concrete sidewalk. "We'll show you the way!" Bethany said.

"Fantastic," Pearl said. "All we need now is the Cowardly Lion."

Bethany chattered to Evan, "You know, I think I did problem six inside out. I don't think we were supposed to figure out the derivative. I think we were supposed to use the formula. But it was such a *neat* problem. . . ."

"You know we weren't assigned problem six, right?" Evan said.

"Oh!" Bethany said. "Really?"

Yellow buses lined the driveway to the school. As they opened their doors, students poured out. Cars whipped into parking spots and disgorged even more students. Humans flowed toward the school from every direction. It was impossible to track them all. Pearl felt as if she'd been caught in the middle of a herd.

Bethany leaned closer until their shoulders bumped. "Don't be nervous, Pearl. Everyone here is as sweet as cinnamon on a Toaster Strudel."

As if on cue, a bottle blonde strode across the sidewalk toward them. She walked with a swagger that was half pop star and half western gunslinger. Her face was too sallow and too angular to be pretty, and her outfit was mismatched plaid and stripes, but she wore it with all the confidence of Cousin Antoinette. Closer, Pearl noticed that she smelled like overripe strawberries. Stopping in front of Bethany, she said, "You parked in my spot."

Pearl watched semifascinated as blood rushed into Bethany's face and spread to her ears. In seconds her cheeks were flushed as red as a tomato. Vampires never blushed like that. Not enough spare blood. "Sorry!" Bethany squeaked.

Evan rolled his eyes. "You don't own the parking lot, Ashlyn."

"Still standing up for the losers, Evan?" Ashlyn said. "You need a new hobby." She fixed her eyes on Pearl. She raked her up and down. Pearl did her the same favor. This girl wasn't the anorexic model type, nor was she Miss Picture Perfect. Pearl noted that her left eyeliner meandered over her lid. Yet the nearby humans fanned out in a semicircle around her as if she were their queen.

"Nice boots," Ashlyn said in a tone that implied Pearl had strapped garbage cans to her feet and clanked out the door.

Snickers spread through the humans.

Without waiting for a response, Ashlyn spun on her heel and strode toward the school. Reaching the doors, she was flanked by a quartet of brunettes, her honor guard. They swung open the double doors and swept through as if going to a grand ball.

Pearl looked down at her knee-high steampunk boots and contemplated the steel tips.

"She boxed me in!" Bethany said. She pointed at a red BMW convertible that had parked sideways behind a squat blue minivan that resembled a lunch box from the seventies.

Pearl spoke, despite her resolution to ignore Bethany. "You drive *that*?"

Bethany wrung her hands. "Ashlyn has volleyball after school. I'll be stuck for hours!"

"Ask her to move it," Evan said. "You need to stand up for yourself."

Bethany shot him a look that was impressively withering, especially for a girl so perky, but Pearl was already striding across the parking lot. She halted next to the red convertible, and then she kicked hard and fast at the driver's side door. Her steel toe slammed into the door, and the metal crunched in a satisfying way.

She surveyed her handiwork: The door had caved in.

Nodding at it, she returned to the sidewalk.

Evan whistled low, and Bethany said, "Uh, thanks, Pearl."

"These *are* nice boots," Pearl said. She swept past them and entered the school. It wasn't until later that it occurred to her to wonder how Bethany knew her name.

The poofed-haired woman in the front office clucked her tongue over the paperwork that Pearl had dutifully filled out, and then handed Pearl a schedule. "Your locker is on C hall," she said. "Your first class is Honors English, room three forty-seven, with Mr. Barstow." She pointed at a map behind Pearl. "Don't worry, sweetie. You'll love it here. And if you don't . . ." She waved her hand in the air. "It won't last forever. Nothing does. Not even Spam."

Pearl smiled with her lips pressed tightly together. She didn't inhale—the woman wore enough perfume to stun a dog. Pearl didn't know how humans handled being around each other with such odors.

"You'd better take this hall pass," the woman said. The sign on her desk said her name was Mrs. Kerry. "First period already started." She scrawled on a pink slip of paper and handed it to Pearl.

Pearl accepted the slip plus a packet of papers. She was careful not to touch the woman's pudgy fingers. She didn't want any of that scent to cling to her. As she exited the front office, she studied her schedule.

"Ooh, yes, we share first period!" Bethany, clearly waiting for her, clapped her hands like a four-year-old delighted with a new dolly. "Come on, let's go!" She grabbed Pearl's elbow and propelled her down the hall.

Blend in, Pearl reminded herself. *Do not chuck the girl into the lockers.*

Inside, Greenbridge High smelled like antiseptic cleaning supplies, mixed with a hint of old socks. The walls were pale-green cement blocks, and the floor was drab gray linoleum, streaked with scuff marks. Stretches of lockers were interrupted by bulletin boards. As they approached a set of double doors, Pearl spotted another picture of the school mascot. Painted in red and silver, this unicorn reared over the doorway with an elongated torso and a slightly bent horn. Its eyes were red with a drip of paint down its cheek that looked like a blood tear. "Nice touch," she said to it.

"Sorry?"

"Your school is a glorious sanctuary," Pearl said.

"Uh, thanks." Pointing at the doors, Bethany said, "Cafetorium. Half cafeteria, half auditorium. We have everything from sloppy joes to Albanian folk dance demonstrations in there. Up ahead is the old gym. The new gym, which is fifteen years old but still newer than the old gym, is in the back." She continued to pull Pearl down the hall. She halted in front of an orange door with a narrow window. She caught her breath. "Don't worry. Mr. Barstow is a petty dictator with a Napoleonic complex, but it only lasts forty-seven minutes. Plus Evan's in the class." Conspiratorially, she whispered, "You know, I think he likes you."

After that extraordinary comment, Bethany pushed the door open.

"Ms. Norton!" a voice boomed.

Bethany shrank back. She seemed frozen between flight and . . . well, not-flight. Pearl rolled her eyes and shoved past her into the classroom. Finally, Bethany piped up from behind Pearl, "New student, Mr. Barstow!"

The owner of the booming voice, Mr. Barstow, bore an uncanny resemblance to a garden gnome. His gnarled white beard lay against a tomato-red shirt. Bits of bread were suspended in the wiry snarls. "Very nice, Ms. Norton, but *you* aren't a new student. You are a late student. Do you have a hall pass?"

Feeling the eyes of the class on her, Pearl presented the pink slip. She pressed her lips together to keep any remark from slipping through (or fangs from slipping out).

He scowled at it. "Take a seat. Welcome to Honors English, Ms. . . ."

"Sange. Pearl Rose Sange." Out of the corner of her eyes, she scanned the classroom and spotted Evan. He'd chosen a chair by the window. Sunlight streamed in, illuminating the dust to create distinct rays so it appeared as if he were highlighted by a halo of angelic light. If he'd been trying to stage it to catch her eye, he couldn't have planned it better. She stared at him, or more specifically at the sunbeams. Clearly enjoying her stare, Evan grinned at her. She contemplated shoving him out of the way to claim the sun seat, but she doubted that was what Mr. Barstow meant by "take a seat." She thought of Bethany's assertion that he liked her. If he truly "liked" her, he'd give her the seat.

"I expect you to borrow notes from another student," Mr. Barstow said. "Catch up as best you can. Finals are in a mere two months, and I can't have the whole class suffer to accommodate you." He shook his head. "Honestly, why do parents think it unimportant to start school at the beginning of the year? Learning is cumulative!" He pounded his fist in his hand for emphasis.

"Ms. Norton will provide me with notes," Pearl said. She raised her eyebrows at Bethany, which was as close to asking for assistance as her pride would allow. She found the idea of asking favors of humans to be repugnant.

"Of course!" Bethany chirped.

Sighing, Mr. Barstow dismissed them with a wave of his hand. "Find seats, you two, and don't make me separate you." He turned his back on them and began to write on the board. "Jealousy, irresponsibility, denial, and insecurity. John Knowles believed that the peace of maturity could not be attained until each of these was addressed."

Pearl threaded through the rows toward an empty seat. Every set of eyes was fixed on her, which made her feel better. It was at least a familiar sensation. She'd been the focus of human attention before. Plus it helped that this class was a controlled environment with everyone seated (or slouching) in rows, rather than the free-for-all cattle call that marked the start of school. She added an extra swish to her step. She checked to be sure that Evan was watching her.

Trailing behind her, Bethany whispered, "Thanks. He scares me."

Pearl suspected a bunny would scare Bethany. "Clearly you have never met my uncle Stefan," she said. She slid into an empty seat.

"Ooh, worse?" Bethany asked.

"You have no idea."

A few students continued to stare at her. Others switched their attention elsewhere: their notebooks, their phones (held by their sides or beneath their desks), their friends, anywhere but at Mr. Barstow. Evan's attention had shifted to the window, as if he were waiting with bated breath for the leaves on the trees to sprout. She didn't blame him—she'd rather stare at the sun-encrusted courtyard than at a chalkboard lit by bluish fluorescent bulbs—but if he was attracted to her, as Bethany had implied, his eyes ought to be riveted on her.

At the front of the class, Mr. Barstow tapped on the chalkboard with a battered copy of *A Separate Peace*. "Please give me examples of each of these. From the book, please, not your lives. I am one hundred percent uninterested in who has wronged whom this week."

Forcing herself to ignore Evan, Pearl clasped her hands in front of her and studied the words on the board. She committed them to memory, along with the other scrawled notes and a nonsensical pie chart. Every other student seemed to have a notebook, though she wasn't sure why it was necessary for so few words. Perhaps human powers of retention were lesser, as well as their base intelligence level. She glanced around the room and saw that half the notebooks were empty and the other half were filled with doodles of hearts and stars or, in the case of a boy with hair flopped over his eyes, an intricate dragon with fingernail-size scales. Evan's notebook—at least what she could see from here—was covered in words that filled every inch of the page in neat script. She wondered if it was poetry after all. He seemed like such the secret poet type. As Evan glanced over at her, Pearl looked away. She supposed she should track down some school supplies, complete this charade. Cousin Jocelyn might have some spare paper and pens to donate to the cause.

Providing examples himself, Mr. Barstow added notes to the board.

Behind her, Pearl heard a student whisper to another, "Going out tonight?"

"Can't," a girl whispered back. "Parents."

All around her she heard soft clicks, so faint they could have been fingernails on flesh. But a peek to the left and right revealed the dance of fingers tapping on phones. Another student sneaked M&M's from his pocket, popping them in his mouth like pills that he swallowed whole. Another lightly snored. Pearl imagined if these students were in one of Aunt Fiona's classes. One banshee shriek and their attention would never wander again.

Mr. Barstow seemed as oblivious to the students as they were to his lecture. "So if Phineas is the personification of innocence"—he scrawled, "Finny = innocent"—"you can see the obvious symbolic importance of the climactic event as a fall. It is a fall from innocence for all the characters. This fall transforms Gene as he moves from childhood to adulthood, but for Phineas—our personification of innocence—he is unable to accept his transformation, to release the innocent, guilt-free view of Gene, and so he is unable to complete his transformation."

One hand was raised. "So he, like, turns into a butterfly?"

A few students in the back laughed. Others, like Bethany, were nearly quivering in their chairs. Pearl realized that some were listening to Mr. Barstow. She had the sense that they wanted to raise their hands. She wondered what kept them from speaking up.

The boy said, "Seriously, there's this one story where the guy wakes up and he's this bug and it's very deep."

A few others tittered. Mr. Barstow's face tinted red. A vein in his neck bulged.

Ugh, this could go on and on. Pearl interrupted, "Kafka's *Metamorphosis*. Boy turns into cockroach. Accurate depiction of man's position in the world."

Mr. Barstow raised both of his woolly eyebrows as he looked at her. His face began to return to its normal paper-pale shade. "Interesting," he said. To the class, he asked, "Can *anyone* tell me what happens after Phineas's failed transformation?"

No one answered.

A few shifted uncomfortably. Several glanced at their watches, the clock, or their phones. One looked at all three, as if by checking everything she'd find a more favorable answer. Again, Pearl noticed a few hands that trembled on the desktop, as if they wanted to reach up but extra gravity held them down. Bethany continued quivering in her seat. Evan was watching Pearl.

Mr. Barstow sighed gustily. "Did anyone finish last night's reading? Climax of the book, people. Even CliffsNotes should mention it." He focused on Pearl, and she tore her attention away from Evan. She didn't know why that human boy kept drawing her attention. It was getting annoying. "Have you read *A Separate Peace*, Ms. Sange? Can you tell everyone the spoiler that somehow evaded their keen reading comprehension skills?"

She shrugged. "Anything that fails to transform, dies."

He exhaled a puff so loudly that it was like a whale spouting. "Finally, an insight. Welcome to my class, Ms. Sange. I pray that you leave here smarter than you enter and that your classmates do not leach intelligence out of you by their proximity."

She glanced around the class. That was a distinct worry. Still . . . "They'd be smarter if you hadn't terrified them into silence." She couldn't comprehend how he had done it. His flabby arms couldn't throw a punch. She could evade him with her eyes squeezed shut and one leg tied back so she had to hop like a flamingo, which she had tried once in training. Results had not been pretty.

He arched his bushy eyebrows. "Here for less than a class, and you have analyzed the full dynamics already."

"Pretty much."

"Yet you don't seem to be terrified into silence."

Pearl shrugged. "That's because I know I'm superior to you."

All the students froze.

Keeping her appearance casual, Pearl readied for an attack. Her feet stayed crossed, but her leg muscles tensed in case she had to spring into action. Her fingers, twirling her hair, touched the steel barrette that she had filed to a point. She watched Mr. Barstow. It was better, she reasoned, to see what the dangers were at the beginning. If the teachers at this school were dangerous, she needed to know sooner rather than later.

Bemused, Mr. Barstow blinked at her. Pearl thought she may have even seen a hint of a smile, but then she convinced herself she'd imagined it. "Since it's your first day, I'll be magnanimous and not hand out a detention. Consider yourself warned."

She wondered what kind of punishment constituted a "detention." Mother had several holding cells, each a lightless nightmare. Pearl had been in one once for shoplifting at the mall. With all the security cameras, Mother had felt it was too high risk. After twenty-four hours in the cell, Pearl hadn't been tempted to repeat the incident—at least not at that mall.

Mr. Barstow proceeded to ignore her for the rest of the class. The other students, however, did not. She heard whispers buzz around her, while every student in the class shot her sidelong glances. She used the opportunity to study them as well. A few boys in the front wore button-up shirts and had their hair carefully combed out of their eyes. A few in back wore strategically ripped jeans and T-shirts with random slogans that she wasn't convinced would make sense even in context. One girl wore a miniskirt so high that it nearly morphed into a blouse. The center of the classroom was occupied by a swath of boys and girls in unmemorable outfits. She studied the power structure by watching body language. For nearly all the students, it was easy to peg their place in the hierarchy: A glance here, a shift there, and she could tell who wanted approval from the teacher and who wanted approval from a nearby student. Only Evan proved difficult to read, but that was primarily because he kept glancing at Pearl. Staring back at him, she decided his expression looked a lot more like amusement than adoration.

A bell rang, and she jerked in her seat.

All the semicomatose kids leaped out of their chairs. Backpacks were slung over shoulders, and notebooks and textbooks were shoved into bags. Pearl stood. In seconds, Bethany and Evan flanked her like bodyguards.

In his deep silky voice, Evan said, "That was impressive. You alienated your first teacher in your first class of your first day."

"Are you kidding?" Bethany said. "She's, like, a hero!" With shining eyes, she turned to Pearl. "You are exactly what this school needs."

"How convenient," Pearl said, "since this school is exactly what I need."

Chapter
EIGHT

A few classes later Pearl joined the salmon stream of juniors heading for the cafetorium—honestly, that was the dumbest name for a room that she'd ever heard. She let the chatter ebb and flow around her and wondered if she would become used to the cacophony of sounds and smells.

She was aware that some of the students were chattering about her. She'd managed to keep her mouth shut in her other classes, but she'd supplied enough fodder by the end of first period to entertain the masses. By third period, her exchange with Mr. Barstow had blossomed in the retelling to become a full-out screaming match, during which she had supposedly insulted his ancestry and his prize Maltese. By fourth period, news of her run-in with Ashlyn's car had spread as well. One variant of that tale involved explosions. If Daddy and Mother expected her to keep a low profile, she was failing. Luckily, Daddy and Mother were zonked out underground.

Pearl let herself be swept with the other students into a line. Kids clustered in front and behind her. She watched as they selected orange plastic trays and then proceeded through the food line. Choosing her own tray, she followed. Newly washed, it dripped water on her hands. Mimicking the other students, she held it away from her to avoid dampening her sweater.

As she reached the front of the line, her nose was assaulted by the sweaty stench of grease. She noticed some of the students were bypassing the line altogether, carrying bags and the occasional knapsack. Next time she'd pretend to bring lunch.

She pursed her lips as she read the scrawled signs above each congealed food item: vegetarian, kosher, lactose-free, low sodium. . . . She bet there wasn't a vampire-friendly option. She'd have to fake eating. Pearl selected a salad that looked as though it would make some rabbit ecstatic and a container of red fruit juice that at least reminded her of something edible.

She wondered if anyone would notice if she packed a thermos of blood. It would be stale, of course, but at least she wouldn't have to worry about hunger pangs at awkward moments. So far she hadn't had a single opportunity to feed. Her stomach growled, and she eyed the neck of a boy in a gym shirt as she followed him to the cashier. Peachlike fuzz covered the back of his neck. She snagged a piece of fruit from a basket.

"Student lunch account number?" the cashier asked.

Pearl frowned at her tray. She was sure her parents hadn't made arrangements for this. They wouldn't have thought of lunch as something she'd need to participate in. "I'll return these."

A voice behind her said, "I'll cover her."

She knew without looking that it was Evan. "No, thanks. I'm not hungry." Last thing she needed was to be beholden to any of these humans, especially Evan. His knight-in-shining-armor act shouldn't be encouraged.

"No one eats alone on their first day," he said. "Ought to be an official rule."

Lousy rule, she thought. She couldn't eat in a crowd, at least not without inspiring a lot of screaming.

He swiped his student ID, and the cashier nodded them through.

"Keep this up, and one of these days you'll be nice to the wrong person," she said. Her Good Samaritan warning of the day delivered, she swept by him.

Following her, he said, "Is it overstepping if I tell you where to find the forks?" He pointed at a display of utensils and napkins right before the entrance to the cafetorium.

Pearl was reasonably certain that he was laughing at her. Glaring at him, she selected a fork and knife. For good measure, she also picked up a spoon. She hoped she remembered how to use them—she'd had training once in a human etiquette class, but she hadn't practiced since then. She brushed past Evan and entered the cafetorium itself.

The noise was nearly deafening, as if several flocks of seagulls were fighting over a whale carcass. It also smelled not unlike a whale carcass.

It took Pearl a second to adjust to the sound and smell before she looked properly at the cafetorium. It was large enough to fit all four hundred students in the junior class. One wall explained the "auditorium" part of the name: It featured a stage with a blue-and-red curtain across it. The red blotches looked more like ketchup stains than an intentional design choice. Two other walls were the same greenish concrete blocks that filled the rest of the school. The fourth wall, however, was a bank of windows. Glorious sunlight spilled from the windows to cover all the tables.

Each table had a flock of students at it. Interestingly, each flock member matched the others, as if they were birds that had congregated based on plumage. But the groups weren't distinguished so much by physical appearance or ethnicity as they were by clothing choices, hairstyles, and mannerisms. One table featured guys in mostly buttoned shirts. Another table held students in T-shirts and torn jeans. Another brimmed with an overabundance of pink. Perhaps Cousin Antoinette's movies weren't so far off.

"Our table is there," Evan said, nodding at a table in the corner.

Bethany hopped up from the table and waved.

As Pearl took a step forward, the bottle-blonde Ashlyn slammed down her lunch bag at her table of shiny-haired girls and then marched across the cafetorium toward Pearl. Her entourage of four brunettes trailed behind her in a V formation like geese. Students fell silent in her wake.

Tray in her hands, Pearl waited.

She studied Ashlyn as she approached and confirmed the impression she'd made outside. Ashlyn wasn't overly pretty. Her makeup was stark against her washed-out skin. Her arms were so skinny that her elbows looked like knots in a tree. She lacked the muscle tone to be exceptionally strong, and she hadn't been in any of the honors classes this morning so she couldn't be particularly intelligent. So what made her queen bee? Every head she passed turned to watch her. She clearly had power, though Pearl couldn't detect its source.

Ashlyn leveled a finger at Pearl's chest. "You dented my car!"

"Yes, I did," Pearl said. She tensed in case the girl flew toward her. After all, Cousin Jocelyn didn't appear to be strong either, yet she could chuck a motorcycle a hundred yards. (She'd done it once. Pearl never knew what the poor bike had done to offend her, except perhaps fail to recite a sonnet in iambic pentameter.)

Ashlyn was momentarily speechless. Whatever response she'd expected, that wasn't it. Her entourage exchanged glances and shifted uneasily. Pearl guessed that she'd veered from the standard script.

Cocking her head, Pearl waited to see what the girl would do next.

"You'll pay for the repairs," Ashlyn said. "I'm having my parents call your parents. They'll make you pay to fix it."

It couldn't be intelligence that fueled Ashlyn's power. Pearl detected nothing superior about her wit. So far, she seemed no more articulate than a cat spitting its fury at a rival. She also lacked the common sense to know she was spitting at a tiger. If Pearl wanted to, she could break the girl in half. "I have a better idea," Pearl said. "How about I send my parents over to your house tonight to discuss it?"

Ashlyn blinked. Again, Pearl obviously hadn't responded as expected. She heard students at nearby tables whisper and titter. "They'll bring a check for the damage?"

"Of course," Pearl said.

"Well . . ." Ashlyn glanced behind her at her entourage. The four brunettes fidgeted, clearly confused about the direction of the conversation.

"Can you tell your parents to expect mine?" Pearl said. Once Ashlyn's parents invited Pearl's parents inside, then they'd be able to come and go as they pleased. This one incident could provide them with multiple meals, as well as contribute to the king's dinner. "What's your address?"

"One fifty Mount Grey Road," Ashlyn said. She seemed a bit dazed, as if trying to figure out when she'd lost control of the conversation.

"Splendid," Pearl said. "Are we done?"

Pearl watched Ashlyn draw her scattered confidence into herself as if drawing breath. It filled the girl as she straightened her shoulders and lifted her chin. Ashlyn plastered a smile on her face, and Pearl could tell it was the sort of smile meant to project out to adoring crowds. Every eye at the nearby tables was riveted to the two of them. Some students had quit walking to their own tables to watch. "I accept your apology," Ashlyn said in a voice that carried. "And please try not to be a bitch again. That's my job."

"You do it well," Pearl said sincerely. She meant it. She didn't know how Ashlyn was commanding the attention of the other students, but they were focused on this girl with all the intensity of mice who had noticed a hawk. Pearl found herself impressed—perhaps not as impressed as she was by, say, Uncle Felix, who once reportedly scaled the outside of the Empire State Building in a late-night, blood-drunk reenactment of King Kong, but she was at least as impressed as she was by the mangy, flea-bitten cat that ruled an alley downtown.

Ashlyn laughed, a real laugh, as if she were delighted with Pearl's response. "I can't decide if you're stupid or crazy. Time will tell, I guess." She tossed her hair and turned back toward her table. Over her shoulder, she said, "Welcome to Greenbridge High."

The brunettes fell into position behind her as they trooped back to their table. The students erupted into chatter again. Pearl hadn't realized how quiet everyone had fallen during their exchange. She watched as Ashlyn strode across the cafetorium with all the confidence of a vampire . . . and Pearl wondered if that was it, if it was the confidence that she radiated that was the source of her power.

If that's all it takes, Pearl thought, *then I'm going to rule this place.*

Softly, Evan said in her ear, "You didn't actually apologize."

"I do *try* not to lie," Pearl said. "It's bad for karma."

She swept forward into a swath of sunlight. As the sun spread over her face, she let out a happy sigh. As if pulled by the light, she turned toward the bank of windows. Formica sparkled from the nearby tables. Young faces glowed with a pinkness she never saw in her relatives.

"Pearl, our table is in the opposite direction. No pressure, of course. . . ."

Ignoring him, she crossed to the door to the courtyard.

A teacher's voice said, "If you take your tray outside, remember to return it. No one will pick up after you. We aren't your servants."

"Pity," Pearl murmured as she pushed open the door and then stepped into the midday sun. As the breeze swept past her, it lifted her hair and tousled it. She felt the sun touch her neck, warm despite the not-quite-spring air. She stood still for a moment as the rays spread over her. The courtyard held a semicircle of picnic tables with graffiti gouged so deeply that the wood looked ready to split. Straggly trees ringed the tables, half blocking the classroom windows. One end of the courtyard opened onto the school parking lot.

A few students were scattered around the picnic tables.

She gravitated toward an empty table. She laid the tray down and then stretched herself out on the bench, face up to the sky. A few minutes later she heard voices.

"Dude, it's so her."

She opened her eyes when shade fell over her face. Shoulder to shoulder, the two wannabe vampire hunters peered down at her. "Whoa, you go here?" Chubby said.

"You're blocking the sun," Pearl said.

Like Tweedledum and Tweedledee, they shifted sideways in unison.

She closed her eyes and focused on the warmth of the sunlight. She continued to hear them breathe. Sighing, she opened her eyes. "Seriously? You're still here?" For a moment she missed the night. She could have a moment alone at night. She never knew humans were so socially needy.

"You're the new girl that everyone's talking about," Tall said. He plopped down on the bench beside her. "You realize you have already achieved mythic status. Kudos."

Pearl sat up.

Chubby sat on the other side of her. "You don't want to eat that," he said, pointing to a shriveled crouton in her salad.

"True," she said.

"So how do you like Greenbridge High?" Tall asked. "Is it not a delightful treasure trove of intellectual splendor?"

"I am delighted beyond belief," Pearl said.

Tall whipped out a paper bag and extracted a sandwich. He plugged his mouth with it, but to Pearl's disappointment, he continued to talk around the bread. "We'd be honored to be your guides as you adjust to this mad, mad world. We know the ins and outs of this school. We can tell you who's safe and who's"—he dropped his voice low—"suspect."

Don't ask, Pearl ordered herself. *Do not engage them further.* But the word just hung there. "'Suspect'?"

"We're crusaders," Chubby said.

"There's more to this world than meets the eye, Horatio," Tall intoned.

Approaching the table, Evan corrected, "'There are more things in heaven and earth, Horatio, than are dreamt of in your philosophy.'" Evan straddled the bench opposite her and grinned. "Looks like you found plenty of people to eat lunch with. Apologies for underestimating you."

Pearl turned her head. Behind her, a semicircle of kids had formed. She tried to pick out which group they were from based on Antoinette's descriptions and the tables she'd seen inside, but these seemed to be a mix. Some wore torn jeans and strings of safety pins. Others wore tight skirts and drooping shirts. Others were in plain shirts and jeans or sweaters and skirts. A few wore flip-flops, despite the chill. A few wore heels. Most wore sneakers. One wore clogs. All of them had their eyes (black, brown, green, blue, hazel, overly mascaraed, kohl-painted, natural) trained on Pearl.

"Yes?" Pearl said to them.

One spoke up, "Heard you went ballistic on Queen Ashlyn's car."

Another said, "You stood up to Mr. Barstow."

"I heard you clog danced across the cars of the entire volleyball team," a third said.

"I heard you punched out Mr. Barstow."

She debated clarifying the rumors and then discarded the idea. She shrugged. "It's been a busy day," she said. A few of them smiled. All of them continued to watch her, including Evan. "What do you want?"

The hunter wannabe Tall spoke up, "You have that shiny new-girl smell. General consensus is you rock, and we want to see what you do next."

Chubby said, "Yeah, we totally want to worship you."

Pearl smiled at them. "That would be lovely."

Chapter
NINE

"You smell of humans," Mother said.

Pearl maneuvered through the stacks of books and papers in Mother's underground office toward the wingback chair. "It's given me a headache," she admitted. The stench was caught in her hair. She'd need a dozen showers with extra-strength soap plus a Brillo pad to scrub herself.

"Stand," Mother said as Pearl reached the chair. "I do not want the smell to seep into the upholstery." She added another name to a yellow legal pad.

Reading upside down, Pearl saw it was an invite list to the Fealty Ceremony. She envisioned a string of nights spent sealing envelopes and suppressed a sigh. "Aren't you worried that invites will fall into the wrong hands?"

Mother nodded at a stack of a hundred or so cards. "Look. Don't touch."

About to reach for one, Pearl froze. She clasped her hands behind her back and looked. The cream-colored cards looked like silk. In the center was a single image: a twist of leaves in front of the crescent moon, the Family seal. Underneath it, there was a date.

"We will add a drop of Family blood to each one to prove its authenticity," Mother said. "As attendees arrive in our territory at sundown, we will escort them through the tunnels to the mansion's cellar. No one outside the Family will know the specific location until the night of the event."

Pearl closed her hands over her wrists. "Whose blood?" She didn't have any to spare right now.

Mother looked up sharply.

She should have kept her mouth shut. Perhaps it was a decent time to change the subject. "I have an address for you. One fifty Mount Grey Road. A girl named Ashlyn has told her parents to expect you and Daddy tonight. So you know, she thinks you'll be bringing a check to pay for a little car damage."

Mother raised her perfectly sculpted eyebrow. Pearl wished she could master that expression. Without a reflection, she couldn't practice in a mirror. "Very well," Mother said. She put down her pen and rose to her feet. "Daddy and I will leave now. It would be a shame to be late when we're expected. And speaking of late, you have a class with Minerva."

Seriously? After all day in human high school, she had to attend more classes? "But . . . ," Pearl began. She saw Mother's lips begin to press together, and she changed what she planned to say. "I'd hoped to accompany you and Daddy. I didn't have a chance to eat today, and Ashlyn—"

"You need the extra etiquette training most of all," Mother said. "We have to erase any bad habits you acquire through consorting with humans." She crossed her office to an ornate wardrobe decorated with Renaissance-like scenes that featured vampires feasting on corseted shepherdesses plus cupids with fiery hands in a shaft of sunlight—Mother's idea of art was not demure. She kept her "work" clothes here, the ones she wore to hunt. Opening the wardrobe, she selected a burgundy suit dress. "Any details I should know? Did you create any alibis we must uphold?"

Pearl shook her head. "Everyone seemed very interested in knowing me. No one seemed at all interested in knowing any-thing about me." *Except for Evan and Bethany,* she amended silently, but she'd told them nothing so it didn't count.

"Excellent," Mother said. "You have learned your lessons well." She held up a finger to forestall Pearl's reply. "Not that that excuses you from class tonight. Shower first. You smell of bathroom stalls and human trash."

Pearl opened her mouth to protest that this wasn't her fault. High school wasn't her idea. But then she saw Mother's expression—her lips curled as if she anticipated Pearl's response—and Pearl wisely didn't speak. Later, if Pearl could catch Daddy alone, she'd ask whether she truly had to attend every day. It seemed a bit overkill, no pun intended.

"Put your towel in the hamper when you finish," Mother said. "Otherwise, we'll find Cousin Jeremiah chomping on it later tonight."

"Yes, Mother."

"Use the upstairs," she said. "I don't want the downstairs showers contaminated."

"Yes, Mother," Pearl repeated.

"And remember: Silence about your daytime activities," Mother said. "Until the king's dinner is secured, other vampires may not look favorably on your new ability. We do not want word to reach His Majesty before the ceremony."

"Of course, Mother." She bowed as she backed out of the office.

Out in the corridor, Pearl leaned against the cool concrete wall. She'd nearly antagonized Mother in there. She had to remember to watch herself. She was back in her world now, and she needed to focus. As a door opened and shut around the corner, Pearl peeled herself off the wall and headed quickly for the stairs. It would be best if she could avoid Family until she was in a more suitable mind-set. Mother was right—these humans had a corrupting influence.

Upstairs in the house, she locked the bathroom door behind her and turned on only the hot water. She let it run until waves of steam poured into the room, and then she shed her pink sweater, black skirt, and steampunk boots. She stepped under the stream. Hot water hissed on her skin, and she let it flow over her. She hadn't drunk enough blood today for her skin to redden in the heat, but she felt it scald away the taint of humanness.

Out there, in the sun, it was alarmingly easy to forget that humans weren't real people. She'd laughed at Evan's jokes. She'd wanted him to look at her. At the library she'd been insulted when he criticized her clothes. Yes, she'd wanted to bite him too, but that didn't make up for the fact that she'd had conversations with humans as if she were one of them.

Grabbing a towel, she scrubbed hard, as if she could scour away every human breath that had touched her body. When she finished, she felt dizzy, and her head hurt. She needed more blood. Tomorrow she had to arrange to bite someone. It was just so impossible to find a student alone. They traveled in flocks like sheep.

Pearl brushed her teeth, popping her fangs out to clean them. She then dressed in her favorite soft black jeans and a nice black blouse. Her headache squeezed harder. If she wanted to make it to dawn without passing out, she'd have to sneak a pint or two of stored blood.

Ugh, that was a disgusting thought.

She headed downstairs after depositing the towel in the laundry, per Mother's request. Downstairs was mostly empty. Since a few of the older vampires were ultraquiet, one could never be sure, but she didn't see any relatives. She crept past the doors that led to each one's private rooms.

Each door in the catacombs was steel and resembled a

bank vault door, except for the one to the storage room, which looked more like the door to a walk-in refrigerator—mainly because it was. Pearl paused by the storage room door and listened. She heard nothing. She shot glances in both directions. She saw no one.

She could *not* believe she was raiding the storage room for spare blood. This was humiliating. She promised herself it was just this once. Easing the door open, she ducked inside. Chill air pricked her still-damp skin. She walked quickly to the back, selected a jar from a shelf at random, and cracked it open. Holding her nose, she chugged it down. The old blood tasted like copper. She felt as if she were sucking on pennies. After she finished the jar, she squeezed her lips shut, forcing the blood to stay down as it churned in her stomach. Slowly, the blood spread through her, warming her arms and legs. Her fingers and toes began to tingle, and she sighed in relief.

Now she was ready.

She sneaked out of the storage room and headed for Minerva's quarters. It was a fifteen-minute trek (and occasionally a crawl through a few of the narrower passageways). Pearl had never had a class with her, but she knew where she lived because of Jadrien. Minerva had been his private tutor. His Family had a lot of ambitions for him.

Minerva was a member of the New Haven clan, but she frequently tutored members of other Families, due to either her venerable age or her overabundance of wrinkles. (Either she was remarkably old or she'd been turned late in life.) Rumor had it she was as old as the king of New England himself. Not a question that was prudent to ask any vampire, even a sweet little old teacher vampire.

Unlike the other steel doors, Minerva's door had been painted a rich purple with gold accents. Pearl paused in front of it to straighten her blouse, smooth her hair, and pluck the spiderwebs off her shoes.

"Come in, child," a voice said through the door. The voice was warm and welcoming. It creaked like an old rocking chair. Pearl pushed the door open and stepped inside.

Inside was decorated with delicate chairs and tables covered in curled gold that looked as if they'd been pinched from Versailles in a postrevolution yard sale. A priceless collection of hideous antiques—china plates painted with pastoral scenes, ornate filigree eggs, and bejeweled vases—filled shelves on the walls. But the most noticeable feature of the room was the crystal chandelier. Suited to a grand ballroom with a cathedral ceiling, rather than an ordinary room, the chandelier dangled so low that the bottom crystals were only three feet above the faded Oriental rug.

Minerva stood next to the chandelier. She held an ivory cane in one hand and was dressed in high-necked lace and damask silk. Around her in a semicircle were two dozen young vampires, including Jadrien. All of them were silent, as if they were sculptures in Minerva's collection too.

"So delighted you could join us," Minerva said with a warm

smile. "This class is specifically for young vampires about to experience their first Fealty Ceremony. I do hope you'll be our first volunteer."

She heard a hiss, and her eyes fixed on Jadrien's face. His eyes slid away from hers to focus on the Oriental rug. Pearl began, "Since I'm late, perhaps—"

"You must learn exactly how to behave in the presence of the king of New England," Minerva said. "One important rule is not to be tardy. The king values punctuality, as do I."

Since she'd been sworn to secrecy, Pearl realized she couldn't explain. She hoped this wasn't going to be a problem. Minerva couldn't be truly angry. She seemed too much like a refined heiress, who surely held herself above such pettiness. "Please accept my apology—"

"You and you," Minerva said as she pointed to two male vampires. Pearl recognized them vaguely. One was Jadrien's brother Chadwick. He had a collection of desiccated bat wings— a collection that, to Pearl's amusement, he'd failed to find at all ironic. She couldn't remember the name of the other vampire, but she thought he was from the Old Saybrook clan. Like her, both were due to complete the Fealty Ceremony for the first time this year. "Please stand on either side of our volunteer."

If this was about how to curtsy to the king, then she could handle it. Thanks to Aunt Lianne's constant badgering, Pearl had perfect posture. She tried again to meet Jadrien's eyes for some hint of what to expect. Avoiding her eyes again, he focused on the chandelier.

"My darlings, if you fail to arrive on time, if you fail to approach the throne in the specified number of steps, if you fail to greet His Majesty with the proper words, if you sip from the wrong side of the Cup of Fealty . . . the reaction will be swift." Minerva nodded to the boys who flanked Pearl. "Hold her steady, please."

The two of them gripped Pearl's arms. Pearl reminded herself not to resist. Minerva was her teacher, and Mother had sent her here with the expectation of obedience. Her expression still pleasant, Minerva picked up a flail. It consisted of a metal bar with three chains dangling from it. Each chain ended in a spiked ball.

Minerva walked in a semicircle around Pearl.

"Really, this isn't necessary. I underst—," Pearl began.

Pain exploded on her skin as the spikes bit into her back.

"Do not scream," Minerva instructed her.

As Pearl clamped her mouth shut, Minerva hit again. And again.

Pearl huddled beneath the chandelier. The other students filed past her as Minerva shooed them into a straight line. "Yes, my jewels, my gems, my delights!" Minerva crowed. "Excellent, keep walking! You all must master the proper walk. . . . Pearl, I said *all*."

As Jadrien walked past her, Pearl thought he'd reach down and help her stand. But his eyes slid over her as if she were invisible. Alone, she struggled to her feet as pain shot from her back down her thighs. She gritted her teeth as her head spun and was grateful that she'd had the stale blood. Without it, she might not have risen at all.

"Shoulders back," Minerva instructed, her voice still cheerful. "Posture. Arms lightly by your side. Your steps should be no more than one and a half feet in length, and you should follow this rhythm." She clapped, and everyone marched in a circle. Their footsteps were soft on the Oriental rug. "His Majesty repeats this ceremony once a century for each state in his domain. Any variation from the proper ritual, and he will notice. Any lapse, and he will notice. Any hesitation, and he will notice. And, kittens, he is not as kind as I."

Gritting her teeth against the pain, Pearl joined the end of the line.

They marched for three hours.

At last, Minerva lined them up against the shelves with the filigree eggs and priceless vases. "At the start of the ceremony, each of you will be announced by name and lineage. You will then proceed forward like so. . . ." She demonstrated by walking toward a thronelike chair. She smoothly knelt on one knee. "Hands on your bent knee. Incline your head. Come on, my delights, let's try the approach."

One by one, the vampires mimicked Minerva.

A few succeeded. Most did not. Their heads weren't bowed, or their heads were too bowed, or they didn't kneel smoothly enough. By the time it was Pearl's turn, eight others had felt the flail.

As Minerva fixed her kindly old eyes on her, Pearl straightened her back. Her split skin burned each time her shirt whispered against it. Swinging her arms lightly, she walked forward. Each step sent a fresh jolt of pain through her, but she didn't flinch or slow. Without pause, she dropped lightly to one knee and tilted her head.

"Very nice, Pearl," Minerva said. She placed a hand on Pearl's back, and Pearl froze. Sweat beaded on her forehead as Minerva's hand rested on her raw wounds. "Once this ritual is complete, the king will summon each of you by name and then drink from you. Stand, Pearl."

Pearl obeyed. Grabbing a fistful of Pearl's hair, Minerva tilted Pearl's head. Minerva leaned close, her fangs extended. Pearl ceased breathing. She felt the tips of Minerva's fangs brush across the skin of her neck. In her head, she knew the venom wouldn't affect her—nature's way of protecting the predators from one another—but her body hadn't received the memo. Every muscle screamed at Pearl to move or fight. She held the pose by sheer willpower.

Minerva withdrew.

"After he drinks from each of you, the king will fill a goblet with his own blood, which his servant will carry to each vampire at the ceremony, both new vampires and old," Minerva said. "Be aware that through all of this, you must never turn your back on your king." She nodded at Pearl. "Demonstrate for us, please, my dove. Return to the line."

Pearl wiped her face of any emotion, and she wiped her

mind of any thought. She concentrated every ounce of energy on retreating backward smoothly. Once in line, she allowed a thought she'd never had before to slip into her mind:

She wished for dawn.

Chapter
TEN

Steel-toed boots clicking on the linoleum, Pearl strode through the high school halls. Students fell into step behind her, as if she were a Goth Pied Piper. By the time she reached her locker, she had a train of a dozen guys and girls. They joined the cluster of humans who were waiting for her arrival, which included the two wannabe hunters.

"Yo, Pearl," Chubby said.

"Really?" Tall said to him. "Did you just say 'yo'? No one says 'yo.'"

"I mean, yo-ho, yo-ho, a pirate's life for me."

As she opened her locker, Pearl wondered whether it would be socially acceptable to hose down the humans around her. She smelled a mix of deodorant and sour perfume. The worst was the spicy sour odor that emanated from the two wannabe hunters. They must have doused themselves in body spray, a stench far worse than the normal human smell. At least the normal odor didn't ruin her appetite.

"Love to chat, boys," Pearl said. "But I have class."

"I'm in your history class and your English class," a girl with an orange shirt said. "I l-loved what you said to Mr. Barstow. He's a b-bully. You were really brave. My name's Melody." She held out her hand for Pearl to shake. Gingerly, Pearl shook it. Perhaps she could invest in some Clorox wipes.

"Dude, we have been utterly remiss in our function as guides," Tall said. "She needs names." The two of them proceeded to rattle off a string of human names while pointing to the people in a semicircle around Pearl's locker. "Casey, Alyson, James-don't-call-him-Jim, Girl with the Tattoo, Bill or Bob or Buddy, Zoe, That Guy, That Other Guy, Mackenzie, Hannah, Emma Z., Emma C., and Emily. . . ." Each of them waved. One of the nameless guys piped up with this own name, but Tall cut him off. "Whatever, dude. You can't expect her to remember everyone. It's her second day. Lay off."

Chubby leaned closer and said, "Want us to clear them out for you?"

Pearl held up her hand to stop them. "Do you two have names?"

Tall smacked himself on the forehead. "Idiots."

"Appropriate," Pearl said.

Chubby executed a deep bow. "I'm Matt, and this is my trusty—"

"If you say 'steed,' I'm kicking your ass," Tall said. "My name's Zeke." He mimicked Matt's bow.

From behind her, Pearl smelled a deep musky scent that caused her fangs to ache. Someone smelled like breakfast. She turned to see that it was Evan.

He smiled at her. "Good morning, Pearl. Are the idiots bothering you?"

Crap, he looked even better than she remembered. Today he'd paired khakis with a white T-shirt, which showed off his delicious arms. As much as she wanted to drool, she had to stay focused. She had an audience. "I believe it's their mission in life," Pearl said.

He considered that. "Most likely," he said. He leaned against the lockers, seemingly oblivious to the audience of other students or his effect on her. "So, what's yours?"

She blinked at him. She'd *thought* she'd been paying attention to the conversation, not the lovely way his chest rose and fell as he breathed, but she'd missed the leap to his question. "Sorry?"

"Your mission in life," Evan said. "Why are you here? Not at your locker. But *here* here, life here." He looked utterly sincere with his black eyes clear and bright.

For a brief second she imagined telling the truth, and that thought made her smile.

Coming up behind Evan, Bethany poked him in the shoulder and said, "No existential questions before nine a.m." Bethany flashed Pearl a smile. "Morning, Pearl! Wasn't that third calc problem a killer? I *think* I have it, but I barely slept last night." She looked remarkably perky for barely sleeping. In fact, she reminded Pearl of a very alert squirrel.

"I didn't look at it," Pearl admitted. "Family stuff."

Bethany's mouth formed an O. "But . . . but it's not optional." If she could have started to chitter like a squirrel, Pearl bet she would have. It was somewhat amusing to watch the shock play across her features.

"This is all new to her," Evan reminded Bethany.

Sympathy spread over Bethany's face. Her moods were so fascinatingly transparent, passing over her face like clouds across the sky. No vampire was ever as readable as this girl. It was as if she'd never encountered the concept of guile. "I'll tutor you," Bethany said. She said it in a poor-lost-lamb voice.

"I'd be happy to tutor you as well," Evan said.

At first Pearl wanted to turn down the offer. She did not need instruction from humans. But then she reconsidered. So far, it had proved impossible to be alone with a student at school for long enough to feed. Maybe she would have better luck with after-school tutoring. "Sounds lovely," Pearl said. She met Evan's eyes. He had warm eyes, the kind that sparkled as if he were inwardly laughing all the time. She didn't intimidate him, she realized. The majority of other humans in the crowd around them wore semiawed expressions, as if she were a rock star, but Evan didn't.

"Oh, you don't want Evan to tutor you," Bethany said. "He's one of those annoying people who never need to study.

Facts just stick in his brain. It's like he has fly traps in there instead of neurons."

"You're the better tutor?" Pearl asked. She couldn't help being amused.

"Not that he's *bad*. But I alphabetize my notes."

"All right. How about after school at your house? You can drive us there in your lovely lunch-box minivan, and I can call my parents to come pick me up when we're done," Pearl said. That should work out perfectly. To Evan, she said, "Sorry. Bethany's pitch was better."

Bethany beamed at her.

"Hey, we can tutor you too!" Matt chimed in.

Pearl patted his cheek. "You'll all have your chance. Don't worry."

Evan continued to lean against Pearl's locker. She wondered what it would take to faze him. Fangs in his neck? Pinch on his ass? Her gaze drifted down to his jeans, and she forced her eyes up as he said, "As a consolation prize, any chance you could give me the name of your parents' mechanic?"

She froze. What had her parents done?

"Ashlyn's car," he said. "It's fixed."

She tried not to let any expression register on her face. Daddy had called in a favor. Pearl wondered if this meant she was in his debt, or if it was merely a thank-you for the treat of Ashlyn's parents. She hoped the latter.

Zeke whistled low. "Queen Ashlyn could use some fixing too." He nodded across the hall toward Ashlyn's locker. Pearl followed his nod and saw the bottle blonde propping herself up against the lockers. Her hair lay stringy on her cheeks, her face was sunken and pale, and her eyes had circles so deep and dark that they looked like bruises. She really, really didn't look that great. Not that Pearl cared, of course. It was just that . . . She'd never seen a meal on the morning after. She wasn't sure what bothered her about it. Maybe it was that she had expected to snack on Ashlyn first. Now the girl was leftovers.

Others seemed to sense it too. Pearl noticed that Ashlyn's flock was clustered at a nearby locker. Ashlyn was on the fringe, not quite listening, as one of the brunettes babbled at the center of the clump. The brunette laughed, a silvery peal that echoed off the cement-block walls.

Pearl looked away from the bedraggled prom queen and her successor and said, "Gotta go listen to Mr. Barstow's monologue." Pearl's own court fell into step around her, and they swept past Ashlyn to class.

Pearl managed to make it through several classes without incident. (*Go, me,* she thought.) She was aided by the fact that she was bone-tired exhausted. Her headache had returned, and it occurred to her that she might have to up her intake to two pints a day if she was going to skip sleep. Her body hadn't had a chance to recharge. Luckily, she had her tutoring session with Bethany to look forward to. She could indulge then.

Last period of the day was new: gym class. According to

her trusty schedule, she had it twice a week, and it was her only class that didn't include Evan, which was a relief. For forty-seven minutes, she wouldn't have to worry about his scent causing her fangs to poke out. She didn't know why he, out of all the humans, had such an effect on her, but it was annoying. She should be functioning at peak concentration, but he and his luminous eyes kept distracting her. *First opportunity I have,* she thought, *I'll bite him.*

Leading the way to the locker room, Bethany bounced like an overeager puppy. Pearl tuned out the bulk of her chatter until Bethany stopped at the locker room door and announced, "Here we are, the portal of pain and misery."

"You don't like gym?" Pearl asked. So far, Bethany had loved every class they had. She cradled her textbooks as if they were babies, and she treated her notebooks like kittens.

Bethany shook her head vigorously. "Really bad asthma. And a fear of objects flying at me at high velocities. But I'm sure you'll be fine."

Unsure whether Bethany was serious or not, Pearl chose not to reply. Instead, she pushed the door open. Inside, she saw row after row of gray lockers, topped by posters of athletic humans chowing on fruits and vegetables. She entered the locker room and was engulfed in a cacophony of babble. In between each set of lockers, students chattered as they stripped off their school clothes and stepped into shorts and T-shirts.

Pearl paused, transfixed, as a brunette tied her hair back

into a ponytail. As the girl swept her hair away from her neck, Pearl was acutely aware that she hadn't eaten since the stale blood before Minerva's class last night.

"Hey, new girl!" a woman called, interrupting her middrool.

Honestly, humans had no manners. That was not a way to greet a member of the Family. She fantasized about teaching them all manners, Minerva-style. Pearl pasted a pleasant smile on her face with her lips closed to cover her partially exposed fangs. "Yes?"

"You need gym clothes." The woman scooped a few items of clothing out of a cardboard box. "Here, these are from the lost and found. Bring your own tomorrow. Shorts must be no higher than six inches above the knee. No logos on the T-shirts. White socks. Sneakers. You go down a half letter grade each time you're unprepared for class."

"Very well," Pearl said.

The woman tossed her the wad of clothes. Pearl's hand shot up, and she caught the clothes without moving the rest of her body. The woman blinked at her. Raising her voice, she said, "Everyone, I want you outside and stretching in three minutes." Her eyes lingered on Pearl for an instant, and then she exited the locker room.

Stepping into the aisle with the long-haired brunette, Pearl changed into the shorts and T-shirt. The clothes stank of human, and she cringed as the fabric touched her skin. She'd need another thorough shower tonight. Lacking sneakers, she happily left her beloved boots on.

"You should do something about your hair," the brunette advised. "Here, take an elastic." She handed Pearl a bright pink hair elastic. "Coach doesn't like hair in the eyes. It's easier to put it back yourself than to have her 'help.'"

Pearl tied her hair into a ponytail. She was immensely grateful that Jadrien slept during the day. At least no one would see her like this. No self-respecting vampire wore a ponytail. She imagined Aunt Lianne in a gym outfit and pigtails and nearly laughed out loud. "Thank you," she said. She eyed the girl's long golden neck and made a mental note to befriend her soon. "I'm Pearl."

"Tara," the girl said.

Coming around the corner of the lockers, the bottle-blonde Ashlyn said to Pearl, "Oh, it is you." Close up, Ashlyn looked even worse than she had across the hallway. Her shoulders sagged, her skin was pale, and her breath sounded shallow. Listening, Pearl heard the beat of her heart, a shade too fast. "Guess I should thank you for the car," Ashlyn said without much enthusiasm.

"You're welcome," Pearl said, but she couldn't stop staring at Ashlyn's hollow eyes. She wondered how much blood her parents had taken.

"Tara, can you tell Coach that I went to the nurse's office?" Ashlyn asked. "I'm feeling less than my divine self. Just need to lie down for a while."

"Oh, sweetie, you look terrible!" Seeing the two of them together, Pearl recognized Tara as the brunette from Ashlyn's entourage. She was the one with the silvery laugh who'd taken center stage by the lockers.

"Your tact is overwhelming," Ashlyn said.

Pearl watched Ashlyn shuffle out of the locker room. It was very disconcerting to see the aftereffects of a bite. Maybe she could limit her victims to students who weren't in her classes.

Dismissing Ashlyn from her mind, Pearl joined the rest of the gym class outside on the field. She noticed that the other girls were shivering in the not-quite-spring air. Most had goose bumps on their bare arms and legs. She didn't feel any chill, of course. She faked a shiver (just to fit in), and then she lifted her face toward the wonderful sun and inhaled to her full lung capacity. So glorious to be outside again!

Clipboard in hand, the coach (who, as far as Pearl could tell, had no other name) took attendance. She paused at Ashlyn's name, and Pearl toyed with the idea of telling the truth: Ashlyn had to go to the nurse's office due to the effects of vampiric blood loss.

Tara spoke up, "Ashlyn went to the nurse's office."

Coach pursed her lips, and another student spoke up, "Yeah, Ashlyn has been out of it all day. She even drooled in the middle of history. It was so disgusting."

Half-awkward laughs spread around Pearl.

"She was vomiting in the bathroom all morning," Tara said. She hit a note right between concerned and disapproving. "Food poisoning is my guess. If it's an eating disorder, she's doing a terrible job hiding it."

Others around her nodded wisely, and a few laughed outright. Pearl realized what she was seeing: a shift in power. Ashlyn had shown weakness, and others were jockeying for her position. She wondered how malleable the social hierarchy was and how far Ashlyn would tumble. Mildly, Pearl said, "I'm sure Ashlyn will be comforted to know she has supportive friends thinking of her."

The snickers died instantly.

Tara nodded as if she were the paragon of supportive friends.

Pearl noticed that Bethany was watching her with a strangely calculating expression on her face. But as soon as Pearl met her eyes, Bethany brightened like a lightbulb. Pearl wondered why she'd felt the need to defend Ashlyn. Obviously, it wasn't guilt. Vampires didn't feel guilt. It had to be scientific curiosity: If she poked at the hierarchy, would it collapse?

"Enough, ladies," the coach said. "Start running. I want to see those legs pumping. Once around the football field. I'm timing you." She took out a timer and waved it in the air.

A groan swept through the ranks, and everyone shuffled into a jog. Pearl kept to the center of the pack, determined to not stand out. Beside her, Bethany puffed like an out-of-shape hamster in a wheel. After a few minutes Pearl let her fall behind. Others lagged behind too. By halfway around the field, more than half the girls had slowed to a stroll. Unwilling to slow, Pearl matched the pace of the student at the front of the pack, a long-legged girl whose ponytail bounced with the rhythm of her steps. Pearl considered striking up a conversation, but the girl was focused on the grass in front of her. Plus it was so nice to simply run.

Pearl felt the wind in her face, cool and caressing, and she felt the sun on her back. Lengthening her strides, she wished the field were miles long. Unfortunately, she had only one more turn before she'd be back with the coach and back to the game of fooling humans.

Pearl rounded the turn.

On the opposite side of the school parking lot, between the pine trees, she saw a flash of shimmering white. Pearl slowed. That white . . . She'd seen it once before. Her hand flew to her chest.

She stared at the trees as if she could will it to appear again. Distantly, she heard the coach yell. She ignored the coach, and she ignored the girls who jogged past her. She walked toward the chain-link fence that surrounded the field.

The unicorn stood between the trees.

A millisecond later it was gone.

Pearl vaulted over the fence and ran after it.

Chapter
ELEVEN

Ignoring the shouts of the coach and the other girls, Pearl pounded through the parking lot. She ran directly over the cars in three strides each: trunk, roof, hood. Her boots dented the metal roofs. As she impacted on the hoods, car alarms blared.

In seconds she reached the trees. She scrambled up the bank and through the underbrush. Branches snagged her hair and scratched her skin, but she ignored them.

"Okay, Mr. Sparkly-and-Pointy, which way did you go?"

Stopping just inside the woods, she held still. She deliberately slowed her breathing and listened. Behind her across the parking lot, she heard the coach rounding up the other girls on the field. Ahead beyond the trees, she heard a truck rumble down a street. Above her, she heard cheerful birds chirp and coo. She focused on each annoying, perky, daytime sound, identified it, and then discarded it. Sorting through the noises, she heard a faint rustle that didn't have an obvious source. Feet soft on the pine needles and dirt, she crept forward.

Rustling again, a squirrel darted out of a bush and up a tree.

Pearl glared at it. "C'mon, roadkill. You saw it too. Which way did it go?"

The squirrel chittered at her from high on a branch. Even rodents were more brazen in the daylight. Pearl extended her fangs and bared them at the squirrel.

It yelped and dived into a hole in the tree.

"Respect the food chain, rodent," she said.

She heard a soft whicker, and she turned her head so fast that her ponytail whipped her cheeks. She spotted a flash of white in between the pine trees.

In a soothing voice, she said, "Stay, horsey. Shh, I won't hurt you . . . much." She barreled toward it, knocking into branches and tearing through the underbrush.

Just ahead, the unicorn danced between the trees. She saw its horn sparkle like a spray of golden water droplets as the unicorn cantered away from her.

Chasing it, she tore through the trees faster than any human could run. When the unicorn broke out of the woods, she was only a few steps behind. She lunged forward. Evading her, it raced across an empty road. She pelted after it. It jumped over a fence, and she vaulted over just behind it.

It disappeared into another patch of trees.

She plunged in between pine trees and birches. Green and white flashed past her in streaks. But as fast as she ran, the unicorn was faster. Every time she thought she'd lost it, she caught another glimpse of silvery white.

It's toying with me, she thought.

As she had the thought, she saw the unicorn again—this time, it slowed and looked back at her, as if it *wanted* her to catch up. Its eyes were brilliant black, swirling with a thousand colors all at once. Caught in those luminous eyes, Pearl stumbled on a root.

The unicorn surged out of the woods and into the back-yard of a house. It clambered onto a low roof over a garage and then vanished over the other side. Seconds behind it, she threw herself onto the garage roof and climbed to the peak—

On the other side, the unicorn was nowhere to be seen.

She scanned the cul-de-sac with its TV-show-neat lawns and decorative mailboxes. . . . Mr. Sparkly-and-Pointy was gone. Slapping the roof tiles, Pearl let out a yell that could have rivaled Aunt Fiona's screech.

She collapsed on the roof and tried to calm herself.

On the plus side, she was certain now that the unicorn was real. She could say "told you so." On the negative side, she still couldn't explain why it had stabbed her—or more interestingly, why it hadn't killed her. She'd been out for the count. A toddler could have staked her. So why hadn't the unicorn finished the job? And who had brought Pearl back to her house? So many questions, and the stupid, shimmery, speedy glorified donkey had escaped without coughing up one single answer!

She continued to lie flat on the roof, working to control her breathing and to resist the urge to yank off all the shingles and toss them in a massive temper tantrum. The sun felt lovely on her skin. In fact, the longer she lay on the roof, the better she felt. It was almost as good as drinking blood.

She sat up with a sudden thought: *Bethany!* Pearl groaned. She'd missed meeting Bethany for her tutoring session. There went another day without a proper meal.

"Unicorn, you so owe me," Pearl said out loud. She'd never skipped so many meals before. She scanned the houses around her and wondered if anyone was home that she could "visit." A UPS truck sped by but didn't stop. She heard a distant radio.

"Pearl?" a voice called from the driveway.

She peered over the edge of the roof and saw Evan. He shielded his eyes from the sun to look up at her. "Evan? Why are you here?"

"I live here."

She studied the house with interest. It was one of those nondescript white houses with manicured shrubs, flower beds filled with newly sprouted crocuses, and a perfect weed-free lawn. It didn't have the standard slightly scummy pool, but it did have the requisite barbecue grill in the backyard, along with a tiny fenced area that would be a vegetable garden in summer.

"Pearl? Why are *you* here?"

"Just taking in the view."

Evan crossed to the porch. Jumping onto the porch railing, he grabbed the lip of the roof. She admired his arm muscles as he pulled himself up. He nearly rivaled Jadrien in muscles, though he obviously lacked the vamp superstrength. He stood on the shingles, steadied himself, and then walked up the slope of the roof to her.

"You missed the excitement," he said, dropping down to sit beside her. "Seems the new girl in school just took off in the middle of gym class. Ran across the parking lot, dented a few cars, and then vanished into the woods. Speculation runs from drug addict to covert CIA agent in hot pursuit of a criminal."

"I'd tell you, but then I'd have to kill you," Pearl said.

"I won't ask." Stretching out beside her, he put his hands behind his head. "Look at me, not asking. I am the picture of self-restraint and civility."

He seemed as relaxed as a sunbather, watching the clouds drift overhead and soaking in the rays of the sun. He looked as if he were made of sunlight. She imagined how warm his skin would be. Hers was marble cold and would stay that way until she fed. "I didn't know it was your roof," Pearl said. "I wouldn't have come here uninvited." She watched him, hoping he would respond with the kind of invitation that would allow her to enter his house.

"You're welcome to visit my roof anytime," he said.

Close, she thought.

Daddy always said he preferred to hunt businesspeople rather than the derelicts that most vampires targeted. It required more finesse to manipulate a human in a social situation than it did to waylay a drunk college student or a homeless drug addict in an alley. Daddy would have told her to enjoy the game. She, however, had always been fond of the direct approach.

She checked the street again—no one there.

Pearl leaned onto her elbow and faced him. "You know, I've never been alone with a boy on a roof before," she purred. Smiling with her teeth hidden, she inched closer.

He sat up abruptly. "Pearl, I hope I haven't given you the wrong impression. I know I've been friendly, but I'm not hitting on you. I didn't mean to lead you on."

She blinked. Okay, she hadn't truly been trying to proposition him, but still. . . . "Why not?"

"You're new," Evan said. "I remember being new. You need a friend right now. Let's just . . . be friends first. Okay? You might not even like me once you get to know me."

"Seriously? You're turning *me* down?" Her kind was supposed to be irresistibly alluring to humans. She was the humanoid equivalent of a Venus flytrap. She'd seen how Brad and the boys at the high school had ogled her.

"I hope I haven't hurt your feelings," he said.

"I don't have feelings, at least not the inconvenient ones."

"Okay," he said. "I hope I haven't hurt your ego."

"Yeah, that part of me is a bit miffed," Pearl said. "What

exactly is not hot about me? You're a teenage boy. I have boobs. What part of the equation is missing?"

He laughed, a surprised sound that burst out of him and seemed to startle him as much as it did her. "I didn't expect you to have a sense of humor."

"See, I have *more* than boobs," she said. "Also keen fashion sense, killer intellect, and more charm than a fluffy little kitten, when I put my mind to it. I am, in fact, the whole package. What exactly are you looking for in a girl?"

His smile faded. "Kindness. Compassion."

Snorting, she lay back on the roof. "Guess I'm not your type after all."

"Guess not," he said.

"Pity," Pearl said. "You have a nice ass."

"Uh, thanks."

She poked his elbow with her index finger. "It's your turn to compliment me. I said 'nice ass,' and you say . . ." She waved her hand at her body to show him the options.

He stared at her. "Nice boots."

Now it was her turn to laugh. "Yes, they are. And very useful. Out of general curiosity and not out of a desire to do anything about it, how many cars did I dent?"

"Five or six, or a hundred fifty, depending on the speed of the rumor mill," he said. "Good thing you have that mechanic."

She winced.

He saw her expression. "I thought you claimed no feelings."

"None," she confirmed.

"I saw you look worried."

"Yeah, well, there are feelings, and then there are parents."

"Ah," he said. "Home-life issues?"

She suddenly realized how odd this was: a conversation with a human. She'd never talked to one like this before. "You have no idea."

"Try me," he said.

She eyed his neck. "Love to," she said, "but you might scream."

An expression flickered across his face so fast she couldn't read it. He couldn't possibly have understood what she'd meant. From his point of view, this had to seem like casual banter. Somewhat to her surprise, she wanted to keep it that way. She hadn't been this entertained in a while. "How about you?" she asked. "You seem to have everything under control. What are your issues?"

"At the moment just you." His voice was serious. "I have a bit of a hero complex, you see, and you need saving."

She tilted her head. "You have no idea how hilarious that statement actually is."

"Tell me why you ran from school," Evan said.

"I am a covert CIA agent in pursuit of a hot suspect," Pearl said.

"Seriously, I can help you."

"Seriously, I doubt that. And I'm not in trouble anyway."

"Who were you chasing?" Evan asked. His black eyes

were intense. She felt as if she could swim in them. She imagined that countless high school girls had gotten lost in them. Luckily, she wasn't some silly human girl to be swept away by an intense look. She'd been around plenty of vampires whose eyes smoldered with repressed power. In fact, she was related to several excellent smolderers.

She considered a half dozen responses and decided that the truth sounded the most innocuous because of its sheer insanity. "I was chasing a unicorn."

Evan nodded sagely. "Isn't everyone, at least on some level?"

She'd expected shock or surprise or amusement or . . . she wasn't sure what. Certainly not philosophy. "I don't think so," she said.

A familiar blue Honda Civic turned into Evan's driveway. Under her, the roof rattled as the garage door rolled up. The Honda drove in, and she heard a car door.

"One of my brothers," Evan said.

I should have bitten him while I had the chance, she thought. Of course, if she had, she would have missed out on the banter. He actually got her jokes. It was refreshing. "You have a lot of siblings?"

"Lost count at six," Evan said. "Our parents kept adopting more of us—long story that I'll bore you with someday. Regardless, it's pretty unusual that we were left alone for this long. I'm not sure I've ever had the house to myself." He sounded wistful. "I could have raided the fridge."

"Sorry to have interrupted," Pearl said. She should be feeling more regret for missing the opportunity to bite him. What had gotten into her? Talking with a human instead of eating him? Humans weren't for conversation.

"No worries. Mom would have killed me if I'd touched Louis's chocolate cake anyway," Evan said. "Louis is the third oldest. I'm the youngest. Do you have siblings?"

"Cousins," she said. "Aunts. Uncles. The house is never empty." She wondered what it would be like to be in the house in daytime with everyone asleep. So far, she'd spent every day outside. She wondered if it would feel as if she had the house to herself or if she'd be too aware of all the silent bodies around her, waiting for the sun to die so they could wake. Probably the latter. "Even when it should feel empty, I still feel all their expectations."

"I know your pain," Evan said. "Even when they're asleep, they're still there, like they're tapped into your subconscious. Makes it tough to figure out which thoughts are your own and which thoughts are the ones you're 'supposed to' think. Sometimes I—"

Whatever he'd been about to confess was interrupted by a shout from the driveway: "Evan?" Pearl looked down and saw a stick-thin older boy with a mop of red-orange curls. "Does Mom know you're up on the roof with a chick?"

Evan sighed. "William, this is Pearl. Pearl, my oldest brother, William."

"That would be a 'no,'" William said. He put his hands on

his hips as if he were a disapproving grandma. "Pearl, does your mother know you're up on the roof with this young rake?"

Pearl rose. "I'll take that as my cue to leave," she said. If more of his family was coming home soon, she'd rather not be here. Six (or more) siblings plus parents . . . She didn't like those odds.

Softly he said, "Good luck finding your unicorn."

"You're really very strange, you know that?" Pearl said.

He grinned. "It's part of my charm."

Pearl took two long steps and then leaped off the edge of the roof. She landed in a crouch, sprang up, and jogged down the street. Since she'd missed her rendezvous with Bethany (aka dinner), she might as well finish what she started.

Somewhere in this town was a unicorn, and she was going to find it.

Chapter
TWELVE

As the sun sank into the horizon, Pearl trudged home without having seen a single sparkly hoofprint or rainbowed poop pile. It wasn't as if she'd expected UNICORN WUZ HERE graffiti. . . . Okay, yes, that would have been nice.

She let herself in the front door and headed downstairs. It was a little later than she would have liked. Already, the Family stirred in the catacombs. She scooted into the storage room. Squeezing herself behind some shelves, she chugged a pint of blood. It tasted like old batteries on her tongue. She downed a second bottle then hid both empty bottles on a shelf behind a few cleaning supplies. As she slipped out into the hall, she hoped no one could tell from her breath that she hadn't had fresh. She also hoped she could make it to her bedroom before anyone sent her to an etiquette class or conscripted her to scrub the mansion cellar.

She strode through the halls. In a bloodred brocade corset and tulle gown, Aunt Lianne stepped out of her room. She had forgotten to style her hair, which was spiked at odd angles as if one section had decided to defy gravity and the other had been mashed against her cheek. But Pearl didn't slow to enlighten her. She nodded to Aunt Lianne and kept walking as if she had a purpose. The key was to look as though someone had already issued her an assignment.

Others emerged from their rooms. Pearl avoided eye contact and limited herself to nods. She tried to wrinkle her forehead as if she were deeply concerned about pressing business. Certainly her mattress was calling to her in an urgent way.

Cousin Antoinette waved cheerily. "In a rush?" She was dressed in her favorite partying/hunting outfit: a pink blouse with ruffles plus a miniskirt that would fit a Barbie doll. If Pearl lingered at all, Antoinette would undoubtedly begin wheedling her to come party.

Pearl shrugged and kept walking. "You know how it is."

"Not really these days," Antoinette said. "You and your double life."

Three more doors and she'd be home free, at least until someone came looking for her.

"Stinking of human," Antoinette continued. She sauntered toward Pearl. "Thinking you're too good to hang with the rest of us."

Oh, fantastic. Another stupid power game. Antoinette wanted to pick a fight. Pearl debated how to handle it. She could keep walking and run the risk of Antoinette escalating matters with a kick into her spine—Antoinette wasn't one you should turn your back on. Or Pearl could prove that she was better right here and now.

It was an easy decision.

Pearl spun around. Her fist sailed through the air. Antoinette ducked to the side and kicked at Pearl's knee. Pearl had seen Jadrien use that move a hundred times. Interestingly, she'd never seen Antoinette try it. They must have been training together. *Talk about not wasting any time,* Pearl thought.

Like she always did when Jadrien pulled that move, Pearl shifted her weight and caught Antoinette's leg with her foot. She yanked, pulling Antoinette off balance. Antoinette stumbled against the wall.

"I don't think I'm better than you," Pearl said. "I know."

Antoinette merely smiled.

Pearl kept her knees bent and hands loose. If she tried another move, Pearl was ready. But Antoinette didn't attack again. Instead, she laughed, a silvery peal that reminded Pearl of Tara, laughing by Ashlyn's locker. "Just teasing you, Pearl," Antoinette said. "You need to lighten up."

Like that, the play for dominance was over.

"I have a lot on my mind," Pearl said. She had to secure the king's dinner, and it wasn't going to be an easy hunt. The king didn't sound like the type that would accept a note from her doctor or any other excuse. She had to deliver.

"Ooh, homework and pop quizzes?" Antoinette said.

"Don't worry about it, sweetie." She waggled her fingers at Pearl in a good-bye wave and sauntered down the hall. Over her shoulder, she called back, "I'll tell Jadrien you said hello."

Pearl sighed. "All right. Where's the party?"

Pearl descended into the basement of a house owned (she guessed) by an elderly woman who was either too deaf to notice or recently deceased. All the junk had been piled up on one side of the basement, including a 1920s baby stroller, an exercise machine that resembled Aunt Maria's favorite torture device, and an assortment of hats with plumage that looked more like dead rodents than bird feathers. Everything stank of mildew.

One of the vampires had rigged a sound system on top of a puce-colored washing machine. The machine vibrated violently as the music pumped out bass notes that shook the basement so hard dust rained from the rafters. In the haze of this dust, vampires danced and kissed and talked and then disappeared into the night either jointly or separately to hunt. It was a prehunt party, the kind thrown to stoke up vampires, to get their bodies moving before the blood started flowing.

Pearl loved these parties. Or at least she used to. Tonight it all seemed a bit . . . She couldn't put her finger on it. She just wasn't in the mood.

As she walked down the basement steps, she recognized the song: "Bloodline" by Slayer, one of Jadrien's prebite favorites. He had to be here. At the bottom, one of the young vampires that she vaguely knew—Bernard or Sebastian—grinded against her side. She patted him absently on the shoulder the way a human would pat a dog. He switched to another vampire who greeted him with more enthusiasm.

She spotted Jadrien in a darkened corner beside a leaking pipe covered in old duct tape. He was dancing with a female vampire that Pearl recognized from Minerva's class. Their hips slinked back and forth, and Pearl watched for a while, admiring how smoothly Jadrien moved and how aware he was of his body. He was the most handsome vampire in the place, and he knew it.

Pearl threaded through the dancing bodies until she reached Jadrien. He saw her approach and fixed his eyes on hers. A smile pulled at his lips as he continued to gyrate with the new girl. Her name was Lauren. Or Laura. Or Laurie. Whatever.

Pearl toyed with asserting her position with Jadrien. She could tear Laurie away and chuck her across the room before the girl could react. She wasn't even aware of Pearl's presence—or if she was, she didn't consider Pearl a threat, which was either a mistake or an insult. *Or both,* Pearl thought. But Pearl wasn't in the mood for a fight, which was odd. She chalked it up to lack of sleep and elected to simply wait the girl out.

It didn't take long.

Every time Jadrien swung Laurie, his eyes sought out Pearl. Every time he nuzzled her hair, he looked at Pearl. Every time he curled his lips and pulled her close, he watched only Pearl. After a few minutes Laurie noticed that Jadrien's attention was fixed elsewhere.

Stopping, the usurper frowned at Pearl. Her eyes raked up and down, as if assessing her competition. Pearl didn't bother tensing. If Laurie attacked, Pearl would pummel her. It was that simple. If she had any sense, though . . .

Laurie launched herself at Pearl.

Pearl lashed out fast, catching Laurie in the stomach with her fist. She doubled over, and then she came up swinging and clawing. Dodging right and left, Pearl evaded each of her strikes. She grabbed Laurie by the arms and slammed her against the concrete wall.

"Daywalker," Laurie spit at her. "You don't deserve him."

"Interesting insult," Pearl said. "You aren't privy to my Family's business. Why would you choose that word?"

Laurie's eyes darted to Jadrien.

"I see," Pearl said. She pressed her lips into a line. If Mother knew that Jadrien had babbled . . . Idiot. Hot idiot, but still an idiot. Pearl released Laurie and began to stalk toward Jadrien.

But Laurie wasn't cowed yet. She lunged for Pearl.

With a sigh, Pearl grabbed her again and slammed her a second time against the wall and then a third and then a fourth. "I can keep this up not only until dawn but through until the next sunset. But I think that would get fairly boring. How about you?" Fifth slam. Sixth. Laurie's eyes were looking cloudy, and the smack of her skull sounded wetter.

A few vampires watched with interest, but none moved to intervene.

Oddly, Pearl began to imagine it was her head smacking on the cement. The back of her scalp itched, and she started to feel nauseous. Before the seventh slam, she hesitated.

"Okay," Laurie gasped.

"Okay to what?" Seventh slam. This time Pearl flinched. She struggled to keep the reaction from registering on her face. *Why is this bothering me?*

"Whatever you want."

Pearl smiled. "Right answer." She stopped. "Now, I have only two little demands. You can handle two little demands, right? That's not too much for your smushed brain, is it? Two?" Blood tears ran down Laurie's cheeks as she nodded. "One, don't talk about the whole daylight thing. It's a bit of a Family secret, a surprise for His Majesty, and I'd hate to have to tell Mother that you have loose lips. She's not as gentle as I am. Oh, and you might want to tell everyone that you told to also keep their lips shut. Two . . ."

Behind her, Jadrien said, "That's already two."

"*Two,*" Pearl said. "Hands off my boyfriend."

Laurie mumbled something very close to agreement, and Pearl let her stumble away through the crowds. Jadrien, leaning against a pole, watched. Pearl turned back to him.

He smiled at her, one of his smoldering just-for-her smiles. "That was sexy."

At the moment she didn't feel sexy. He deserved to have

his head bounced against concrete a few times too. For one thing, if he hadn't danced with that girl, Pearl wouldn't have had to prove her dominance. These power games were tiring and oddly nauseating, and Pearl was short on sleep. For another . . . Mother had implied that Pearl's safety depended on secrecy, and he should have respected that.

Stepping in close, Jadrien ran his fingers down her arm. He lifted her hand to his mouth and gently sucked Laurie's blood from Pearl's fingers. He kept his eyes on her face as his tongue lapped around her nails.

Pearl smelled the sweat on his skin, some of it his and some of it hers. She also smelled fresh blood—he'd already drunk from someone tonight. She wondered again about the woman who owned the house, and then wondered why she cared. Judging by the junk in the basement, the home owner was old anyway. She was in for a shock the next time she came down to do her laundry, and that could be enough to kill her. Pearl looked at the smear of blood that she'd left on the cement. One of the other vampires was dragging his finger through the blood and then licking his finger. Despite the fact that she'd only had stale blood for the past couple of days, Pearl wasn't tempted to join him or Jadrien. She told herself it was because the wall was coated in grime and spiderwebs, which it was. She couldn't possibly be feeling guilty. Vampires didn't feel guilt. It was a perk, along with the immortality thing. Besides, it was Laurie's fault. She had attacked first. Pearl had reacted the only way she could have, the only way the idiot girl would understand. Pearl shook herself. She didn't know why she was second-guessing herself. It wasn't like her at all. She needed sleep.

"Missed you," Jadrien said. With his arm around her waist, he pulled her close and nuzzled her hair with his fangs.

She put her hand on his chest and pushed back. "You told."

He shrugged. "People were asking about you."

"You could have been cryptic and mysterious," she said. The Rolling Stones' "Paint It Black" kicked in, and she had to shout in his ear over the music. "Mother is not going to be happy."

"Good thing you aren't going to tell her," Jadrien said.

A few days ago she would have found this charming, but now. . . . Maybe Antoinette was right. Maybe she did see herself as superior. She certainly was busier. Pearl flicked her hand at the party. "Let's get out of here."

"But it's just getting started!" Jadrien said.

"Then stay." She shrugged. "See how many girls dance with you with that"—she pointed at the blood smear—"as their object lesson."

"Sounds like a challenge to me," he said. He surveyed the partyers. His eyes flickered over the girls, particularly their midriffs and their legs.

Pearl narrowed her eyes at him. She'd thought perhaps they'd spend a little time together. After all, she had experienced daylight and high school. She'd expected that he'd at least want to hear about it. "Whatever," she said. "Have fun."

He smiled at her. "Come on, Pearly, you know you're the only one for me. Your heart is my heart, forever and all time. Stay and party with me. Don't make me dance with women who don't appreciate me." He waved his hand at all the vampires who were dancing around them. "You know they're nothing compared to you."

She smiled back. "Pretty words," she said. She let the smile slide off her face. "Let's see if you mean them when I'm not here."

"Pearl . . ."

"I'm tired of games, Jadrien," she said. "I play them all night and now all day. But you know what?" She stepped closer to him. "If I have to play . . . I play to win. You should know that about me by now."

He swallowed, and she held his gaze. And then she deliberately brushed past him and ran her finger through the blood on the wall. She didn't lift it to her lips, though. Instead, she turned back to Jadrien and ran her finger down his cheek, leaving a blood trail.

"Have a lovely night, Jadrien," she said.

She walked out of the basement without looking back.

Chapter

THIRTEEN

The next morning Pearl marched through the school halls. She wasn't trailed by an entourage this time. In fact, the students widened a path for her as she passed. She heard whispers and felt stares.

Up ahead, Bethany was at her locker. She was counting out pencils—she had a separate one for each class (pink for history, blue for English, yellow for calculus). Seeing Pearl, she smiled and waved. She was the only one.

"Fickle," Pearl commented as she reached Bethany. She gestured at the other students, who all pretended they hadn't been staring at her.

Behind her, Evan said, "You made them afraid to drive their cars to school."

She supposed she hadn't behaved like Ashlyn or Tara. In fact, she probably hadn't behaved very humanlike. But then, she wasn't human. "Fear can be fun." She smiled (full teeth but no fangs) across the hall at the girl named Melody, who whispered to her friend and then scurried away. At least this reaction was much more appropriate than the original new-girl worship. As a bloodsucking fiend of the night, she was sup- posed to be feared.

Leaning against the lockers, Evan looked entertained. She wondered if anything ever ruffled him. She bet she could wipe that expression off his face. She pictured sliding her hands around his back and kissing his soft lips. . . . She met his eyes, and his smile enveloped her like a warm wind. Pearl shook herself. He wasn't Jadrien; he was human. She shouldn't be picturing doing anything but drinking from him. Ugh, what was wrong with her? She needed soap for her brain.

"Ta-da!" Bethany said. She presented Pearl with a notebook. "I noticed you didn't have one. It's kind of one of those all-important school-supply things." She selected a pencil from her collection and handed it to Pearl as well. "You use it to jot down the highlights. Dates, names, formulas . . ."

"Eighties song lyrics," a voice said behind her. Zeke.

"Plans for world domination," Matt said, also behind her.

"Doodles of . . . anatomy," Zeke said. Evan raised his eyebrows at him. "Hey, what? I'm not about to draw puppies and rainbows."

Pearl examined the notebook. It was cherry red, which was a reasonable color, and she didn't see any illustrations of the aforementioned puppies and rainbows. Given that all of Bethany's notebooks boasted smiley faces, ballet slippers, or silvery mountains, Pearl counted herself lucky. "How much do I owe you?"

Bethany laughed. "It's a present, silly. It's for you."

She studied Bethany and wondered what she really expected out of all this niceness. "Sorry to miss tutoring. Can we reschedule?"

"Of course!" Bethany said. "Can you meet me after school in the reading room of the public library?"

"Fine." Pearl had been hoping for Bethany's house, but at least this was a start. "I love the reading room. . . ." She trailed off as she realized that she'd seen Bethany there before. Bethany was the girl with the strawberry-blonde hair who had read a book in one of the leather chairs while Pearl had marveled at the sun through the stained glass. "You were there. The first day I . . ." She trailed off, unable to describe why it was a monumental day.

"It has beautiful windows," Bethany said. Her eyes were wide and guileless, as if she had no memory of that day. Perhaps she didn't. It would have been an ordinary day for her, though it was odd that she'd been in the library instead of school. She must have had a project.

The bell rang.

Zeke and Matt darted in the opposite direction, and Evan and Bethany flanked Pearl on the way to their class. All the while Pearl wondered what game Bethany was playing. Or if she was even playing a game at all. That thought was so shocking that Pearl was silent for the entire walk.

Three-quarters of the way through English class, Pearl was called to the principal's office. Everyone, even Mr. Barstow, was silent as she exited. Evan mouthed the words, "Good luck," and Bethany looked worried, which caused the pit of Pearl's stomach to clench—no one had ever looked worried for her before, and she'd been called to Mother's office dozens of times for punishment for various offenses.

She carried her new notebook with her, not because she expected to take notes but because . . . she wasn't sure why. She just didn't want one of the humans to scoop it up.

As she walked to the office, it occurred to her that she could bolt. It would be easy to switch directions, walk out the door, and keep going. But her parents expected her to stay, and she had yet to locate dinner for His Majesty.

She wondered what the punishment would be. She thought of how she'd punished Laurie last night, and then she wondered why she'd thought of her. Usually she dismissed incidents like that without a second's thought.

These humans were making her irritatingly introspective.

Attempting to wipe her mind clear, Pearl lengthened her stride. She didn't look at the classrooms on either side or the murals that covered the concrete blocks with images of beaches and mountains in bright sun.

As Pearl entered the school office, the poofed-haired

lady, Mrs. Kerry, smiled, and her perfume wafted through the air. Pearl switched to breathing only through her mouth. She could still taste the perfume on her tongue, but at least it didn't instantly squeeze her skull. "I'm supposed to see the principal?" Pearl said.

Mrs. Kerry's smile fell, and she clucked her tongue. "Oh, yes, they're expecting you. Go on in." She reached across the desk and patted Pearl's shoulder. "Don't be scared, sweetie. They know you're new."

Pearl almost laughed. Her? Scared of humans?

She felt sweat on her palms, but it wasn't because of fear of any humans. She was afraid of Mother's reaction if she failed here—and of the king's—but she didn't care what humans thought of her. If worse came to worst, she could always bite the principal. Actually, that wasn't a terrible idea. She pushed through the door to the principal's office.

Belatedly, she realized that the receptionist had said "they."

Three people sat in the office: the principal, the coach, and a woman in an olive-drab suit dress and too-bright makeup. *I'm outnumbered,* she thought. *Crap.*

"Pearl, please have a seat," the principal said. "I'm Principal Shapiro. You've met Coach Enlow. And this is our school counselor, Ms. Delancey."

Studying Ms. Delancey, Pearl wondered what a counselor was. She'd heard of camp counselors—Uncle Felix spoke fondly of a few delicious ones he'd visited for several summers by a lake in Maine. She'd also heard of guidance counselors, but she doubted they were going to discuss college plans. Keeping an eye on the counselor, Pearl perched on a blue chair with upholstery worn to threads on the arms and seat.

Leaning forward, Ms. Delancey said, "Pearl, would you like to tell us what happened yesterday in gym class?" Her voice was soft and even, and Pearl tensed. In her experience, the soft ones were the most dangerous.

Pearl's eyes slid to the coach, and she wondered what she was expected to say. She wondered what Mother would want her to say. "I wasn't supposed to leave class."

"Correct," the coach said. Her voice was a rumble. Her arms were crossed in front of her chest. Coach, Pearl guessed, was a yeller. She wasn't sure yet about the principal.

She told herself to relax. There wasn't much these humans could do to her that would hurt her permanently. Even Laurie was most likely healed by now. With the exception of a stake through the heart or a beheading, her kind was pretty much indestructible. Besides, she was a well-trained fighter with vamp strength and speed. Even with three-to-one odds, chances were that these people couldn't touch her if they tried.

But they *could* kick her out of school. She could lose this hunting ground for herself, her parents, and the Family. She couldn't let that happen. The Family was counting on her. She debated options: Scare the pants off the humans (i.e., start with flipping the table, attack the principal, rough them all up a bit), argue her way out of it (i.e., convince them that it wasn't such a terrible infraction and bargain for a lesser sentence), or . . . she could use their humanness against them.

She went for option number three: the truth.

Pearl knotted her hands together. "I'm sorry," she said. "A lot has changed for me lately. School. And at home. My parents expect a lot. And my boyfriend hates that I'm here. He and the rest of my family . . . Last night my cousin said . . . She accused me of thinking I'm better than them. They demand that I change, but they hate that I'm changing. And I don't know what to think about it, what I want. The people here are so different from anything I'm used to. Everything here is different. It was just . . . too much. And so I ran. I think I thought that if I ran, I could find some understanding. . . ." She trailed off.

It would never have worked with a vampire, but these weren't vampires.

All three humans nodded their heads.

The principal spoke first. "Believe me, we are not unsympathetic. We know how difficult transitions can be."

"Change can be frightening," the counselor said. "But you should know that you're not in this alone. We are, all of us, here to help you. Pearl, I'd like you to start coming to see me, once a week. We'll look at your schedule and find a free period."

Pearl tensed. "See you for what?"

"To talk," Ms. Delancey said. "Just talk about whatever is on your mind. That's my job. That's what I'm here for. I'm your safe haven."

Pearl couldn't help gawking at her. "Seriously? That's your job? To listen to me talk?"

"You and other students who need someone who won't judge, who won't play games with you. Don't mistake me—if I think you're out of line, I will tell you. But our conversations will be strictly confidential."

It was such a bizarre concept that Pearl couldn't think of a response. This was her punishment? Weekly "talks"?

"You understand that this sort of behavior—leaving school property without parental permission—is not to be repeated," the principal said.

"Do you plan to tell my parents?" Pearl asked.

Principal Shapiro shook his head. "I think we can overlook it this time. So long as we can expect better of you in the future, and so long as you meet your appointments with Ms. Delancey without fail."

This was a genuine miracle. For whatever reason (either stupidity or kindness), these humans were sparing her from facing Mother's wrath. "It won't happen again," she said. "And I'll make the appointments." She felt an odd twinge inside her rib cage. Her eyes felt hot, but she didn't dare let any tears leak out. They couldn't see her cry blood.

Coach Enlow spoke up. "One more thing . . ."

Okay, now the ax would fall.

"I'd like you to consider joining one of our sports teams."

Wait . . . what? Instead of being punished, she was being asked to join a team?

"It might make your transition easier," Ms. Delancey said. "Sports are a great way to make friends. You can form bonds with other students by sharing a common experience."

"The track team trains after school today," the coach said. "Join us in the gym, and we'll assess your skill level."

Pearl found herself nodding. *Humans,* she thought, *are certifiably insane.*

The principal said, "We want your high school experience to be as rewarding and successful as possible."

Ms. Delancey added, "We want you to be happy here."

The coach smiled. "And I would like to win at regionals."

Pearl left the office feeling dazed. Mrs. Kerry at the front desk waved at her as she half walked and half stumbled back toward class. Glancing over her shoulder multiple times, she watched for an attack that never came.

Chapter
FOURTEEN

After school, Pearl poked her head into the gym. She saw a collection of girls stretching on the floor. A couple of them she recognized from classes or the cafetorium (like the thin girl with pink-lemonade-colored hair), but most she didn't, which was perfect—she needed a fresh batch of humans. Maybe now she'd have better luck with securing the king's dinner.

Everyone recognized her instantly, of course. As soon as they noticed that she wore gym clothes (with sneakers, this time), the whispers started. She ignored them and walked across the gym to the coach.

Coach Enlow smiled like a shark. "Pearl! Delighted you could join us. This"—she waved her hands at the girls—"is my varsity track team. Everyone, this is Pearl. She'll be trying out for us today."

The whispers intensified.

The coach clapped her hands. "Okay, we're going to start with an easy run around the field. Everyone, out the door! Pearl, show me what you've got, but don't tap yourself out. I already know you can sprint. We'll be heading off-road shortly to see how you do on long distance."

Pearl joined the pack. She stuck to the middle at first. Around her, the girls chattered about their day: quizzes, boys, and the upcoming prom. One of them had picked out her dress already, and the others demanded details, which led to a discussion of how many sequins were too many and a consensus that no girl should risk being mistaken for a disco ball.

Listening, she studied the hierarchy of the girls around her. There was the opinionated one (at the center of the pack) and the quieter ones (on the edges). The witty ones flanked the center girl, while the focused runners took the lead. Their physical positions mirrored the conversation dynamics. Pearl debated which kind of girl would be the best prey.

"All right, ladies," the coach shouted. "Let's take it off campus!" Jogging, she led the way through a break in the fence (rather than over it, as Pearl had done the day before). They crossed the parking lot in a pack. "Three miles today, ladies! Stay together, and don't let the cars smush you."

They jogged across a crosswalk that someone had over-enthusiastically marked with yellow Xs bright enough to be seen from an airplane, and then they spread out over an uneven sidewalk. Their run involved multiple streets in the wooded section of Greenbridge, aka the dull half of town.

On the second mile Pearl spotted the unicorn.

He was a white shadow that flitted between the pine trees. At first the flashes of white were so fast that she thought she was seeing reflections from the cars that zoomed past them. But then she saw the horn, sparkling in the sun.

A second later it was gone.

Searching for another glimpse of the unicorn, she didn't realize she was pulling into the lead. She'd meant to stay in the middle of the main pack, perhaps start up a conversation and become one of the girls.

"Nice stride," the girl in the front said.

Pearl kept her eyes on the woods, watching for more flashes of silvery white. "Thanks."

"You holding back?" the girl asked.

She heard the challenge in the girl's voice, and she looked away from the woods to fix her eyes on the girl. She was taller than Pearl, mostly legs, and she ran like a loping gazelle. Her coffee-colored skin had a sheen of sweat on it, but she talked as evenly as if they'd been walking. "Clearly," Pearl said. "You?"

"Obviously," the girl said.

Side by side, they reached the stop sign at the end of the street. Over her shoulder, the girl called, "Coach? Can me and the Goth chick stretch our legs?"

"Go for it, Sana," the coach said. "Just don't lose her."

Smiling fiercely, Sana put on a burst of speed. Pearl lengthened her stride and matched her. Together, they ran through a neighborhood. The girl's ponytail flapped on her back, and her breathing stayed even. Her breath control was impressive, for a human.

In minutes, they'd left the pack behind.

Pearl wished she could run like this for hours. It felt lovely to simply move, even better than it had felt in gym class since she wasn't confined to a fenced-in field. But she was here to do a job. This was an opportunity: She had alone time with one of the runners. She needed to chat her up, befriend her, and then figure out the best trap to lay. It would be good if she could learn about how the practices worked, if the team normally left the campus, if they ever varied their route, if they ever ran at dusk. Jogging at the same pace as Sana, Pearl tried to think of a casual opening. "So . . . do you like track?" Pearl asked.

"Running time," the girl said in a perfect imitation of the coach, "not chatting time." She increased her speed, and Pearl matched her. They ran silently past yards and fences, as well as thick swaths of trees. Pearl felt the sun warm her shoulders, and she relaxed into her stride.

"Yes, I like it," Sana said. It took Pearl a second to remember what question she'd asked. "It's just *you* in track, you know? Just your muscles and the ground. You can forget everything else."

Pearl wished that were true.

She saw another flash of white between the trees. She was certain that the dratted beast was following her. She gritted her teeth and told herself to ignore it. Her parents needed her to complete this hunt. If she could make herself part of this team, perhaps she could deliver the whole pack of joggers for the ceremony. That was a lovely idea: nine girls plus a coach.

Liking that plan, she ran a little faster, just fast enough so that Sana fell behind her as they raced by the school sign, through the parking lot, and to the field by the gym.

"Nice," Sana said, panting as they reached the bleachers.

"Think Coach will let me in?"

"Definitely," Sana said. "She wants to win regionals this year. Hey, I don't mean to pry, but is it true you bashed all the cars in the parking lot?"

"Not exactly all," Pearl said. "Is that a problem?"

"Do you plan to do it again?"

"I didn't plan it the first time," Pearl said. "The cars were just in my way."

Sana stared at her for a second, and then she burst out laughing. She doubled over, hands on her knees. She had one of those half-silent, half-donkey-bray sorts of laugh.

Frowning, Pearl said, "What's so funny?"

"The cars . . . ," Sana sputtered, " . . . just in your way . . ." She kept laughing. Oddly, Pearl felt a laugh bubble up inside her, too. Her mouth tipped into a smile. " . . . so you just . . ." Sana mimed with her fingers the act of hopping over them, and Pearl couldn't help it: She started laughing too.

By the time the coach and the other runners panted their way onto the field, both Sana and Pearl had recovered from laughing and were stretching side by side.

Sana pointed at Pearl. "You need to let this girl on the team, Coach."

The coach flashed a smile. "Done. You're in."

Pearl smiled back, but she couldn't look at Sana. Hunting was so much easier when she hadn't heard her prey laugh.

The other morning in the library reading room, the light had pierced through the colors and played over the wood. Now, in late afternoon, the light was a rich amber that danced with the blue, green, and red stained glass in a subdued waltz. It spread across the wood panels, chairs, and tables, warming them with jeweled colors. Pearl couldn't blame Bethany for wanting to meet here. Standing in the middle of the room, she let the light fall over her skin.

"You're here!" Bethany said behind her.

"Anxious to fulfill my academic potential," Pearl said without turning from the sun.

"I thought you'd decide I'm too much of a nerd to be seen with," Bethany said. "I'm not. I mean, I kind of am. But it's not all of me."

"I know," Pearl said. She looked over her shoulder at Bethany. "You're also the human equivalent of a puppy: eager, trusting, and overly friendly."

Bethany's face fell.

"Believe it or not, that wasn't an insult."

"I can identify a gerund, a dangling participle, and an insult at a hundred paces." Bethany dropped her backpack on one of the tables and unloaded a stack of textbooks.

"Shakespeare has the best insults," Pearl said. She laid her one notebook on the table. "'Truly thou art damned, like an ill-roasted egg, all on one side.'"

Both of Bethany's eyebrows shot up. "You read Shakespeare?"

"I think I'm insulted that you're so surprised." Pearl picked a chair and sat. "I have an uncle who loves him. I had to read to participate in dinner conversations. My other favorite: 'Teeth hadst thou in thy head when thou wast born, to signify thou camest to bite the world.'" In actual conversation, that quote had been used as a compliment, but Bethany didn't need to know that detail.

"What's your favorite?" Bethany asked.

"Midsummer Night's Dream."

Bethany again looked surprised. On her, the expression was a bit like one of those anime characters with the enormous eyes and mouth in a perfect O. "Really?" She sank into the chair opposite Pearl.

"Puck is kind of badass," Pearl said.

"Huh," Bethany said. "I would have picked you more for *Hamlet.*"

Pearl shook her head vehemently. "Too whiny. Just get on with it. Though I do appreciate the body count at the end. Old Will was quite thorough."

"So what exactly do you need help with?" Bethany asked.

Pearl's eyes fixed on Bethany's neck. She forced herself to

look up at the girl's face. She couldn't snack with the librarians and patrons wandering in and out of the reading room. *Might as well do what I came here to do,* she thought. She went with the truth again: "I can't flunk out. My parents would be very, very displeased. So I need you to bring me up to speed. My education has been . . . nontraditional."

"You honestly want to be tutored?" Bethany asked.

"Um, yes," Pearl said. "Did you think I came to dance?"

"I didn't think you'd show at all."

Pearl shook her head. "You have a serious confidence issue, do you know that? If you were in my family, you'd be eaten alive."

"How do you do it?" Bethany asked. "You walk through the school halls as if you own the place, even though you upset half the student body so that they're not sure if you're stable enough to be near. . . . No offense meant. I mean, I know you're totally cool and stuff, but . . ." She began to dither as she backtracked over her words.

Pearl held up her hand. "Can we just do some tutoring?"

"Oh. Right." Bethany selected a textbook. She flipped to the middle. "Let's start with history." Bethany switched to sit next to her. Pearl focused on the book and tried to ignore her tutor's neck.

After about two hours, Pearl's stomach began to roll, and her notes became erratic. Oblivious, Bethany continued through the textbooks, switching from history to English to bio.

Finally, she paused.

"Can you excuse me for a second?" Bethany said. "Just have to run to the ladies' room." She darted out of the reading room.

Pearl rose to follow. At last, she could snack! Bathrooms were (mostly) private. She could easily gulp down a pint and then . . . she pictured the bubbliness draining out of Bethany's eyes.

For an instant the image stopped her.

She shook herself. So what if Bethany lost her perkiness? Carbonated sodas lost their fizz too, but that didn't stop humans from popping them open and slurping them down. Leaving her notebook behind, Pearl strode toward the restrooms.

As she entered, Bethany was stuffing her cell phone back into her pocket. "Oh, hi! You, too? Power of suggestion, I guess," Bethany said. Her voice jumped as she spoke, as if she was nervous. Pearl wondered whom she'd called and then decided she didn't care.

"Guess so." Pearl smiled tightly. She listened for any sounds from the toilet stalls. No flushes. No visible feet below the stalls. If she pulled Bethany into a stall . . . it would be quick and easy.

"You're doing better with the bio," Bethany said.

Of course, it would also end the tutoring session. It would be a shame if that smart leached out of her before Pearl was finished with it. Then again, she did have other volunteers to tutor her, such as Evan. Pearl stepped closer to Bethany.

For an instant Pearl thought she saw a flicker of fear, as if

Bethany had somehow sensed the predator in Pearl. But then the expression vanished, and Pearl decided she must have imagined the skittish-rabbit look.

"I wish I could make my hair behave like yours," Bethany said as she lifted her strawberry-blonde waves up. They bounced back down. "Yours looks all sleek and not tangled. You practically shine."

Pearl realized that they stood in front of a mirror. Any second, Bethany would notice that Pearl had a ghostly reflection (at best) or no reflection at all (at worst). Inching backward, Pearl glanced at the mirror.

She froze.

Reflected in the mirror beside Bethany was a tall, thin girl with sleek black hair. Her face was pale, and her eyes were bright blue black, like a fresh bruise, brilliant against the paleness of her skin. In a detached way, Pearl noted that she was quite beautiful, though she'd never pass for "cute" in the way that Bethany did. She also noted that she didn't look as much like Mother as she'd always imagined.

"Ever try wearing your hair up?" Bethany asked. "If I had yours, I think I'd try a new twist every day if my hair would cooperate. I know, I know, call me shallow, but I'm a girly-girl when it comes to hair."

Pearl shook her head, and the girl in the mirror mimicked her. She had never tried a different hairstyle because she'd never seen her hair to style it. She touched her hair and then her face.

After a moment of silence, Bethany smiled brightly and then said, "Okay then, meet you back in the reading room."

Pearl barely heard her exit.

She had a full, solid reflection, not the hint of one that she'd seen at the Dairy Hut. Whatever that unicorn had done to her . . . What had he done? And why? She had to catch him. Even if he couldn't talk, he could pound his hoof yes or no. She'd throttle the answers out of him, if necessary.

She wished she knew more about unicorns. It was impossible to hunt something when she didn't know its habits or habitats. She wondered if anyone did. If so . . . well, she was in a library.

New goal in mind, Pearl strode out of the bathroom without a backward glance at the mirror. She crossed to the computer, brought up a search on the keyword "unicorn," and then headed to the folklore section. She immediately began pulling out book after book. Dropping down to sit cross-legged in the aisle, she flipped through them.

After fifteen minutes of this, she decided it was pointless. No book was going to conveniently fall open to just the page she needed. After all, unicorns were supposed to be mythical. Like vampires.

Feeling like an idiot, she left the pile of books on the floor. All she'd learned was that unicorns had a thing for virgin girls. Also, judging by the plethora of tapestries, medieval people had a lot of spare time on their hands.

Pearl returned to Bethany, who was humming to herself as

she completed her math homework. Stopping, Bethany asked, "Is everything okay?" There was real concern in her voice, which was unsettling.

"Just needed to look something up," Pearl said as she sat. "Out of curiosity, are you a virgin?"

"Isn't that kind of a personal question?" Bethany asked.

"Yep," Pearl said. "Are you? Or are you and Evan . . ."

"Me and Evan?" Bethany laughed. "He's like a brother to me. Seriously, we grew up together. It's not . . ." Her laugh faded. "Wait, are you interested in him?"

"Me?" Pearl said.

Bethany looked delighted. "You are! You like him!"

Pearl had no idea what to say.

Bethany patted Pearl's hand. "Don't worry. Your secret is safe with me." She mimed locking her lips with an imaginary key.

"Uh, thanks," Pearl said.

Chapter

FIFTEEN

Over the next two weeks Pearl fell into a routine. In the mornings she had school. She spent lunch period outside in the brightest patch of sunlight she could find with Evan, Bethany, Zeke, and Matt, and she studiously avoided damaging any more cars. In the afternoons she ran track with Sana and the team and then she met Bethany in the library for tutoring. At night she attended Minerva's etiquette classes, sparred with Jadrien, and assisted with cleanup of the mansion's cellar. Once in a while she managed to steal a couple hours of sleep plus a few pints from the storage room to keep her upright as she juggled both lives. And every other minute she had to spare (which wasn't many), she searched for the unicorn.

She had zero luck.

One evening she walked home from the library (rather

than accepting a ride from Evan or Bethany) so that she could search for the elusive hoofed wonder. She didn't see anything more mythical than an elderly lady shooting hoops with her young grandson (a feat so impressive, given the woman's age, that Pearl had wondered if she were supernatural). She half-seriously considered asking the woman if she'd seen a unicorn—for all Pearl knew, humans had been spotting unicorns for decades, and no one had bothered to tell the vampires.

It wasn't as if her kind and their kind talked frequently. Until Evan and Bethany, Pearl had never had an intelligent conversation with a human. Brad didn't count, given the adjective "intelligent." She wondered if Brad had been capable of stringing sentences together before he'd met her fangs. She doubted it.

Still thinking about the unicorn, Pearl let herself into the house. She dumped her backpack by the door and headed toward the hall.

"Pearl."

She halted halfway across the living room.

Daddy rose to his feet. He'd been sitting in a leather chair. She hadn't noticed him. She mentally slapped herself. That sort of lack of awareness was the kind of thing that got you killed. Or, at the very least, surprised in an embarrassing way. "Daddy, you're home." She tried to muster up enthusiasm to fill her voice and failed. He didn't look happy to see her. He was frowning in that perfect movie-star way of his, with one tiny crease between his eyebrows and with his mouth in the shape of a perfect circumflex.

"I thought we could have a little chat about how everything is going," he said.

"It's fine," Pearl said.

"You haven't reported in lately."

"Not much to report," she said. "I've been laying groundwork, developing plans, making connections. Generally integrating myself with the student body. Learning the rhythm of the hunt. This is a complex hunt, not the quick snatch and grab, so I am trying to be smart."

He seemed to like that response. Lowering himself back into the leather chair, he indicated the wood chair next to him. Pearl elected to pretend she hadn't seen the gesture.

"I would love to hear about your experiences," Daddy said. "No vampire has ever seen what you see."

"It's . . . loud," she said. "Humans like to talk."

"They're a surprisingly social animal," Daddy said. "You could almost grow fond of them, like pets who perform interesting tricks." He clasped his hands on his knees and leaned forward, the picture of intensity. "Pearl . . . there is a danger to what you are doing."

"I'm careful," Pearl said. "No one knows what I am . . . what *we* are."

Daddy shook his head. "Not the obvious danger. I am worried about a much more insidious danger. Pearl, you are undercover now, which means you run the risk all undercover operatives run: identifying too much with your targets. To fit in, you must make yourself like them on the outside, and too often that can spill over onto the inside. You must hold on to the core of who and what you are."

"Of course," Pearl said. "I know who and what I am."

"Good," Daddy said. "Keep hold of that. And, Pearl, I hate to pressure you, but your performance so far . . . You have gained us access to only one family, and while they have been delightful enough for multiple visits, one family is not enough to satisfy His Majesty at the ceremony." *So that's why Ashlyn continues to worsen,* Pearl thought. Lately the former queen of Greenbridge High resembled a hollow-eyed mannequin. Pearl opened her mouth to respond, but Daddy wasn't finished: "Also, Uncle Felix tells me that the supply of stored blood has diminished. You haven't even been feeding yourself."

She should have guessed that Uncle Felix would notice the empty pint bottles. She'd tried to stash them out of sight, but obviously that hadn't worked. Humiliation squeezed her throat shut.

"You *must* do better," Daddy said. "I say this with only your own good in mind. You've never met His Majesty, have you?"

She shook her head.

"You've heard stories, though, haven't you?"

This time she nodded. Stories about the king of New England were whispered like ghost stories, just before the break of day. Before he became king and confined himself to his domain, he'd built an illustrious and global reputation. In Venice, he'd drowned his victims in the Grand Canal as he'd drained them. In Mexico, at the old Aztec temples, he'd sliced out his victims' hearts. He'd feasted on plague survivors in the Middle Ages, and he'd dined on artist models in the Renaissance. Rumor had it that he'd wiped the smile from the real Mona Lisa's face. He'd participated in the Spanish Inquisition, and he'd reveled in countless unspeakable atrocities that everyone loved to both count and speak about. He'd traveled from country to country, fostering conflict as if it were a plant to be nurtured, before he'd challenged (aka butchered) the prior king of New England and took up residency in his stronghold.

"The stories are not exaggerated," Daddy said.

"Really? Even the Mona Lisa one?"

"His Majesty is an old-style vampire, and he is not fond of change. What happened to you . . . He will accept it if he sees the benefits. Everyone will accept you if they see the benefits. Do you understand what I'm saying?" She'd never seen Daddy this serious. "If he doesn't see the benefits . . . You do not want him to consider you a problem."

"I understand," she said.

"Good." Daddy smiled, and the warmth in his eyes washed over her. "You're needed below. Your mother has begun to work on seating assignments."

"Oh," Pearl said. Her eyes slid to the door. Perhaps she had come home too soon.

He laughed. "I guarantee she already knows you're here. Better go down." Sighing, she headed for the hall with the concealed door. "And, Pearl . . . if you do not prove your worth to His Majesty, then he will blame us for allowing you to continue." His voice was again low and serious. "Our fate is tied to yours. Don't let us down."

Downstairs, in the basement dining room, Mother leaned across the table and said, "Mmm." She then cocked her head to view it sideways and repeated, "Mmm."

Pearl waited silently in the doorway.

The dining room had been converted into a command center. All the antique sconces had been switched out for office desk lamps. The table was covered in charts and lists. Cousin Jocelyn was positioned at one end of the table, and Cousin Antoinette was stationed at the other. Cousin Jeremiah was curled up like a cat underneath the table. Pearl doubted he was helping much.

"Switch Meli for Antony," Mother said.

Jocelyn scurried around the table, moving pieces of paper from one circle to another. Each circle represented a table. Each slip of paper was a vampire.

"Aren't they in a feud?" Antoinette asked, pointing to two slips of paper.

Mother shook her head. "Resolved with a duel. But those two should *not* be seated with Lucien. Jocelyn, fetch Rocco's name and add Juan to table number six."

Pearl watched them for a few more minutes, calculating how long she could stand here before it would be all right to quietly withdraw. She could claim she hadn't been needed.

"Antoinette, swap table five for table eleven minus the three cousins from Bridgeport." Mother looked like a general. Dressed in a black suit, she defined "severe." Pearl inched backward. Without raising her head, Mother asked, "Did your father speak to you?"

Pearl halted. "Yes."

"Excellent," Mother said. "Report to dojo number three. You need another training session. Your focus must improve. We have received word that His Majesty is bringing two dozen guards to the ceremony. Each will need to be served with a blood donor."

"Two dozen?" Pearl said. She tried to keep her voice lower than a squeak and failed. Both Jocelyn and Antoinette raised their heads at the note of panic in her voice and regarded her with interest. Pearl modulated her tone to sound confident. "Of course, two dozen. You'll have them."

"Good," Mother said. "We are all counting on you."

Bowing, Pearl retreated from the dining room before Mother could change her mind about the training and assign her a mind-numbing, nonvampiric task like folding napkins instead.

She headed for the training rooms. Before entering the dojo, she changed into a flexible cotton outfit, and she tried to force the number twenty-four out of her mind. She just needed to try twice as hard.

Pearl didn't bother to knock. Sliding the rice-paper door open, she stepped inside. Jadrien was midpractice. She watched as he swung a staff in a fanlike circle so fast that it blurred in the air. Continuing to spin the staff with one hand, he executed a series of hands-free cartwheels. He landed in a crouch and struck the floor with the staff.

"Nice view?" he asked.

"You know it is."

"I prefer to see through your eyes," Jadrien said. "You're my mirror."

Pearl wondered if he knew about her reflection and then decided there was no double meaning. She examined him. His skin glistened with the sheen of sweat. "You're pretty and shiny," she told him.

"Dance with me, Pearl," he said.

She should have stopped for a pint from the storage room, but Daddy's knowledge had rattled her more than she wanted to admit. She'd expected that to stay her dirty little secret. She wondered if Jadrien knew. She wondered how she was going to find twenty-four victims (twenty-five, counting one for His Majesty) when she couldn't even manage to feed herself. "Let me warm up first."

Slowly at first and then faster, Pearl worked through her warm-up routine. She stretched. She kicked. She punched. She ran up a wall and flipped over.

"Sloppy kicks," Jadrien observed. "You should retract faster."

"Stand back," Pearl said. He dutifully retreated, and she sprang forward into a series of handsprings across the dojo. She closed the tumbling pass with a midair somersault. She landed solidly on two feet and straightened to face Jadrien. "First to pin wins."

"Let's up the stakes," he said. "First blood."

Pearl hesitated. She didn't have so much extra to spare. But refusing would signal she was weak, and she refused to show weakness in front of Jadrien. He'd proven that he'd talk even if it endangered her. For a moment she felt a strange pang near her breastbone. Just a couple weeks ago she wouldn't have cared what Jadrien said or did. He was hers, and that was enough. Now his games were tiring. "Agreed," she said, and she charged at him.

He reacted by springing into the air and flipping over her, which, while impressive, was a stupid move because it gave her ample time to switch directions and be there with a kick to his stomach as he landed from his fancy aerial. He let out an *oof* as he flew backward. Crossing the dojo in two strides, she followed up with a flurry of kicks and punches. He warded them off with his arms and countered with his own kicks and punches. She dodged his feet and fists as he drove her backward.

"You lack the fire tonight, sunshine girl," Jadrien said. "Are those humans making you soft and slow?"

Just sleep-deprived and stressed, she thought. *Also, thirsty.* A thought occurred to her: If she drew first blood, she could snack. She'd never drunk from Jadrien before, but there was no reason (other than etiquette) why she couldn't—vampire venom didn't affect other vampires. He'd said first blood but hadn't specified what to do with that blood. With new energy, she slapped his fist away and then clipped him hard on the chin.

"That's my girl," he said as he rubbed his jaw.

She didn't reply. Instead, she advanced on him. She aimed each strike at a new area, confounding his defenses. She gained ground on him.

"Nice," he said.

He sprang into the air in a flawless spinning kick. She didn't duck. Instead, when his leg sliced toward her, she dived forward and bit into his thigh, hard. He collapsed to the ground, and she fell on top of him. She took a deep long pull of blood from his femoral artery before she released him.

"Ow," he said. Blood trickled down his thigh and spread across the sheen of sweat. "I fail to understand how you continue to win. You're smaller. You're weaker. I'm faster, and my technique is flawless." She tossed him a towel to mop the sweaty blood.

"I want it more," she said.

"That's kind of profound," he said.

"Thanks."

"So, can we make out now?"

She looked at him, still splayed on the floor with blood drying on his leg. He was shirtless, and his muscles were still flexed from the tension of the fight. Except for the blood, he could have been on the cover of a supermarket romance novel.

But her stomach spasmed, awakened again by the drops of blood.

"You're lovely," she told him, "but it's a school night."

Chapter
SIXTEEN

Ms. Delancey, the school counselor, was overly fond of her mechanical pencil, in Pearl's opinion. If she clicked it one more time . . . She clicked, and Pearl reached over, whipped it out of her hands, and snapped it in half. She handed back the pieces.

"So . . . ," Ms. Delancey said as she studied the two halves of her pencil. "I see we still have a few items to work through."

"I think my boyfriend is going to break up with me," Pearl said.

Ms. Delancey tucked the pencil into her drawer and pulled out a fresh one. Glancing at Pearl, she appeared to reconsider. She returned the new pencil to her drawer and selected a pen instead. She clicked the top so that the pen popped out. "Why?" she asked.

That was one of the things that Pearl liked about Ms.

Delancey. She didn't express sympathy or disapproval, and she was required to listen to whatever answer Pearl gave. *Every vampire should have a counselor,* Pearl thought, *and not for dinner.*

"He doesn't understand my choices," Pearl said. Jadrien would have already snacked on the counselor, on Bethany, on Evan, on Sana. . . . It wasn't that they didn't look tasty, but there always seemed to be a reason not to bite. She needed Bethany to tutor her, and Sana entertained her during track practice. As for Evan . . . the time just never seemed right. "I have a lot of pressure on me right now, and he . . . well, he's the same."

"And how does that make you feel?" Ms. Delancey clicked the pen top twice.

"Irritated," Pearl said. She focused on the pen.

Ms. Delancey quit clicking.

"I didn't ask for this," Pearl said. The ceremony feast shouldn't be her responsibility. She was supposed to be an honored attendee, concerned only with swearing allegiance for the first time without humiliating herself in any way. The older vampires were supposed to worry about the details of the event. None of them understood how different the hunt was in daylight. She kept having to exclude people as victims. It was a lot easier when the concerns were merely logistics. "I liked the way it was."

"Do you want to return to that?" Ms. Delancey asked.

Pearl considered it. She studied the photos on Ms.

Delancey's desk: two children in sundresses at a park, a bride in a garden with Ms. Delancey in a drab-olive bridesmaid dress, a man on a sailboat with a two-foot-long fish in a net. She saw a hint of her own reflection in the glass of the photo frames. "Yes," she said.

"What makes you feel . . ."

"I don't belong here," Pearl said. She felt as if a cartoon lightbulb had snapped on over her head. Suddenly, everything was clear: the reason she felt so much stress, the reason things felt off with Jadrien. . . . She shouldn't be here. This shouldn't be her hunt.

"You've been here more than two weeks," Ms. Delancey said. "Is this feeling better or worse now than it was when you started? Are you more comfortable here after two weeks?"

Pearl stood. "Yes, I am!" And that defined the whole problem. She wasn't supposed to be comfortable here. She was supposed to be in the catacombs, either asleep or with Jadrien. She thought of how she'd turned him down last night. That wasn't right. He was supposed to be her future consort, yet she'd drunk from him and then blown him off. Two weeks ago she'd never have done that. She'd never have resorted to stored blood or refrained from snacking on a human.

"In two more weeks we can assess this again," Ms. Delancey said. "Sometimes these things take time. You've never been in a public school environment before. The adjustment can't be easy, and we shouldn't expect it to be quick."

Pearl didn't want to adjust. She wanted humans to revert

to being merely meals again. She wanted to stop pretending to fit in. She wanted to return to being the ordinary child she was born to be, not a special miracle charged with this impossible task. Daddy was right—she was too far undercover. She needed to break out of this and return to being herself. "Thanks, Ms. Delancey," she said as the end-of-day bell rang. "You helped me clarify something that's been bothering me."

Ms. Delancey looked delighted.

Striding out of the counselor's office, Pearl beelined for Bethany's locker. The strawberry blonde was already there, backpack open at her feet. "Hey, Bethany," Pearl said, "I was wondering if you could help me with a project."

"Of course!" Bethany said. She loaded her backpack with every textbook in her locker and then hefted it onto her shoulder. She staggered from the weight.

Pearl rolled her eyes. "Let me." She took Bethany's backpack and tossed it over her shoulder. She led her out of the school and past the buses. Bethany half skipped and half jogged to keep up with her. A few of the students watched them warily, but Pearl didn't touch any of the cars.

"Wait, we passed my—" Bethany pointed back at her minivan.

"It's sort of a back-to-nature project," Pearl said as she propelled Bethany into the woods that ringed the school. "Extra credit. Ms. Delancey's idea, really."

"Oh!" Bethany said. "I was worried I'd missed an assignment. I mean, I know I don't technically need extra credit, but my parents say I need to bump my GPA higher than 4.0 if I want to have a prayer at the top colleges. I want to ask Mr. Barstow if I could write a term paper, but that requires actually talking to him outside of class. . . ." She puffed as she climbed up the incline and over the bushes.

"Seriously, you need to grow a backbone," Pearl said. She waited for Bethany between the trees. Over the past few days, the trees had begun to bud. Every branch sported tiny leaves, some in clumps. With the sunlight streaming down, the woods looked a murky pale green, as if they were underwater. "It's not like he's going to eat you." She turned and tromped over the forest floor. The brambles had begun to spread and grow. They snagged at Pearl's feet. "You'll never make it through life if you let irrational fears freeze you all the time."

Bethany let out a laugh. "I can't believe *you* are giving me life advice." She climbed onto a fallen tree. Straddling it, she was stuck for a moment, and then she wiggled herself over to the other side.

Scowling, Pearl waited again for Bethany to catch up. "What's that supposed to mean?"

"Totally no offense meant," Bethany said quickly. Changing the subject, she looked around them and said, "Where exactly are we going?"

"Over there," Pearl said. She pointed to a clearing. It was only a few yards from a fence that hemmed in a house, but it qualified: open grass ringed by trees. All the myths had the virgin in a clearing, usually weaving flowers into a garland, as if she had nothing better to do with her time. "You don't happen to know how to make a garland, do you?"

"Are you taking up a craft?"

Grabbing Bethany's elbow, Pearl steered her into the clearing. Sunlight hit the grasses, creating a cheerful spring-green glow. There was even a convenient rock in the center plus a few oh-so-picturesque crocuses and snowdrops. "Sit here. Just . . . pretend that I'm about to take a photograph."

Bethany didn't sit. "Pearl, what's this about?"

Pearl debated a couple of different answers. Each wasn't much more plausible than the truth. "I want to see if you can lure a unicorn." Bethany's mouth fell open, and Pearl thought perhaps the other answers would have been slightly more plausible, but it was too late now. Pearl shrugged as if it were no big deal. "I need to talk to it."

"Oh," Bethany said.

"It always lurks near me after school, but it never comes close. According to myth, it's attracted to virgins. So, here you are." Pearl tossed Bethany against the rock, spinning her so that she'd sit. Bethany hit the rock hard and fell to the ground. She yelped and then moaned. "If you want, you can sing. Maybe a medieval tune will draw Mr. Sparkly-and-Pointy. Remind him of all the medieval tapestries. Do you know 'Greensleeves'?"

Bethany's face was pale, and her voice quivered. "I . . . I think so. Same tune as 'What Child Is This?'" Her eyes were wide. Pearl ignored the fear that rolled off the girl as pungent as sweat. "'Alas, my love, you do me wrong to cast me off discourteously. . . .'" Her voice broke.

Pearl motioned for her to keep singing and added the next line. "'For I have loved you well and long, delighting in your company. . . .'" Tentatively, Bethany joined in and they both sang, "'Greensleeves was all my joy. Greensleeves was my delight. Greensleeves . . .'" Pearl held up a hand, breaking it off, and said, "Okay, this is idiotic." She looked at Bethany, quivering against the rock. Sighing, Pearl sank to the ground. The dirt and moss felt cool beneath her knees. "This is so far from right. I shouldn't be here. I shouldn't be out. I shouldn't even be awake." All she wanted was for that stupid unicorn to undo whatever it was it had done to her. She wanted her old self back.

She expected Bethany to bolt. It would have been the sensible thing to do. But, instead, Bethany got shakily to her feet and crossed to Pearl. "Do you . . . want to talk about it?" Bethany asked.

"Always talk, talk, talk with you people," Pearl said. "You know, sometimes violence really is the answer." She shot Bethany a look that should have sent her scurrying away like a squirrel.

Bethany laid her hand on Pearl's shoulder, lightly, like a bird landing on a live wire. "Who's hurting you, Pearl?" she asked softly. "Is it your family?"

Pearl had never, ever had anyone ask her a question like that. For a moment she simply stared at Bethany, at her wide eyes as clear and innocent as the morning sky. "You're either the bravest or the stupidest person I've ever met. You should really have run." She let all lightness drain out of her face.

Bethany began to shake.

Pearl knew what she was seeing: a killer's empty eyes. It was a look that Pearl had seen perfected on the faces of her uncles, cousins, and parents.

"You won't hurt me," Bethany said. Her voice was a whisper, and her heart raced so fast and loud that Pearl could hear it above the distant whoosh of cars from the street beyond the houses and the perky chitter of birds in the trees around them. "You need to pass AP History."

Pearl couldn't help it; she laughed out loud.

"Pearl . . ." Bethany licked her lips and began again. "Pearl, you don't get to choose what family you're born into. But you can choose not to stay. There are safe houses. Shelters with people who can help. You don't have to do it alone."

Her laugh faded. Even if she wanted to leave the Family— which she didn't, of course—no human could help. "I'm fine," Pearl said. "They're fine. And no one in my family is ever alone." As she said the words, she realized that for the first time, it wasn't true. In a way, she was alone. The Family slept. All her uncles, aunts, and cousins were trapped in the shadows until dusk. Only she was out in the world.

"You have friends, if you want them," Bethany said. "Me. Evan. Zeke and Matt. Whatever you're going through, we're here for you. Just . . . you need to let us in."

She almost laughed again. Vampires weren't "friends" with humans. Vampires didn't have friends. They had alliances. They had Family. Relationships between vampires and humans only happened on TV. "And here I was hoping that one of you would let *me* in."

"Talk to Ms. Delancey tomorrow," Bethany said. "She can help you leave. She'll know how to find a shelter. We can talk to her together, if you'd like."

Pearl took a deep breath and let it fill her as if she were human. "If you really want to be my friend . . . stay here in the clearing with me. And if the unicorn doesn't appear, I'll talk to Ms. Delancey tomorrow."

Bethany smiled. "All right." She perched on the rock. "Do I have to sing 'Greensleeves'?"

"Guess not."

Bethany tucked her knees up under her chin. Above, the afternoon birds chattered to each other. A breeze rustled the branches, shaking the baby spring leaves on the trees. "Um, Pearl?"

"Yes?"

"Are we talking about a literal unicorn or a metaphorical one?"

"Literal."

"Uh-huh," Bethany said.

"Just sit there," Pearl said.

Bethany was silent for a few minutes. "Hey, do you want to study?"

* * *

By sundown, Pearl knew more about the Federalist Papers than she'd ever wanted to know. She also knew that the unicorn was a no-show. As Bethany packed up her backpack, Pearl climbed on top of the rock and scanned the woods in all directions.

"Sorry for . . . You really expected a unicorn?" Bethany asked.

Pearl jumped off the rock without replying. She strode out of the clearing. She punched a tree trunk as she passed. Chips of bark sailed off where her knuckles impacted.

Hauling her backpack, Bethany scurried after her. "You'll think about leaving, right? Your family clearly isn't healthy for you."

Pearl dodged the question. "I appreciate the lack of mocking about the unicorn. In your shoes, I would have mocked relentlessly."

"You're welcome," Bethany said. "I mean, I understand. Sort of. I mean, we all have issues, right? So, it's okay."

"You don't have 'issues.'"

Bethany snorted. "Public speaking terrifies me. Authority figures intimidate me. I'm an obsessive perfectionist who cares too much about grades. . . ."

"Real issues."

Quietly she said, "My parents don't notice me."

Pearl raised her eyebrows at her.

As Bethany's toe caught on a root disguised by the

growing shadows, Pearl shot her hand out to steady her. "Thanks," Bethany said. "Once, when I was four, they forgot to fetch me from preschool. . . . It was a common thing for them. They missed pickup about once a week, and a friend's mom would bring me home and babysit me. But once, I had this idea—you know, one of those stupid ideas that seem perfectly logical when you're four—that I'd walk home myself. Of course, preschool was about five miles away, and of course, I got lost. I was found several hours after dark by this silver-haired man in a pin-striped suit. He wore a silver loop in his ear. I remember asking him if he was a pirate."

Pearl slowed. She felt as if the blood inside her veins had turned to sludge. *Silver-haired man in a pin-striped suit. Silver loop in his ear.*

"He laughed and said no, he's a vampire."

Pearl stopped altogether.

"Long story short, he hurt me, and then as he was putting me in his car, I was rescued by one of the preschool mommies. Evan's mom. But the worst part . . . my parents didn't change. I almost died because they forgot me, and it didn't faze them. Oh, they fussed for a week or two, but then they went right back to pretending they didn't have a daughter. Evan's mother started picking me up from preschool every day. I pretty much grew up in their house."

Silent, Pearl started walking again. She didn't know what to say to that story. As childhood traumas went, she'd heard worse. Honestly, she'd probably caused worse. But she hadn't expected Bethany to have encountered Daddy.

They reached the school parking lot. Shadows from the scattered few cars fell across the lot, but it was mostly an empty field of cracked pavement. Bethany's ancient minivan was on the opposite side.

Streetlights flickered on, creating pools of sickly yellow light. Above, the sky was matte gray.

As they crossed the parking lot, Pearl tried to figure out why it bothered her so much, the idea of Daddy with a young Bethany. She kept hearing Bethany's voice in her head asking, *Who's hurting you, Pearl?* She was focusing so hard on her thoughts that she failed to hear the footsteps behind them.

Bethany heard them first. She swung around. Only a millisecond later, Pearl reacted too. Behind them, Jadrien smiled and spread his hands to show he was innocent. "Pearl, jewel of my life, aren't you going to introduce me to your little school friend?"

Chapter
SEVENTEEN

Jadrien leaned against a streetlamp in the middle of the parking lot. Amber light spilled over him, casting shadows across his pale face. His own shadow pooled at his feet. Bethany shot a look at her minivan—still several rows away.

Pearl saw Jadrien's lips quirk into a half smile. His eyes were pinned on Bethany.

Without thinking about it, Pearl slid in front of Bethany. "Bethany, this is Jadrien. He's what is known as a 'bad boy.'"

"Ah, Pearl, you flatter me," Jadrien said. He flashed a full smile at Bethany over Pearl's shoulder and oozed the usual bad-boy kind of charm. "I'm the baddest boy."

Pearl rolled her eyes. "Bet that sounded cooler in your head."

Jadrien picked up Pearl's hand, turned it over, and kissed her wrist. "So, where were you headed, and may I join you?"

Pearl listened hard for any other vampires. Wind blew a

stray crumpled paper across the parking lot. It somersaulted until it hit a streetlamp. "Mmm, no."

"Pearly." He clucked his tongue in disapproval. "Remember what we learned from that kindergarten teacher we once had dinner with: 'Share, care, and always be fair.'"

"Not in a sharing mood today, Jadrien."

"Tonight," he corrected. He continued to hold her wrist. "Interesting slip of the tongue, Pearl. You really seem to be embracing your new lifestyle. Exactly where are you taking this lovely lamb? Are you heading out for an ice-cream soda together? Oh, Pearl, are you and little Bethany now BFFs?"

"She's not for sharing."

Behind her, Pearl heard Bethany shift as if preparing to run. She wouldn't make it three feet if she did run. Pearl hoped she had enough sense to keep still and quiet.

Bethany whispered, "Pearl, what's going on?"

"Good question, Pearl," Jadrien said. "What's going on? Level with your new BFF." He drifted closer, still smiling.

"She's *mine*," Pearl said. It was her choice when and where to drink from Bethany. She'd do it when she was good and ready, not a moment before. "Back off."

"'Back off'? That's your witty repartee?" He laughed, a hollow sound that skittered like wind across the silent parking lot. "I expect better of you, Pearl. We all do. What would your parents say if they knew you'd taken in a stray pet?"

She kept her arms by her sides. If he attacked, she'd be ready.

Bethany bristled. "I'm not a pet!"

"Your pet needs some lessons in manners," Jadrien said. "Let me help you train her, Pearl." He reached past Pearl and let his finger brush against Bethany's cheek. Bethany leaped backward. She clutched her backpack in front of her as if it were a shield.

"Should I run?" Bethany asked Pearl.

The human asks the vampire for advice? What next, flying pigs? Pearl thought. After their escapade in the woods, Bethany shouldn't trust her. Still, Pearl gauged the distance between them and the minivan. . . . She frowned at the rust-pocked vehicle. The tires had been slashed. Clever boy.

Jadrien was practically purring. "By all means. I love when they run."

Pearl put her hand on Jadrien's chest. "I said no." He didn't deserve to be the one to destroy Bethany's intelligence and her perkiness and her ridiculous innocent friendliness.

"Ooh, so forceful," he said. "Sexy."

"You know I can kick your ass, right?"

"And hand it to me on a platter," he breathed. He took a step toward her, closing the gap. "Come on, Pearl, you have to admit that we're a good team. I've missed that. I'm not complete without you."

"I've been around," Pearl said.

"But you haven't been yourself," Jadrien said. "Not since—"

She jabbed him hard on the shoulder before he could spill

Family secrets in front of a human. Mind-boggling that he hadn't yet learned to think before he spoke.

"She won't remember," he said. He pouted at his shoulder and rubbed it as if she'd wounded him instead of poked him.

Pearl said to Bethany, "You heard me say 'no,' right? I'm speaking English. I'm talking out loud." She shook her head. "You wouldn't think from looking at him that he'd be this slow."

"I hesitate to even suggest this," Jadrien said, "but you aren't protecting her, are you, Pearl?" His voice was bland, as if the whole situation were only mildly interesting to him, but Pearl knew him better. He was as tense as a tiger who'd spotted an antelope. "Why would you do that?"

Bethany spoke up, "Because she's my friend."

Both Pearl and Jadrien looked at her.

Bethany lifted her chin and glared at Jadrien. "Fine. Then I'm *her* friend."

"Weird," Jadrien commented.

"Seriously," Pearl said.

"I could just . . ."

"No," Pearl said.

"It would only take a—"

"No."

"Just a—"

"No."

"You're no fun anymore, Pearl." He pouted. "What if I asked for her as a token of your affection? Prove that you care about me, that you want to be with me."

Bethany yelped. "I'm not a token! Pearl, your boyfriend is a psychopath. Did you notice that? We need to leave. Come with me." She tugged on Pearl's sleeve as a car whipped through the parking lot. Bethany must have thought she was safe since they weren't alone—

Car wheels squealing, the driver slammed on the brakes only a few yards from them. Evan stuck his head out the car window. "Pearl? Bethany? You okay?"

"How cute," Jadrien said. "You called for reinforcements. Let me guess: text messaging? What will kids think of next?" He clenched his fists so that his muscles tensed under his shirt, and he turned toward the Honda Civic.

Evan stepped out of the car but didn't close the door. He held his hands palm out as if to show he came in peace. He nodded at Jadrien. "Hi, I'm Evan. Bethany, Pearl, need a ride?"

"Yes!" Bethany squeaked.

At the same time Jadrien said, "Thanks, man, but I have them all taken care of."

Bethany darted toward Evan's car. Pearl sensed Jadrien decide to intercept Bethany. Before his muscles could begin his lunge, Pearl struck with her foot flat into Jadrien's rib cage.

He flew backward.

"Pearl, come on!" Bethany yelled. "Into the car!"

Pearl ignored her. Concentrating on Jadrien, she said to Evan, "Go."

From the car, Bethany called, "Run, Pearl!"

"Can you take him?" Evan asked her.

"Yes," Pearl said.

Jadrien picked himself off the pavement. Out of the corner of her eye, Pearl saw Evan back toward the car, smartly not turning away from Jadrien. Her opinion of Evan rose a notch. Without moving, Jadrien watched them as if they were putting on an amusing play.

Evan climbed into the driver's seat.

Pearl could hear Bethany protesting, "We can't leave her!"

"She can handle him," Evan said, earning another point from Pearl—he not only hadn't underestimated Jadrien, but he wasn't underestimating her. Evan floored it to zoom out of the parking lot. The tires squealed as he rounded the corner and then disappeared.

Conversationally, Jadrien said, "You know I could have caught that car."

She rolled her eyes. "If I let you."

He smiled. "Right. Because you're that much stronger and faster. How can you be so certain I haven't been letting you win in the training room?"

He said it with so much surety that her breath caught in her throat. For a full ten seconds, she didn't breathe as she ran through the latest match in her head. Had there been an intentional mistake, a moment when he'd chosen to be too slow? She shook herself. He was playing mind games, and she was letting him. "Clever," she said. "Almost believed you there."

Jadrien said nothing. He circled her slowly as if she were a work of art that he wished to examine from all angles. She rotated, watching him. She kept her arms limp by her sides and her knees a little bent, as if they were in the dojo.

He halted after one revolution. "Why?"

She opened her mouth to make a snappy retort and then stopped. It was a valid question.

"You and I, we could have taken both of them easily," Jadrien said. "Helped ourselves to a snack and then had a nice joyride in their car. A mere two weeks ago you wouldn't have hesitated. In fact, it would have been your idea."

She thought of the unicorn in the parking lot, and her hand automatically went to her breastbone. "I haven't changed," she said. "I just . . . I have to think long term. I'm on a complicated hunt."

Jadrien shook his head. "You let two suspicious humans leave. I don't buy it, Pearl. You aren't hunting. I've seen you hunt. You're relentless. You're spontaneous. You're all the things that I love about you." Closing the distance between them, he cupped her face in his hand. "You're changing, Pearl. Whatever happened that night by the Dairy Hut . . . You're losing your taste for the hunt."

"No," she said. It was nearly a whisper, as much to herself as to him.

"If you don't hunt . . ." He caressed her face. Leaning in, his lips brushed against hers. ". . . I can't be with you. You know that, right? I'm a hunter. I deserve to be with a hunter. Everyone expects it of me. I have a reputation to maintain, you know, and a future to consider."

"I'm still a hunter," she said. Her voice was stronger. She was still herself. Just because everything had become more complicated . . . The unicorn hadn't changed who she was.

"Prove it," he said. "Hunt with me. Your choice of prey. It doesn't need to be those two new shiny friends of yours. It could be your ice-cream boy. Just bite him. Suck a pint or two. Show me you're still you, that we're still us. Please, Pearl." He kissed her. "Make someone bleed. For me."

Pearl peered through the window of the Dairy Hut.

"You don't need it to be vacant," Jadrien said into her ear.

"I hate standing in line," she said. She also hated that she felt nervous and that Jadrien could undoubtedly smell her nervousness on her skin. She should never have agreed to this. The very idea that she had to prove her vampireness was insulting. She should have rejected the whole premise by attacking Jadrien right there in the school parking lot. If she'd done that, then by now they could have been tucked away somewhere, getting sweaty for nonviolent reasons.

She watched a family buy heaping sundaes for each kid, including for a toddler who dug into his face-first before they'd finished paying.

"How can you like humans?" Jadrien asked. "Makes me want to shower just watching them. They're filthy animals. Varmints. We do the earth a favor by culling their numbers." The family left the store and headed for an SUV that was large enough to squash a rhinoceros. "Yet still they breed."

Smeared with chocolate sauce, the toddler howled as the parents strapped him into his car seat. The two older children raced around the SUV in an impromptu game of if-I-catch-you-I-punch-you. Laughing, the parents shooed them inside. They sealed the door and smiled goofily at each other.

"Disgusting," Jadrien said. "Someday we won't skulk in the shadows. We won't fear these vermin. We will put them in their rightful place as our chattel, our sheep."

Pearl gawked at him. She'd never heard him talk like this.

He sang softly, "'You may say I'm a dreamer. . . .'"

"Humans will always outnumber us," Pearl said. She couldn't believe he bought into the rule-the-world crap that radical vampires spouted. "We might be their predators, but if we come out of the shadows, then the advantage shifts to the humans." Besides, who really wanted to rule the world? Talk about too much pressure. Just high school was bad enough.

"Exactly why it's a lousy idea for you to pal around with them," Jadrien said. "Until we're ready to rule the world, we have to stay in the shadows."

She began to reply and then stopped. She *could* stay in the shadows voluntarily. She could choose to give up the sun. She'd tell her parents that the hunt was too difficult for a lone vampire in daylight. Humans were too aware in the day. They ran in packs. She'd quit attending high school, and no one outside the Family would ever know—aside, of course, from the hundred nearest-and-dearest buddies that Jadrien elected to tell.

Okay, so that wouldn't work. Too many vampires knew. Someone would tell the king, and he might not see her "ability" as an asset. He might see it as a sign of betrayal, especially if the Family failed to deliver his dinner and someone with loose lips reported that it was her fault.

She wondered if Jadrien's loose lips could help her. He could report back that nothing had changed about her. Of course, that first required her proving that nothing had.

There was no reason that she should hesitate. She'd done this dozens of times. Out of all her meals, Brad was her most dependable snack. Pretty much all he needed was a little cleavage.

Pearl pushed through the door. The bell rang, and the sound was so familiar that it calmed her. She knew this hunt. She flashed a smile at Brad, the kind that was aimed at one person and one person alone. As he always did, he faltered in the act of closing the cash register.

"Um, can I h-help you?" Brad asked.

Her smile froze as she saw her reflection in the glass over the ice cream. Behind her, she heard the door ring again. Jadrien. Oh, great, she had an audience. She slid sideways, away from the glass, so that he wouldn't see her reflection.

"Two scoops of vanilla," she said. "And you."

He blinked. "Excuse me?"

She winced at herself. She was off her game. She told herself it was because she wasn't used to an audience, especially a judgmental one. Pearl faked a laugh and tried to channel Bethany's cute innocence. "I don't like to eat alone, but you see, I'm new here, and I don't know anyone so I was trying to very awkwardly ask if you'd like to have some ice cream with me?"

"Uh, s-sure, I guess," he said. "I'm not really hungry."

"I'm hungry enough for both of us." Smiling sunnily, she rounded the counter and hooked her arm through his. "Be my friend for the night?"

"I . . . uh . . . have other customers."

The bell rang as Jadrien exited.

She looked at the empty store. "No, you don't. Please come outside with me."

For the first time she wondered why Brad always agreed. Perhaps he was lonely. Or maybe he just liked that she was female. She wondered if any girls ever saw him as more than the ice-cream scooper, an extension of a spoon.

Pearl wanted to slap herself. She should *not* be thinking about Brad as anything other than a snack. Certainly Uncle Stefan hadn't when he'd savaged Brad's neck. The boy still bore scars that looked like a knot of rubber bands in his skin. She wondered how he'd explained that to himself the next morning. She wondered if his family had asked about it.

He scooped the ice cream fast and let her lead him out the back door.

Outside, the night was cool. Stars speckled the sky, and the moon was a crescent above the dumpsters. "This, uh, is where I take my breaks," he said. "It's not very . . . nice. I mean, we could go out front. But I'm not really supposed to . . ."

"This is fine," she said. She took the cup of ice cream out of his hands, and then she sat cross-legged on the stoop by the door. She patted the step beside her. Obediently, he sat. "Do you attend Greenbridge High?" She hadn't noticed him there. Granted, it was a large school.

He shook his head. "Left. It wasn't . . . meeting my needs." He was trying to sound suave and failing. He looked up at the sky and tried again. "Just seemed so pointless, you know? It's not as if I'll ever be anything or anyone. Dad says I'm a waste of space . . . so I made some room in the school. If you look at it the right way, it was downright altruistic."

She studied him. If she were really channeling Bethany, she'd be advising him to seek counseling. Evan, too, would have prompted him to talk more and offered some wisdom. Zeke and Matt would have joked him out of his funk and had him laughing. But Pearl wasn't them. More important, she didn't want to be them. As she'd told Daddy, she knew who and what she was.

"Hold still," she told him.

And then she leaned toward him and bit his neck.

He jerked back as her fangs sank through his skin. Her fangs tore the skin as he moved, and she clamped both her hands hard on his shoulders. In seconds, the venom in her fangs hit his bloodstream, and he quit struggling. His breathing slowed, and she felt his muscles relax under her fingers.

Warm blood spilled into her mouth. She hadn't had fresh in so long that her head began to buzz. She licked with her tongue to catch the stray drops, fast like a cat with milk. Her veins heated, and she felt her skin start to burn. Her head swirled. It was hard to focus.

She felt his heartbeat, each pulse sending a wave of fresh blood into her mouth. It poured down her chin. His breathing was soft and shallow. She thought of the breathing of the students in school. She seemed to hear them echoed in the breathing of this boy.

A part of her knew that she should detach. She'd proved her point. She was still a predator. But that part was a whisper underneath the beat of his heart. She heard a thousand heartbeats under the thrum. *Lub-dub, lub-dub.* She heard voices, all the students in the school, talking to her all at once. She heard Bethany and Evan and Zeke and Matt and Sana, all telling her, *Stop, stop, stop.*

A hand shook her shoulder. "Enough, Pearl."

But it wasn't enough. She had to swallow them all. She had to drink them all down so they stopped talking to her, so she stopped hearing them. She didn't want to listen. She was a vampire. She didn't want to hear human voices inside her. She didn't want to care.

She *shouldn't* care.

And she shouldn't walk in sunlight or have a reflection.

"Stop, Pearl," a voice said. She didn't know whether the voice was inside or outside. But she heard it, and she knew it was right. She had to stop it. She had to stop listening. She had to stop the breathing. She had to stop the heartbeats.

Only then would she have herself back. Only then would she have peace.

Brad slumped down, slipping out of her grasp. She felt his skin tear as he fell, her fangs clamped on his veins. Blood poured over her chin and neck, and she opened her eyes to see the last of his lifeblood spill out of him and over the sidewalk.

He lay silent.

Chapter
EIGHTEEN

Blood filled her mouth, her throat, her nose. It blinded and deafened her. She tasted it, and she breathed it. Filling her, it spread through every inch of her body until she felt saturated. She felt as if she held an ocean inside her, and she felt as powerful as that ocean. She was the tides and the currents, and waves crashed inside of her. Her skin couldn't possibly hold it all in. She felt as if she'd burst.

"Pearl."

The voice was distant.

Mother's voice.

It cut through the red haze. Her voice sliced through the waves. "You part the Red Sea," Pearl said, and then she laughed in a high-pitched cascade.

"She's blood drunk," Mother said. "Clean her."

Dimly, Pearl felt her clothes peeled from her, but she

didn't care. The blood thrummed so close to the surface that her skin felt hot. Cold water hit her. It slammed against her throat, her chest, her stomach, her legs. It drenched her hair and dripped over her face. She laughed again as the drops sizzled on her skin.

She heard other voices and began to be able to separate them: Daddy, Uncle Felix, Aunt Lianne, and Uncle Stefan. Uncle Stefan barked orders. Gradually, the blood receded like the tide pulled back from her mind. She saw the parking lot of Dairy Hut. She saw her cousins scrubbing the step where she had drunk from Brad.

"Every drop gone," Uncle Stefan said. "It must be untraceable."

Through the back-door window, Pearl saw Daddy inside with Uncle Pascha. Both of them held gasoline containers. She saw Brad. He was slumped across a table. His cheek was pressed against the plastic surface. His arm hung limp over the side. His eyes were open and very, very dead.

A dozen memories flashed through her mind. She saw him as he was a few hours ago, talking about high school. She saw him on the day Zeke and Matt had caught her. She saw him on the day the unicorn had staked her. She saw him again and again: standing behind the ice-cream counter captivated by her, scooping ice cream with shaking hands, and then following her behind the store . . . all the way back in her memories to the first time she'd waltzed into the Dairy Hut. But she couldn't remember what he'd said or what she'd said that first time. She couldn't remember if he'd been different before he'd met her. This night, his last night, was the first time she had talked to him really and the first that she'd listened to him.

And she'd killed him.

All of a sudden, the red haze dissipated. She shivered as the water prickled her skin, ice cold. Inside, she felt herself begin to scream. Silent and without end.

"You killed him," Uncle Stefan said, as if echoing her thoughts. He was suddenly in front of her, though she hadn't seen him move. Last she'd seen he'd been in front of the dumpsters. "You'll bring police attention, press attention, *human* attention here, before the Fealty Ceremony. You have failed the Family at this most important of times."

"She can't hear you," Mother said. "She's lost in the blood."

"She's lost to us," Uncle Stefan said. "She must be destroyed. She's a danger."

"She will be contained," Mother said.

"We can't afford this kind of disaster at this time. All eyes will be on us."

Daddy joined the conversation, minus the gasoline container. "We know. It will be dealt with, Stefan."

"With fire? You risk us all for her mistake."

"Fire will destroy all evidence of her," Daddy said. "And no vampire hunter in the world would expect us to use it."

Pearl held very still. For some reason they thought she was unaware. She wondered why she was aware, but shoved that mystery away with all the others to be addressed later. Right now . . . this was bad. Very, very bad.

She watched without even flickering her eyes as Mother, Daddy, and Uncle Stefan went inside to finish laying the stage for covering up her mistake. The cousins added bleach to the step and then dirt to disguise the area. Uncle Pascha spread gasoline throughout the store as Pearl attempted to stave off panic. She'd never seen or heard of vampires using fire to cover a scene before. Fire was anathema to them. One lick of flame, and a vampire could burst into a blaze as fast as if touched by sunlight. The fact that they were willing to risk it . . .

Pearl didn't wait to see what would happen next. She had to flee. She didn't let the decision show in her face or register in her muscles first. She simply ran.

Vaulting over the nearest dumpster, she bolted into the woods between the houses. She left her clothes behind. She left everyone behind. Full of fresh blood, she had more power in her than any other vampire in Connecticut. She let it fuel her as she ran faster and faster, beyond the speed of a human, beyond the speed of a car, until she felt as if she'd melded with the wind.

Her cousins fell quickly behind her.

She laughed out loud as the blood surged through her. Stolen blood. Lifeblood. At this moment she felt as if she was the most powerful and fastest being on the face of the planet. She couldn't be stopped.

She ran barefoot and naked without feeling the pavement

beneath her feet. All she felt was the wind on her skin as she ran across town. Red tinted her sight again.

Somewhere in the glory of running, conscious thought crept back in. They'd be after her. Her Family. They'd chase her. She couldn't run forever. At some point she'd have to run *toward* somewhere, instead of merely away.

She had to find a place to hide.

She knew one place where she could go, one place that her Family didn't know about. Pearl switched direction and let the blood push her faster and farther. She didn't think the Family could track her—they'd hosed her down specifically to erase all hint of her—but she wasn't about to take the risk. She crossed through backyards, swam through swimming pools to confuse any scent, splashed through every stream and gutter puddle. She wove through the streets, ran over the rooftops, and climbed through the trees.

Only when she was sure that no one, not even a vampire, could track her did she let herself approach Evan's house.

Chapter
NINETEEN

As fast as a speeding bullet (but without any shred of a cape), Pearl darted across the street and plunged into the bushes beside Evan's house. Branches scraped her skin, and she felt blood rise to the surface. Quickly, she licked the scrapes, and the skin healed smooth. She checked the tips of the branches. She hadn't left any traces. She was still safe.

Hidden in the bushes, she studied Evan's house. She saw shadows through the blinds and curtains: the silhouette of a man, a woman, a teenage girl. She didn't see Evan.

She crept into his backyard. She'd regained enough rational thought to realize that she could not walk naked up to his front door and ring the bell. She had to find Evan and convince him to invite her inside without anyone else noticing her. Once she was inside . . . then she could figure out the rest.

Up on the second floor, third window to the right, Pearl

spotted him. He was hunched over a desk. She stared at his silhouette for a moment, unable to process the idea that anyone could do so mundane a task as homework on a night like this, but then she sprang into action. She ran across his yard. Moonlight reflected on her skin, but she was fast. Like a cat, she leaped silently onto the garage and then scurried across the roof. She then lay down and leaned over the side of the house so that she hung upside down by Evan's window. She knocked lightly on the glass.

She saw his silhouette startle, and then the blinds opened. Pearl withdrew so that she was perched on the roof above him. She heard the window being raised. Evan poked his face out.

"Above you," she whispered.

He twisted to look up. When he saw her, a series of emotions flickered across his face so fast that she couldn't read any of them. "You're on my roof again," he whispered.

"I know," she said.

He stuck his head farther out. "You're naked."

"I know," she said. For the first time, she felt naked. She was conscious of the night wind licking her skin, and she felt the stolen blood rush into her cheeks in an almost-human blush.

For a millisecond he stared at her, and then he visibly forced himself to stare down at the lawn instead. "Would I be totally out of line if I asked what you're doing here?"

She entertained several retorts but rejected all of them. She was exposed here in more ways than one, and she didn't have time for games. Hating herself for what she was about to say, Pearl blurted out the words: "I need help."

So softly that Pearl was certain she wasn't meant to hear it, Evan whispered, "And lo, Hell freezes over."

The night wind swirled over her back, and her hair tangled as it swept against her neck. She shivered. "Please," she said. Saying the word made her feel as if she were cracking open bones inside of her. It hurt like a wound.

"Come in," he said. He lifted the window higher and then turned his back as she lowered herself inside. She landed on his desk and climbed off it. He tossed her a shirt, and she slipped it on. It fell down to midthigh. The cotton felt rough on her scoured skin.

She noticed he was wearing boxers and a T-shirt, ready for bed. Automatically, her eyes slid over to his bed. Blue sheets were crisp and flat. He followed her gaze. "Um, I don't . . . ," he began, taking a step backward toward his door.

"I ran away," Pearl said.

It was the simplest explanation, and it had the added benefit of being true.

"Naked?" he asked.

"They took my clothes," Pearl said. Also true.

His eyes widened. "Are you . . . okay? Do you need a hospital?"

She shook her head. "I need . . ." She trailed off. She wasn't sure what she needed. No one ran from the Family.

What had she done?

What was she going to do?

She kept picturing Brad, slumped on the table, as the vampires prepared to disguise his death. If she hadn't lost control . . . What was wrong with her?

Evan caught her elbow as she sank onto the bed. The crisp sheets dented beneath her. Her muscles shook, and her thoughts felt as if they were chasing each other in tight circles. In a hollow voice, she said, "I think I made a very, very big mistake."

It was a statement that she'd never uttered in her life and that she never thought she would utter to a human, but with that statement, Evan switched into hero mode. "You'll be safe here. You did the right thing by leaving. Do you want to tell me what happened?"

She did *not* do the right thing by anyone's definition of the word. "I didn't mean to run away." As soon as the words were out of her mouth, she knew they were true. She also knew that the Family would never believe her.

The rush of Brad's blood was beginning to wear off, and the ramifications of what she'd done were beginning to sink in. She'd never committed such a major infraction. Killing someone when the Family was trying so hard to maintain a low profile and then fleeing punishment . . .

"You needed to leave," Evan said with his usual certainty back in his voice. "You can stay here until we decide what to do. We'll help you." He rose. "Let me explain to my parents—"

Her hand shot out and seized his wrist. "Don't. Please. I

don't . . . trust anyone else. I need tonight. I have to be safe for one night. To think."

He held still, as if she were a skittish rabbit. "You trust me?"

"Yes," she said simply.

Looking as if she'd knocked the air out of him, he sank down on the bed beside her. She released his wrist. "You continue to surprise me." He fell silent, and she looked around at his room for the first time. His bedroom was as sparse as a modernist painting. His walls were white, and his furniture was sleek black. His dresser had a flat mirror on top of it with zero clutter around it. Bookshelves jutted out of the wall. Rows of books were sorted by height and alphabetized. His room looked like a photograph in a home-decor magazine. The only sign that anyone real lived here were the scattered papers on his desk. Seeing her looking at them, he jumped to his feet and shuffled them into his backpack. "Sorry for the mess." She caught a glimpse of a page covered in short lines of words, like in a poem.

"You *are* a poet," Pearl said.

He flashed her half a smile. "You know my deep, dark secret. Funny, you're the only one who ever guessed."

"I knew the day I met you."

She couldn't read his expression. Softly, he asked, "Pearl . . . your family . . . do they know you're here? Does anyone?"

She shook her head.

"Could anyone have followed you?"

Again, she shook her head. She wondered what was happening at the Dairy Hut. By now Mother and Daddy must have torched it. Most likely, fire trucks and ambulances were arriving, and her relatives had disappeared into the night, assuming none of them had combusted from the flames. She wondered how many of them were searching for her. Oh, who was she kidding? All of them were searching for her.

"You don't have to talk about it if you don't want to," Evan said. "But if you want to . . . Are you sure you don't need a hospital? Or the police?"

"You call them, and I'll run," Pearl said. In truth, she would rip the phone out of his hands and crush it before the call was complete, but there was no need to say that.

"Can I call Bethany? She'll want to know you're here," Evan said.

She considered it and then nodded.

He fetched his cell phone from his bedside table. He dialed. She heard the phone click and a faint *hello* from the other line. "Bethany? She's here. You were right."

Pearl heard silence on the other end and then Bethany unmistakably saying, "I can be there first thing in the morning. Can you handle it until then?"

His eyes were again fixed on Pearl's face. "Sure."

I shouldn't be here, Pearl thought. If she returned right now and begged for forgiveness . . . Even as she had the thought, Pearl knew it was too late. She'd run. No amount of groveling could erase that.

Pearl heard footsteps in the hall. Her first thought was: They found me. She leaped to her feet, ready to bolt, but Evan held out his hands to calm her. A second later her brain caught up with her instincts. She'd known Evan wasn't alone in the house.

"Evan, are you on the phone?" It was a girl's voice. "You know what Mom said."

"Bethany needed homework help," Evan called back as he clicked off the phone.

The girl snorted, loud enough to be heard through the door. She sounded like a horse whinnying. "From you? Ha!"

"Can you tell Mom that Bethany will be here in the morning?" Evan asked.

"Tell her yourself. I'm not your message service. And don't you have school tomorrow?"

"Lizzie, can't you just . . ." He ran his hands through his hair. To Pearl, he said softly, "She's right—I'm a terrible liar. I am improving, though. Practice makes perfect."

The doorknob rattled. "Evan, do you have someone in there with you?"

"Naked girl climbed in my window."

"Ha-ha," Lizzie said. "You are full of wit tonight. Go to sleep."

Pearl listened to her footsteps retreat.

"Sisters." Evan tried to smile to lighten the mood.

Now that the threat was gone, Pearl felt as if every ounce of energy had sapped out of her. She sank back down on the bed.

He sat beside her. "Pearl . . . I'll do whatever I can to help."

His eyes were intense and serious, and she found herself wanting to believe him. She also found herself wishing he'd put his arms around her so she could bury her face against him. The feeling was so strong and so unnatural that she recoiled from him. He added, "And I will never hurt you."

But I might hurt you, Pearl thought. She was inside a student's house, which had been the goal of her high school matriculation. She looked at Evan, the trusting boy who had invited in a vampire, and she pictured Brad's blank eyes overlaid on Evan's beautiful black eyes.

All of a sudden her stomach flipped. Pearl clenched her teeth tight as she felt the hot blood boil up into her throat. She swallowed hard, forcing it back down. For the first time ever, blood tasted as vile as battery acid.

"Pearl? Are you okay?" Evan asked.

She was very much not okay. She put her face in her hands and tried to push the nausea away. She'd seen death before. She'd helped *cause* death before. So why were her insides shaking and swirling? Why did the thought of drinking from Evan make her feel like spitting out every bit of blood inside her? She should be blood drunk, so full that all she could think about was blood and all she wanted was more blood. But she wasn't, and she didn't.

"It's okay, it's okay," he said. "I'm here. You're not alone."

Pearl shook her head. She *was* alone. None of the Family would forgive her for this. Even if she called her parents right now and offered up Evan's entire household, it wouldn't make up for what she'd done. She'd endangered the Fealty Ceremony by risking exposure. She'd shown a lack of control. She'd killed unintentionally. She hadn't behaved like Family. Uncle Stefan would stake her as soon as Mother gave the word.

"What's wrong with me?" Pearl asked. How would she ever undo what she'd done? She wanted to reverse time so badly that it felt like a stake inside her guts, twisting and twisting.

Evan touched her shoulder. "Maybe it's not that there's something wrong with you," he said. "Maybe there's something finally *right*."

Lifting her head, she stared at him. There was nothing right about this, absolutely nothing right in the way that she didn't want to bite him, absolutely nothing right in the way she wanted to lean against him and let him comfort her as if she were a human. Only a few weeks ago he'd been the tastiest morsel she'd ever seen. Her fangs had threatened to pop every time she was near him. But now she looked at him and saw comfort and safety and kindness and all sorts of other human bullshit that she wasn't supposed to care about. It wasn't him; he hadn't changed. It was her. "There's something wrong with me," she said. "But I'll fix it. I just need . . ."

"You need to rest," Evan said firmly. "We'll figure out what to do next in the morning, okay? Just . . . you should sleep. How long since you last slept?"

"I think I slept an hour or two on Thursday."

"You take the bed; I'll sleep on the floor."

As Evan bustled around the room, establishing a nest for himself of spare pillows and sheets and sweatshirts, Pearl lay down on top of Evan's bed. The sheets smelled like him. Wrapping her arms around his pillow, she breathed in his scent. It was almost as if he were holding her, and for an instant she felt oddly safe. But then she remembered Brad and she shuddered against the sheets.

"If you want to talk . . ."

"No," she said.

"All right," he said. He fell silent. She listened to him breathe. She wondered if she should say anything. She didn't want comfort from a human. Or maybe she did, but she shouldn't. *I hunt humans,* she reminded herself. *I don't hug them.* Evan was nothing more than a friendly pet, keeping her company on an upsetting night. She shouldn't want to have heartfelt conversations with him.

Evan asked, "Can I get you anything? Water? Snack? Spare toothbrush?"

"Nothing, thanks." Except for a way to click undo. She squeezed her eyes shut and tried to stop picturing Brad inside the gasoline-drenched Dairy Hut.

"Okay, then," Evan said. "Hold on one sec." He darted into the hall. When he returned, he handed Pearl a pair of girl's underwear. They were red with a heart emblazoned on the back. "I liberated these from my sister's dresser."

"My hero," she said. She'd intended it as a joke, but it came out serious. He met her eyes, and for a long moment neither of them spoke or moved. He broke the moment by looking away. Standing, she took the underwear. She slipped it on while he averted his eyes.

Returning to his bed, she slid in between the sheets. He switched off the lights. Lying in the dark, she listened to him breathe.

"Good night, Pearl."

"Good night."

She didn't sleep for a long time.

She was very certain that he didn't either.

Chapter
TWENTY

Pearl woke to a knock on the door. She lay still, momentarily unsure of where she was, and then it rushed back: Brad, blood, Evan's roof, his bed. On the floor, Evan sprang to his feet.

"It's me," Bethany called through the door.

Evan leaped across the room and opened the door just wide enough for Bethany to scoot in. Bethany scurried to Pearl's side. She plopped down on the bed and squeezed Pearl's hands. "Are you okay?" she asked. "What do you need? How can we help? I'm so proud of you, Pearl. You did the right thing."

Brad's face flashed into Pearl's mind. She couldn't return Bethany's smile. For one insanely long millisecond, Pearl wanted to tell Bethany everything, and then the moment passed, like indigestion. She pried her hands out of Bethany's.

"Evan!" Bethany said. "You should have told me to bring her some clothes."

"My sisters have clothes," Evan said. "She's wearing Lizzie's underwear."

Bethany leveled a look at him. For someone normally so chipper, it was a surprisingly laser-beam-like look.

"I didn't peek!" he said, a little too fast.

Bethany rolled her eyes. "Go borrow more clothes. And tell your parents we were right." She may have had problems talking to her English teacher, but she certainly didn't hesitate to boss Evan around.

Pearl asked, "Right about what?" She wondered if she should flee out the window. She'd run from her parents. She wasn't all that keen to meet Evan's.

Bethany squeezed her hand again. "That you need help! Don't worry. We're helping kind of people. Evan's whole family is. They're super nice. You'll love them. Except don't try to pet the cat. She's evil."

"She likes everyone but you," Evan said.

"She's evil and a poor judge of character."

Evan hesitated in the doorway. "Are you two going to be okay? . . ."

"Go," Bethany said. She shooed him with her hands. "The sooner we can get your family to welcome her, the sooner she'll feel safe."

He left the door cracked open. Pearl heard his footsteps retreat downstairs. Voices drifted up. Before she could distinguish the words, Bethany hopped up, crossed the room, and shut the door. The voices faded to a hum, and then they rose again as Evan and his parents began to shout. She heard a few scattered words—"reckless" and "responsibility"—and she heard Evan's voice, louder than all of them, say, "Everything was fine the entire night!"

One of them hollered, "Lizzie!"

"Don't worry," Bethany said to Pearl. "I'm sure they'll come around. They really are very nice people. They just don't like surprises."

"Neither does my family," Pearl said. "I should introduce them." She'd meant it as a joke, but even saying the words caused her mind to conjure an image of Brad's neck, torn open. She shuddered. "Or not."

She wondered what this oh-so-nice family would say if they knew about Brad. Why couldn't she banish him from her mind? She should be thinking about the Family and how she could avoid whatever fate they had planned for her. But instead she kept tasting the blood and thinking about ice cream.

"You did right to leave," Bethany said. "That was a toxic environment. Home shouldn't be like that. Home is supposed to be safe. And if it's not, then you need to find a new one. Everyone deserves to be safe."

Home was the opposite of safe and always had been. She'd made it, of course, a million times worse. How was she going to fix this? Somehow she had to find a way to prove that she didn't need to be destroyed. She was an asset, not a wild card. There had to be a way!

The bedroom door bashed open, and Pearl leaped to her feet.

An older girl filled the doorway. She was a platinum blonde, sun-kissed tan all over. She wore workout shorts and a T-shirt. "Whoa, little brother told the truth," she said. Pearl recognized the voice from last night—it was Evan's sister, the one he'd called Lizzie. To Bethany, Lizzie said, "You okay? You shouldn't be in here alone."

Smiling sunnily, Bethany said, "I'm not alone. I'm with Pearl."

"You know what I meant."

"How's it going downstairs?" Bethany asked.

Lizzie snorted. "Eh, they're primarily upset that Evan didn't introduce her last night. Also, the whole unchaperoned slumber party is wigging them out. But Evan can charm the pinfeathers off a duck. They'll be offering her a lease on the master bedroom before breakfast is over." Her eyes raked over Pearl. "You're wearing my baby brother's clothes. And, I assume, my missing underwear."

Under her glare, Pearl suddenly felt more naked than she had last night. "I lost my clothes."

"I'll fetch you some more." Lizzie exited without waiting for a response. Pearl inched toward the window. If she left now, she could avoid any parental interaction. It wasn't as if Bethany could stop her. But if she left . . . where would she hide next nightfall? Before Pearl could come up with a reasonable solution, Lizzie returned with a stack of clothes. "I doubt they'll fit you, but you shouldn't meet the 'rents wearing his."

Pearl expected them to give her privacy, but they didn't. Instead, Lizzie plopped herself in Evan's desk chair and swirled around once before glaring again at Pearl. "Little brother said you were pretty. You'd better not mess with his head. He's too nice for his own good."

Pearl picked her words carefully. "I'm not planning to hurt him." It was disturbing how true that was. She didn't want to pierce that lovely skin or see the light fade from his luminous eyes.

"Good," Lizzie said. "Don't. He always looks for the good in everyone. It's a strength and a weakness. If I hear you're taking advantage of him . . ."

Bethany yelped. "Lizzie! She just left home. She needs our help, not threats."

Lizzie snorted again.

"So . . . he thinks I'm pretty," Pearl said.

"Beautiful, actually."

That cheered her up a little. "Good to know he has taste." Pearl pulled on the clothes. The skirt was loose on her and sat low on her hips, but the shirt was fine, albeit hot pink.

They waited in an uncomfortable silence, listening as the voices rose and fell downstairs. Pearl began to contemplate the window again. Surely she could find someplace else to hide.

Lizzie cocked her head as footsteps thudded upstairs. "Told you," she said.

Evan burst into the room. His eyes were so bright they seemed to spark. "All set! You can stay." He darted across the room with all the energy of a hummingbird, and he closed the window. "You take Lizzie's room."

"Hey!" Lizzie said. "What about me? Dog pen?"

"You'll share."

Lizzie raised both eyebrows, and Evan waited as if daring her to object. Pearl felt as if she'd missed a piece of the conversation. Finally, Lizzie said, "I don't sleep well with others."

"They said you girls could take turns," he said.

"This sucks," Lizzie said. Pearl felt a prickling on her spine from Lizzie's word choice. *Just an expression,* Pearl told herself. Obviously, Lizzie didn't know the truth.

Breaking up the staring match between Evan and Lizzie, Bethany asked, "Do Sandy and Donald want to meet her?"

He nodded. "They're waiting for us to be dressed and ready." He grabbed clothes from his drawers. "Lizzie, I'm going to change in your room."

"Resist the urge to alphabetize anything," Lizzie said. "I like my clutter exactly the way it is. And don't open the closet. And stay out of my desk."

"I won't touch anything," Evan said. "You . . . behave too."

Lizzie glared at him. "Believe it or not, I have some manners. Don't squish the spider in the corner. He's not hurting anyone, and he catches the other bugs."

"Charming," Evan said. He walked out the door and crossed the hall. Pearl heard another bedroom door open and shut.

Lizzie grinned, and then she flopped down on the bed. "Apologies in advance about the spider roommate," she said to Pearl.

"I won't be here long," Pearl said. Somehow she'd find a way to return home. She'd earn the Family's forgiveness without having to suffer horrendous pain, dismemberment, or death. She just needed to quit thinking about Brad for long enough to plan.

They lapsed into silence again.

A few awkward minutes later, Evan reappeared, looking both slightly rumpled and startlingly handsome, as if he'd walked off the set of a windblown fashion shoot rather than out of his sister's room. "Ready?" he asked. Lizzie and Bethany sprang for the door. Pearl followed behind. Gentlemanlike, Evan waited for her. "Don't worry. I think you'll surprise them."

"You know, that's more cryptic than comforting," Pearl said.

Ahead of her, Lizzie and Bethany trooped down the stairs. "Ooh, I smell waffles!" Bethany said. Lizzie sniffed and corrected, "Pancakes." Bethany shook her head and said, "Banana waffles with maple syrup."

"Better with honey," Evan said from behind Pearl.

Lizzie faked a shudder. "Next, you're going to tell me you put margarine on it. You know that's like dipping caviar in ketchup."

I should have jumped out the window, Pearl thought. But it was too late. Sandwiched between Lizzie, Bethany, and Evan, Pearl was swept into the kitchen.

She saw a picture-perfect, magazine-cover kitchen. Brass pots gleamed above a stainless-steel stove. Marble counters shone in the morning sunlight that poured through the bay window. Herbs grew in hand-painted pots on the windowsill.

By the counter, Evan's mother was peering into the toaster oven as if it were an oracle. She raised her head as they entered. She was, hands down, the most beautiful woman Pearl had ever seen. She had honey-colored hair with white streaks so bright they nearly glowed. Smile lines creased her cheeks and highlighted her coffee-warm eyes. *So this is the woman who raised Evan,* Pearl thought. She could see it. Even though they didn't share genes, Evan had adopted her smile. Like him, she radiated warmth in all directions. Evan's mother smiled at Bethany. "Lovely to see you so early, Bethany. What an unexpected treat!"

Evan shot a look at Lizzie at the word "unexpected."

Bethany skipped across the kitchen and threw her arms around the woman's waist as if she were four years old and this were her real mother. Pearl thought of what Bethany had told her, about Evan's mother rescuing her from Daddy. It looked as if the duckling had imprinted. For the first time, it occurred to Pearl to wonder how that rescue had occurred. Evan's mom looked like she could flip a mean pancake, but Pearl doubted she could out-kung-fu a grown male vampire. Unfortunately, that question wasn't exactly acceptable breakfast conversation.

"Hello, Pearl," Evan's mother said. "Welcome to our house. You may call me Sandy."

Evan's father was at the stove. He flipped three pancakes into the air in rapid succession and then caught them in the pan. "Hi, Pearl! I'm Donald, Evan's dad. Stay as long as you like. Any friend of Evan's is a friend of the Karkadanns."

He actually seemed to mean it.

Evan leaned toward Pearl and said, "Melinda." He pointed to a pencil-thin girl who towered over their mother. "She's one year older than me but adopted five years later. She's a tap dancer, special dance school in the city. Don't play her in Scrabble."

"Heard that," Melinda said. Crossing to them, she pecked her brother on the cheek and then sniffed. "You used my shampoo."

"Mine ran out."

"You smell like magnolias. It's lovely." She ruffled his hair with a fond smile. "Welcome, Pearl. We've heard a lot about you."

"Oh?" Pearl said to Evan.

In a superchipper voice, Evan said, "Dad, those pancakes look great!"

A college-age boy bounded into the room, scooped up five slices of bread, and disappeared down a hall. Pearl heard the front door bang shut. "That was Marcus," Bethany said. "You'll get to meet him in three, two, one . . ."

The front door banged again and Marcus skidded back into the kitchen and stopped in front of Pearl. "Whoa," he said.

"Marcus, this is Pearl," Evan said.

Marcus stared at her. For the first time since she walked into the kitchen, she saw an expression that wasn't warm and fuzzy. "Jesus H. Christ," he said.

Pearl suppressed a wince. Religious names hurt vampiric ears. It wasn't anything like holy water on the skin, but it did make her want to scratch her ears with a Brillo pad. "Nope," she said. "Just Pearl."

"Marcus," their mother said sharply. "Manners. She's our guest."

Evan placed his hand on Pearl's shoulder, as if to protect or claim her or something. "It's a girl, Marcus. Ever seen one before?"

"Uh, sorry." Marcus's face turned flame red. "You just surprised me. No one in this family tells me anything!"

Lizzie swept by him and said, "Your fly is down." She winked at Pearl. "There. I told you something. Happy?"

He examined his fly, which was up, and said, "Not so much."

"Aren't you late?" Lizzie asked.

"Right." Marcus snagged an apple from a bowl that more resembled an arrangement for a still life than an actual fruit bowl. "Tell me everything later," he ordered Evan. He nodded his head at Pearl. "Interesting to meet you." He darted out of the house again.

Lizzie smirked.

Evan looked at her. "You changed his clock again, didn't you?"

"Falls for it every time," she said happily. "He's a full hour early."

During this exchange, two more boys, another girl, and a fluffy gray cat had entered the kitchen. Bethany pointed to each of them. "Brooke, Louis, and Allen. The cat's Molly."

Another boy, also older, followed them, scooped up a plateful of pancakes, and dug in while he leaned against the refrigerator. "And that's William," Bethany said.

He waved at Bethany. "Hey, Bethy-babe. Still hanging out with us squares?" Pearl recognized him from his curls—he'd seen her on the roof with Evan. He nodded at Evan. "Good to see you this morning, bro." Pearl noticed that he didn't look at her. The cat, on the other hand, minced across the kitchen floor to investigate Pearl.

"You know that no one says 'squares' anymore, right?" Bethany said.

"Well, gag me with a spoon, I'll be hornswoggled."

To Pearl, Bethany said, "He thinks he's funny." William grinned at Bethany, and she stuck her tongue back at him like a four-year-old. Pearl felt as if she'd fallen into a vat of wet sugar. All of them were so sickeningly sweet. "No one tells him he's not because he's the oldest."

Lizzie chimed in, "Seems impolite seeing as how he'll go gray first."

Evan pulled out a seat at the table. "Have a seat," he said to Pearl.

She sat, and the cat jumped into her lap.

"He likes you!" Bethany said, delighted.

The cat hissed at Bethany, kneaded Pearl's lap, and then settled down.

"Pancakes?" Donald offered Pearl.

For an instant the kitchen was silent as everyone looked at her. The so-called evil cat purred in her lap, perhaps recognizing a kindred spirit. "No, thanks," Pearl said. "I'm not a real breakfast person."

Bethany cleared her throat. "Donald, those pancakes smell wonderful."

Still smiling at Pearl, Evan's father presented Bethany with a plate piled with three oblong pancakes. Sandy added a scoop of mushed strawberries. One of the other brothers—Allen or perhaps Louis, Pearl had missed who was who—handed her a fork and napkin. As everyone ate, Pearl felt the sidelong glances from Evan's brothers and sisters, as well as the encouraging smiles of his parents. She tried to think of a way to shift the focus off herself. Turning to Melinda, she asked, "So . . . honey or maple syrup for your pancakes?"

This had the desired effect: She touched off a family-wide debate on the relative merits of pancake condiments. Pearl stayed quiet and listened, trying to feel out the undercurrents. Usually, she could spot the power structure in a group, which ones tensed when another approached, which ones watched the others, which ones smiled too much or kept too silent. But all the normal clues were missing here. Evan's family . . . they *liked* one another.

As she watched them banter, she wondered what it would feel like to be a part—*Oh, shut up, Pearl,* she told herself. These were humans, for goodness' sake. There was nothing admirable in all this sweet, loving crap.

Cutting off the condiment discussion, one of the sisters asked, "Did you hear the Dairy Hut burned down last night?"

Don't react, Pearl thought.

The sister who'd spoken, Melinda, had found a perch on the counter next to the sink. She talked around mouthfuls of pancake. A patch of maple syrup was stuck to her cheek.

Everyone expressed dismay at the news.

"Was anyone hurt?" Evan's mother, Sandy, asked.

Pearl stood before she even realized she had. Everyone looked at her. The cat, who had slipped to the floor, stalked away with her tail high. The kitchen was silent except for the sizzle of the pancake griddle on the stove. "We should leave for school, shouldn't we?"

"Pearl . . ." Evan's dad spoke. "We hope you know that you are welcome to stay here for as long as you need. As you can see . . . we're a *made* family, not a *born* family." Pearl looked around—as Evan had told her once, all the siblings were adopted.

Evan's mother said, "All of us know at least a little of what you are going through, even though the specifics may be different." Sandy held up a hand to forestall anyone from speaking. "You don't have to talk about it until you're ready. Just know that you've come to a place that understands."

Pearl had to look away. For reasons that she couldn't identify, she felt a lump in her throat, and her chest ached. She swallowed hard and tried to force the achy feeling to stop. No matter how lovely the words were, these people didn't understand, and she couldn't stay.

Staying could destroy her more thoroughly than a stake through the heart ever could.

Chapter
TWENTY-ONE

At first Pearl was oddly happy to be in school. Every-thing about this place was so distant from her problems that she might as well have traveled to another planet. But then she heard the whispers in the hall, everyone talking about the Dairy Hut and the horrible fire. It had been contained, thanks to the speed of the fire department, but there had been one casualty.

One casualty.

No one seemed to know his name. Ted. Or Todd. Or Ben. Or Brett. "Brad," Pearl wanted to say. He'd been an idiot who couldn't stammer out a complete sentence. He'd been a boy who was easily distracted by cleavage. He'd been a skinny kid in an ice-cream store, a dropout whom no one really knew and no one really remembered and no one really cared about, until he became fodder for conversation up and down the halls of Greenbridge High.

Every time she overheard another student whispering about him, she wanted to rip the lockers off the walls and kick the concrete until it cracked. And then she wanted to rip and kick herself for feeling like this. She'd never felt this way about a victim before. Maybe it was because he'd been her victim alone, not shared with the Family. Maybe it was because she hadn't meant to kill him. Or maybe it was simply the corrosive influence of all these humans.

She had to stop this feeling. But every time she tried to shut it off, her brain replayed the bite-suck-die cycle from last night. She felt as if she were suffocating on the memory, and she stumbled through the morning with little awareness of her surroundings.

At the end of third period Pearl shuffled back to her locker with so little enthusiasm that she might as well have crawled. She shoved her books inside and then leaned her forehead against the cool metal. She wished she could run fast and far away from her memory, her Family, and all the voices around her. But where could she flee that they wouldn't find her? Vampires were immortal and very, very stubborn. Someday they'd catch her. One night she'd be late returning to shelter. Dusk would come early, or dawn would come late. Or they'd find a way to trap her. No, she had to find a way to fix this mess, reclaim her place in the Family, leave this daylight world, and forget about Brad.

Behind her, she heard two voices.

"Dude, you ask her."

"Nuh-uh, you ask."

"Rock paper scissors?"

"You cheat, man," Matt said.

"How is it possible to cheat at rock paper scissors?" Zeke asked.

"You game the system," Matt said.

"It's not my fault you always choose rock."

"My manly strength will not allow me to choose a less unyielding material," Matt said. "I have rocks for muscles. You fear my strength."

"Whatever," Zeke said. "You never choose scissors."

"Sometimes I choose paper," Matt said. "You can't predict me. I'm cagey."

"You always choose rock or paper," Zeke said. "So long as I always choose paper, I can't lose."

"See, I knew you gamed the system."

Pearl did not turn around.

"On the count of three?" Zeke asked. Together, they said, "One. Two. Three." There was a brief pause. "You should have chosen scissors."

"That would have been too obvious," Matt said. "You just said I never choose scissors so you had to know I would choose scissors so I couldn't choose scissors because you'd know it. Hence, the rock."

"Hence the paper, covering your rock. You ask her."

"Well played, my friend," Matt said. "Well played."

Pearl lifted her head from her locker and looked at Matt and

Zeke. Both boys shifted nervously as she studied them. Matt smelled like cheesesteak, and Zeke smelled like extrastrong mouthwash. Both needed to locate a comb for their hair, but they'd shaved meticulously. Every chin hair had been mowed down to a dot. She appreciated the improvement.

"So . . . Pearl . . . hi," Matt said.

"Hello," she said. She didn't say anything further. She wasn't in the mood for a conversation with Tweedledum and Tweedledee. All she wanted to do was find a bed, burrow under the covers, and sleep a dreamless and memoryless sleep until the safety of the next day's sunrise. She didn't know how humans handled the weight of their memories and losses.

"Oh, fine, I'll do it," Zeke said. "You're new here—new, in fact, to the whole high school experience—and you may not know that there's this delightful soiree in the spring of junior year known as junior prom."

"Prom," Pearl said. According to Antoinette and her beloved eighties movies, it was the crowning jewel of every teen's life. "I may have heard of it."

The two boys missed the sarcasm. "It's a dance," Matt said. "Fancy dress. Guys do the tux-penguin thing. Girls do the"—he started to gesture toward his chest to indicate cleavage and then apparently thought better of it and pointed to his feet—"high heels thing."

"So?" Pearl said.

Zeke patted Matt on the shoulder and said, "What my

esteemed colleague is trying to say is: Will you be our date to the prom?"

"Both of us," Matt said.

"We couldn't decide which of us should have the honor, and it seemed cruel to make you choose," Zeke said.

"Let me think about it a minute. . . . Um, no."

Their faces fell. "No expectations," Matt said. "Totally platonic."

"We just thought . . ." For once, Zeke seemed out of words.

"I'm not going," Pearl said.

"But it's a rite of passage," Zeke said. "One of those moments that you will talk about to your children and your children's children. Everyone must have at least one mind-blowing prom memory."

"Or a totally embarrassing one," Matt said. "Either will work so long as the story's good."

"It's at night," Pearl said. "For the near future I'm strictly a daytime girl." She tried to keep her voice light, but saying it made her throat constrict.

They looked confused. "Grounded?" Matt asked.

She shook her head.

"Then why?"

Glancing both ways down the hall, Pearl leaned closer to them and said in a fake whisper, "Vampires."

After messing with Zeke's and Matt's heads, Pearl felt better. She nearly whistled on her way to her next class. But by lunchtime she felt the familiar ugly whirlpool of her own thoughts tug at her. As she entered the cafetorium, she looked over the churning press of students, jostling in the lunch lines, and thought, *Is this my existence now?* If she didn't find a way to return to the Family, she'd have to pretend to be one of them—gossiping about the teachers, hunkering down over homework, worrying about the prom—for eternity.

She didn't want this! She'd *never* wanted this.

Pearl closed her eyes and wished she could close out all these humans with their blood flowing through their veins, so close to spilling out of their skin. The amount of blood between these four greenish walls was staggering. It helped if she remembered that's what they all were: vessels for blood. While they obsessed over their minutiae, they were just prey, sheep obsessing about their grass, completely unaware that she was the proverbial wolf in sheep's clothing. Daddy was right; she couldn't forget who she was or why she'd come here.

Her eyes flew open as a sudden glorious idea came to her.

"Pearl, are you all right?" Bethany asked. She stood next to her with a tray of congealed food in her hands. Of all the items on her tray, the plastic fork and knife looked the most edible.

"Tell me about prom," Pearl said.

"Sorry?"

"I need to get my mind off my . . . situation," Pearl said.

"Right." Bethany began to walk toward a table, and Pearl joined her. "Prom is this arcane ritualistic celebration. . . .

Okay, really, it's just a dance with food and a DJ. But we rent out this fancy hall and everyone wears uncomfortable shoes. Also, guys give the girls corsages."

"Interesting," Pearl said. "What fancy hall?"

"Actually, it's even more pathetic than usual this year," Bethany said. "Prom committee was late reserving a space so all the good places were gone. Our junior prom is in the school gym."

"Prom committee?" Pearl asked.

"Student volunteers who plan the event," Bethany said. "Ashlyn's the head of it."

Without another word, Pearl left Bethany. She crossed the cafetorium directly to where Ashlyn and her friends were. She stopped beside Ashlyn, who looked up at her with shadow-rimmed eyes. Pearl felt a jolt as she looked into those eyes—they held the same vagueness that she'd seen time and time again in Brad's eyes. All of a sudden she was seeing his vacant eyes again. She rocked backward, unable to speak for an instant.

Tara spoke first. "Come to stomp on our table instead of cars?"

Pearl switched her attention from Ashlyn to Tara—she'd been right the other day; the power in the group had changed. "I heard you were on the prom committee."

"We *are* the prom committee," Tara said. "I'm the new head."

Ashlyn displayed zero reaction to this pronouncement.

She swirled her lettuce with a fork but didn't eat. With her sunken cheeks, she didn't look as if she'd eaten much lately. Addressing Tara, Pearl said, "I'd like to join."

Tara laughed, and a half second later, the girls around the table joined in. "No offense, but you're homeschooled. What would you know about planning a prom?"

"I know a little about event management," Pearl said. She allowed a small smile to creep onto her face. "I know how important location is."

The laughter died. "The gym will be fine," one of the girls said. "We have great plans to decorate it. You'll see—it will be transformed!"

Pearl sat down at the table, forcing one of the other girls to scoot over. "I have an alternative," she said. "Do you know the mansion on the east side of Greenbridge, between the apple orchard and the nature preserve?"

Tara's eyes widened. "That place is expensive. And booked years in advance."

Pearl smiled. "My daddy owns it. It's possible that I could convince him to make a deal. All we'd have to do is shift the date of the prom."

"If you could do that, you'd have our undying gratitude."

"Just gratitude would be fine," Pearl said. Undying was already taken care of.

Chapter
TWENTY-TWO

Pearl let herself into the house before sunset. She spread the prom posters on the coffee table. She brewed a pot of blood tea and laid out the china teacups. And then she sat down on Uncle Felix's leather couch to wait for her Family to wake.

She tried to keep her mind blank. Concentrating on her breathing, she focused her eyes on the "Nighthawks" print over the mantel. Uncle Felix always talked about the isolation in the print, but it seemed to her as if the figures weren't lonely at all. The woman in the red dress sat beside the man. Their hands lay on the counter next to each other, nearly touching, so they were clearly aware of each other. Both of them focused on the waiter, who bent to fetch a drink or a napkin or whatever they'd requested. The man around the corner of the counter looked lost in his thoughts, surrounded by memories.

All of them were cocooned in the light of the diner, safe from the night outside.

It was, she decided, the most antivampire painting she'd ever seen.

Still contemplating the print, she was discovered first by Cousin Charlaine. Charlaine froze in the doorway and stared. Pearl stared right back. The burns on her face had healed into tight knots of pale flesh. Charlaine reached up a hand and touched the scars with her fingertips. Pearl saw her begin to tremble and knew it wasn't with fear. That was anger.

"You'd better head downstairs, Charlaine," Pearl said. "I'm waiting for Daddy and Mother. I'll open the shades until they arrive if I have to."

Charlaine fled downstairs. Pearl wondered if her cousin realized it was nighttime. Open shades wouldn't hurt her. But Charlaine had a nice little phobia developing, as well as most likely a murderous rage toward Pearl. Pearl added Charlaine to her "deal later" list.

Next to enter were Aunt Lianne and Aunt Rose. Neither of them paused at the threshold like Charlaine had. Seeing Pearl, they raised arched eyebrows in unison, but they didn't say a word. They glided across the floor, their footsteps so silent they could have been hovering an inch off the ground. It was impossible to see their feet under their voluminous skirts. Both of them assumed their customary seats. Aunt Rose picked up her embroidery. Aunt Lianne selected a crossword puzzle in a yellowed newspaper.

Cousin Jeremiah crawled into the living room on all fours and then curled up in front of the hearth. He watched Pearl with half-lowered eyes.

Uncle Felix halted in the doorway, looked at Pearl on his couch, took in the teacups with the cooling blood tea, and said nothing. He chose a chair, folded his hands in his lap, and waited. Entering after him, Uncle Stefan scowled at her and stood with arms crossed, leaning against a bookshelf. Uncle Pascha resumed his chess game.

Finally, Mother and Daddy joined them.

Crossing the room, they chose to sit on either side of Pearl. She felt the hairs on her skin stand up straight as they sat, but she didn't let herself shake as she poured first Mother and then Daddy a cup of tea. They accepted the tea but didn't drink.

"There are formalities we must follow for your punishment," Mother said.

"She returned of her own accord," Daddy said.

Mother nodded. "You understand that it is too late for excuses."

"I don't have excuses," Pearl said. "I have a proposal." She pointed to the posters in front of her on the coffee table. "Junior prom."

Mother took a sip of tea.

"It's a spring ritual that involves fancy dress and—"

"We're aware of the event," Daddy said mildly.

"She should be staked," Uncle Stefan said. He didn't move

from the bookcase, but she saw his muscles were tense, ready to spring at her. "She's a wild card at a time we can't afford it. She's disobedient, and she's reckless."

"I have a plan," Pearl said. She didn't meet Uncle Stefan's eyes. She didn't want to see her own death in them. Uncle Stefan didn't bluff. "I've joined the prom committee."

Uncle Stefan wasn't finished. "It would be doing her a kindness. The king is not kind."

"You asked for a drink for the king and his retinue, but you're thinking too small," Pearl said. She tapped the poster with her fingernail. "Four hundred kids equals four hundred pints."

Mother held up a hand to stop whatever Uncle Stefan planned to say next. Pearl risked a peek at him. He still hadn't budged, but she could feel the waves of power rolling off him. Uncle Stefan was the oldest vampire she'd ever met. If he had had the temperament for it, he could have challenged His Majesty. But Uncle Stefan didn't like to be tied to a place. He'd been known to disappear for months on end. Pearl thought it was a pity that now wasn't one of those times. "Continue, Pearl," Mother said.

"All we need to do is allow the prom to occur in the mansion's ballroom on the night of the ceremony," Pearl said. "Close the exits, and it's done. If we drink a pint or two from everyone, then no one will remember anything. We'll have our feast with no one the wiser."

Mother and Daddy stared at her. Aunt Rose laid down

her embroidery. Uncle Felix chuckled softly. Jeremiah crawled closer.

"Simple, elegant, and brilliant," Daddy said.

"Forget last night happened, and it's done," Pearl said.

Mother fixed her eyes on Uncle Stefan. "It's done."

"Oh, my little girl," Daddy said. "I'm so very proud of you."

Standing on a pedestal and wearing a swath of black lace and satin, Pearl wasn't entirely convinced that this was better than punishment. Aunt Lianne and Aunt Rose flanked her. Aunt Lianne held a pair of scissors so oversize that they resembled hedge trimmers. Aunt Rose had the pins. They cut and pinned the fabric while Pearl felt like a reluctant mummy.

"Remember it has to pass for human fashion," Pearl said, "not Queen of the Dead."

"Undead," Aunt Lianne corrected.

Cousin Antoinette waved her hand in the air as if she were Cinderella's fairy godmother. "You will be magnificent! Fashion-forward, a vision in black."

"Everyone will be wearing black," Cousin Jocelyn said. On her own pedestal, she was also mummified in a stretch of black fabric, pinned up to her neck. "The entire event is designed to eliminate individuality and erase artistic expression."

Pearl gestured at the black lace. "You didn't model this after one of your Molly Ringwald movies, did you?" She told herself that she didn't care what the humans thought of her clothes, but it was important not to set off alarm bells, such as being out of touch with today's fashion due to the immortality of the dress designers.

Aunt Rose jabbed a pin into her thigh, and Pearl swallowed a yelp. "Do not move," she said. "You will be the jewel of both balls."

Cousin Antoinette sighed happily. "Teenagers! So angsty and so tasty! Do you think we'll be allowed to drink? After all, we planned everything, which means in essence it's our party."

"Of course we will. Honestly, it's not difficult math," Jocelyn said. She attempted to squirm her arms into a more comfortable position. Pivoting, Aunt Rose stabbed her in the arm with a pin. Jocelyn flinched but didn't bleed—clearly, she hadn't eaten in a while. "Four hundred or so juniors in the class, minus whoever chooses not to attend the capitalist antifeminist peacock display of adolescent humanity. One hundred or so vampires, minus those who choose not to attend due to death, dismemberment, or insanity. We will have a true feast."

"Unless the king wants them all for himself," Aunt Rose said. "He is known for his penchant for mass feedings."

Jocelyn picked at the ruffles on her dress, and Aunt Rose smacked her knuckles. "I heard he once drained every monk in a monastery in a single night," Jocelyn said in a dreamy tone. "And I heard he bought a brothel in New Orleans in the eighteen hundreds that he emptied out once a month with his appetite."

"Oh, Pearl, this is going to be the most magnificent ceremony ever!" Antoinette said. "And you will be its crown jewel. I am so proud of you I could burst into flames right now." She giggled. "Sorry, Charlaine."

Cousin Charlaine growled deep in her throat.

"How very animalistic, Charlaine!" Antoinette said. "I'm shivering in my boots. Simply shivering. I may faint from all the excitement. Wouldn't that be dramatic?"

Aunt Lianne patted Pearl's hand. "We're all proud of you, my dear."

"I think as the hostesses of the ball we should be allowed to drain a few dry," Antoinette said.

Pearl felt her insides flop as she thought of Brad's eyes imposed on Evan's. "No." All the vampires in the room looked at her. "Everyone in town will know where they are. All the parents. All the teachers. If any wind up dead, it will draw too much attention. Eventually, someone will blame us. But if everyone simply loses an hour of memory and a pint or two . . . all they'll blame is the spiked punch."

Cousin Antoinette sighed dramatically. "So sensible. So boring."

"I've learned my lesson," Pearl said. "I won't endanger the clan again." Saying it out loud, she believed it. Her caution had zero to do with Evan or Bethany or any of the other sheep. Allowing them to live was a practical choice that benefited the Family, nothing more.

All the aunts nodded approval.

"Still . . . ," Antoinette said, "a girl can hope."

For the first time, a tendril of doubt crept into Pearl. What if this was a mistake? Pearl firmly pushed the doubt aside. She was going to be the jewel of the ball and deliver a fealty feast (and prom) the likes of which no one had ever seen before.

Chapter
TWENTY-THREE

Armed with a stapler, Pearl prowled the high school halls in search of bulletin boards. She had a stack of flyers under her arm with the new junior prom location and date. She felt as if she were succeeding in the greatest jewel heist of all time, or more accurately, blood heist. She grinned as she passed classrooms and lockers.

Pausing at a bulletin board, she stapled three flyers across random ads and on top of sign-up sheets. She added a fourth one for good measure over a set of fire-safety regulations. The theme of the prom was "A Night to Remember," which Pearl loved for its delicious irony. If everything went as planned, none of the students would remember a thing, but she would be remembered in her Family's history for centuries to come: the daywalker who delivered the feast.

She caressed the words in her mind as she continued on

toward the school library. The library door was flanked by bulletin boards. As she posted flyers on the first bulletin board, the library door opened. Pearl didn't bother to glance at the student—until she realized the student hadn't left.

Arms crossed over her chest, Bethany blocked the second bulletin board. "You returned home," Bethany said.

"They forgave me," Pearl said. Instantly she wished she hadn't spoken. She didn't have to defend her actions to anyone, especially a human.

"And you forgave them? Just like that? Pearl, I know you can't see it, but that environment . . . I'm sorry to say bad things about your family, but you know I'm right. You can't stay there. You aren't like them."

Pearl slammed the flyer onto the bulletin board right next to Bethany's head. Bethany flinched. "Yes, I am," Pearl said. Instantly she wished she'd held her temper. The last thing she wanted to do was provoke suspicion. She softened her voice. "I can't leave my family. They're part of who I am."

"They're part of who you *were*. You've changed, and that's okay," Bethany said. "You said yourself: 'Anything that fails to transform'—"

The bell rang, and students began to pour out of the classrooms. "I have to finish up before next period starts." She strode away from Bethany, but the persistent girl galloped after her.

Students waved and smiled as Pearl passed.

Bethany gawked at them. "Zero to hero? What happened?

Just a few days ago you were the girl who stomped on cars."

"Another power shift," Pearl said. "Didn't you feel the earthquake in second period? Administration approved the change in venue and date for the junior prom." She waved the flyers at Bethany. "It'll be a night to remember, or so it says in print. And print never lies."

Bethany wrinkled her nose at the flyer. "You're organizing prom?"

"To save it from sheer patheticness," Pearl said. "It was slated for the school gym. I must be developing Evan's hero complex."

Behind her, Evan said, "I do not have a hero complex." He plucked a flyer out of Pearl's hands, and she let him. She felt a pang inside her rib cage as she inhaled. He smelled especially good today. He must have used a new soap, instead of his sister's shampoo. She thought of the smell of the sheets on his bed and the night she'd spent listening to him breathe in the darkness. "You had us worried," Evan said. "All the time you were out organizing prom?"

"She also returned home," Bethany put in.

Zeke and Matt joined them before Pearl could reply. They scooped the flyer out of Evan's hands and read it together. "Hey, does this mean you are going to prom?" Zeke asked. At the same time Matt said, "Whoo-hoo, date night is on!"

Uh-oh, she had to think of a way out of this. She couldn't attend prom with two wannabe vampire hunters at her side. As inept as they were, that was too much risk. "I don't—"

"She's going with me," Evan said.

All of them turned to look at Evan, and then they all looked at Pearl. She debated turning him down—it was his hero complex again, trying to come to her rescue. This time, though, she decided to let him save her. She didn't have a better idea. "Sorry, boys," she said to Zeke and Matt. "Taken."

Evan smiled at her, the kind of smile that erased everyone else. She had the unsettling feeling that he knew what she'd been thinking, that she'd chosen to let him be her knight in shining armor.

Zeke raised his eyebrows at Matt, and Matt nodded. As one, they turned to Bethany. "Would you do us the honor, Miss Bethany?" Zeke asked.

Bethany blinked. "Both of you are asking me to prom?"

"Otherwise we'd have to duel to the death," Matt said. "Wouldn't be pretty."

"Uh, okay, I think," she said.

Zeke and Matt high-fived, and then they headed off down the hall conferring with each other about tuxedos.

"Just as friends, right?" she called after them.

Swallowed up by the press of students, they didn't answer.

"Why do I suddenly feel like this is a bad idea?" Bethany asked no one in particular.

As Evan met her eyes, Pearl asked herself the same question.

Days and nights became a blur of preparation. During the night, Pearl continued to assist with the cleanup of the mansion cellar. All the gunk had been scrubbed, scoured, and chipped away to reveal a black stone floor that Mother insisted they polish until it gleamed. The walls were polished too, so that the mica in the stone twinkled like stars. Each wine bottle was replaced with a bottle of blood, in case the guests felt peckish before the feast. Each table was decorated with crystal vases that Mother planned to use for night-blooming flowers. Strands of tiny Christmas lights were strung throughout the cellar, after Uncle Stefan nixed the medieval torches as too flammable. With the addition of the lights, even Pearl had to admit that it was beginning to look beautiful.

In daylight hours, in addition to school and track, Pearl cut out decorations with the prom committee: silver stars and crescent moons, as well as silhouettes of dancers. She argued over DJ playlists, and she helped organize student car pools for the prom—ostensibly to cut down on drunkenness but really to cut down on the number of limo drivers outside the mansion that the vampires would have to contend with. She talked up the prom with everyone: the track team, the soccer team, the debate club, the theater kids, the band. . . .

She discovered she was looking forward to both events, a development that disturbed her. She was worrying over that revelation as she loaded up her backpack at the end of school one day. "Pearl?" Bethany asked. "I think I need your help."

"You know I haven't done homework all week, right?" Pearl said. "You should ask Evan."

As if on cue, Evan appeared beside them. "Ask Evan what?"

"How do you do that?" Pearl asked.

"Do what?"

"Always appear when we're talking about you."

He shrugged. "I like to stalk you. Plus you're standing next to my locker." Reaching past her, he opened his locker and switched out his books. On the inside of his locker door, Pearl noticed he had a slip of paper stuck between the photos of his family: a few lines of a poem. *She walks in beauty, like the night,* she read. He shut the locker, and she thought about how Lizzie had told her that he thought she was beautiful. She wished she didn't know that, and she wished she didn't know he liked poetry. All of this would be easier if she'd met boorish humans instead.

"Not homework help," Bethany said. "Prom help. And lately, you're the prom expert. I don't have a dress yet. Are you any good at dress shopping?"

"Sorry." That was more Cousin Antoinette's province. "My aunts made me a dress."

Bethany wrung her hands like the star of a melodrama. "Prom is in two days!"

Evan began to back up. "Uh-uh, don't look at me. Malls terrify me to the core of my being." He faked a shudder.

Pearl heard a high-pitched squeal-like laugh from across the hallway, and her eyes slid over to Tara and her entourage. "I know someone who knows about shopping." She grabbed Bethany's wrist and pulled her across the hall.

"But I don't really know them . . . ," Bethany protested.

"Good time to start," Pearl said. She halted in front of Tara. Ashlyn, she noticed, was nowhere to be seen. She tried to think when she'd last seen the girl with her haunted eyes and couldn't remember. Instead, she thought of Brad's eyes. She pushed the memory firmly down. "Bethany here is in need of a makeover."

All the girls focused on Bethany, who shrank back.

"Really, I'm fine," Bethany said. "Just was wondering about where to shop. . . ."

"A prom dress," Pearl said. "You guys free after school? Feel like a trip to the mall? Bethany has a minivan. She'll drive."

All the girls broke out in smiles. Chattering to Bethany about colors and styles and fabrics, they swept her down the hall. Feeling like patting herself on the back, Pearl watched them.

"That was nice of you," Evan said softly behind her. "Bethany always saw them as the popular kids, the untouchables, like they're some stock characters from an eighties movie."

Pearl shrugged. "They're just people. She shouldn't be afraid of them."

Softly, so softly that Pearl thought it could have been in her own mind, Evan said, "Who should she be afraid of, Pearl?"

Pearl was not prepared for the mall. She'd been here before, but only at closing when the kiosks were packaged up and the chain gates were rolled down. Employees were an easy catch at the end of the day when the mall was nearly vacant. She especially loved the ones who worked at Cinnabon. But you couldn't hunt them when they had customers, so she'd never bothered to come any earlier. She hadn't anticipated how much of a crowd there would be midafternoon. She halted in the department store entrance as the force of the noise hit her like a wave. Canned mall air blasted in her face from the vents by the door.

"You okay?" Bethany asked.

"I feel like I fell inside a pinball machine," Pearl said.

Bethany laughed. "You see why I prefer the library."

Tara and her friend Kelli pushed through the doors without pause, dancing around a mother with a double stroller and a woman with a walker. Both girls wore matching yellow-and-white shirts plus jeans. They only varied in their jewelry: Tara wore hoop earrings that could have doubled as bracelets, and Kelli wore three strands of bead necklaces. Their conversation had been going since the end of school without any help from Pearl or Bethany.

"Strapless?" Kelli asked.

Tara said, "You need balls to wear strapless."

Behind her, Pearl said, "Not literally."

Bethany giggled.

Ignoring both Pearl and Bethany, Kelli considered the matter and proposed with the air of someone making a grand concession: "Spaghetti straps, then. Or halter?"

"Depends on her shoulders," Tara said. She glanced back

at Bethany, who tiptoed around a howling toddler as if he were a live wire about to electrocute her. "No halter."

"Sequins or satin? Ooh, I so want these jeans!" Kelli scurried over to a mannequin that wore a pair of jeans that looked to Pearl exactly like every other pair of jeans in the department store.

"Sequins," Tara said, "and your hips are too narrow for those jeans."

Following the two of them, Bethany whispered to Pearl, "Are you sure this is a good idea? I don't want to look like a cheap disco ball."

At the dress department, Tara took command. Kelli rummaged through the aisles and returned with dresses. Tara would issue thumbs-up or thumbs-down. "Arms out," she ordered Bethany. Dress after dress was piled on top of her outstretched arms.

As yet another orange dress landed on top of her, Bethany ventured to say, "I like pink."

"Not with that hair you don't," Tara told her.

Leaning against a wall, Pearl admired the growing pile of dresses. She was beginning to understand how one could spend the whole day at the mall. This was kind of amusing, especially watching Bethany's increasingly pained expression.

When the stack of dresses reached Bethany's chin, Tara marched her into the fitting area and gave her a little push toward the first room. "Go on," she said. "And come out when you have them on. We want to see them."

Kelli nodded in solemn agreement.

"All of them?" Bethany squeaked.

"Not all," Tara said. She scooped a midnight-blue dress off the top of Bethany's stack and shoved it toward Pearl. "This one is for you."

Satin, it slid over Pearl's arms as she caught it. "I told you I have a dress." She discarded it onto the floor. Her skin tingled from the touch of the satin.

"You'll like this one better." Tara scooped up the dress and hung it on a hook. She then shot a look at Bethany. "Shoo."

Bethany disappeared into the room.

The three of them waited in the hall between the fitting rooms. Pearl hoped that Mother didn't ask for a report on the day. *Shopped at the mall* was not going to sound overly impressive.

After a few minutes Tara knocked on the dressing room door. "Are you changed yet?"

"I tried a few," Bethany called back, "but I don't think—"

Tara let out a long-suffering sigh. "Put the first one back on, and show them to us one at a time. You wanted our help. You do this our way."

"Yeah, we need to see," Kelli said. "You can't shop without verification."

There was a pause, the sound of fabric rustling, and then Bethany opened the door. The dress was yellow and very tight. It hugged her from her armpits to her knees.

"Hmm," Tara said.

"Well . . . ," Kelli said.

Tara shook her head. "Clearly, no."

Bethany's cheeks tinted pink. "For the record, I didn't pick it out."

"I did," Kelli said. "Apparently, I have horrible taste."

Bethany blushed harder until her skin was redder than her strawberry-blonde hair. "Oh, I didn't mean to imply—"

Tara waved her hand. "You aren't getting it. Whole point of going to the mall is to mock. So, let her have it. What do you think of Kelli's choice for a dress?"

Bethany looked down at herself and then at the three-paneled mirror that reflected her and the brilliant yellow over and over again. "I look like a banana."

Tara nodded. "Not bad."

Pearl said, "Toss in an adjective and you may even have yourself an insult. How about: You look like a latex banana."

The side of Bethany's mouth quirked up into a half smile. "I look like a number two pencil after it's been chewed on."

Kelli clapped her hands in approval.

Smiling fully, Bethany ducked back into the changing room. The next dress was declared to look like a purple porcupine with indigestion. The third dress resembled a sailor suit worn by a drunk toddler. The fourth was a napkin. The fifth . . .

Pearl studied her in the green dress. "That's it. This one's gorgeous."

Both human girls nodded.

"Perfect," Tara proclaimed.

"Keeper," Kelli said with two thumbs up.

Tara had Bethany twirl once and then said, "Don't you dare wear flats with this. Two-inch heel at least. Four, preferable." She then turned to Pearl. "Your turn."

Pearl began to protest but then stopped. Honestly, there was no real reason not to try on the dress. Until Mother woke, she could do as she pleased. "All right." Scooping up the satin dress, she swept into an open changing room. Her reflection met her, and Pearl deliberately turned her back on the unsettling image of a second Pearl.

She slipped off her clothes and stepped into the dress. It was a sheath dress in midnight blue satin with a single ruffle flare at the bottom. Also, it was strapless, which made Pearl smile—Tara thought she had balls. It slid on easily. She hopped a few times as she zipped up the back.

From the other side of the door, Kelli said, "Don't just admire yourself. Come out and show us."

Without checking her appearance in the dressing room mirror, Pearl swung open the door. "It's nice, but my aunts made a dress and they'd literally kill me if—"

All three girls stared at her.

"What?" Pearl looked down. It seemed to fit.

"You're wearing that," Tara said. She took Pearl's shoulders and turned her around to face the mirrors.

Pearl looked at herself. The midnight blue made her skin glow, and the shape of it made her look . . . She pivoted as she examined herself from all angles.

She looked beautiful.

"I'm wearing this," Pearl declared.

Bethany beamed at her, and the other three girls looked as pleased as cats with milk. She met their smiles with her own until a terrible thought occurred to her:

Oh, crap. I have friends.

Chapter
TWENTY-FOUR

The mansion shone like a fairy-tale castle in the light of the nearly full moon. Pearl climbed the marble steps to the carved wood door and understood why the prom committee had nearly peed themselves when she'd offered up this place. She imagined the expressions on the students' faces as they walked up to the entrance. It was not only better than the school gym; it was perfect. Except, of course, for the bloodthirsty vampire horde that would be in the basement. "Details, details," she said. All she had to do was convince said horde to exclude just a few humans from the feast. Surely, that wasn't too much to ask.

At the door she heard a buzz saw. She frowned and wondered why she could hear work from the basement all the way out here. She'd thought the soundproofing was better than that. If the prom-goers could hear the vampires downstairs, that could be a serious problem. She pushed the door open and entered the ballroom. All sound ceased.

A half dozen vampires stared at her.

A second later, work resumed as she was deemed not a threat. She shut the door behind her and surveyed the stacks of lumber, tools, metal bars, and paint. She hadn't thought the ballroom needed any work. Upstairs was always kept in perfect order for corporate events and weddings. Besides, Mother had a to-do list for downstairs that had to be giving her nightmares, especially since the ceremony was only two nights away.

"Ah, the author of our triumph," Uncle Felix said. He crossed to Pearl in three large strides. "You can take the north side ballroom windows." He poured a pile of nails into her hand.

"And do what?" she asked.

"Nail them shut, of course."

Looking around again, Pearl realized the goal of all this cheerful industriousness. The vampires weren't improving the cosmetics; they were improving the trap.

Uncle Pascha was sealing shut an emergency exit on the opposite side of the ballroom. Using lumber and then strategically positioned furniture, Cousin Jocelyn and Aunt Fiona were blocking the hallways that led to the remainder of the mansion. In case the humans became creative, Cousin Charlaine was nailing shut the windows on the south side of the ballroom. Uncle Stefan and Cousin Jeremiah were adding iron bars to the window design. (Or rather, Jeremiah was sucking on the bars, and Uncle Stefan was installing them.) Together, the vampires were transforming the mansion's ballroom into a cage.

All the gilded mirrors had been draped in tapestries. One emerald tapestry hid the door to the cellar. A second door to the cellar was in the hall with the bathrooms—Cousin Jocelyn and Aunt Fiona had deliberately left that hall unblocked.

Also, a magnificent clock covered in gold-leaf swirls had been added above the orchestra area, where the DJ would blast undoubtedly cheesy party music for the prom. The clock ticked loudly, as if it were the mansion's heartbeat. Pearl thought of all the heartbeats that would be in this ballroom soon. "Uncle Felix . . . if we wanted to spare a few students . . ."

He laughed. "Oh, don't worry, Pearl. We won't let the king's vamps hog them all."

"It just seems a little greedy for just one night," Pearl said. With so many students and chaperones, His Majesty would be sufficiently sated even if he sucked a pint each from dozens, wouldn't he? He didn't need everyone.

"It's not an ordinary night. It's the Ceremony!" He threw out his arms like the ringmaster of the circus. "This will be a night to remember!"

She turned away before Uncle Felix could read her expression. She should be as gleeful as he was. This was her victory! For the hundredth time since the unicorn stabbed her, she asked herself, *What's wrong with me?*

"Idiot!" Uncle Stefan shouted. He clocked Jeremiah on the head with an iron bar.

Uncle Felix excused himself from Pearl and scurried across the ballroom to assist Uncle Stefan while Jeremiah whimpered on the floor. Pearl didn't follow. It was useless to talk to him while he was with Uncle Stefan. She watched them for a moment and a new question popped into her head: *What's wrong with them?*

The question shocked her. To erase it, Pearl crossed the ballroom and began to hammer nails into the windows, securing them to the windowsills.

Several windows away, Cousin Charlaine was muttering to herself as she hammered. Scooting along the wall to the next window, she flinched when the moonlight touched her skin. As if she felt Pearl looking at her, Charlaine whipped around and bared her fangs at Pearl. She then returned to hammering.

Pearl resumed her own hammering and tried not to imagine Charlaine draining Bethany. She added another nail. She hadn't let Jadrien drink from Bethany; she wasn't about to let Charlaine or any of her other relatives sap the light from her eyes.

She had to talk to Mother.

After nailing shut one more window, she returned the hammer to Uncle Felix and told him she was wanted downstairs. She crossed to the cellar door, hidden by its tapestry, and she descended into the cellar.

Downstairs had been transformed into a beautiful ballroom, worthy of a dozen kings. Thousands of crystal strands dripped from the ceiling so that the cellar looked drenched in glitter. Elegantly bedecked tables bordered the room, leaving a wide-open floor in the center for both the ceremony and the waltzing. The aunts had constructed a dais of wood stained so dark that it looked like stone. It was decorated with curls of gold filigree. Pearl walked toward it, replicating Minerva's lesson. She practiced kneeling in one fluid motion.

"Passable," Mother said as she swept past Pearl. Her red velvet gown whispered against the stone floor. She repositioned a vase on one of the tables. "It will have to do, of course. We are out of time."

"Mother . . . I have a request that I believe you'll agree will be in the best interests of the Family," Pearl said, choosing her words carefully. "A few of the humans have the potential to be valuable in terms of establishing Greenbridge High as a long-term hunting ground, but the toxin would render them useless. Can we find a way to avoid drinking from a select few of the humans?"

Mother weaved between the tables, dusting invisible crumbs and straightening tablecloths. "Everyone will be drained. Leaving anyone alive would be a security risk."

Pearl felt as if all the borrowed blood in her veins had frozen.

"We will find a new hunting ground for you," Mother said. "Your father has contacts throughout Connecticut. He will pull the necessary strings. Perhaps a private school next time."

Careful to control her voice, Pearl said, "The plan was to take a pint from each, let the toxin cloud their memories, and then send them on their way none the wiser."

"His Majesty amended the plan," Mother said. She raised her voice and said, "Cousin Shirley, please refold the napkins on table fifteen." Shirley, who had been polishing one of the wine racks, scurried to table fifteen.

Pearl asked, "Amended the plan?"

"He wants a bloodbath," Mother said.

Pearl couldn't speak.

Mother continued, "Burning the Dairy Hut was so effective at hiding the evidence of a vampire kill that we decided we could repeat that on a larger scale here. After the feast, we burn the mansion. Your father even has plans for it to look accidental." She laughed.

"Oh," Pearl said. She felt as if her mind were swimming. Everything was drowning in a red haze. Her insides felt as if they'd cramped into knots.

"The king will be very pleased with you," Mother said. "I already am." She kissed Pearl's cheek. Her lips were cold. "Help fold napkins, dear."

As the bell rang for lunch period, Pearl leaned her forehead against the cool metal locker. She heard the thunder of all the juniors around her as they slammed their lockers and headed for the cafetorium. After Saturday, this hall would be silent. Of course, she wouldn't be here to know. She wouldn't be able to return as the sole surviving junior. Oh, no, she'd be starting over at another school. Mother and Daddy would enroll her elsewhere so she could befriend the humans and then betray them. At this thought, her stomach lurched inside her, and her grip tightened on the locker door until the metal creaked under her hand.

"Pearl, coming to lunch?" Bethany asked.

She lifted her head. "Yeah." Shoving her books into her locker, she touched the notebook that Bethany had given her. Her vision blurred as if she were underwater.

"Pearl . . . are you okay? You're crying."

Pearl's hands flew to her eyes. She wiped quickly, expecting to see a smear of blood tears. Instead, she saw only a sheen of water. She brought the tears to her lips and tasted salt. "Real tears," she said.

"Is it your family?" Bethany asked. "What did they do? I've never seen you cry before."

To herself as much as to Bethany, Pearl said, "I never have." Her tongue went to her gums, and she felt the skin that covered her fangs. *I'm still a vampire,* she thought.

"Come to lunch. We'll figure it out together," Bethany said. She put her arm around Pearl. "They don't own you or control you. You can make your own choices."

Pearl shook her head. She had no choices. She'd lost control of the situation. The ceremony and the prom were moving forward regardless of how she felt. Shrugging off Bethany's arm, Pearl walked past the line for food and into the cafetorium. Sunlight streamed over all the students. *I've doomed them all,* she thought.

Holding a tray with a salad and three apples, Sana from the track team breezed past her and said over her shoulder, "5K today, yes? Of course yes. Otherwise, you forfeit and must admit that I am clearly faster than you."

Pearl caught her arm. "Are you going to prom?"

"Absolutely," Sana said. "Half of us from the team are going together. Want in?"

Mutely, Pearl shook her head.

Joining them, Zeke said, "She has a date." He had a bag lunch in one hand and a two-liter soda in the other.

Matt carried an old Atari Pac-Man lunch bag and was sucking on a juice box. She thought of Uncle Stefan and how he sucked blood. She felt the wetness in her eyes again. "Ooh, yes, hot date," Matt said. "Hubba-hubba."

Zeke raised his eyebrows at Matt. "Did you really just say that?"

"Unfortunately, yes," Matt said. "Dude, it just slipped out."

"'Hubba-hubba' never slips out," Zeke said. "You selected those words with deliberate intent, and I question your commitment to the respectable use of the English language."

Catching up (with a limp sandwich on her tray), Bethany said, "And these are my date. Or dates, rather." She faked a sigh but couldn't erase her smile. *After tomorrow night,* Pearl thought, *she won't ever smile again.*

Sana nodded hello to Bethany. "So who's your hot date?"

she asked Pearl. "I didn't know you had a boyfriend."

She pictured Jadrien. He saw them all as sheep, ready for the slaughter. Pearl squeezed her eyes shut and tried to will herself to stop these thoughts, these images, these *feelings*.

Sana said, "If your date's a jerk, then come with us. Zero dates. Zero pressure."

Evan joined them. "Hey, who's a jerk?" Pearl opened her eyes to look at him, really look at him. His eyes were beautiful black with colors dancing around his irises. His skin looked warm. If she touched him, she knew she'd feel the pulse beating just below the surface. He was the most alive person she'd ever met.

She felt the pressure in her eyes again, the strange water that threatened to spill out.

Evan touched her arm. "Pearl?"

His touch was like a jolt of electricity, waking the blood under her skin. Pearl said, in a louder voice than she'd meant to, "We have to cancel prom."

All conversation near them ceased.

A few whispers spread across the cafetorium, and a hush fell over all the students.

Bethany touched Pearl's other arm. "Pearl, what are you talking about?"

She looked at Bethany and then at Evan and then at the students at the tables. She recognized so many of the faces, a few from each of the crowds she even knew by name: Tara, Kelli, Melody, Emily, Emma. "Vampires," Pearl said. Everyone was silent. Everyone could hear her. "Beneath your prom, in the mansion's cellars, the vampires of Connecticut will be holding their Fealty Ceremony. At the conclusion of it, they will feast upon you. They plan to kill everyone at prom."

A few laughed, and then the laughter spread like a wave across the cafetorium.

"You can't go!" she said. "It's not safe!" Of course they wouldn't believe her. Concentrating, she pushed her fangs out through her gums. She'd *show* them the truth. She'd undo what she'd done, and she'd fix everything.

Evan slapped his hand over her mouth.

Chapter
TWENTY-FIVE

"We need to talk," Evan said into her ear.

Bethany jumped forward. Her face was bright red as all eyes focused on her. "New prom theme! Vampires! Do you like it?"

Most of the students cheered. Some groaned. A few catcalled. Conversations burst out across all the tables.

"Outside," Evan said to Pearl. She thought about flinging him away. It would be easy, a quick maneuver that she'd done a thousand times with Jadrien. One twist of her arm, and he'd be splayed across the nearest cafeteria table. "Please, don't fight me," he whispered. He took his hand off her mouth. "And keep your fangs in."

Pearl froze. *Fangs?* He knew?

"Trust me, okay?"

She let herself be shepherded across the cafetorium. As

she passed by tables, various students called out to her, "Great theme!" "You rock!" "This will be the best prom ever!" "Can we wear fangs?" "Will there be fake blood?" "Can I wear fake blood?" "Does blood come out of tuxedos? Mine's a rental. . . ."

As they reached the courtyard doors, Mr. Barstow, their English teacher, intercepted them. "Am I right to think you're planning a dinner-theater kind of show with this 'Fealty Ceremony' during the prom? I love the concept of imposing a story structure on a free-form event."

"Still need to work out a few details," Evan said. "We need to do a little planning where the rest of the junior class can't hear." He reached past Mr. Barstow to open the door. "Lots of surprises to be staged, you know."

"It just started raining out there," Mr. Barstow said.

"We'll stay under the trees," Evan promised.

"All right," Mr. Barstow said. "You know, I used to be involved in amateur dinner theater, improv with audience participation. Let me know if you'd like any advice."

"Uh, thanks," Evan said. He pushed through the door and propelled Pearl outside in front of him. Drizzle hit her skin. "Come on, vampire girl, this way."

She followed him across the courtyard to the trees. She expected him to stop there, as he'd told Mr. Barstow, but he kept walking out of the courtyard and through the parking lot. She caught his arm as he headed into the woods. "Enough," she said.

He shot a look back at the school.

"Unless Superman is in our school, no one can hear you from here," she said. Rain snaked down her cheeks and wormed down the back of her shirt. "I've been patient enough."

"A little farther," he said. "I can't be seen. Please, Pearl, you've trusted me before." His eyes were so ridiculously earnest. She sighed and gestured for him to continue. He plunged into the woods and led her in between the trees. Rain hit the leaves in soft smacks. The pine-needle floor squished under her boots.

Evan halted in a clearing with a rock in the center. It was the same clearing she'd chosen to wait with Bethany for the unicorn. She frowned at him.

"That afternoon when you took Bethany here, I watched you from those bushes," he said, pointing to a thicket of brambles. "We weren't sure you were safe yet."

"Excuse me?" Pearl said.

"Just . . . wait a minute, okay?" he said. "Easier if I show you first."

He closed his eyes and held still. Rain drew streaks down his face. It flattened his shirt and curved across his arms. Slowly, Evan began to glow. Soft white light emanated from him as if he were in a cheesy religious movie.

"Huh," Pearl said. "Super Glow Boy. Unexpected but interesting."

The glow brightened, washing out the features of his face and the outline of his body. He looked like a white blur, and then light flashed so bright that Pearl flinched.

An instant later, Evan was gone.

In his place, in the center of the clearing, was a unicorn.

Like water poured from a pitcher, all thought ran out of her head. "You're . . . you . . ." She pointed at him, out of words. He shimmered again. This time, there was no flash. After a blur of light, Evan knelt in front of her, sweating and panting.

Pearl stared at him. "Seriously? You? You're Mr. Sparkly-and-Pointy?"

"Not the nickname I would have picked," Evan said. He straightened and winced, as if the new shape of his bones hurt. "You've heard of werewolves, right? Well, I'm . . . kind of like that, except I don't need to wait for the full moon."

"You're a were-unicorn?" Pearl asked.

"Basically, yes."

"Do you have any idea how stupid that sounds?"

Evan's lips quirked into a smile. "It's not as if I . . . how did you put it? Poop rainbows."

Pearl pointed her finger at him. "You stabbed me through the heart."

"And healed you," he said. "And carried you home. Pearl, I can explain—"

She knew her mouth had dropped open, but she couldn't help it. He was the knight in shining armor who had placed her on the porch that dawn. "Whatever you did, the stabbing or the healing, you're the reason that I can walk in sunlight. You're the reason that I have a reflection. You're the reason that I—"

"Have developed a conscience," Evan said. "Yes."

"You . . . you . . . ," she sputtered. Out of words, Pearl launched herself at him. She aimed for his shoulders, intending to slam him against a tree. Instead, he dodged faster than she would have thought possible for a human. *Okay, so he's not human,* she thought. Adjusting, she switched to fighting as if he were Jadrien. She kicked low and shot out her fist at the same time. He danced backward and swung his arm to intercept her punch. She grabbed his wrist and yanked. He leaned back and kicked at her knee. She twisted and flipped up, using his arm to propel her up into the tree branches. She landed on the branches and perched above him for a fraction of a second before she dived toward him. He dodged, and she landed and rolled across the roots and underbrush. Rain soaked into her skin. She sprang up, her fangs out.

"You're fast," she growled. "I'm faster."

She exploded into movement, a frenzied swirl of kicks and punches. She felt rather than saw them impact. She drove him out of the clearing into the woods—and then she saw a flash of gold shoot from his arm.

Pearl leaped backward as Evan sliced through the air with a sword of swirled gold. "Good," she said, grinning with her fangs out. "With my new 'conscience,' I'd hate to beat up a defenseless boy."

She kicked fast and hard, and he spun and swung with the sword. She dodged it, and then he attacked, cutting through the branches and leaves as he stabbed and sliced.

The sword didn't have a hilt. Instead, his hand was wrapped around the base. And it didn't have an edge. It was a spiral of gold that ended in a sharp tip, exactly like . . . Pearl faltered, and Evan stabbed the unicorn horn through her sleeve, grazing her skin. She fingered the cut and said conversationally, "You know you have a unicorn horn coming out of your wrist."

He withdrew the horn. "Uh, yeah." Horn raised in front of him, he waited for her to attack again. When she didn't, he held out his arm and rotated it to show her. The horn emerged from his wrist at the base of his palm as if it were an extension of his bones. "It's an adaptation so we can fight better. Not always efficient to turn horse. Really, it's not any more strange than your fangs."

"Um, yes, it is. You have a horn coming out of your wrist. And did you say 'we'? There are more of you?"

He nodded.

"Your family?" she guessed.

He hesitated and then nodded again. "Our birth families all rejected us when we began exhibiting signs of what we were. The Karkadanns adopted us."

"I spent the night with unicorns?"

"I spent the night with a vampire."

He'd known what she was all along. He'd known what she was when she'd appeared at his window. He'd known what she was earlier when he'd found her on his roof . . . when he'd *led* her to his roof. She thought back to that chase. He'd wanted her to know where he lived. But why? "You knew what I was, and you still invited me in."

"I had to be sure," he said.

"Sure of what?"

"That you'd changed enough," he said. "That it had worked. You were next to me all night, and you never so much as looked at my neck. So I knew."

She remembered when he'd picked her up that first morning after she'd left Zeke and Matt. He'd driven her to the library and then watched her while she was out on the field. He'd been the first person she'd met at high school. None of that was an accident or a coincidence. "You . . ."

"You're going to attack again, aren't you?" He raised his sword-horn a split second before she punched him. Her fist impacted on the side of the horn. It felt like punching steel. She winced, but she didn't stop.

"Do you"—she hit again—"have any"—hit—"idea what you've done?" Lunging low, she knocked his feet out from under him. He lost his balance. She leaped onto him. He wasn't fast enough to flip away. "You changed me! You've made me lose who I am. Lose my Family. Lose my world!" With each accusation, she landed a blow. Her eyes blurred until she couldn't see him. Her strikes lost power. She put her hands over her face.

And she cried.

She felt his arms slip around her as he sat up. He drew her against his chest and held her as she wept. She heard his heart beat as she leaned against him, and she felt him breathing, as deeply and evenly as the human that she'd thought he was.

"I'm sorry," he said.

"Are you?" she demanded.

He hesitated. "No."

Pearl drew away from him. "Why? Why do it? Was it to save lives? I'm a minor vampire. Before you came along, I sipped from a few here and there." She thought of Brad, and she felt the strange ache that she could now name—her conscience. "But now I've endangered four hundred lives."

"You were trying to save them in there," Evan said. "You were about to reveal yourself, sacrifice your safety, for them." He sounded admiring.

"Until you stopped me," Pearl said.

Evan looked over Pearl's head. "Until *we* stopped you," he corrected.

Pearl turned around to see Bethany walking through the woods toward them. Her strawberry-blonde curls had been flattened by the rain so they clung to her forehead and cheeks like limp yarn. The pine needles squished and crunched under her feet. She ducked under tree branches that rained more water down on her.

"Don't tell me she's a were-unicorn too?" Pearl asked.

"One hundred percent human." Bethany beamed at Pearl. "So I assume he showed you his fancy horse trick? Pretty neat, huh?"

Pearl crossed her arms.

Bethany's smile faded. "You're mad at us. I knew you'd be mad at us! But you were a psychotic killer before. Aren't you so much happier this way? You can feel emotions! You can have friends! You can experience love!"

"And loss," Pearl said softly. "Either I lose my Family, or all those people die."

Bethany looked over her shoulder at Evan. "You didn't tell her?"

"Been busy," he said, standing. He dusted the leaves and dirt off his clothes.

"So you were in on this with him?" Pearl asked.

Bethany raised her hand as if in class. "Actually, it was my idea."

Evan caught Pearl's arms to prevent her from lunging at Bethany. Bethany let out a shriek and scurried behind a tree. Pearl shrugged him off. "I'm not going to hurt her," Pearl said. "She gave me a notebook."

He released her. "Wish I'd thought of that."

"You stabbed me," Pearl said. "I'd need a whole stationery store to fix that." She glared at Bethany. "Come out and tell me what the master plan for world domination is."

"No domination," Bethany said. "We're the good guys."

"Debatable," Pearl said. "But go on."

"Do you promise you won't attack me?" Bethany asked. She clutched the tree trunk as if it would protect her.

"Depends on what you say," Pearl said.

Bethany looked at Evan.

In a grave voice, as if he were narrating for the History Channel, Evan said, "For centuries were-unicorns have fought and killed vampires. It's why we exist. We're your natural enemy." He sounded as if he expected an orchestra to play an ominous chord at this revelation.

"Huh," Pearl said. "No offense, but you guys aren't very good at it. Everyone in my Family thinks you're mythical."

"That's intentional," Evan said. "We planted the myths. It made our hunt easier."

"Interesting," Pearl said. "And the whole virgin-in-a-clearing thing?"

"Look, what kills vampires? Stake through the heart, right? And what do unicorns have?" Evan tapped his forehead. "Built-in stakes. All the other legends are just to obscure the truth."

Pearl digested that. "Okay. So you stake vampires. Why did I live?"

"Well, the healing part of our myth is true," Evan said.

Bethany burst in. "When they heal, they kind of, you know, make people more good. Wake up their conscience a bit more. At least, that's what happened to me, when Evan's mother saved me." Pearl supposed this explained how the quintessential mom had saved little Bethany from Daddy: Mrs. Karkadann was a vampire slayer. *Handy hobby*, she thought. Bethany continued, "I should have turned out like my parents, but I didn't. So I had an idea. What if you tried that with a vampire? Kind of insert goodness directly in. What would happen?"

"So you basically infected me," Pearl said. "I was your lab rat."

"Oh, no!" Bethany gasped in horror. "We never thought of you like that! You're the first of your kind! Dawn of a new species!"

"Right," Pearl said. "Species of one."

Both of them shook their heads. "Only until the Fealty Ceremony," Evan said. "It's a brilliant plan, really. Even my mother agreed."

Bethany blushed. "It *is* pretty clever. See, you're like a carrier now. You have unicorn in your veins. So when the king drinks from you . . ."

Pearl felt her mouth drop open. "You know about the blood exchange?" The details of the Fealty Ceremony were a closely guarded vampire secret. No matter how hard Bethany studied, she couldn't have learned about it in any library.

"We know a lot," Evan said. "We've been hunting your kind for centuries. But in all those centuries, we've never been able to touch royalty. They're too well guarded."

Bethany jumped in again. "But they're the key, you see! In the Fealty Ceremonies, all the vampires share the king's blood. If that blood is—"

"Tainted," Pearl interrupted. It *was* a rather brilliant plan. "You planned to use me to infect all the vampires at the ceremony. Out of curiosity, at what point did you intend to tell me all of this?"

Bethany and Evan looked at each other.

"Nice," Pearl said. "So your plan was to let everything proceed. I go to the ceremony. King drinks my blood. Everyone drinks the king's blood. Everyone becomes nice, shiny, happy friends." She shook her head. "You realize your plan has an enormous gaping hole? Prom."

"That is a complication," Bethany agreed.

"Serious complication," Pearl said. "Even after they're 'tainted,' the vampires will still want their feast. They won't change instantly. I didn't. In fact, I'm not convinced I shouldn't tear both your throats out right now."

Bethany skipped backward a few steps, but Evan merely smiled.

Pearl glared at him. "What?"

"I like how direct you are," he said. "I don't know. It's different from my family."

"I mean it," she said.

"I know."

His smile was highly disconcerting. "You're an idiot," she told him. "We have to cancel the prom. Your 'brilliant' plan isn't worth—"

Bethany interrupted. "If we cancel prom, how will the vampires react?"

Pearl hesitated, remembering what Daddy had once said. "The king would most likely cancel the ceremony. And the Family would most definitely kill me." Uncle Stefan would be thrilled to do the honors.

"If we could cancel the prom and still ensure that you

participated in the ceremony, we'd do it in a second," Bethany said. "But if there's no prom and no ceremony and you're killed . . ."

"If we lose you, we lose the best chance in centuries to prove that it's possible to change the power dynamic between humans and vampires," Evan said.

Bethany was nearly hopping up and down. "It could lead to the end of hunting! It could show the way to peace! We've never had an opportunity like this before!"

"It's worth the risk," Evan said.

Both of them looked so ridiculously innocent and excited. It would have been sweet if it weren't so idiotic.

"We'll find a way to ensure the students' safety," Bethany promised. "Evan, think your family would be willing to chaperone?"

Pearl wanted to shake both of them. "Have you ever seen a horde of bloodthirsty vampires? You'd better have one very extended family."

"We can do it," Evan said. "Really, how many vampires are we talking about? A dozen or so young vampires, your family, and the royal retinue, right?"

Pearl wanted to smack him again. "No. It's me, my Family, the royal retinue, and every last vamp in the grand ol' state of Connecticut. At the last RSVP count, we were up to one hundred five."

Both Bethany and Evan were silent.

"We may need to amend the plan a bit," Bethany squeaked.

TWENTY-SIX

The funny thing was that even despite the dire seriousness of the situation, Pearl could tell it bothered Bethany to cut class. She'd insisted that she had to participate in the emergency meeting with Evan's family, and she'd offered to drive, but every few minutes Bethany glanced in the rearview mirror as if she expected the principal to charge up the street behind them, brandishing a pitchfork and a detention slip.

Pearl rolled her eyes. "The teachers are not the big bad scary monsters. Take it from me, one of the big bad scary monsters."

At a red light, Bethany looked at Pearl with ridiculously wide, innocent eyes. "You aren't a monster. Not anymore. I'm not scared of you."

"You should be," Pearl said. "This isn't natural. What I

feel . . . what I think . . . your pet horsey put this all inside of me. I'm your Frankenstein's monster."

Behind her in the backseat, Evan said, "Your thoughts are your own. All I did was . . . heal the broken parts inside you. I woke up your soul, that's all."

Pearl turned her head away from both of them. She looked at her reflection in the window, as if it could show her her soul. Rain continued to fall, tracing jagged lines down her reflection as if she were covered in tears.

"Also, I'm not a 'pet horsey,'" Evan said.

A few minutes later they reached Evan's house. They spilled out of the minivan and into the house. Evan's parents plus three of his siblings were already in the kitchen.

Without any preamble, Evan said, "We discovered when and where the Connecticut Fealty Ceremony will be." He gestured to Pearl. "Go on, you can tell them."

The words stuck in her throat. She looked at these faces— vampire hunter faces—and she couldn't speak. Sandy, Evan's mother, smiled at her encouragingly, as if she were a sitcom mom urging her wayward daughter to tell the truth about a bad report card. Evan's father, Donald, kept his face neutral, an expression Pearl was sure he'd had to practice. Like Sandy's, his face was lined with smile marks, and his pink nose marked him as someone who blushed easily. At the table Evan's siblings were not so calm. Lizzie folded her hands on the table in front of her. Her knuckles were as white as pearls. One brother, Marcus, fidgeted in his chair, rocking back and forth so that the chair legs squeaked on the linoleum. A second brother, Allen or Alex or another A name, looked tense enough to leap up like a cat if Pearl so much as twitched.

"I can't," Pearl said to Evan. She bolted outside into the rain.

"Stay. Explain," Evan ordered Bethany. Pearl heard his footsteps behind her. But she had a head start. She threw the door open. Twisting around, she grabbed the porch gutter. She propelled herself up onto the roof, and she scrambled up to the peak. The roof tiles were slick, and she slipped twice before she stood at the top.

A few seconds later Evan launched himself onto the roof. "You like roofs," he grunted as he scrambled up the wet slope.

"Roofs are dramatic," she said. "Vampires have a fine sense of drama."

He stood next to her, balancing with bent knees. Rain spattered him as if the clouds were spitting. "So . . ." He let the word dangle, as if this were a casual conversation.

"So," she said.

"You okay?" he asked.

She considered it. "No, really not okay. You know, this conscience thing is a bitch. I don't want the humans to die." Blinking away raindrops, she looked at him. "Yes, I can admit that."

He half smiled. "Happy to hear it."

"But I'd rather not aid in the slaughter of my Family, either," she said.

"The goal is to change them, not kill them."

"Your family . . . they're vampire hunters. It's what they do, what they're designed to do," Pearl said. "You said so yourself."

He nodded. "Then help us find a way to do this with the least number of casualties."

"That's a ridiculously unvampiric goal," Pearl said.

"For this to work, we need you," Evan said. "Otherwise . . ."

Pearl waved her hand. "Bloodbath. Vampires and humans die. You sure know how to sweet-talk a girl, don't you?" She started down the roof, deliberately skidding down the slick shingles.

Evan didn't move. "Pearl."

At the lip of the roof, she looked back up at him. His shirt, wet from the rain, stuck to his chest and arms. Drops of water clung to his hair.

"I meant what I said. Your thoughts are your own. Your choices . . . your own. And you . . ." He looked down at the roof tiles as if embarrassed to meet her eyes. "You impress me."

She almost smiled. "Getting better at the sweet talk." She turned and leaped off the roof. As she landed, she called up, "A bit more practice, and you'll find me in your bed again."

She heard him slip and then slide his way to the edge of the roof with a loud "Oof!" She laughed. He jumped down next to her, landing with a splash in a puddle. They went inside together.

Pearl didn't offer an explanation or an apology. She didn't owe them either, as far as she was concerned. She was doing this for Bethany, Evan, Sana, Tara, Matt, and Zeke—and, she hoped, for her Family too, though she doubted they'd see it that way. Marching into the kitchen, she said, "Paper?" Evan fetched her a pad of paper covered in smiley faces. She scowled at it. "Pen?" He handed her a pen, and she began to draw a blueprint of the mansion, as well as the tunnel system that led into the cellar. "At sundown the ceremony guests will enter the mansion's cellar via an underground tunnel. Meanwhile, upstairs, the prom-goers will arrive through the main entrance to the mansion." She dripped on the paper, blurring the ink.

"And you?" Evan's brother Marcus asked. "Are you with the vampires or the humans?" He fingered his wrist, and Pearl thought of Evan's swordlike horn. She tensed, calculating the distance to the exit.

Evan glared at him. "She's helping us."

Marcus spread his hands to show innocence. "Just working through the logistics."

Evan's father, Donald, spoke, his voice gentle, as if Pearl were a deer he didn't want to startle. His mannerisms reminded her of Evan. "Can you walk us through the ceremony timeline?"

"First, the king and his retinue will make their grand entrance," Pearl said. "All of the young vampires will be introduced, and the king will drink from each of us. Then the king will share his blood with the full assembly."

Evan's brother Allen swallowed hard, as if attempting not to gag.

Sandy jotted a few notes. "How much time will there be between the ritual drinking of blood and the feast?" She was all business, and Pearl suddenly could imagine her as a woman who could go toe-to-toe with Daddy.

"An hour," Pearl said. "There's a lot of waltzing."

"And where will your attack begin?" Marcus asked.

Evan bristled at the word "your," but it didn't faze Pearl. He wasn't wrong. She had set all this in motion. Pearl said, "There are two sets of stairs from the cellar into the mansion. One of them leads directly into the ballroom—it's here, obscured by a tapestry. And the other is down this hall near the restrooms." She pointed at her drawing. "My Family has blocked access to the bulk of the mansion so that once the front door is closed, the feast can't flee."

Sandy tapped the map. "Marcus, after Pearl goes downstairs, you and Melinda will barricade the cellar door in the hall. Evan and Lizzie, after Pearl completes her mission and rejoins us, you will barricade the cellar door in the ballroom. Allen, you'll patrol the grounds with William. Brooke and Louis will assist Donald and me with the evacuation."

All of the Karkadanns in the kitchen straightened like soldiers who had received their orders.

"All we need to do is hold the cellar entrances until the students are evacuated," Evan said. "We don't need to kill the vampires." He looked directly at Pearl. "Killing them isn't the goal here."

Marcus cleared his throat. "What about the tunnel?" he

asked. "What if the vamps make a run for it, come up to the surface somewhere else, and then double back to the mansion?"

"The nearest tunnel system entrance is a mile away," Pearl said. "Once we—I mean they—notice there's a problem with the feast, some may try. And, as you probably know, we're fast."

Sandy nodded briskly. "So we complete the evacuation before any of the vampires notice. We have more than an hour to do it. If we're careful, we won't need to hold the entrances or worry about the tunnels. Zero casualties on either side."

"Sandy," Donald said. His voice was quiet and intense, like Evan's. His eyes were fixed on his wife's face. "Are you sure about this? We're risking a lot of kids."

"We do it quietly over the course of the hour, and the risk will be minimal," Sandy said. "Especially in comparison to the potential rewards. We've waited a long time for a moment like this."

They held each other's gazes, and Pearl was suddenly reminded of Mother and Daddy and how they knew each other so well that they sometimes communicated just through their eyes. She wondered what her parents would think of the Karkadanns. *They'd think they're tasty,* she thought.

Lizzie interrupted their staring contest. "You're assuming the students cooperate. They're not going to want to leave their prom. They won't understand, and they won't leave quietly."

Everyone around the table fell silent.

"Sure they will," Pearl said, "if their friends are. I've studied the social dynamics. Peer pressure is a powerful thing. All we need to do is tell the truth to a few select people, ideally some from each clique, and the rest will follow their lead." She knew a few of the key players in each branch of the social hierarchy. She bet Evan knew more.

Lizzie rolled her eyes. "Seriously? You want to tell kids about vampires?"

"She kind of already did," Bethany said. Her cheeks blushed pink, matching her hair. "Everyone pretty much laughed. And I . . . I told them it was the new prom theme."

Evan nodded. "Mr. Barstow assumed we were planning a kind of improv dinner theater show around a vampire theme. We could spread the word that the evacuation is part of the show."

"Convince a few to sneak away, and the rest will follow," Pearl said. "Like good sheep."

"Absolutely not," Sandy said. Her tone was as firm as Mother's, and Pearl instinctively straightened her posture. She had to remind herself that this was *not* Mother. "You're talking about trusting children to—"

"You trust them," Pearl said, waving her hand to indicate Bethany, and Evan and his siblings. She excluded herself. She doubted they trusted her. In their shoes, she wouldn't.

Gently—Pearl had the sense he did everything gently— Evan's father, Donald, said, "We raised them. Of course we trust them. Plus, they aren't minors. With the exception of Evan, all of our children have been hunting vampires on their own since they turned eighteen. Your classmates, however, are minors who have no knowledge of vampires."

Pearl rolled her eyes. "Sharp fangs. Suck blood. Lot easier concept to grasp than the purpose of the Federalist Papers. And for the record, I'd like to point out that it's deeply ironic that I'm the one arguing in favor of trusting humans."

"It's our job to protect and save them," Donald said.

"Can you?" Pearl countered.

Silence. Evan's family studied the kitchen table. His parents exchanged glances that seemed loaded with unspoken words. Pearl glared at each of them and said, "You're perfectly fine with using four hundred kids as bait, but not with trusting any of them to help save their own skins. I may be new to this whole having-a-conscience thing, but I'm thinking that doesn't sit right."

Bethany said, "She has a point." Her cheeks flared bright red as everyone looked at her. "Truth is, the math doesn't work. There aren't enough of us. We need more allies."

Pearl watched their faces and knew she'd won. Even Evan's parents reluctantly nodded. Smiling, Pearl said, "Good. I know where to start."

Pearl spotted Zeke and Matt lounging in the rain on the bleachers by the athletic field, instead of in sixth period, where they were supposed to be. Each had an umbrella propped up over his head. Zeke was typing on his phone. Matt was reading a book. Neither noticed Pearl.

Ducking under the bleachers, Pearl poked her finger up at Zeke's leg. "Boo," she said.

He tumbled off the bench onto the next bleacher, and then he sprang to his feet. Matt dropped his book. He retrieved it and dried it off frantically with the bottom of his T-shirt. "Pearl!" Matt said. "Are you trying to give us heart failure?"

"Big bad vamp hunters should be more alert," she said. She slithered through a gap in the bleachers and then boosted herself onto the bench beside them. Rain wormed through her hair. She ignored it.

"It's daylight," Matt said. "No vampires now."

Briefly, Pearl considered displaying her fangs with no prelude. He'd given her such a beautiful opening. But it wasn't worth the dramatic value. "Boys, I need your help."

"Your wish is our command," Zeke said, executing a half bow.

"The vampires are plotting to attack the junior prom, feed, and then torch the place to hide the evidence," Pearl said.

"I knew it!" Matt said. "Always a bad idea to have large social events. Totally tempting fate. Vampires love proms. Look at the original *Buffy the Vampire Slayer* movie. I mean, don't look at it, because it's seriously bad, like in an awesome way, but the climax? Giant vampire attack at prom. Also, *Carrie*. No vampire attack there, but lots of blood and carnage. And don't forget *Mean Girls*. The horror, the horror!"

Zeke frowned at her. "You're mocking us. Not cool, Pearl."

"Obvious option is to cancel the prom, but we can't," Pearl said. "A bunch of slayers think it's a brilliant opportunity.

The plan is to hold the prom as normal so that the vampires don't figure out something is wrong while I infect them with special grow-your-own-soul juice. Meanwhile, the slayers will evacuate everyone from the prom so that when the vampires come up for their feast, the food has left the building."

"She *is* mocking us," Matt said. Zeke nodded.

"I wish I were," Pearl said. "But the slayers need your help with the evacuation." She sat down next to them and looked out at the field. Rain drizzled down her cheeks. Her clothes stuck to her skin. "And I need your help if it fails."

"Our help?" Matt asked.

"The evacuation needs to be silent and gradual so that the vampires don't notice," Pearl said. "But if they *do* notice . . . we need to slow them down."

Zeke lifted his umbrella over her head. "What's this all about, Pearl? Level with us. You can't expect us to believe that you ditched class and came out here in the rain to poke at our hobby."

"Apparently, I'm the first vampire with a conscience," Pearl said without looking at them.

"You can't be a vampire." Matt pointed at the sky. "Daytime."

"Yes, I can." Pearl pointed at her mouth. "Fangs." She concentrated for a second and then displayed her fangs. She then retracted them and didn't move.

"Whoa," Zeke said.

"Do we stake her?" Matt asked. He tried to sound cool but failed. Inching away, he scooted across the wet bleachers.

"She's not trying to bite us," Zeke said. "And it's Pearl. Wait, when we first met you . . . that guy behind the Dairy Hut . . . you weren't really . . . All right, who put you up to this?"

"I'd like to try to avoid being responsible for the deaths of everyone in the junior class. I think you guys can help. But if I'm wrong, let me know, and I'll head back to history class. Or, more accurately, I'll ditch and try to come up with a better idea. Ideas aren't really my strong suit, though. Apparently, it's Bethany who is the mastermind genius." She decided not to mention Evan's role in this. Zeke and Matt were confused enough already.

They were staring at her. "So not following you," Zeke said.

Pearl stood up. "If you want to help, we're meeting at the mansion tomorrow after dawn to prepare. Bring whomever you want, so long as you can guarantee they won't panic."

At the start of seventh period, Pearl intercepted Tara en route to the mall—the head of the prom committee had a pass to leave campus to buy prom supplies. Climbing into the passenger seat of Tara's car, Pearl said, "Do you believe in vampires? Not the sparkly variety."

"You!" Tara screeched.

Pearl blinked. She hadn't expected her to figure it out so quickly. "How—"

"You changed the prom theme without even consulting

the prom committee!" Tara said. "I thought we were friends. You need to get out of the car. Now. I'm not speaking to you." She pointed at the car door and tossed her hair to show she meant it.

"Tara, I'm a vampire," Pearl said.

"Yeah, whatever, and I'm queen of the sea."

"Your Marine Majesty, I'm a vampire," Pearl said.

"Look, I like the theme, okay?" Tara said. "I think it's brilliant. I wish I'd thought of it. But you could have told me! I was fending off questions the whole rest of the day, and where were you, by the way?" She continued her tirade.

Pearl sighed. Concentrating, she slid her fangs out. "Tara. Tara!" She curled back her lips to expose the points. "See."

Tara screamed.

"I won't hurt you," Pearl said. "Calm down. Sheesh."

Tara continued to scream.

Pearl contemplated biting her merely to shut her up. Regrettably, that would be counterproductive. Studying her nails, she waited for Tara to quit screaming. She noticed that Tara didn't try to exit the car, which was an interesting choice. "You aren't running away," Pearl said.

"Duh, it's raining outside," Tara said. "Someone is supposed to hear my screams, run over, see your fangs, and then spread the word about our commitment to the prom theme. Pearl, if you'd just let me in on your idea sooner, we could have rolled it out with style!"

Pearl reminded herself that it was her brilliant idea to

involve the humans. She hadn't thought they'd be quite so dense. "Tara . . . My parents fed on Ashlyn. That's why she . . . that's what's wrong with her and her parents. Vampire bites hurt humans' minds."

Tara was silent.

It was such an unexpected sound that Pearl felt her muscles tense, ready to defend herself. She tried to read Tara's expression, but Tara's face betrayed nothing. She merely studied Pearl. At last, when Tara spoke, all traces of her usual ditzy act were gone. "Ashlyn's my best friend. Or was. She changed a few weeks ago, about the time you appeared here. I don't think it's nice of you to joke about her like this."

"It doesn't really matter if you believe me or not," Pearl said, "so long as you help at the prom. Before the end of the night, about a hundred vampires plan to chow down on the prom-goers. We need to evacuate everyone before that happens."

"Evacuate prom?"

"Alternative is we cancel it. But then we lose our shot at stopping the vampires permanently. Plus, I'll be killed, which would suck both literally and figuratively."

Tara's eyes were as wide as if she were watching a horror movie. "You're serious about this. You aren't staging some elaborate practical joke on me, are you? If so, I warn you I have zero sense of humor. I will not be humiliated in public."

"If this works, you'll be a hero," Pearl said. "All we need you to do is convince everyone to leave once Evan gives the signal. Get them out quietly and tell them to find a house that vampires can't enter. Any nonpublic place works. Vampires can only enter a house that we've been invited into by a resident."

Tara was quiet for a moment. Rain battered the windshield. "You're telling me that vampires have been sucking on Ashlyn."

"Ever since I damaged her car," Pearl said. "I believe my parents have visited her and her family multiple times."

Tara reached into her shirt and pulled out a necklace: a diamond-encrusted crucifix. Instinctively, Pearl flinched. Tara's eyes widened. She looked at the crucifix, and then she looked at Pearl. "Seriously?"

Pearl nodded and put it in a language she knew Tara would understand: "As serious as a Manolo Blahnik shoe sale."

"Ha, very funny," Tara said. "For the record, no vampire is ruining *my* prom. I won't allow it. Canceling is not an option."

"Then you need to lead the evacuation," Pearl said. "If you do it, it will become cool, and a certain percentage of the class will follow. Just lead them home or to after parties or whatever. So long as everyone is inside until dawn, you'll all be fine."

"After parties are a cool idea," Tara said.

"Exactly," Pearl said.

"You know, of course, that I don't believe you," Tara said. "I'm doing it because it fits the theme. This will be the best junior prom ever. Totally blow those seniors out of the water."

* * *

It was easiest to talk to Sana while they were jogging through the drizzle after school. Side by side, their sneakers sloshed on the field. Muddy water splashed their calves. Sana had taken the news surprisingly well, especially after Pearl demonstrated her natural speed. "So what you're telling me is . . . I am actually the fastest human student at Greenbridge High?" she asked.

"Humans have such odd priorities sometimes," Pearl said.

"Coping mechanism," Sana said.

"Goal is to get everyone out before the vampires notice," Pearl said. "Quietly round up all your friends and get them to the cars. Herd as many other students as you can too."

"Or we could skip prom and avoid the entire risk-of-bleeding thing," Sana said.

"Or that," Pearl agreed.

"But you aren't planning to cancel," Sana said. "And these vampires in the cellar . . . if they notice the evacuation, they'll come for whoever's there."

"Pretty much. No one will blame you if you ditch."

Sana ran silently for a while. Puddles spattered under their feet. "Coach just couldn't have let us run inside today. Had to make us slosh. Despite the perfectly nice track inside."

Pearl agreed.

"You know this is nuts, right?" Sana said. "There are about a hundred things that could go wrong with your plan."

Pearl agreed with that, too. She'd considered and reconsidered the plan. With so many vampires and humans involved, the potential for disaster was enormous. But she didn't have any better ideas. "If this doesn't work . . ."

"Think I can run fast enough?" Sana asked.

"I hope so," Pearl said.

"That's not reassuring."

Rain began to fall harder, and Pearl wiped it out of her eyes. "I'm a bloodsucking fiend," she said. "I'm not supposed to be reassuring."

Chapter
TWENTY-SEVEN

At dawn on Saturday, the morning of the prom, Pearl sat on the front steps of the mansion and waited. Earlier in the week a fleet of gardeners had trimmed the shrubs and planted a swath of tulips and daffodils. The petals shimmered as the light danced over them. Yesterday's rain still dotted their leaves, and the earth smelled like moist mulch. Beyond the manicured gardens, the nature preserve glistened with raindrops so that it looked as though a jeweler had spilled diamonds on the grasses, bushes, and wild apple trees. Really, the sky should have stayed gray and damp. It would have been a lot more appropriate for an impending massacre than this cheerful lemony sunrise.

On the plus side, at least she would die in a pretty place.

Out loud, Pearl said, "This will never work."

Evan sat down next to her. He slipped his arm around her

waist. On her other side, Bethany sat too and put her arm over Pearl's shoulders.

"Okay, that's really too touchy-feely for the vampire," Pearl said. She shrugged them both off. "I don't need sympathy; I need plans."

Both of them were quiet.

Bethany spoke first. "If you want to quit, no one will blame you."

Pearl snorted. That was just about the most inane thing she'd ever heard. "If I don't show at the ceremony, my Family will kill me."

"Only if they catch you," Bethany said. "You can stay with us after sundown. Evan's family can keep you safe."

"Splendid," Pearl said. "I've always wanted to be a pet." She waved off their objections. "Besides, the Karkadanns won't be so fond of me if I ruin their master plan."

Down the narrow, twisty gravel driveway, Pearl heard the crunch of tires. She grinned as the pickup truck rattled into view. "Enough with the melodrama. Here comes the cavalry." She stood as Zeke parked. Matt plus three friends rode in the bed of the truck, crammed between shovels, wheelbarrows, gas cans, and boxes of metal junk. It looked as if they'd carted their backyards to the mansion.

Zeke climbed out of the cab while Matt and their friends hopped out of the truck bed. Efficiently, they handed out shovels. They had easily twenty more shovels piled in the back.

Bethany skipped over to them. "You came! Ooh, you have a plan?"

Zeke held up a hand to forestall Matt. "Safe to talk here?"

Pearl pointed at the sun, which now hovered above the horizon. "Clearly."

"Always pays to be careful," Zeke said. "You said the vamps plan to torch the place to hide the evidence. So that got our creative juices going, inspired our muse, so to speak. . . ."

"Out with it," Pearl said.

"A trench of fire!" Matt said. He waved his arms dramatically in the air.

Zeke nodded. "We dig a trench around the mansion, fill it with wood, disguise it with flowers, drench it with gasoline, and then light it as soon as we all cross to the parking lot. If the vamps notice that we're leaving, this should slow them down." He patted one of the boxes of junk fondly. "Plus we have a few other ideas."

"Remember one of the mission parameters is to limit casualties," Evan said, "including vampires." He laid his hand on Pearl's shoulder.

"Ooh," Matt and Zeke said simultaneously.

Wistfully, Matt asked, "So, no stake crossbows?"

Face filled with sorrow, Zeke shook his head. "You don't comprehend the awesome glory that is a stake crossbow."

Pearl raised both eyebrows in a fair imitation of Mother.

"Okay, okay," Zeke said. "We can adjust. We are masters of flexibility and spontaneity. No plan ever survives contact with the enemy, and all that." He patted another crate. "Good ol' bucket of holy water over the door trick. Rig one over each cellar door in case the barricades fail. Slow down any vamp without causing permanent death and disintegration."

Evan leaned toward Pearl. "Will it work?"

Just as conspiratorially, Pearl faux whispered, "Holy water hurts, and we're very, very flammable. So trench of fire . . . kind of brilliant. But don't tell them I said that. It'll go to their heads."

Matt beamed.

Zeke said, "I always wondered what the difference was between flammable and inflammable. Why have two words that look like opposites but mean the same thing?"

"Just give me a shovel," Pearl said.

As Bethany calculated the exact location for the trench— it had to be far enough from the house to be hidden by the greenery but close enough so that it wouldn't cut too close to the parked cars—other cars with students began to arrive at the mansion.

Zeke and Matt had enlisted the Goth kids, the smokers, and a few theater types. Sana brought the track team. Tara led the prom committee (minus Ashlyn). Shovel in hand, Pearl met them all on the walkway to the mansion.

"You guys all know about . . . well, you know?" Pearl mimed fangs.

Everyone nodded.

"Huh," Pearl said. "And you still came?"

Tara shrugged. "It's *prom*."

Pearl studied them, unsure if they really understood this was real. She supposed it didn't matter. If all went as planned, she'd be the only vampire they ever saw. "Okay then," she said. "A few guests are already in the cellar, asleep for the day. Keep the conversation banal. We have excellent hearing."

She sent Sana and the team, plus a selection of the Goth kids, to assist Bethany with the trench. Zeke went inside with a few of the theater kids, hauling in the buckets of holy water.

"We have supplies," Tara announced to Pearl. "Center-pieces with garlic. Your kind hate garlic, right? Also, garlands of crucifixes and Stars of David and a bunch of other religious doodads. . . . I wasn't sure what would work so we made them all."

Pearl began to shake her head. "Subtlety is key—"

Tara beckoned to Kelli. "Bring them out!"

Kelli opened the back of her SUV, and she and another member of the prom committee carried out six life-size foam cutouts of Edward Cullen, four of Jacob, and one panorama of the entire cast. Another prom committee member—Emma or Emily—fetched an armful of *Twilight* posters. Another carried Party City bags full of *New Moon*, *Eclipse*, and *Breaking Dawn* cups, plates, napkins, and plastic tablecloths. "Theme!" Kelli said happily.

Pearl began to smile. "Have fun," she said as she swung the door to the ballroom open to let them inside. Each of the girls oohed and aahed.

Tara marched past them. "Come on, ladies. Let's make it gaudy."

As work commenced inside, Pearl joined the trench crew.

Bethany had identified the location for the trench and calculated the best width and depth. Leading the other students, she'd begun to peck at the dirt with her shovel. So far, she'd chipped out about three inches of dirt. Stepping in front of her, Pearl slammed her shovel into the ground and began to dig. She didn't bother to hide her strength. She powered through the dirt as if she were a living bulldozer. The students stared at her with jaws dropped open. Feeling their gazes on her back, she leveled a glare at them over her shoulder. "This isn't performance art, people. Fill the trench with branches."

Silently, they followed behind her, filling the trench with branches that they fetched from around the mansion's land. Evan led forays for dry wood in the nearby nature preserve.

Bethany lugged over a pile of brush. Her face was flushed bright red between her freckles, and she looked as if she was going to keel over any second. "Bethany," Pearl called to her. "Can you check on everyone inside? Keep them from going downstairs or doing anything else idiotic."

Bethany dropped her branch and fled inside without protest.

Pearl continued to dig. After Bethany left, she didn't talk to the other students. It was enough to listen to her own thoughts. She'd done a lot of avoiding her thoughts in the past twenty-four hours, mostly because they were a snarl: If she did this, she was betraying her Family and would lose them.

But if she didn't do this and left, then her Family would betray her and she'd lose them.

She had to admit the whole situation was rather brilliant of Bethany and rather brave of Evan. He'd taken a massive risk. He'd let her into his life, his house, and his family's secret. He trusted her with the truth of their plan. She couldn't decide whether that was idiotic or sexy. Glancing over at Evan, she watched him haul brush into the trench. As if he felt her eyes on him, he looked up. For an instant they stared at each other, and then Pearl turned back to the dirt.

After three hours Pearl completed the trench. She climbed the front steps of the mansion to survey her work. Zeke and Bethany joined her. "Nice," he said. "Pile it higher, everyone! We want it to burn until dawn. Plus it's supposed to look like shrubbery, people, not a superobvious trap."

As the students trotted into the nature preserve to fetch more brush, Pearl said, "The fire department will never let it burn until dawn."

Bethany said, "With luck, we won't need to light it. But if we do . . . it only needs to last until everyone is safely home. Anyway, Evan's family will take care of the fire department. Some of them work there."

Pearl rolled her eyes. "Of course they do. It's the hero family."

Smiling, Evan bowed at her.

"Technically, you're doing the hero thing too," Bethany said.

"I'm digging a hole," Pearl said.

"Trench," Zeke said. "Huge difference. Trench has a battle-worn poetry to it. Hole . . . kind of more a gopher thing." He strode down the walkway to assist with arranging the branches.

Bethany tugged on her sleeve. "Come see what the prom committee did inside."

Inside . . . the ballroom sparkled. Glittery tulle and black lace were draped over every chandelier. Movie posters covered every wall. The *Twilight* cutouts framed the windows, and every centerpiece featured bloodred roses ringed by garlic bulbs. It was garish. It was over-the-top. It was perfect.

"Bloody brilliant," Pearl said in a fake British accent.

"Done!" Tara said. "Just in time to begin to beautify us." She beckoned to the committee. "Ashlyn's house, fifteen minutes." She pointed at Bethany and Pearl. "You too."

"R-really?" Bethany said.

At the mention of Ashlyn, Pearl felt her stomach clench. "Thanks, but I'll prepare at home." At home she might be forced into her aunts' monstrosity of a black lace dress, but that was preferable to facing the zombielike Ashlyn.

"Ashlyn won't be coming to prom, but her house is close to here," Tara said. Her smile didn't reach her eyes. Pearl stared at her. *She understands,* Pearl thought suddenly. *She knows this is real.* "You should come with us."

"Pearl . . . ," Bethany began. Her eyes slid to the cellar door, and she changed whatever she was going to say. "Your dress is in my car. I . . . I thought we'd get ready together. I kind of promised Sandy."

Pearl looked from Bethany to Tara. "You don't trust me," she said softly.

Bethany studied her sneakers as her cheeks flushed bright red. Tara, though, wasn't the least bit embarrassed. "Bingo," Tara said. "Just want to keep your loyalties straight. No one, and I mean no one, is ruining this prom."

On a treeless hill, Ashlyn's house gleamed with shiny new paint. It was the crown jewel of her cul-de-sac with gaudy White House pillars and a fake widow's walk at the peak. Bethany and Tara sandwiched Pearl between them as they walked past daffodils toward the front porch.

"Does she know?" Pearl asked.

Tara snorted. "Do you want to be the one to tell her?"

"If you expect me to be all contrite, it's not going to happen," Pearl said. "I am what I am. Or was what I was." They walked up the porch steps.

After ringing the bell, Tara tried the door. Oddly, it wasn't locked. Or maybe it wasn't odd. If your worst nightmare could enter your house at will, locking the door had to seem futile. She wondered how aware of their fate Ashlyn's family was.

As Tara, Sana, and the others piled inside, Pearl halted at the threshold. "My parents were invited in, but technically I wasn't."

"So?" Sana said.

"It's a vampire thing," Pearl said. She demonstrated by reaching toward the doorway. At the threshold, her hand hit what felt like an invisible wall. She knocked on solid air. "We need to be invited in by a resident before we can enter a home."

"Weird," Sana said. "Also, good to know."

"Wait here," said Tara. Without waiting for a response from Pearl, she disappeared inside. A few seconds later she reappeared, propelling a haggard woman in a half-buttoned blouse toward the doorway.

Reaching them, the woman leaned against the door frame as if she needed its support in order to stay vertical. "Not buying, not selling, please leave us alone," Ashlyn's mother said. Her eyes didn't focus anywhere in particular. Pearl noticed that her makeup was smeared down her cheek into a puddle of bluish rouge. She wore mascara on her left eyelashes only.

"This is one of Ashlyn's friends," Tara said loudly and clearly. "May she come in?"

Ashlyn's mother focused on her. "Ashlyn's upstairs. Won't talk to us anymore. Mopey teenager. Never should have had kids. Was meant to be an actress. You know I was in a commercial once, toothpaste. I had a beautiful smile. Still do."

Wow, the venom hit her hard, Pearl thought. Her brains were dribbling out her mouth, metaphorically speaking.

Bethany elbowed Pearl. Pearl asked, "May I visit Ashlyn?"

"If you want, come on in," Ashlyn's mother said.

Pearl tried walking forward. She felt a fizzle as she crossed the threshold. Inside, she peered at Ashlyn's mother's neck. Multiple scars bunched the skin. Her parents had visited often. Very often. "I'm sorry," Pearl said without meaning to.

Bethany patted her shoulder.

Together they all went upstairs. Ashlyn lay on her stomach on her bed. She had a remote control in one hand. She switched channels as the girls piled into her bedroom.

Ignoring Ashlyn, Tara pointed at Pearl. "You need a shower. You have dirt on you." She confiscated a towel from a closet and pushed Pearl toward a marble bathroom. "Clean up well. You need to perform tonight." Pearl glanced over her shoulder at Ashlyn, who had yet to acknowledge them. "Consider her your object lesson. You can't fail us again." It occurred to Pearl that Tara was smarter than she looked.

Pearl nodded and obeyed.

As she showered, she listened to the chatter from Ashlyn's bedroom. There were eight girls total: They'd brought along not just the prom committee but Sana and a theater girl. A few days ago the sound of so many humans would have made Pearl's head pound. Now . . . all of them were wrapped up in the unicorns' plan together.

Feeling fond (or at least protective) of the humans, Pearl came out of the shower wrapped in a towel and said, "Now what?" Immediately, Kelli and another girl descended on her. One of them grabbed a comb while the other sat her down and began painting her toenails. Pearl let them manhandle her.

Chatter washed over her. Everyone was discussing who

would come with dates and who wouldn't, who would wear what dress, and whether so-and-so would look good in a tux. No one mentioned vampires or ceremonies or blood.

Of course, Pearl couldn't help smelling all the blood in the room, fresh and pounding through veins, but every time she began to think about blood, she looked at Ashlyn, and her stomach churned inside of her. Tara was right—Ashlyn made an excellent object lesson. Pearl kept her lips firmly pressed together, fangs in, as Tara applied makeup to her face.

"Done," Tara said. She turned Pearl's head so she could look in the mirror.

Pearl's eyes widened. Tara had applied blush to her cheeks to mimic human coloring. She had eyes that sparkled and lips that looked out of a magazine. "I look like you." She smiled. *Just one of the girls,* she thought.

"Not as pretty, but you'll do."

Bethany brought over the blue satin dress. Pearl slipped it on. Tara donated the shoes from Ashlyn's closet. Ashlyn didn't even notice. She hadn't budged. As Pearl twirled so the others could admire her, Bethany clapped. Soon, others began to pull on their dresses.

Tara darted out of the room. She returned with a bag of tortilla chips, as well as Ashlyn's cat. She tossed the bag on the bed. "Anyone hungry?" The other girls dived into the bag. Pearl eyed their young fresh necks and tried to remember when she'd had her last pint from the storage room. She told herself firmly that she could manage.

Tara thrust the cat toward Pearl. "I think it's purebred. Maybe that will make it taste better?" On the bed, Ashlyn stared at the ceiling and didn't speak.

Sana coughed on a chip. "Seriously?"

"This is insulting," Pearl said, catching the cat before Tara dropped it.

"Imagine how it must be for the cat," Sana said drily.

"Please try it," Bethany said. "We don't want you hungry." All the girls stared at her. Some looked revolted. Others looked fascinated.

All her warm, fuzzy, one-of-the-girls feelings fled. Pearl retreated into the bathroom. She didn't realize until after she'd shut the door that she had the cat tucked under her arm.

"Don't mess up the lipstick," Tara called through the door. "And don't get fur on the dress!"

Outside the room, she heard silence. Everyone was waiting to see what she'd do. This was, she thought, single-handedly her most embarrassing moment ever. She held the cat up under its armpits and looked at it.

The cat looked back at her. It was one of those ridiculous fluffy white cats, Persian or something, with the flattened nose and the wide cartoonish eyes. It meowed.

"Oh, quit it," Pearl said. She wasn't going to become some pathetic cat-eating pseudovampire. She dropped the cat in the bathtub, and then she opened the bathroom window, hiked up her dress, stepped on the toilet to boost herself up, and climbed out onto the roof.

Pearl sidled down to the edge of the roof and then leaped off. She landed on the grass, and her heels sank into the lawn. She unstuck herself and readjusted her dress. Cat fur clung to the satin. She spent a few seconds plucking it off, and then she started to run.

She didn't have a destination in mind. Her legs just needed to be moving. So she ran, at half-speed thanks to heels and a prom dress intended for slinky shimmying. She felt the sun on her bare shoulders and on her face, and she breathed in the air even though she didn't have to. Soon, she slowed because she knew where she'd come: the Dairy Hut, or what was left of it.

She halted on the sidewalk.

"Hey," a voice said. She knew the voice, of course. It was as warm as a caress, a voice that made her entire body want to turn toward the voice's owner.

"You have some serious stalker tendencies," Pearl said without turning around. "It's not very attractive."

"I have a tux on," Evan said. "Shouldn't that help?"

"Every guy thinks he looks good in a tux," Pearl said. "But it's not true. Some look like overstuffed emperor penguins." She still didn't turn around. The Dairy Hut was a brown shell. The windows were plywood. The sign was charred. The picnic tables were absent. Only the dumpsters in the back remained untouched. She smelled smoke in the air, or maybe she imagined it. "This was my fault. That night that I came to your house . . ."

He was silent.

"I killed him," Pearl said. "Believe it or not, it was an accident. I was trying . . . well, it doesn't matter. I killed him, and my Family torched the place to hide the evidence. That's what gave them the idea to do it with the prom . . . after, of course, I offered up the prom to them to atone for the accident."

Still Evan didn't say anything.

"I killed *after* your little experiment," Pearl said. "I'm still a killer. You didn't cure that."

"I woke your soul. What you choose to do with it . . . that's up to you."

"I chose to kill," she said.

"You said it was an accident."

"Well, yes," Pearl said. She hadn't meant to kill him. "I'd only meant to take a pint. It didn't . . . turn out that way. And I am feeling this horrible wrenching guilt, and I hate it. I hate what you've made me feel. I hate what you've turned me into." She spun to face Evan.

He stood there in his tux, and he looked more handsome than anyone she'd ever seen, human or vampire. She supposed that made sense since he was neither. But she couldn't help gawking at him as if her eyes were drinking him in. He was gazing at her too, in her satin blue prom dress with her human makeup and her hair that had only slipped a little on her run. She wished she knew how this boy had the power to unsettle her with just his eyes. More than anything, she wanted him to keep looking at her like that.

"I don't hate what you've turned into," Evan said softly.

"That's nice," Pearl said. "Frankenstein likes his monster."

"You aren't a monster."

"Yes, as a matter of fact, I am, both on a theoretical level and on a literal level."

"You are whoever you make yourself to be," he said.

Pearl rolled her eyes.

"Then let me put it this way: You have a chance to make up for this," Evan said. He nodded at the Dairy Hut. "You have the chance to change the world."

Pearl studied the burnt shell of the Dairy Hut.

"And you have a chance to dance with me," he said. "There's also that incentive."

Gravely she said, "There's also that."

Chapter

TWENTY-EIGHT

Prom night.

Everyone drove up to the mansion at eight o'clock. Pearl and Evan joined Bethany, Zeke, and Matt, plus half the prom committee in the minivan. Kelli and her date followed. Others arrived in a steady stream of taillights down the narrow, winding driveway. In the minivan no one talked much as they pulled in behind the other prom-goers. Thankfully, Pearl didn't see any limos—they'd done a good job discouraging that complication.

"Sorry about the cat," Bethany said. "We didn't mean it as an insult."

Pearl said, "I don't eat fluff. Or Fluffy."

From the backseat, Tara said, "That was cool what you did for Ashlyn's family." After returning with Evan, Pearl had told Ashlyn and her parents the phrase to say to uninvite vampires. And to prevent nonvampiric visitors, she told them to lock their door. In her opinion, it was too little too late.

Everyone fell silent again.

Bethany parked in the gravel lot in front of the mansion. Red, green, and yellow strobe lights flashed through the windows, and disco-ball lights spun by. As she shut off the engine, the beat of the music inside thrummed through the parking lot. Song lyrics were muffled. Without moving, Pearl stared at the mansion.

"Everybody ready?" Zeke asked. Even his normal exuberance felt tamped down.

A stream of prom-goers flowed toward the entrance. Red satin and blue tulle, black gowns and tuxedos . . . A few of the girls hobbled on their high heels as they crossed the gravel. Pearl promised herself that she'd ensure as many of them survived the night as possible. Payment for Brad and for Ashlyn. "Ready," Pearl said.

She reached for the door handle, but Evan said, "Wait!" He hopped out and then swung the door open and held out his hand. "Chivalry, alive and well."

"I am swooning at your feet," Pearl said, but she let her hand rest on his as she stepped out of the minivan. A cool breeze swirled over her skin but didn't budge her hair, thanks to Kelli's enthusiastic use of hair products. Everyone else piled out of the minivan in a flurry of formal wear. Together, they joined the stream of prom-goers.

Tiny white Christmas lights outlined the doorway. They

winked and sparkled. The prom committee had interspersed aluminum foil bats in between the lights. At the bottom step, Sana and another member of the track team (Claire) collected car keys to the SUVs and other large vehicles, ostensibly to prevent drunk driving but really to prepare the evacuation vehicles. Bethany silently handed over her key. The mansion's entrance was flanked by Sandy and Donald on one side and Mr. Barstow and a second teacher on the other. Evan nodded to his parents as he passed. Both of them watched Pearl.

"Dude," Matt said behind her and Evan. "You forgot something."

Pearl wondered what they'd forgotten: weapons, common sense.

Stopping on the threshold, Matt handed Evan a clear box with a single rose bud inside it. The bud lay in a nest of lace and green leaves. "It's a corsage," Tara said as she breezed past them into the ballroom. "You wear it on your wrist, and you pretend it doesn't itch like hell."

Evan managed a smile. "I meant to buy you one. I've been preoccupied."

"I'll excuse you this time," Pearl said as Evan slid the corsage onto her wrist. The leaves tickled her skin.

"Whoa," Matt said. "I think she just asked you for a second date."

Pearl opened her mouth to protest but then shut it. Evan was looking at her with his warm eyes. A smile played on his soft lips. "Whatever," she said. She was unlikely to survive the night anyway. She walked into the ballroom with her date in tow.

The DJ pumped music so loud that Pearl felt it through her toes as she entered. To her amusement, it was the Doors's "People Are Strange." (Tara had insisted that the DJ play theme-appropriate music.) Halting by the door, Pearl surveyed the scene: The dance floor was empty. Some students clustered around the tables with the rose-and-garlic centerpieces. Others, mostly boys in ill-fitting tuxedos, leaned against a wall in between the cutouts of Cullens. A few couples hovered by the appropriately bloodred punch. Other couples waited in line for a photographer who snapped photos in front of a cheesy crescent-moon backdrop. "Reminds me of middle school," Bethany commented, as she entered behind them. "I kind of expected more. . . . I don't know."

"Hey, why is no one dancing?" Tara said. "This is a prom, people!" She plucked one of the tuxedo boys off the wall and dragged him to the center of the ballroom. Kelli followed her lead, pulling her date onto the dance floor. Others joined them. The dancers bobbed stiffly up and down. As Pearl watched from the sidelines with Evan, one student attempted to break-dance. He toppled over.

Zeke and Matt swept by with Bethany in tow. "Prom photos!" Zeke called to Pearl and Evan. "Height of cheesy artistry! Must participate!"

Evan caught Matt's arm as he passed. "Keep an eye

on the punch bowl, okay? Last thing we need is everyone tipsy."

"I can think of other 'last things we need,' but sure." He veered toward the punch bowl. "Sustenance first," he said to Zeke and Bethany. "Cheese squares are calling our name. *Eat me, Matt. Eat me, Bethany.*"

Pearl watched the prom-goers smile stiffly for the photographer. Every smile looked as fake as a mask. "You don't want a photo, do you?"

"Only if you do," Evan said.

She wasn't one hundred percent sure she'd show up in a photo. Ordinary vampires didn't. On the other hand, ordinary vampires didn't attend junior proms with were-unicorn dates while plotting to sabotage plans for a mass murder. "I can live without a photo. Or, you know, not *live* per se."

"Good," he said, his voice serious.

"Evan . . . ," she began.

He put his fingertips on her lips. "It's okay. You don't have to say anything. I understand."

Both of Pearl's eyebrows shot into the air. "I could have been about to say that your fly is down."

"But you weren't," he said. He held her gaze, and then he broke the moment by not-so-subtly glancing down at his tuxedo pants. The fly was up.

Pearl peeked at the golden clock. She had a half hour before she was supposed to sneak downstairs. Her Family should be there already, guiding attendees to the cellar, waiting for the king and his guards to make their grand entrance. Pearl touched the rose on her wrist. Plucked, it was dying, but it smelled like sunset.

Softly, into her ear, Evan said, "I'm coming with you."

She felt his breath on her skin. "Nicely heroic, but no."

"You aren't facing this alone."

"You're an idiot."

"So I've been told," he said. "Dance with me anyway?"

It was a slow song, and the couples had paired up, pressing against each other and swaying. Evan looped his arm around her waist and led her onto the dance floor. After a moment's hesitation, she put her arms around his neck. His skin felt soft under her hands, like caressing silk. "You don't trust me," Pearl said as they swayed to the music.

He shook his head. "You shouldn't have to be down there alone. Plus, you might need me." His arms tightened around her.

She studied his face, so lovely and perfect. "You still want to save me, even after . . . what I told you I did."

"Of course," he said.

Gently, she touched the side of his face, cradling his cheek in her hand. She felt his warmth against her cool-as-a-serpent skin. "But you already have."

He quit swaying, and he stared at her with his brilliant eyes, so earnest and pure. "You mean that?"

She wished he hadn't asked. It had been such a perfect line. "No." Pressing closer to him, she said in a whisper that was barely above a breath, "You messed up my life in a high-handed, daddy-knows-best, alpha-male way and reshaped me to suit your own ideals without any regard for my culture or family background, not to mention my personal wants and needs—and that's if I'm being charitable. If I'm *not* being charitable . . ." Her lips touched his ear as she breathed the words. "No matter how you rationalize it or how wide you open those shining eyes of yours, you treated me like a lab rat. Worse, an expendable lab rat."

"We can call this off right now," Evan said just as softly. "Evacuate now."

Drawing back a few inches, Pearl shook her head.

"You'll make it through this," he said.

She studied his eyes, trying to read him. "Why do you care?" She got why he cared before the ceremony was complete—he needed her to cooperate—but there was no earthly reason for him to care if she survived it. Maybe he was drinking his own Kool-Aid: Too much unicornness was making him over-kind to puppies and babies and reformed vampires.

Evan twirled her in a circle and then spun her close. He touched her cheek with his cheek. She felt her skin tingle, and she inhaled his scent. He smelled like the forest. His lips next to her ear, he said, "It's because you wanted to see the light in the library."

The slow song ended, and a fast dance started. Around them, couples broke apart and began to wiggle. In the center of the dance floor, Tara shimmied with her arms in the air.

Kelli and the prom committee circled around her. But Evan didn't release Pearl, and Pearl didn't move away. "Explain," she said.

"That first morning, it was too soon for . . . any effect," he said. "But you didn't hunt. You wanted to see the sun through the stained glass. You stopped being a 'lab rat' for me then."

Pearl didn't know what to say. "Don't come downstairs."

"Why not?" he asked. "You just finished telling me how much you hate me."

She considered several answers and rejected them all. Finally, she settled on the truth. "I have no idea," she said.

"Very persuasive argument," he said.

"If you try to come with me, I'll break your arms."

"Obviously, you secretly love me and have a difficult time expressing it."

She swatted his arm but not hard. He faked a wince.

"Tell me, fair maiden," he said, and bowed, "how do I earn your love?"

Out of the corner of her eye, Pearl saw a new couple walk into the ballroom. She felt the blood inside her slow, and the music seemed to fade. "Stay up here," she said to Evan. "Keep everyone safe." He followed her gaze to the door, where Jadrien stood in a tuxedo with Cousin Antoinette in a shimmery pink 1980s dress. Beaming, Antoinette surveyed the assembly. She looked as happy as a cat in a catnip field. Jadrien looked only at Pearl. His eyes seemed to blaze.

"For your love, I will," Evan said.

She glared at him. "I'm serious."

"And I'm not?" Deliberately turning his back on the two vampires by the main entrance, Evan looked into her eyes. For an instant she felt as if the world had shrunk to only them. Music cocooned them, blocking out all other sound. His eyes were luminous, full of dark rainbows, like the eyes of his unicorn self.

"Are you?" she asked.

"Ask me again in the morning," he said.

He spun her in a circle with the music, and the moment was broken. She noticed the dancers around them had slowed. Smiles drained from their faces as they watched Jadrien and Antoinette sashay onto the dance floor. Pearl watched Jadrien and Antoinette progress toward her through the dancers. The students shifted aside, parting for the vampire couple—as if the humans could sense the predators in their midst. Stationed throughout the ballroom, the Karkadanns watched their every move.

Pearl hoped no one, vampire or human or otherwise, would do anything stupid.

Evan's hands tightened on her waist as Jadrien and Antoinette halted beside them. Pearl really, really hoped she wasn't about to get everyone killed.

Antoinette wore a replica of a Molly Ringwald dress. She'd twirled her hair up in a bird's-nest style, complete with pink feathers. Gloves covered her arms up to her elbows. Jadrien looked handsome, as always.

"May I cut in?" Jadrien said. His voice was smooth, exactly

the cultured gentleman that Evan had been imitating a few minutes earlier.

"Sorry," Evan said, clearly not meaning it. "She's my date tonight."

Pearl saw the muscle in Jadrien's cheek twitch. Antoinette looked delighted, backing up as if she expected a fight to break out in front of her. Pearl shot a don't-be-an-idiot look at Evan. If she could have subtly whacked him on the head, she would have. Now was not the time for territorial macho crap. "It's all right," Pearl said to Evan. "He's a friend. How about you dance with Bethany for a while?" She spun him by the shoulders and gave him a shove toward Bethany, who was sandwiched between Zeke and Matt by the punch bowl. Pasting a smile on her face, she turned back to Jadrien and Antoinette as Kool and the Gang's "Celebrate" came on.

"Ooh, I love this song!" Antoinette said.

For a second the absurdity of that statement derailed Pearl. "Seriously?"

Antoinette began hopping up and down. Waving her arms, she gathered a circle of students around her. The students danced stiffly, shooting glances at Pearl.

"Humans really don't know how to party," Jadrien said. He wrapped his arm around Pearl's waist, and she had to force herself not to chuck him across the dance floor. "Oh, Pearly, my jewel, don't look so mad. You know we can't resist a decent shindig. By the way, the theme is hilarious. And suitably sparkly."

"You'll tip them off," Pearl said. She swung her arm up around his neck and breathed the words into his ear. "Humans aren't that stupid. No one living likes this song, at least not unironically." She'd been thoroughly briefed by the prom committee on this topic.

"Oh, yes, they are stupid, my delectable delight," Jadrien said. "And by the way, you reek of them. Shower before we next kiss, m'kay? You may want to rethink cuddling them quite so much."

"Always the charmer."

He dipped her, and then swung her up and pressed her against his chest. "Forgive me. I just hate to see you having to play nice with sheep."

"It will be worth it," Pearl said. Over his shoulder, she spotted Cousin Shirley across the dance floor. She wore sleek black silk and moved like a ribbon, dancing to the music between two slightly stunned boys. She ruined the effect by continually checking to see if Antoinette had noticed her, obviously seeking her approval. "You can't all crash the prom. You'll be noticed." This had such potential for disaster.

"Relax." Jadrien brushed his lips against her cheek as he ground his hips against hers. "This is *our* night. Revel in it!"

She danced close with Jadrien until the song switched (abruptly, as Tara scolded the DJ) to the more thematically appropriate "Blood Roses." Jadrien adjusted his and Pearl's arms to a waltz position and proceeded to spiral with her across the dance floor. Couples scattered out of their way as they spun. He hummed under his breath, half in tune with the music.

Into her ear he breathed, "I suppose an appetizer is out of the question?"

"You really need to develop a self-preservation instinct," Pearl said. He had to know that if he ruined the feast, either the king or Mother would skewer him. Of course, Evan's family would skewer him long before that, especially if his interference led to the cancellation of the ceremony. She wished he'd stayed downstairs like a good little vampire. "You at least left Jeremiah downstairs, I hope?"

"Chewing on the tablecloths, last I saw," Jadrien said. "Your uncle Stefan should put him down. He gives your Family a bad name."

"Uncle Stefan's decision," Pearl said. She often wondered why Uncle Stefan didn't eliminate Jeremiah. He normally didn't tolerate any deviation from vampire perfection— witness his reaction to her. Perhaps he felt a connection with or sense of responsibility for Jeremiah since he'd turned him. If so, if even Uncle Stefan had the potential for empathy, then maybe this plan wasn't totally insane.

She glanced at the golden clock. *Nah,* she thought, *still totally insane.*

"Pumpkin time," Jadrien said. He looked across the dance floor. Cousin Shirley and Cousin Antoinette drifted away from their dance partners. Pearl watched them hook arms and head off chatting, as if on a trip to the ladies' room. One of the entrances to the cellar was in the hall across from the rest-rooms. She had to trust that the Karkadanns stationed there wouldn't try to stop them.

She and Jadrien danced across the ballroom. "Follow my lead," he said. He pushed her against the wall and began to kiss her. She kissed back, eyes open. She scanned the ball-room, filled with hundreds of prom-goers, and her eyes locked onto Evan's. His fists were clenched. Bethany's hand was on his shoulder, and she was whispering in his ear. But his eyes didn't leave Pearl's.

He mouthed the words, "Good luck."

Jadrien maneuvered her closer to the door, as if the goal was a more private make-out session behind the tapestries that covered the mirrors. Unlocking his lips from hers, he smiled at her in the shadows. "See, easy-peasy." He opened the door and slipped inside. She followed him down into the cellar.

Chapter
TWENTY-NINE

On Jadrien's arm, Pearl walked down the stairs. Even intensive scrubbing hadn't scoured away all hints of the mildew scent. The walls stank of centuries-old dust—or maybe that was the stench of the guests.

As she reached the bottom steps, she saw them: one hundred vampires drifting, slinking, and sliding through the cellar with silent grace. No footsteps, no sighs, no rustles, no spare sounds at all. She heard only the murmur of voices.

Around the vampires, a thousand crystals danced in the light of the electric sconces that Mother had installed. Each bulb imitated a candlelike flame, waving with amber light and casting shadows that wove and writhed on the cellar walls. Swaths of black satin were draped over the beams in the ceiling, a tasteful echo of the tacky glitter lace upstairs.

Tiny Christmas lights twinkled from within the satin. The floor had been cleaned and polished so it was as sharp and clear as obsidian. Pearl stepped lightly off the last step. The air nearly crackled with age and power, and she smelled jasmine and dahlias mixed with the mildew.

Flat and empty eyes fixed on her blue satin dress and painted face. She lifted her chin and adopted her favorite don't-mess-with-me expression. Her fingers rested lightly on Jadrien's sleeve. As her escort, he guided her across the cellar to her Family, who flanked the empty dais—the king had not yet arrived, which was a relief. Her back still remembered the feel of Minerva's flail. His Majesty, she'd been warned, would not be so gentle with latecomers.

Jadrien bowed to Mother and Daddy and then retreated to join his Family, several tables removed from the dais, a status that undoubtedly chafed at Jadrien. Cousin Antoinette lingered to speak softly with him, while Cousin Shirley darted to the Family table.

Mother raised her eyebrows in a perfect arch at Pearl's dress. Pearl met Mother's eyes and didn't flinch. She might feel guilt over a lot of things, thanks to Evan, but this dress wasn't one of them. If she hadn't seen how good she looked in her own reflection, she would have seen it in Evan's eyes outside the burnt Dairy Hut.

Aunt Rose's mouth was pressed into a thin line. Her nostrils flared, a deliberate expression of her displeasure, since she hadn't breathed in several decades.

Aunt Lianne wore a similar look of distaste. "You wound me," she began.

"I approve," Mother cut in. "She's dressed for her hunt."

"As do I," Daddy chimed in too. "She looks lovely."

Uncle Felix nestled his nose in her hair. "She smells like humans." He inhaled deeply, and Pearl scowled at him until he backed away with hands raised in surrender. "You honor us with your hunt. Tonight will be unique!"

Of all the adjectives that he could have selected, that one was apt. "A night to remember," Pearl said. She swept her gaze across her Family and wondered if she should say something profound. Nothing came to mind. She noticed that Aunt Maria wore black lace roses clustered at her throat. Daddy looked dapper in his cravat and Dracula-esque cape. Mother, of course, was the most elegant, in a shimmering black dress that looked like a reflection of the night sky. But it seemed anticlimactic to compliment their clothes. And anything else would sound suspiciously like good-bye.

Jocelyn said, "I will record lines for posterity. And if the feast is a success, perhaps I'll even compose a poem in your honor, Cousin Pearl."

Shirley clapped her hands. "Ooh! But wait, what if she fails?"

"Then, a eulogy."

Pearl tried to resist an eye roll. Obviously, Jocelyn had coached Shirley to set her up for that punch line.

Uncle Pascha favored her with a faint smile, the closest she'd ever come to affection from him. "'Thy eternal summer shall not fade, nor lose possession of that fair thou ow'st, nor shall death brag thou wander'st in his shade, when in eternal lines to time thou grow'st.'" Pearl recognized the quote instantly—Evan had quoted part of the same sonnet to her on the day they first met. She wondered if Evan had ever written a poem about her. She should have asked.

"Exactly," Jocelyn said.

She wished . . . *Never mind,* she told herself. She was not going to launch into mushy regrets, not now and not ever.

Daddy laid his hand on Pearl's shoulder. "We are all proud of you, and we are all glad you are here with us on this very special night."

She managed a false smile.

Aunt Rose sniffed again but was wise enough to say nothing. Charlaine merely glared. The fake candlelight darkened her face with new shadows.

Antoinette breezed up to them. "Never fear. We rescued her, even though I didn't dance either the Electric Slide or the Macarena." Smiling brightly, she joined the other cousins clustered around a table that overflowed with night-blooming jasmine and black irises. Antoinette kicked Jeremiah as she squeezed herself in between Charlaine and Jocelyn. Jeremiah scurried underneath the table. He peered out from beneath the tablecloth and eyed Pearl's leg as if it were tasty.

Pearl looked from Antoinette to Daddy. "You sent them up? To check on me?"

"It's an important night," Daddy said. "We wanted to

be sure you were not delayed. Forgive us, but it is our last opportunity to parent you." He assumed a fatherly expression. It didn't quite fill his eyes. Pearl thought of Evan's father, who leaked authentic fatherliness from his pores. "Our jewel, grown at last. You will shine the brightest of them all, fulfilling the promise of your birth."

Pearl felt a lump in her throat, a very nonvampire reaction. She tried to swallow it down. The last thing she needed was to show human emotion. "It has been an honor to be your daughter," Pearl said. "I will always remember your teachings."

"See that you do," Mother said.

She wondered if these would be the last words she ever exchanged with her parents, aside from whatever insults and death threats would follow later tonight once her betrayal was discovered. If she was lucky, she'd be too far away to hear them. Most likely she'd be too dead.

Her eyes slid to the stairs. She estimated thirty vampires were between her and the upstairs, not counting her own Family. All of them were older and stronger than she was. She needed to be much closer to the stairs when the missing feast was discovered, if she was to have any chance of surviving this.

Truthfully, survival didn't seem likely.

Surrounded by their own kind, the vampires did not need to pretend to be human. As they waited, they held themselves with a stillness that was not unlike the stone that surrounded them. All the faces were blank masks. Death masks.

Silence spread across the cellar like a blanket, muffling

every murmur. If she'd closed her eyes, she would have thought she was alone. Even the younger set controlled their breath.

Opposite the dais, double doors (installed at the tunnel entrance purely for this moment—Mother loved little touches of drama) were thrown open. They made no sound as they hit the velvet that had been draped over the stone walls on either side.

At first Pearl saw only empty darkness.

One dramatic pause later, two guards marched out of the tunnel and into the cellar. Each of them wore black leather armor. Spikes protruded from their wrists and knees. They carried spears with silver points on black wood staffs—silver to cause pain and wood to kill. Red silk capes swirled behind them as they strode across the cellar toward the dais. As they passed, Pearl saw their faces were mangled with holy-water scars that twisted their cheeks and distorted their eyes. The effect was faces that were closer to monster than man, completely unreadable. Their bodies were pure muscle, each bulge visible against the body armor. Every muscle was tense. Halting at the foot of the dais, they swiveled and slammed their staffs into the floor.

Another set of guards, equal parts muscle and menace, filled the doorway. They marched across the cellar, slammed down their spears, and waited. They were joined by another set, and then another, until twelve sets of vampire guards lined the path between the doorway and the dais.

She knew there were to be twenty-four guards, but seeing

them . . . *That is a* lot *of muscles and menace,* she thought. If these guards were set loose in the ballroom before the evacuation was complete . . . *Not going to happen.*

Without a signal that Pearl could detect, the guards en masse pivoted to face the audience, a barrier between the Connecticut vampires and the path to the dais. As one, the guards slapped both hands onto the spears and bent their knees, ready to defend.

This was it. No backing out now. Without thinking, Pearl sucked in oxygen. She felt as if her breath was as loud as thunder in the silent cellar. Seconds passed, and then minutes. The guards did not move. No one moved. She didn't breathe again.

A shadow crossed the doorway, and then the vampire king swept through the door. Silence greeted him, but all eyes were riveted on him as he slid soundlessly across the black stone floor toward the dais.

As he passed by Pearl, she saw his face and nearly gasped.

In the looks department, he blew Jadrien out of the water. Despite having lived through several centuries (or more), he looked no older than seventeen. His cheeks were smooth, and his lips were full and soft. His eyes were as green and bright as emeralds. He'd slicked his black hair back, and he wore only black, a variation on the same black leather body armor that his guards wore.

He climbed onto the dais. As he turned to face the vampire assembly, Pearl saw he was scarred above his left eyebrow. It flared into five lines, as if someone had laid a burning hand on his face. Or a hand dipped in holy water. She tried to let the scar reassure her: He wasn't invulnerable.

She didn't feel reassured.

The king lowered himself onto the throne.

Mother bowed low. "You honor us with your presence."

"I do," the king said. His voice was like silk. It unfurled through the room, soft on the ears. Pearl suppressed a shudder. His voice caused her bones to ache. "I am your master, your lord, your universe."

As one, every adult vampire chanted together, "You are ours, and we are yours."

He said, "I am your light, your shadow, your sun, your moon."

Again, the vampires chanted, "You are ours, and we are yours."

He said, "I come before you to receive your pledge. You are my children, pieces of me given movement and voice."

Again: "You are ours, and we are yours."

The voices were swallowed by the stone.

Silence echoed. And for the first time, perhaps the first time in her entire undead life, Pearl felt terrified. She wanted to run. Or vomit. Or scream. But somehow, through sheer willpower, she managed to hold herself still and silent.

"Very well. Let us begin," His Majesty said. "But first, one bit of business. *You* disappoint me." He raised his hand and pointed at a vampire in a green cape and Victorian suit. Pearl recognized him as a member of the New London clan. One guard leveled a spear at him.

Aunt Fiona began to wail. Uncle Stefan clamped a hand firmly over her mouth.

Silent, the vampire spun and ran toward the open double doors. With a whistle, the spear flew through the air. It pierced the vampire in the back, hitting his heart. The vampire fell to his knees, and then he crumbled into black dust.

The spear clattered to the ground.

The guard crossed to it and picked it up. He returned to his position. Pearl felt her rib cage hurt as she pictured the spear sliding through her skin and finding her heart. Her fingers touched satin as she covered her heart.

No one spoke. No one moved. Even Aunt Fiona was silent.

The vampire king offered no explanation. He opened his hand toward Mother. She stepped forward. The guards permitted her to pass. She knelt before the king. "Please allow me to present your newest children."

That was their cue. Minerva had drilled them on this a hundred times. Each young vampire left his or her Family and proceeded forward to form a line. Forcing her feet to obey, Pearl crossed the black stone floor. She assumed her spot beside Jadrien. She was conscious of his perfect stillness beside her, but she didn't dare look at him. None of them looked at each other. All eyes were fixed on His Majesty.

One by one, Mother introduced the young vampires. As she stated their names and lineage, each vampire walked between the guards to the dais, knelt, and then retreated.

The young vampire on the other side of Jadrien proceeded forward. His toe caught the hem of his cape, and he began to stumble. He hid the mistake in a flourish of his cape and bowed. Miraculously, he returned to the line unscathed.

Beside her, Jadrien executed the maneuver flawlessly. Next, it was her turn.

She wished she'd worn the black dress. She wished she'd stayed upstairs at the prom. She wished she'd run fast and far when she'd had the chance. Stilling her breathing and blanking her expression, she drifted across the obsidian-like floor toward the dais. She knelt in one smooth movement, and then she rose and returned to the line, next to Jadrien, her eyes fixed on the floor. She did not raise her head until she was back in the line.

All of them survived the introduction.

Maybe everything will be okay, Pearl thought.

His Majesty rose from his throne. "Your youth adds to our strength. Your power increases ours. I will join you to us and bid you welcome, my children." Out of the corner of her eye, she saw each vampire tremble under his gaze. She didn't dare turn her head. As Minerva had instructed, she stared straight ahead at the gilded throne. Beside her, she felt Jadrien quiver, and then the king's eyes slid to meet Pearl's.

Staring into the king's eyes felt as if she were looking into a telescope at a distant galaxy. She heard roaring deep within her, as if she could hear the echo of that distance. He held a vastness in his eyes—a vastness of years and of power—as if he were his own galaxy. Pressure built in her head. She felt her borrowed blood hot inside of her. Suddenly, the king broke the gaze, focusing on the next vampire in the line. Despite her resolve, Pearl sagged. She heard her own breath whoosh out of her. She wished immediately she could suck it back in. Instead, she summoned her strength and straightened her shoulders. She couldn't afford to show any weakness.

One by one, the king summoned them to the dais. The first vampire hobbled up, as awkward as a just-born foal. His knees wobbled, and his hands twitched. Pearl's eyes flicked to him—it was Chadwick, Jadrien's brother, the one with the bat collection and without a sense of humor. The king descended the steps of the dais.

Chadwick fell to his knees and bowed his head.

All the young vampires sucked in air. Pearl heard the collective gasp like a sigh of wind. He'd violated protocol. You were supposed to stand to donate the blood.

Gently, the king stroked Chadwick's hair. He took his head in both hands and tilted it as if to access the boy's neck. Then in one quick motion he twisted his neck. Pearl heard the snap. The body slumped to the floor, and a guard drove a spear into his heart. The boy disintegrated into dust.

Looking up from the pile of ash, the king said, "Lauranne Colleen, made by Evelyn Anne Vincent of Hartford, approach."

Laurie, the girl who had been Jadrien's fling, scooted forward. She halted just before the dais and held her head high enough to pinch her neck muscles. He swept her hair to the side and tilted her neck. She kept her hands straight by her side. Pearl saw her hands tremble.

Leaning forward, the king plunged his fangs into her throat. Her hands curled into fists. He drank from her for five seconds, ten seconds, thirty, one minute, one minute and a half. . . . Pearl began to wonder if he intended to drain her dry. Her eyes flicked to the audience of older vampires, but she couldn't identify Laurie's sire. No one stepped forward to interfere. As he passed the two-minute mark, he released her. She staggered and then fell to her knees.

"The first child is now forgiven," he said. "Return to the line."

Laurie was unable to stand. Two guards grabbed her arms and tossed her back toward the line. She collapsed into a heap like a broken doll. Vampires could resist the venom, but lose enough blood . . . Pearl tried to remember the last time she had drunk. She'd taken two pints from the storage room the night before last. She wondered how many pints she had in her and how long she could last.

On the plus side, if the king drank deeply from her, then he would absorb more of Evan's power. *If I had any balls at all,* she thought, *I'd tell him to drain me.*

He summoned the next vampire. This one, he drank from for only thirty seconds. He kept to that amount as he proceeded down the line. As Jadrien was summoned to the dais, Pearl risked a glance at Daddy. His eyes were on her, not the king and not Jadrien, but she couldn't tell what he was thinking. She looked back at His Majesty and hoped Daddy would understand someday.

"Approach, Pearl Rose Sange, born daughter of Isabel Sange and Mickey Sange of Greenbridge." His voice slid over her skin. She walked forward with the precision that Minerva had taught her. The guards permitted her to pass, and she halted at the base of the dais.

She felt the blood inside her as if it were acid beneath her skin. It burned in her veins. A weaker vampire might have broken and confessed. *Not going to happen,* she thought. As the blue strapless dress proved, she *did* have balls.

"Drink your fill, Your Majesty," Pearl said.

He smiled with his fangs out. "How delightful."

Leaning close to her, he cupped her elbows with his hands. His fingers felt skeletal against her skin. She smelled the leather of his armor, like spiced, rotting meat. Or perhaps that was the scent of his flesh. This close, his eyes looked like pools of liquid emerald. She kept her gaze on his until he bent his head to touch his lips to her neck.

She closed her eyes and tried not to think at all as his fangs sank deep into her skin. Pain shot through her neck into her spine, her skull, her muscles. She felt as if nails were being drawn through the inside of her body. She abandoned thinking of nothing and instead tried to cocoon her mind in thoughts, as if wrapping it in gauze. She pictured school and replayed Bethany's tutoring lessons in her head. She imagined jogging across a field in sunlight. She thought of sitting on the roof next to Evan with the sun on her shoulders, warm instead of the cold that crept through her limbs.

I'm dying, she thought. *Huh.* A laugh bubbled to her lips. As a member of the undead, she hadn't thought much about the sensation of dying. She'd expected it to come with a stake or a shot of sunlight, something instantaneous. This was leisurely in its slowness. If it weren't for the pain that skittered through her veins . . . *Don't think about the pain.* She switched her thoughts back to Evan.

All of this was Evan's fault. She wouldn't be here, dying, if not for him. He'd wanted to use her. And he'd wanted to save her. She felt her muscles shake and her legs sag. The king's hands on her elbows kept her upright.

Oh, yes, she was angry at Evan, except that she wasn't. At any point she could have walked away. Gone to California or flown to Europe. She could have changed her identity, melted into the human world, and created a new life for herself. She could have avoided the pesky tug of her new conscience by not drinking from anyone else and survived like that for at least a few decades, even centuries if she was careful, before the Family found her. It wasn't her responsibility to "save" other vampires. No handsome were-unicorns with luminous eyes were here now forcing her to stand still while the king slowly killed her.

"Stand still" wasn't quite accurate anymore. As her head spun, she felt as if she were floating. She couldn't feel her hands or her feet. Her legs felt like pools of jelly. She wondered if she had a shape anymore. She felt like a cloud, floating on red pain. It permeated her cells, yet her mind rose above it. She'd chosen this. Evan had simply shown her the choices. She thought of him lying awake all night while she'd lain in his bed. She thought of dancing with him, and how he'd tried to keep her from Jadrien. Both instances, sweet. Also stupid, which pretty much defined Evan: sweet and stupid. She hoped he didn't feel too bad about her death.

After that her thoughts became clouded. She saw red haze and sank into the pain. It surrounded her and caressed her. Her thoughts scattered as they formed. She felt herself sinking into blackness, and then her arms were jerked backward. She felt stone scrape against the back of her legs as she was dragged from the dais. She felt her cheek hit the stone.

She wasn't dead.

She lay there for a long while. Her arms and legs felt distant, as if her body ended at her torso. She felt heavy and empty at the same time, floating yet glued to the floor. Eventually, she heard the king speak, "My children, I bid you welcome and accept you. As you are now unto me, I will be unto you." His voice was muffled, as if he were underwater. He repeated the ritual words in Latin.

Sideways, cheek pressed against the stone, she watched the king slice his arm. He let the blood dribble into a jeweled chalice. Royal blood, mixed with the strength of every young vampire, including her. He widened the cut, and the blood flowed out until the cup brimmed with the jewel-like red. He then pressed silk to the wound. Blood stained the silk instantly, and her fangs extended at the sight.

One of the guards accepted the chalice and carried it to the first young vampire in line. Still weak from the excessive blood loss, Laurie lay on the stone floor with the black lace and tulle of her dress piled around her like a black puddle. She lifted her head.

The guard held out the chalice at shoulder height. She strained her neck upward toward it. The gashes had begun to heal, but dried blood laced her throat. Pearl saw her arms tremble as she tried to push herself upward. The guard did not lower the chalice. He did not even move to glance down at her. Finally, Laurie's arms collapsed under her and she sank into the stone.

The guard proceeded to the second vampire as another guard drove a spear through Laurie's back. She crumbled to ash.

Oh, crap, Pearl thought. *More vampire macho games.*

She counted six vampires who had to drink before it was her turn. As the young vampires drank, she saw life rush into their skin, lighting their cheeks. The king's blood was powerful. If she could sip it, she had a chance.

Come on, Pearl, she thought. She prided herself on being tough. She could do this! *Stand up!* She forced her muscles to curl her legs under her. She couldn't feel her feet, but that didn't mean they weren't there. Agonizingly slowly, she drew her arms in. She laid her palms flat on the stone. *Push.* She thought of Evan and Bethany and Sana and Tara. If she lived, she could help them. She could see this thing through. She could greet her parents in the sunlight. *Blah, blah, blah,* she thought. She needed *real* inspiration. Opening her eyes, Pearl looked across the cellar floor. She saw the hems of dresses and polished shoes. Underneath a tablecloth, Cousin Jeremiah peered out. She met his wide and crazed bloodshot eyes. He winked at her. *If that crazy bastard can survive, so can you. Now, stand!*

That worked.

As the guard's polished boots stepped in front of her, Pearl pushed herself slowly, painfully to her knees. Out of the corner of her eye, she saw Jadrien watching her. She let that fuel her too. He would not see her weak!

She shook, she ached, but she rose. Standing, she lifted her head. The guard held the chalice to her lips and tilted it. A few drops of blood touched her tongue. They tasted like fire. She licked her lips as the flames spread through her mouth and scorched her throat. The blood touched her lungs and her heart, and then it burst outward into her body. She felt her arms and her legs again. Her muscles burst into a flare of pain, but she could feel them! She felt strength return to her body, and she smiled.

She met the king's gaze and kept on smiling. As the chalice moved to the next vampire, the king shifted his focus to his next "child." After all the young vampires had drunk, the guard carried the chalice to the older vampires.

One by one, they drank.

She wondered how much of the unicorn magic had touched the blood they drank. There may not have been enough time for it to disperse throughout the king's blood. Or it could be too diluted to have any effect. There was no way to know.

She watched the progression of the chalice around the room. She saw Mother sip and then Daddy. Uncle Stefan kicked Cousin Jeremiah until he emerged from the table and sipped. Aunt Maria was next and then Uncle Felix. After them, Cousin Antoinette tossed her hair back and sipped. She then beamed a smile directly at Jadrien. Pearl didn't bother to look at Jadrien to see his response. She could tell from the satisfied look that filled Antoinette's face. Aunt Rose drank. Aunt Lianne. Uncle Pascha. Cousin Shirley. The chalice continued to weave through the room. Minerva drank. Jadrien's Family. The New Haven vampires. New London. Hartford. Bridgeport. Mystic. The only sound was the footsteps of the guard who carried the chalice. From his throne, the king acknowledged each sip with a nod of his head, as if affirming his acceptance of the drinker. As the chalice progressed through the room, the guard had to tilt it higher for the vampires to drink.

At last, the final vampire drank.

The king rose from his throne. "Tonight, we are one. Let the celebration begin!"

Three vampires lifted instruments—a violin, a viola, and a cello. Softly, sweetly, a waltz drifted across the cellar. The heads of each Family bowed and curtsied to each other and then began to swirl around the room. Their footsteps were silent on the stone. Others paired up and danced. Soon the cellar was a swirl of black. No one spoke.

Pearl wove between the dancers, aiming for the wall. She'd watch from the side, a demure wallflower, and then, when all the vampires were dancing, she'd slip toward the stairs. If she was very, very lucky, she could join the exodus upstairs while the vampires celebrated.

Before she'd made it halfway across the floor, Jadrien intercepted her. Bowing, he held out his hand toward her. *Oh, crap,* she thought. *Why couldn't he have chosen Antoinette?* From the glares that Antoinette was shooting her, Pearl knew that her cousin had expected it.

Glancing around at the waltzing vampires, she knew there was no option but to accept. Wordlessly, Pearl laid her hand in his. He placed his other hand on the small of her back.

Under his breath, intended for her ears only, he whispered, "I saw you. You were *reflected.*"

His voice was soft, but his were the only words in the cellar.

Every vampire heard him.

Chapter
THIRTY

On the dais, the king raised his hand.

The music ceased, and every dancer froze. No one spoke. No one even breathed. Pearl shot a look at the stairs. She could reach it in three strides, but it might as well have been three miles away. If she ran upstairs, the vampires would follow her, and the humans would die. She couldn't let that happen.

I'm not going to make it, she thought. She hadn't realized until that moment how much she'd hoped to escape and survive the night. It hurt to release that hope.

"You," the king said. He leveled his finger at Jadrien. "Speak."

Jadrien threw himself down in a prostrate bow. His face touched the stone floor. "Your Majesty, please forgive—"

"Tell me what you said." His voice was like molten stone,

dripping and burning where it touched as it oozed across the cellar.

"She has a reflection," Jadrien said quickly. He didn't even hesitate before condemning her. "I saw it in the chalice. I see it now in the polished stone beneath us." She couldn't blame him—he'd always looked out for himself first, like any good vampire—but she still wished she could kick his ass across the cellar and pound his head against the lovely, clean stone wall.

The king fixed his burning eyes on Pearl, and Pearl was suddenly grateful that she didn't need to breathe. She felt as if all the oxygen in her lungs had ignited. His eyes were intense enough to scald. "I drank your blood tonight," the king said.

"Yes," Pearl whispered. Her voice carried in the silence. She hoped the evacuation was moving fast. It was only a matter of time now. Given how quickly the king had killed when he first entered the ballroom, she estimated her life expectancy was about five seconds.

"You begged me to drink my fill. Yet you are no vampire."

Pearl's tongue felt thick as she tried to wrap it around her words. "Yes, I am." Her eyes slid to Mother. His eyes followed hers.

To Mother, he said, "You allowed this . . . this abomination . . . into my Fealty Ceremony." His voice dipped lower, slithering through the room as if it were a snake. Pearl felt her skin crawl.

"You were informed of the feast," Mother said, her voice shockingly calm. "She is the author of it. May I present my daughter, Pearl, true child of my body and the jewel of our Family. She will bring honor to you—"

The king asked Pearl, "Child, have you seen the sunrise?"

"Yes," she said, wishing for even a third of Mother's poise. Silence punctuated her answer.

"She is our miracle," Daddy said, breaking the silence. "She has proven her worth and loyalty through the feast that she has delivered to us. Above, four hundred young bodies await us."

"Check the upstairs," the king ordered his guards. Two of them strode toward the stairs, so fast that the air rippled around them.

"No, wait!" Pearl said.

The king commanded, "Hold." The two guards halted. They looked as if they'd suddenly transformed into stone. "Speak, daywalker."

All eyes turned toward Pearl. She reeled back, the power of all those ancient eyes searing into her skull, and then she forced herself to stand straight and focus on His Majesty. "The feast . . . if we don't spring the trap carefully, they'll suspect. They'll flee. If any of them escape, it will ruin us! This will only work if we catch them all."

Mother bowed. "Of course, the insolence of her manner of speech will be punished severely, Your Majesty. But in essence, she is correct. This hunt must be executed with precision."

Everyone watched the king while he considered it.

"I will accept this risk," the king said. "You could be in

league with the humans. Hunters could await us instead of a feast. This could be a trap. I have not lived this long by being trusting. Proceed." He flicked his wrist, and the two guards unfroze.

Pearl sprang into action.

The other guards leaped in front of their king, but she wasn't targeting him. She ran at the two guards on the stairs. But she was far too slow.

As the first guard opened the door, she yelled, "They're coming!"

A unicorn horn skewered the vampire guard through the chest. He toppled backward down the stairs. Evan leaped over the vampire's body as it disintegrated into char. He drove his horn toward the second guard as Pearl slammed into the guard's back, forcing him into the point of the horn. He crumbled to ash too.

"Hey," Evan said to Pearl. "Just wondered if you'd like to finish our dance."

"Love to," Pearl said.

Side by side, Pearl and Evan faced the vampires below them. For an instant no one moved or spoke.

"Betrayer!" the king howled. "Punish her!" Half his guards closed ranks around him, and the rest raced for the stairs.

"Up!" Evan shouted.

Both of them pivoted and ran.

At the top of the stairs they spilled out into the ballroom. Pearl swung the door shut, and Evan's sister Lizzie slid the bolt home. There wasn't time to barricade the door. *Oh, crap,* Pearl thought. The evacuation wasn't finished. At least half the prom-goers were still inside.

"Go, now!" Pearl shouted.

Grabbing the DJ's microphone, Tara shouted, "Vampires, coming to suck your blood. Everyone without a death wish, out!" To the DJ, she said, "We'll double your fee if you play along. You can fetch your gear in the morning."

"Got it," he said. He switched the song to "Bela Lugosi's Dead." Taking his microphone back, he said, "Sharpen your stakes and grab your garlic. It's time to run for your lives!" He then abandoned his DJ station and jogged to the door, joining the press of students. A few of the students were screaming. Some were laughing, clearly still believing this was an act. Tara and the prom committee, working with the Karkadanns, shooed them toward the door.

The teachers and parents shouted for order.

Mr. Barstow commandeered the microphone. "Students, there is no need to panic. This is all part of the show! You can return inside—"

Bethany (of all people) plucked the microphone out of his hands. "I'm sorry, Mr. Barstow. Suspend me if you have to, but this is not optional. Everyone must leave now. Please, go with the other chaperones and assist the students outside." She continued, but Pearl didn't have the chance to listen more— the vampires were bashing at the door.

Evan's sister Lizzie handed Pearl a sword.

Pearl swung it in a circle to flex her sword arm as the vampires continued to slam into the door. "Thanks," she said. "How very prepared."

"We were all Boy and Girl Scouts," Evan said.

"Of course you were."

"We have stakes, if you'd rather," Lizzie said. "The sword has more range, though, and no vampire can survive a beheading."

"I am somewhat familiar with vampire facts," Pearl said drily.

The lock bent, and the door creaked.

Pearl glanced over her shoulder. Another hundred students had exited, but a quarter of the junior class still remained. Most faces were pale. A few were crying. Shepherded by several of the Karkadanns, they were funneling out the mansion door.

"Get ready," Evan said.

Pearl kicked off her high heels and sliced a slit in her dress. She then lifted her sword and faced the door.

The door shattered. All the students screamed.

As the first vampire (one of the king's guards) pushed through the broken door, a torrent of water released from a bucket suspended above. The vampire shrieked as holy water scalded his skin. He collapsed and writhed on the floor.

A few yards away, holding a rope, Matt whooped. "One down!"

Evan stabbed the guard through the heart, and he exploded in a cloud of char. The second guard met the same fate. By the third vampire, a woman from the New Haven Family, the water was a trickle. The drops scalded her cheeks, but she barreled forward. Pearl swung her sword at the vampire's neck. The vampire dodged—directly into Evan's horn. As the vampire disintegrated, Pearl spun around and hacked at the next vampire who tried to push through the hole. He fell back.

Matt and Zeke refilled the buckets with holy water. "Pour, pour, pour!"

Hands clawed at the door shards, trying to pry them back, to widen the hole. Pearl hacked at their hands and fingers. From below, she heard Aunt Fiona's banshee wail. Lizzie lopped off the head of the next vampire who poked her head through the hole. Beyond her, through the press of vampires on the stairs, Pearl spotted Antoinette and Shirley. If Pearl didn't end this soon, she'd have to fight Family.

"Leave the water," Pearl called to Matt. "Get it lit!"

"But you guys—"

"Do it," Evan said. "Lizzie, help them. We'll catch up. Go!"

Pearl heard Zeke, Matt, and Lizzie run toward the door, but she didn't dare take a second to check over her shoulder. Vampires were piling against the broken door. In concert, Pearl and Evan fought them back. But the wood splintered.

Seconds later the vampires burst through it. Pearl plunged her sword into the closest one, another royal guard. He grabbed the hilt and yanked the sword out of her hands. He pulled the sword out of his body and swung it at Pearl.

"Time to run," Pearl said.

She grabbed Evan's arm and spun him. Together, they raced for the door. Behind them, the vampires spilled into the ballroom with a roar like a hundred tigers. Evan and Pearl pelted across the dance floor. Ahead of them the way was clear—the humans were all outside. *Yes!* Pearl thought. It fueled her, and she increased speed.

Bursting outside, Pearl saw that the humans were still trickling across the yard. The trench wasn't lit yet. She skidded to a stop. "Can't let them out! Not yet!"

Swordless, she crouched, hands ready to strike, in front of the door.

Behind her, Evan plus his parents and siblings raced up the front steps to her side. They collided with the vampires that spilled out of the mansion. Kicking and spinning and hitting, Pearl fought with every trick she'd ever learned. On either side of her, Evan's family stabbed and sliced with their horn-swords.

Out of the corner of her eye, Pearl saw a flash of red orange. Fire surged into a ring around the mansion, brightness racing around the perimeter. "Go now!" Pearl shouted to Evan and his family. "I'll hold them as long as I can!"

"Not leaving you!" Evan said.

"Can't cross the flames anyway," Pearl said. She spotted Uncle Stefan inside. His gaze fixed on her, and his face twisted into an ugly mask. "Go, you idiot!" she ordered Evan.

Uncle Stefan raced toward her, knocking vampires out of the way. Pearl readied herself as she blocked another vampire's attack. If she was lucky, she'd last long enough for Evan and his family to escape.

"Ride on me," Evan ordered. Stepping backward off the steps, he shimmered, and a unicorn stood beside her. She leaped onto his back, and he galloped away from the mansion.

She glanced over her shoulder. Uncle Stefan charged down the steps. Behind him, Cousin Jeremiah ran on all fours.

"Faster!" she shouted.

Evan leaped over the flames. Pearl squeezed her legs as high onto his back as she could. She felt the heat lick at her.

With a thud, he landed on the other side.

Pearl twisted again to see behind her. Flames roared into the air. By the roses, though, the fire sputtered only two feet high. "More fire!" she cried as Uncle Stefan raced toward the roses.

Bethany hauled a branch toward the roses. Matt tossed gasoline on the branch and onto the rosebushes. Fire raced through the green leaves, crackling and popping, but in the split second before the flame roared upward, Uncle Stefan leaped over the trench.

He knocked Bethany aside. She flew backward and crashed hard on the gravel driveway. She didn't move. He charged toward Pearl.

On the back of the unicorn Evan, Pearl prepared to leap to meet him in three, two . . .

She heard a twang.

A stake protruded from Uncle Stefan's chest. He fell

forward. The stake hit the driveway and rammed through his body. He crumbled to ash.

From the roof of Bethany's minivan, Zeke cheered. "Stake crossbow! Made of awesome!"

Jeremiah howled. Hate filled his eyes as he ran toward them, his sire's killers. Leaping, he threw himself through the fire. Flames curled around him, claiming him. Red-orange fire engulfed his body as if his skin were gasoline. He screamed like a dying pig, a horrible sound that rose above the beat of the music inside.

All the vampires on the lawn stopped.

On the front steps Aunt Fiona began to keen again, a rising banshee wail. Mother stood beside her. Through the flames, Pearl met her eyes. Then Mother turned her back on her only born daughter and walked into the mansion. Other vampires turned and bolted inside.

"Go!" Pearl shouted to the students. "They're heading for the tunnel!"

Matt helped Bethany to her feet. She stumbled toward the minivan, clutching her side. He hoisted her in. Sandy, Evan's mother, strode toward Evan. "Keep everyone moving. We'll lead the cars to safety and rendezvous with you at home. Understood?"

Unicorn Evan whinnied at her.

Sandy patted his mane, and then Evan's parents took off with a cadre of his brothers and sisters, running as fast as vampires into the night.

Pearl continued to herd students into cars and issue instructions: Go to the closest house you know, lock the doors, let no one in, don't leave until sunrise. A row of cars sped single file down the narrow, winding driveway.

Last to go was the minivan with Bethany, Zeke, Matt, Tara, Kelli, and three others. As they started down the driveway, Pearl glanced back at the mansion.

Across the flames, Daddy approached the ring of fire. "Pearl. Stop this. Come home."

"I can't," Pearl said. "I'm sorry."

He studied her. "You really are. How interesting."

Behind him, only two or three vampires remained. Any minute now the night could be crawling with very pissed-off vamps. Out of words, she stared at Daddy. "I'll see you again," she said.

"I hope you won't," he said sadly.

Beneath her, the unicorn Evan broke into a walk, then a trot, then a gallop. Halfway down the driveway, he caught up to the minivan and raced alongside it. Night wind in her face, Pearl held on as he ran away from the mansion, the fire, and her past.

Chapter
THIRTY-ONE

"Faster!" Pearl called to the minivan. If the vampires had breached the tunnels, Bethany and the others would never make it to Evan's house. Clutching Evan's mane with one hand, she leaned toward the minivan and pounded on the window. "Find a closer safe haven!"

In the driver's seat, Tara nodded. Her hands gripped the steering wheel so hard that her knuckles looked like exposed bone. Beside her, Bethany slumped against the passenger window. Eyes half open, she breathed shallowly, cringing with every inhale. Zeke, Matt, and the others were crammed into the back of the minivan. One of them, Kelli from the sound of it, was shrieking like a scared cat.

As they reached the end of the mansion's winding driveway, five vampires burst into view: one of Jadrien's cousins, three vamps Pearl didn't know, and Cousin Antoinette in her prom dress. From inside the minivan, Zeke shouted, "Evasive maneuvers!"

"What?" Tara said.

"Avoid them!"

She swerved to the right as unicorn Evan broke to the left. Pearl shouted in his ear, "I can hold them! Stay with Tara!" But he didn't listen. He leaped over the nearest fence. Racing through a backyard, he increased speed so that wind hit her face and stung her eyes. Four of the vampires chased them, all except Antoinette. Veering toward a house, Evan leaped onto a roof and over it. One of the vampires fell behind. The other three scrambled over the roof and then hit the ground running. Pearl clung to Evan's mane. "Get back to the minivan, you stupid horse!" She knew what Antoinette would do once she caught the minivan.

He pounded down the street and across lawns. At the end of the cul-de-sac, he plunged into a patch of woods. Branches flew at her face. She ducked her head. Behind her, she heard the remaining three vampires trample bushes. Evan ran faster, weaving between the trees. In seconds the forest was a brown blur around them, and she could no longer hear the sounds of their pursuers. This was how she'd always failed to catch Evan—he was *fast,* faster than the cars she liked to drive. Under any other circumstances, she would have loved this. Evan burst back onto the road.

They raced alone through the streets and the woods.

"Okay, fine, you lost them! But Antoinette is still with

Bethany and the others." She hoped Tara had floored it. She didn't know if that clunker had enough juice to outrun a pissed-off vampire, though, even one in heels and a tacky dress. She tried to think what safe haven they could have chosen. "Go to Ashlyn's!" she shouted in Evan's ear.

He switched course.

A few minutes later they emerged onto Ashlyn's street. Ahead, Pearl saw that the minivan was parked sideways on the lawn by the front door, crushing the daffodils. Zeke and Matt were on opposite sides of Bethany, helping her up the steps to the porch. Tara pounded on the door, shouting for Ashlyn.

A shape crouched on top of the minivan.

One of the boys screamed and pointed at it.

Reaching the lawn, Pearl flung herself off Evan's back. She landed in a crouch, sprang up, and ran toward the minivan. She threw herself between the minivan and the porch, shielding the humans.

The front door opened, and Ashlyn poked her head outside. "Tara? Is prom over already?"

Tara shoved inside, and the others piled in with her. Evan transformed into a human, scooped up Bethany, and carried her up the remaining steps and into the house.

Guarding them, Pearl backed up the stairs. The shadow on the minivan didn't move. As soon as she was sure the humans were inside, Pearl turned and sprinted for the door. She halted on the threshold—the air was solid in front of her, as if it were a wall instead of an open doorway. "Ashlyn, invite me in!"

The bottle blonde tilted her head as if considering it. Pearl saw a hint of Ashlyn's old self behind her hollow eyes. "Oh, I don't think so. This is your fault." Ashlyn shut the door.

Evan yanked the door open. "Invite her in!"

A faint smile on her lips, Ashlyn shook her head.

Tara, Bethany, Zeke, Matt . . . all of them pleaded with her.

The shadows on top of the minivan laughed. Pearl spun around in a crouch as Cousin Charlaine drew herself to her full height on the roof of the minivan. Cousin Antoinette sat in the driver's seat. "Ooh, poor Pearly, stuck outside like a mangy dog. How very appropriate."

"Hi, cousins," Pearl said. She strolled down the steps and stopped on the brick walkway. "Looking for me?"

"Not really," Antoinette said. "Just peckish."

Charlaine snarled.

"Okay, I lied," Antoinette said. "For some reason, Charlaine doesn't like you much. Come to think of it, I don't like you much anymore either."

Charlaine launched herself off the minivan roof toward Pearl.

Pearl held still as her cousin dived, fangs out and arms reaching toward her. At the last second, she dodged. Charlaine impacted on the bricks. Before she could recover, Pearl kicked at her stomach hard enough to flip her over onto her back like a turtle. Jumping on her, Pearl grabbed Charlaine's arm and twisted it. She heard a crack. As Charlaine shrieked from the break, Pearl bit her neck. As her cousin thrashed and struggled under her, Pearl sucked until Charlaine lost consciousness. Pearl released her into the damaged daffodils.

"Wow," Antoinette said. "That was really interesting. You do realize she isn't dead, right? If you don't kill her, she'll probably hunt you forever. She's like that."

"She'll get over it," Pearl said, wiping her mouth with the back of her hand. She felt the blood buzz inside of her. Feeling powerful, she stalked toward the minivan and yanked open the door.

Antoinette faked a shriek. "Ooh, Pearly, I'm so scared! Don't hurt me!"

"Behind you!" Evan shouted.

She heard Evan run down the porch steps as she spun and ducked underneath Jadrien's fist. Jadrien's knuckles impacted on the minivan door, denting it. Jadrien kicked backward as Evan lunged for him. He caught Evan in the knee, and Evan collapsed on the walkway.

"Boy for me!" Antoinette said. She swung herself out the car window and landed near Evan. Evan jumped to his feet in time to dodge her kick. She laughed and then skipped around him. "Come play, pretty boy." She jabbed at him. Evan knocked her fist aside. Pearl shifted her attention to Jadrien.

He smiled at her. "Jewel of my heart, just what do you think you are doing?"

"Among other things, I'm breaking up with you," she said.

"Very dramatic," Jadrien said. "Couldn't you have just texted me?" His tone was friendly, even conversational, but the porch light glinted off his fangs, and he had a streak of blood running down his arm that glistened, fresh and wet. She doubted it was his. "You didn't need to try to assassinate the king to impress me. You failed, by the way. His Majesty escaped. By now he's halfway to Massachusetts."

"Go home, Jadrien," Pearl said. "I'd really rather not kill you."

He shook his head in mock pity. "Oh, Pearly, it's a shame to end things this way. We had fun, didn't we? But if I don't take you out, it's *my* reputation that will suffer. Guilt by association. Can't have that."

Without any further warning, he struck. He whipped out every move she'd ever seen him make: leap kicks, spinning kicks, punches, jabs. She blocked and dodged, and she struck back. They danced across Ashlyn's lawn, punching and kicking so fast that wind whipped around them. They were their own tornado, spinning around each other.

Out of the corner of her eye, she saw the driveway: Evan lay on the pavement. He wasn't moving. Laughing, Antoinette kicked at his side.

Enough, Pearl thought. "It's over," she said.

"Not by a long shot, dewdrop," Jadrien said. "We aren't in the practice ring. You can't beat—"

She unleashed a flurry of kicks and punches. No fancy tricks. No spins. No leaps. With fast, economical strikes, she pounded Jadrien to his knees. "Just for the record, you never let me win," Pearl said. "I'm simply better than you." She hit him one more time, and he crumpled to the side, unconscious on the lawn. "Deserve better too."

Leaping over him, she raced to Evan.

In a delighted voice, Antoinette said, "Pearly! Come play with me!"

Ignoring her, Pearl knelt beside Evan. He cracked open his eyes to look at her. "Get your horn ready," she whispered in his ear. Hidden from Antoinette by his body, he extended his horn from his wrist.

"I can't move," he said.

"I'll move for you."

As Antoinette lunged toward Pearl, Pearl somersaulted over Evan and lifted his arm with the horn.

It plunged into Antoinette's heart.

"Heal her," Pearl ordered.

White light flowed from Evan's horn. It buried itself in Antoinette's chest as her eyes glazed and her body slumped forward.

Evan's eyes closed, and the light faded. Pearl kicked Antoinette off his horn. Antoinette collapsed on the driveway, but she didn't disintegrate.

Pearl touched Evan's neck to check his pulse. Still okay. She lifted her head to look at the house. All of the humans were pressed against the windows and wedged into the doorway, just inside the threshold. "I need rope," she called.

"Excuse me, move, please," Bethany said. She hobbled to

the front of the pack. "Bungees. Back of minivan." She pointed and then sagged against the porch wall.

Pearl fetched them. One at a time, she trussed up Antoinette, Jadrien, and Charlaine and tossed them in the back of the minivan. Carefully, she lifted Evan and laid him in the passenger seat. His head lolled to the side, but he continued to breathe evenly, albeit shallowly.

Limping toward the minivan, Bethany said, "Help me in."

"Stay here," Pearl told her. "It'll be safer. You can go home at sunrise."

"I won't abandon you. You saved our lives. That makes us close now. We're *made* family." Though each movement caused her to wince, Bethany reached out to grasp Pearl's arm. "My new sister."

"Whatever," Pearl said. But she carefully lifted Bethany into the minivan. She then pointed her finger at Zeke and Matt. "You two, stay here. Keep everyone safe until dawn."

Matt nodded. Zeke saluted.

Coming outside onto the porch, Tara said, "Are you sure? You could—"

Pearl pointed. "Go inside and stay inside. We have school on Monday. Try not to die before then." She climbed into the driver's seat. "Buckle up, Bethany." Bethany snapped a buckle around the unconscious Evan and then around herself, wincing with every movement.

Pearl peeled out of the driveway.

She dumped Jadrien, Antoinette, and Charlaine in the safest

place she could think of: in the dumpsters behind the burnt shell of the Dairy Hut. They'd be protected from sunlight and could return home next nightfall. For poetry's sake, she would have preferred to leave them on the porch of the Family's house as she'd been left, but that would have been a stupid risk.

Leaving the Dairy Hut, she drove faster than she'd ever driven to Evan's house. The minivan shook on the turns. Tires squealing, she spun into the Karkadanns' driveway, after flattening a shrub.

Easing herself out of the minivan, Bethany limped toward the house. Pearl scooped up the still-unconscious Evan and carried him to the front door. She wondered what she'd do if Evan's family rescinded their invitation to her. She wouldn't blame them if they did. After all, their youngest son lay limp in her arms.

But Evan's mother threw the door open, and within seconds Pearl, Evan, and Bethany were inside. As Sandy took her son, Pearl locked the door behind them.

Chapter
THIRTY-TWO

On Monday Pearl drove Bethany to school in the minivan. Reporters lined the street, but the police kept them off school property.

So far, the popular theory in the press was that a few kids had used the prom's theme to perpetrate a prank. The prank had spun out of control when the student body panicked. Alternate theories included drug-induced gangs and rival football teams.

Pearl had stuck to the prank story when she was interviewed, and the bulk of the junior class had followed her lead. The few who did tell the truth had been instantly discredited by "expert" psychologists and trauma specialists, though some websites believed them.

She wondered how quickly the students would begin to believe the lies. *People,* Pearl thought, *can be so stupid.* Their need to protect their precious little minds from the truth . . .

She parked and watched the students spill out of the school buses and cars.

"Weird that everything looks so normal," Bethany said. "I feel like the world should have changed." One of the students trampled a patch of daffodils. Others jostled as they squeezed through the school doors. Muffled laughter and chatter wafted across the parking lot.

Someone knocked on Bethany's window, and she jumped.

"Tense much?" Pearl asked.

Bethany rolled down her window. Tara poked her head in. "Everyone still alive?"

"Evan's not well enough for school yet," Bethany said. "But he'll be fine."

"Sweet!" Tara said. "Come on, first bell is going to ring. We've got a lot to do before then." She didn't stay to explain what she meant by "a lot to do." Instead, she sauntered across the parking lot to meet Kelli, who waved at the minivan.

"I suppose the world did change a little," Bethany said.

"Redefining the high school social hierarchy was not exactly the master plan." Opening her door, Pearl jumped outside. She crossed to the opposite side of the car and helped Bethany ease out of her seat.

"Change will happen." Bethany held her ribs and winced as she moved. "Be patient. It may take a while before your blood has a real effect. Each vampire received only a few diluted drops. Also, keep in mind that we still need to find a way to introduce the vampires into the normal world."

"For a perky person, you're lousy at pep talks," Pearl said. She carried Bethany's book bag as well as her own, both slung over one shoulder. Hooking her arm under Bethany's, Pearl helped her across the parking lot and through the doors. Other students raced by them into the school.

At first everything felt the same as they walked through the halls. But once they reached the junior class lockers, Pearl felt the stares. Students quieted as they passed. A few whispered. No one spoke to them.

But then a junior Pearl recognized from track—the girl with pink-lemonade hair, Claire—darted over. "Wow, you were so awesome. Where did you learn to fight like that? Can you teach me?" After that a second student approached them. "I saw one of them in my driveway Saturday night," she said in a whisper. A third, a boy from the football team, said, "I've never driven so fast in my life." One of his friends added, "I think I hit a mailbox."

One by one, the students began to talk about Saturday: how they'd run for their cars, how they'd seen the vampires, how they'd driven faster than fast . . . as if seeing Pearl had freed them to admit the truth. Pearl and Bethany walked and hobbled toward their lockers through a cyclone of stories.

Zeke and Matt were waiting for them.

"Dudes," Matt said. "This is awesome. We're like heroes."

"At least until everyone gets sick of staying home after sunset," Zeke said.

"Right," Matt said. "Until then. After that, tar and feathers."

"It won't be forever," Bethany said. "People just have to be sensible until the tainted blood takes effect."

Pearl propped Bethany up against the lockers and watched the students swirl around them. Some of the students sported bandages, which they showed off to their friends. Several of them waved at Pearl, Bethany, Matt, and Zeke. A few of them said "thanks." One of them even asked Pearl for her autograph. She scrawled her signature on the back of his notebook. She drew miniature fangs under her name.

As she handed the pen back to her admirer, Tara scurried over. "Wait, keep the pen! You'll need it for the sign-up sheet."

"Sign-up sheet?" Pearl asked.

Tara thrust a clipboard under Pearl's nose. "Once the blood thingy works, the vamps are going to need help adjusting, right? So . . . we need volunteers." She pointed at the list of names. There were already more than two dozen signatures underneath the header: VAMPIRE REHAB.

Behind Pearl, Zeke and Matt began to laugh.

"You cannot be serious," Pearl said.

Gasping for air midlaugh, Matt said, "Best. Extracurricular. Activity. Ever."

Pearl rolled her eyes, but she added her name to the sign-up sheet.

Instead of joining the Karkadann family for a dinner she couldn't eat, Pearl perched on their roof. She wrapped her arms around her knees and let the first rosy rays of sunset caress her face. A few seconds later Evan swung himself up onto the roof.

She raised her eyebrows at him. "They let you out of bed?"

"Actually, no," he said. "I feigned sleep and then slipped out."

"Clearly, I am a good influence on you."

"You tried to come see me after school," he said, as if that was enough of an explanation. Maybe it was. He handed her a thermos. "I swung by the fridge in the garage on the way. B-positive on the rocks, courtesy of William and the blood bank."

She'd learned on Saturday night that William worked at a hospital. He'd wrapped up Bethany's fractured ribs and pronounced Evan exhausted. The healing, she'd been informed, was a ridiculous strain on the body. Even after nearly forty-eight hours of sleep, Evan still looked as if he'd been hollowed out by a melon scooper. "Thanks," she said. "You look half dead."

"So says the undead chick." Stretching himself out on the roof next to her, Evan closed his eyes. "I have felt better," he admitted. "If you could avoid pummeling me for a day or two, I'd appreciate it."

"No promises." Watching the dying sunlight spill over the other houses, she drank the blood. The ice added an interesting texture, kind of a blood smoothie.

"Any word on the king?" he asked.

"Apparently, Jadrien was right—the king left through the tunnels and didn't look back," Pearl said. "According to your parents, he's holed up in his Boston stronghold again. No sign of any symptoms yet."

"Give it a chance to work. It took you time, and you had a direct hit," Evan said. "Even your cousin Antoinette won't show signs for a while."

"And if it doesn't work?" Pearl asked. She watched the sun spread across the horizon as if it were melting into a puddle of red gold. A few stars poked through the deepening blue. She felt the coming night like an itch on her skin. "One thing with vampires . . . you're never alone. There's always the Family. But if this doesn't work, I *will* be alone. Just me in the sunlight forever. Literally, forever. You get the vampire-immortal thing, right?"

"You aren't alone." He sat up. He sounded angry. "You haven't figured that out yet?" She looked at him and saw his scowl, a sharp contrast to his usual affable smile.

Without warning, he kissed her. It felt like sunlight on her lips.

He drew back. For a long moment she didn't breathe.

"I heard about the new after-school student activity," Evan said conversationally, as if he hadn't just kissed her. "You know it won't be that simple or fast. Rehabilitating several entire clans is likely to take a while. Are you up for this as a long-term thing?"

She was certain he wasn't talking just about vampire rehab. She felt as if her eyes were drawn to his lips. "Depends. How 'long-term' are you? Do were-unicorns come with an expiration date? Because I'm not getting involved with anyone who is going to do the old-age thing while I remain young and cute. That's just inappropriate."

A smile twitched over his lips. "Does this mean you don't hate me anymore?"

"Maybe."

"No expiration date. Mythical, remember?" He scooted down the shingles and lowered himself in through his bedroom window.

She followed him, swinging through his window and over his desk. She landed catlike next to him. "I don't hate you anymore," she said.

"That's a start." He was only inches from her, but he didn't move. She felt his breath, soft and warm on her face. "I don't hate you either," he said softly.

"For the record, you're still an idiot."

"And you're still a bloodsucking fiend."

"Kiss me again," she ordered.

Outside, the sun sank, and the night began.